STAND AND DELIVER

Declan Farrell, earl of Dungannon and the son of the duke of Arlington, is a nobleman of the highest order, dissolute and a thief. He is a drinker and a lover, and at night he is "the Gypsy," a highwayman who prowls from the city of Boreas to Chappendale Forest.

And yet, his heart is true. Impelled by a tragic past, he steals from the rich and gives to the poor, offers hope to those who cannot fight their fate. So much was taken from him, which is why he gives. He himself is undeserving of love and happiness, but there are those who are worthy, like Lady Althea Standfield, daughter to the duke of Oxmoor. Independent and kind, beautiful and smart, she must be freed from the obligation of marrying him. His heart might be stolen by a woman of such fine form and finer character…but his heart is all that he has left, and it is perfectly protected.

PRAISE FOR THE WORK OF CHARLOTTE BOYETT-COMPO!

30 DAYS TO SIN

"Whether it is the smooth writing style or the way the author chose to spin the storyline, this is one of those unforgettable stories that will have a lasting place on my keeper shelf. 5 stars!"

—Romancing the Book

"A true but unconventional love story. Highly recommended! 5 stars and a Top Pick Award!"

—Night Owl Reviews

HARDWIND

"Charlotte Boyett-Compo has once again made me cry before the end of the first chapter. She has such a mastery of the written word that she can, and will, rip your heart out. To have your emotions rollercoaster the way that they do while reading her books makes each one a bittersweet experience."

—Fallen Angels Reviews

"Looking for a story wrought with danger, insanity and a love worth dying for? Then you need look no further.... Sit down, buckle up and be prepared to be taken."

—Love Romances Reviews

IN THE ARMS OF THE WIND

"This book is terrific if you love mystery and romance combined.... Another hit on [Charlotte Boyett-Compo's] long list of wonderful reads."

—Romance Junkies Reviews

DANCING ON THE WIND

"A wonderful offering…. There is just something so compelling about Charlotte Boyett-Compo's writing that catches me up and keeps me reading, regardless of the material."

—ParaNormal Romance Reviews

"One hell of a book. If you have never read anything written by this author then I suggest you do, and if you're already a fan make sure you don't miss this one." An A+ Rating and an Outstanding Read Award

—Simply Romance Reviews

MOONLIGHT RIDER

Charlotte Boyett-Compo

www.BOROUGHSPUBLISHINGGROUP.com

ISBN 978-1-942886-47-1

Dedicated to Tommy

Marriage is a Three-Course Meal
(On the occasion of our 31st anniversary)

In our salad days, at the beginning of our married life, everything was crisp and fresh, delightful to the taste and we were eager to dive right into the meal. Like personalities, the oil and vinegar didn't always mix, but without them, the salad would have been so bland.

In our entree years, the meat and potatoes of our married life, the fare was robust and hearty and satisfying. Our plate was full with children and jobs and communal activities. Sometimes the meat got a little tough and the potatoes a bit mushy, but we were nourished by them all the same.

In our dessert years, the time when we are now once more alone— the children grown, the jobs nearing an end, the activities only what entertain and sustain us—we can enjoy the sweet accomplishments we've wrought. We can sit back, eat slowly and talk about the meals we have enjoyed through the years.

But what would any good meal be without the coffee? Warm and toasty, a bracing taste that calms us and allows us to relax, to finish the meal with a good companion at our side. To finish our drinks and ponder how wonderful it was that we had tasted and savored all the precious meals of life with someone we loved and admired and liked. Our best friend. The love of our life.

I am looking forward to our coffee, my love.

* * *

I never got to enjoy that coffee because my lovemate, lifemate, soulmate, heartmate, the wind beneath my wings, my everything passed away on April 18, 2009. If you have read this, read it to the one you hold most dear as well. Never let a day pass that you don't reaffirm your commitment to him or her. Who knows when the meal will end?

Table of Contents

MOONLIGHT RIDER

Chapter One

He stood on the cliff overlooking the windswept sea. One booted foot was braced on a rock and his wrists were crossed over his knee as he stared out over the heaving waves. Far below him the crash of the breakers washing over the rocks helped to calm the wildness within him. It was four of the clock and the sun was beginning its slow descent, its rays flickering in the rapier strapped to his waist. Behind him the edgy stamp of a hoof on stone made him look around.

"Nearly time, boy," he said to the steed. "Be patient."

The coach from Warrington to Wexford would just be leaving the open road and entering the thick greensward of the Chappendale forest. In his mind he heard the rattle of the harnesses, the rhythmic pounding of the hooves, the squeaking of the struts, the sharp crack of a whip over the heads of the horses as the coach lumbered along. He closed his eyes and saw the driver and guard sitting atop the high seat, the two unarmed, uniformed footmen clinging precariously to the back of the coach. Inside were the Earl and Countess of Warrington, their houseguest Lady Althea Standfield—only daughter of Alastair Standfield, the Duke of Oxmoor—and Lady Standfield's maid.

He imagined the women dressed in their finest frocks with fashionable bonnets perched upon expertly coiffed hair. Jewels sparkled on fingers atop lacy gloves, on their wrists, around their necks and at their ears. Gold coin would be inside the silken reticules hanging from their wrists and in the pompous earl's purse.

Baubles and gold for the taking.

He straightened, adjusted the heavy pistols at his waist then walked to his mount. The steed nickered, bobbed its head and once more struck a hoof to the ground. It was ready to run.

Pulling the black handkerchief up from his neck to cover the lower portion of his face, he swung into the saddle. He clucked his tongue and the horse sprang forward eagerly.

With the breeze whipping under his cavalier hat, he rode with one gloved hand on the reins and the other doubled into a fist pressed against his thigh. Ramrod straight in the saddle, his body flowed comfortably with the rocking motion of his steed. The stallion was sure-footed in the gathering dusk, its long neck stretching toward their destination.

Over the rise ahead came the sound of the coach. He directed the beast to the stand of trees to their right and slowed him down with a gentle tug on the reins. When the beast was moving no faster than a walk, he pulled it to a halt. The sound of the wheels on the loose stones was louder now. From his position amid the trees he would not be seen until he urged his horse into the middle of the roadway, his pistol pointed at the lone guard.

The coach was almost upon him when he gently kicked the steed and it moved to the center of the road. In the fading light he saw the driver's eyes widen as he pulled on the reins. The guard raised his musket but never got it to his shoulder before a pistol shot rang out and the reckless man snatched back a stinging hand where the musket ball had grazed him.

Hat pulled low over his forehead, mask in place, he pointed the three-barrel revolving flintlock directly at the guard. "Stand and deliver," he commanded. "The next shot will find its target."

"Aye, milord," the driver said and tossed his musket to the ground.

The driver's hands were still on the reins to keep the horses in check, but there would be no trouble from him. He was too fat to move fast and too old to try.

"What the divil is going on out there?" came an imperious voice from inside the coach. "Are we being robbed?"

"Aye, Your Grace, you are," the driver called out.

"Bloody hell," the man in the coach snapped. "We are late as it is."

The two footmen were standing together with their hands above their heads, their knees shaking. The highwayman motioned with the barrel of his pistol and they took off running. Where they would go he had no idea, but they were no problem for him, either.

"Down," he told the driver and guard, and both men scrambled to leave the high seat. Once they were on the ground, he ordered them to start walking back the way they had come. They obeyed without a moment's hesitation and he chuckled as he threw a leg over the steed and dropped to the ground.

He knew the earl would have a percussion derringer upon his person, but he doubted either the countess or the ladies' maid would have a weapon. Nevertheless, he would take no chances.

"Toss out your weapon, Your Grace," he ordered.

"I've no weapon on me," the pompous old man stated.

"Aye, but you do," he said. "Toss it out now or you won't live to regret not having done so."

"Oh, for the love of God, Jacob, throw out the pistol," an older woman demanded. "Is a few gold coins and pieces of jewelry worth your life?"

"I'd listen to your lady, Your Grace," he told the earl. "I'm after the gold and jewels, but if I need to take a life, I have no qualms about doing so."

There was a series of low protests from inside the coach but then two derringers were flung from the window.

"My thanks," he said and advanced cautiously to the coach door.

"I've three ladies herein," the earl said.

"Aye, I know," he replied. He took hold of the handle and opened the door. "Ladies, if you please?"

Another series of protests, and then the coach shifted toward him as a large woman appeared in the doorway. He held out his hand and she slipped her sausage-like fingers into his palm. He helped her down the steps as she flounced her skirt around her.

"You are a detestable young man," she said, looking him in the eye.

"So I have been told on numerous occasions, Your Grace," he replied to the countess. At her harrumph, he switched his attention back to the door. The younger woman who descended the steps next batted his hand away as he tried to help her from the coach.

"Don't you dare touch me, you ruffian," she hissed. She was as thin as a rail with a face only a horse could love. Well, maybe not his horse—his steed had discriminating tastes where fillies were concerned. Her hair was an odd color of red that actually made his eyes hurt as he looked at it. She stomped over to the countess and stood there glaring at him.

The next to appear in the doorway was the earl. His bulk all but filled the opening and he had to turn sideways and suck in his pendulous belly in order to exit the coach. He came down the stairs huffing and puffing and waddled over to his wife who was a good foot taller than he.

"Take whatever you like and let us be on our way," the earl said. "There's no need for more violence." He straightened his jabot and reached up to adjust his hat.

"I believe there is one more person in the coach," he said. "Milady, will you join us?"

A shapely ankle appeared beneath the hem of a plain grey gown. He held out his hand and the young woman who stepped down from the coach allowed him to help her down. She did not glance his way but kept her eyes on the steps then on the ground. When she would have pulled her hand free of his grip, he tightened his hold then brought her hand to his lips. Her head came up as he pressed his mouth to her fingers.

"Lady Standfield," he said softly, looking through his lashes into her vibrant green eyes.

"You are mistaken," the countess spoke up. "The lady beside me is—"

"This lady's maid," he said. "Your ruse might have worked for others, but not for me."

She was staring at him with curiosity instead of fear. Her hair was tucked beneath a nondescript bonnet but the broad ribbons holding it atop her head framed her softly oval face to perfection. No man with a discerning eye would mistake her for anything other than the aristocrat she was.

"I am at a disadvantage, milord," she said and her voice was as sweet as honey.

Still holding her hand in his, he put his free hand over his heart. "Alas, it would be unwise for me to provide my true identity to you, milady."

"Then what shall I call you?" she asked.

"What I am," he replied. "The Highwayman."

She smiled. "Indeed," she said and tugged gently. This time he allowed her to break free of his hold. "And I suppose you are here to abduct me for ransom."

"That is my intent, aye," he acknowledged. "And to rid these good folks of their baubles."

"Take whatever you want but you shall not abscond with the Lady Standfield," the earl said. "The entire might of the British Army will descend upon you."

"The entire might of the British Army has been after me for months now, Your Grace," he said. "I have no doubt they'll come after me, but they won't find me nor will they ever catch me."

"You are that sure of yourself?" Lady Althea inquired.

"I am, milady."

She cocked her head to one side. "Yes, I believe you are." She turned to look at the earl and countess. "Pray give the man what he wants, Your Grace, and I am sure he will allow you to be on your way."

"How?" the earl asked. "Who will drive the coach?"

"I will," the horse-faced woman said. "Ain't nothin' to drivin' a coach and four." She lifted her chin. "And if I had a pistol, I would put a hole between this brigand's pretty blue eyes." She glanced at the pistols lying on the ground nearby.

"I am sure you would try," he told her. "Now, if you will, Your Grace, I will have your coin and your wife's jewelry as well as the borrowed ones Lady Althea's maid is wearing. You may place in them in Her Grace's reticle."

"Do you want mine as well?" Lady Althea queried. She put a hand to her throat were a crucifix hung.

He lowered his voice where only she heard. "What I want from you, milady, will be taken in private."

Her soft gasp made him grin behind the kerchief.

Necklaces adorned with diamonds and sapphires fell into the countess's reticle along with the huge garnet and gold signet ring that belonged to the earl. Earrings, rings and bracelets were added to the cache then the earl's purse stuffed atop the take.

"My thanks," he told them. "Now if you will return to the coach, you may be on your way." He looked at the thin woman who had been posing as Lady Standfield. "Do you need a hand to climb into the driver's seat?"

"Touch me and I'll scratch your eyes out, boy," she snapped at him. Hiking the skirt of her borrowed silk gown, she put a sensible boot to the rail and pulled herself easily into the driver's seat.

"A very manly woman, is she not?" he asked Lady Althea.

"Teresa Ann has a certain way about her, aye," the young woman replied.

Reaching into the pocket of his coat, he pulled out a single silver dollar. He flipped it into the air toward the earl. When the older man caught it nimbly, he tugged the brim of his hat in compliment. The coin was his calling card, what he left behind at each robbery.

"Never let it be said I left you with nothing, Your Grace," he quipped then clucked to his horse. The beast neighed in reply and leapt into motion.

"Insolent little bastard," the earl grumbled.

Once the earl had helped his wife into the coach and huffed and puffed his way inside as well, the thin woman barely gave him time to shut the door before she snapped the reins, shouted haw at the horses and the coach lurched forward with a discordant shriek.

He shook his head as the coach disappeared down the road in a plume of billowing dust. "She's a menace on the highway," he quipped.

"You have no idea," Lady Althea replied.

He turned to face her. "I will see no harm come to you, milady," he said quietly. "Once I have the ransom, you will be free to go. You have my word as a gentleman on it."

She nodded as though they were accomplishing a business deal. "I trust you will be true to that word, milord," she said.

He held out his arm and she hooked hers through it then led her to his mount.

"He's quite a handsome beast," she said, patting his neck.

"And docile enough when he wants to be," he replied.

She looked up at him. "And when he doesn't want to be?"

"He can be the very devil himself," he told her.

Before she could comment, he bent his knees, swept his arms under her knees and back and hoisted her with ease into the saddle. The serviceable skirt rode up her shapely calf and he felt his cock stir at the sight. Not giving himself time to contemplate long on that silken limb, he swung into the saddle, trapped her within the circle of his arms and put his heel to the steed's flanks.

He took her to a cabin deep in the woods by which ran a moonbeam-shot stream that trickled pleasantly over shimmering rocks. Smoke rose in a ghostly shroud from the fieldstone chimney and the smell of evergreen was thick in the air.

"Who lives here, milord?" she asked as he drew his mount to a halt.

"Someone I trust," he said and swung his leg from the horse to slide to the ground then tugged the kerchief from his face.

Her eyes widened at the sight of him and she smiled.

"Like what you see?" he asked.

"Indeed," she replied.

He held his arms up to her.

She put her soft hands on his shoulders and he lifted her from the saddle. Her body slid down his and he kept possession of her waist as he gazed down into her eyes. The glow of the moonlight was caught in the verdant depths as she stared back at him.

"Are you going to compromise me before you return me, milord?" she asked on a breathless note.

"Would you like me to, milady?" he countered.

"I do not believe my father will either pay to get me back or want me back if you do," she said.

He wrapped his arms around her and pressed her tightly to him then crooked a finger under her chin. His eyes dropped to her mouth. "Even if I compromise you just a tiny bit with a fleeting kiss?"

Her lips parted and her hands tightened on his shoulders. "Would it be only a fleeting kiss, milord?"

"I'm not sure. Why don't we see?"

He lowered his head and hesitantly moved in then gently covered her mouth with his. He had to caution himself not to ease his tongue past her soft lips for he did not want to offend her. He made the kiss brief—a mere touch of his mouth to hers—and respectful, as gentle and soft as he could make it despite the raging desire that was speeding through his body.

"That was, I believe, the most fleeting of kisses, milord," she said then pursed her lips before adding. "I have a cousin whose kisses are more to the point."

He arched a brow. "You want me to make a point with my kiss, milady?" He knew damned well she felt the flick of his cock against her abdomen as he spoke.

"I would have you make a statement at the very least," she replied.

He stared into her lovely face and got lost in the green depths of her eyes. His body was on fire with need. It was all he could do to force his passion under control.

"I don't think you would like what I have to say, milady," he said huskily.

"Why don't you let me be the judge of that, milord?" she countered. "I have been kissed before."

"Have you now?"

Whether it was by design or nervousness, her gaze fell to his lips. "I have," she said. "I am not unknowledgeable in the art."

He knew better and he seriously doubted any man had ever put his lips to hers. She was unspoiled, untried and she was playing at something she did not fully comprehend or understand. But he would enter her game if only to show her what a real man's kiss could do.

But not standing in front of his friend's cabin.

He released her and stepped back. "We'd best get inside," he said.

She nodded and he walked her to the door, opening it for her. She went in, looking around her with the curiosity of a woman.

"It is well kept," she said, putting a hand to her bonnet strings. She took off the bonnet and placed it on a table. "Lovingly so."

"When a man owns only a little, he takes extra care of it," he replied. He watched her move about the room, taking in all that she viewed.

"We were speaking of what you might have to say to me," she said as turned to face him.

"You're sure you want me to make my case?" he asked, removing his hat and pistol to lay them on the table beside her bonnet. He went to her and once more encircled her in his arms, unable to prevent his body from needing the closeness of hers.

"Yes," she whispered.

"Then I give you fair warning, milady, my statement will be bold and it will not be brief." He spread his hands up her back to anchor her to him. "I can be a bit longwinded when it comes to speeches."

"All I can ask is that you not put me to sleep with your discourse," she said with a tilt of her chin.

That, he thought, was a challenge he could not and would not let pass. He lowered his head and slanted his mouth over hers, pressed his tongue between her lips and delved deep. The sharp intake of her breath brought her breasts hard against his chest and he moved his hands to her sweet little rump to press her against his erection. Her groan was like music to his ears.

Her hands moved into his hair as she became bolder with her kissing. She was a fast learner and obviously knew what she wanted and how she wanted it. There was a moment of shocked surprise when she thrust her sweet little tongue into his mouth and his groan made her chuckle.

He pulled his mouth from hers and looked at her. "Am I amusing you, milady?" he asked, a bit hurt by her mirth.

"Nay, milord. I just realized I have as much power over you as you have over me," she said with a saucy grin. Her fingers raked lightly along his scalp. "You're not going to give me back, are you?"

Slowly, he shook his head but did not answer.

"Is it your intention to compromise me so that giving me back is not an option?" she queried, that adorable little face tilted to one side.

"Do you want me to compromise you?" he countered.

"I would hear your argument for that option," she replied.

He took a step back so he could look down into her face. "Milady, when a man makes that kind of argument it is a one-sided proposition. He knows what he wants and can only hope the lady wants the same."

She looked up at him through her lashes. "And if she does?"

"Milady," he said and pulled his arms from around her so he could take her hands in his. "I cannot promise what will be argued can easily be stopped once started. I cannot swear I can control my…" He took a deep breath. "My words."

"Mayhap I do not want you to control your…" She smiled. "Words, milord."

He tightened his hold on her hands. "Let me be clear with you on the matter, milady."

"Please do," she responded.

"Once a woman is spoken to in such a way, what is said cannot be taken back. The die will be cast. The—"

"You talk entirely too much, Highwayman," she said and pulled him to her, bent his captive arms behind him as she rubbed her body suggestively against his.

"Milady," he said, shocked by her actions.

"Will you marry me?" she asked, shocking him to the very foundation of his being.

"Marry you?" he repeated.

"Yes, milord. Will you make of me an honest woman after our…talk?" she questioned.

He stared into her beautiful face—got lost in her those mesmerizing eyes.

"Marriage is not an option for me," he stated.

"Then let's retire to yonder bed and I will listen very carefully to your argument against it," she said in a business-like tone. She released her hold on his hands, turned and headed for the bed. "I've something I've been itching to get off my…" She swiveled her head around to give him a sultry look and her hands went to the buttons of her plain bodice. "My chest."

Like a man in a trance he followed behind her. His gaze was steady on her swaying hips as she neared the narrow bed. Though his friend's wife kept the cabin scrupulously clean, it was no fitting place for a woman of Lady Standfield's rank to lose her virginity. He stopped in the middle of the floor.

What the hell was he thinking? He could not deflower the woman.

She looked around and frowned at him. Her bodice was unbuttoned all the way to the waist and he saw her chemise. He clenched his hands into fists, released them, clenched them again and felt all the moisture evaporate from his mouth.

"Is something amiss, milord?" she asked.

"I…I…" He couldn't find the words to tell her that he could not—nay, would not—violate her. He was a knave of the highest order, a rake of the lowest degree, but she was a lady of substance, of breeding. Though she was well past the age of consent, she was pure. He knew it in his heart. In the very marrow of his bones.

"Milord?" she questioned. "Why are you so pale?" She took a step toward him. "Are you ill?"

He shot his hand up, palm outward, to stay her advance. "Milady, I do not believe you have thought this through," he said, hating every word that fell from his lips. "In good conscience, I cannot despoil you here in this place."

Her eyebrows lifted. "And pray tell what is wrong with this place?"

"It is not a fitting place for a lady such as you to—"

"Milord, stop," she said sternly, and before he could say another word, she was peeling the bodice from her creamy shoulders. "I am a woman full grown and I know what I want. And what I want is you, Highwayman."

The sight of her silken shoulders, the gown falling down her arms, past her fingertips, gliding down her hips to pool at her feet flooded his entire body with molten heat. He could not look away from the swell of her breasts above the neckline of the chemise. Every breath she took lifted those delightful mounds and he saw the dark shadow of her areolas outlined beneath the lace.

And he was, he thought, as much a male as the next man and just as easily tempted by the sight of a woman's naked charms.

"Merciful God," he whispered.

"I want you, Highwayman," she repeated. "Do you want me or not?"

"Not like this," he heard himself say.

"Then pray how do you want me?" she demanded. "In yon forest on a bed of pine needles? On the banks of the stream? Beneath a—"

He took five steps and put his hands to her waist, lifted her up then grabbed her under her thighs to pull her legs around him. With his gaze fused with hers, he walked her to the wall to press her back against it. He took her in a kiss with a fierceness that barely registered as he ground his lips to hers and inserted his tongue into the warm cavern of her mouth.

Her arms were around his neck. Her ankles were locked at the small of his back. He pushed against her with his hips, ground his cock to her center. His shaft was hard as steel and aching—burning with need. His palms itched to mold around her bare breasts. His tongue wanted to taste the very core of her.

"Milord, do not torture me," she whispered against his mouth. "Let me know what it is to be a woman." She put her hands to his chest to push him. "Let me know what it is to be your woman."

He searched her eyes. "Are you sure?"

"As sure as I live and breathe," she stated emphatically. "I've wanted you—and you alone—from the moment I laid eyes on you."

"Once done…"

"Cannot be undone," she said with a roll of her eyes. "I know."

Her comical expression, the hot desire in those green eyes, was his undoing. He lost all contact with what was morally and ethically right. All resistance went out the window and he surrendered. Hefting her higher against him, he turned and took her to the bed. He hesitated only a second longer before leaning forward to lay her upon the mattress. Stepping back, he moved to the foot of the bed to remove her slippers.

She had small feet with high arches within the opaque cotton of her stockings. The hem of her petticoat was rucked up to her knees and the sight of her shapely calves made his mouth water. Gently— so as not to frighten her—he eased the hem higher until he could get to the garters that held the stockings in place. They were about six inches above her knees and the higher he pushed the hem of her petticoat, the harder his cock became.

As he began to peel the garter and stocking down her leg, his body clenched with such raging lust he was all but salivating. The soft, creamy skin revealed inch by inch to his sight was the stuff of wet dreams. By the time he removed her other stocking and her legs were bare from knee to cute little toes he was barely cognizant of anything save her silken limbs. He swallowed hard, for his attention had gone to the V of her legs and he wanted more than anything to see what lay hidden under the petticoat.

"You may remove the petticoat, milord," she said.

He'd had many women in his life, was no novice to the realm of Aphrodite. A skilled lover who had undertaken dozens upon dozens of conquests in his lifetime, he knew what he was about. Each woman had been a delightful invasion, but this woman was different. He knew it in his soul—what there was left of it. He knew he had to tread carefully for how she was led this night would either make or break the relationship he found he desperately wanted with her.

Realizing his hands were shaking, he put his fingers to the drawstring of her petticoat.

You shouldn't be doing this. It is wrong. You know it is wrong, a voice said inside his head.

"Shut up," he snapped.

"I beg your pardon?" she queried.

"Not you," he said.

Jaw clenched, he fumbled with the ribbon and was tempted to tear the blasted thing apart. When it came undone, he stilled his hands. It was like unwrapping a present and there was a right way and a wrong way to do it. You did not unwrap a package from the bottom up. You unwrapped it from the top down. You peeled the paper away inch by inch until the entire gift was revealed. He looked up at her then extended his hand.

A puzzled look passed over her face but she slipped her hand into his and he pulled her to a sitting position. The chemise should come off first, he decided, and it should be slipped down her shoulders slowly instead of pulled over her head. Why that was important, he wasn't sure. In the past he'd all but torn the undergarments from the women he seduced, but Lady Standfield was different. He needed to treat her with the respect and adoration she deserved.

So he came to the side of the bed, sat down and took her hand in his. He brought it to his lips. "Don't be nervous," he said.

"How can I not be, milord?" she said. "'Tis a monumental enterprise I am about to experience."

"Life altering," he admitted. "And one you should be absolutely sure you wish to have." He reached up his free hand to tuck behind her ear a loose strand of hair that had escaped the serviceable bun at the nape of her neck.

"I am absolutely sure," she said breathlessly and leaned her cheek into the cup of his hand. As he caressed her, she lowered her lashes. "I would have it be no other man save you with whom to undertake the enterprise."

"Why me?" he asked. "Why not wait for that titled lord your father has waiting in the wings?"

She pursed her lips and gave him a droll look. "If you were thirsty, milord, and someone gave you the choice of a fine wine or a cup of sour milk, which would you want?"

"You liken me to fine wine, milady?" he queried.

"Well, you're not sour milk," she said. "And then there is the adventure of it, my bold highwayman. What maid would not prefer a handsome brigand over a mule-faced milksop?"

"I see your point," he acknowledged with a twitch of his lips.

"Besides, there is the forbidden involved to make it all the more exciting," she said, curling that sweet little tongue over her bottom lip. "The clandestine rendezvous. The illicit liaison. The wicked temptation." She swept her unengaged hand to the side. "All those things we maidens read about in our lonely beds and dream about when we lay our heads upon our pillows."

As she spoke he released her hand and reached up to remove the pins from her hair. He wanted to see the ebony tresses tumbling down. When they fell, he fanned the heavy locks around her shoulders, the living cape cascading to her hips.

"Beautiful," he told her, fingering one curl.

"It is my pride and joy," she said.

"And rightly so," he agreed. He brought the lock to his face and inhaled the heady scent of gardenia.

"Do I compare to the other women you have bedded, milord?" she asked and he looked up to see her cheeks blazing with color. There was apprehension in her gaze. "Would you prefer one of them instead of me?"

"Ah, milady, what need have I to pluck the feathers from those gaggling geese when I have the treasures of Kublai Khan here before me?" He stroked her hair. "Here are strands of onyx." His finger trailed to the corner of her eye. "And brilliant emeralds." He cupped her cheek. "Flawless alabaster." He eased his thumb across her upper lip then grazed it over her front teeth. "And here rubies and pearls." He glided his hand down her neck onto the swell of her breast. "And beneath this lacy garment, there will be peaks of rich coral."

"I believe you have missed your calling, milord," she said, sucking in a breath at his bold touch. "You have the soul of a poet within you."

"I know beauty and rich treasure when I behold them, milady," he replied. He took her cheeks between his palms and brought her lips to his.

It was a chaste kiss as kisses went, but it held all the passion he wanted her to taste. She put a hand on his biceps and her touch sent a tremor through him. He slid his hands from her cheeks to her shoulders—to the capped sleeves of her chemise. He held her gaze—silently asking for her permission to continue. When she nodded, he eased his hand along her collarbones to the ribbon tie between her breasts. Her indrawn breath made his cock shift again.

"I will go slowly, milady," he promised.

You need to leave. Now. Not slowly but as fast as you can, run. Go, before it is too late! that inner voice hissed at him.

He pushed the voice to the back of his mind for she was nodding again and seemed to be trying to relax, although her lovely eyes were filled with apprehension.

"I will not hurt you, Althea," he told her. "I will never hurt you."

"I know," she whispered.

He lowered the chemise slowly until it caught on the tips of her breasts. The blood was hammering in his ears and he wanted to pull it all the way down to her neatly tucked waist but controlled the urge. Instead, he leaned in to place a soft kiss on the sensitive spot where neck met shoulder.

"Ah," she moaned, letting her head fall back.

That was the incentive he needed to move his lips to the hollow of her throat where a frantic pulse was beating madly. A succession of light kisses across her left collarbone to the curve of her shoulder elicited another low moan. He trailed kisses from that shoulder to the other then back to the center of her upper chest before tugging the chemise lower until the peaks of her breasts were revealed.

"Sweet Lord," he said on a long breath. Her nipples were hard little pebbles standing erect and beckoning his mouth, his tongue, his teeth. A ripple of desire undulated through him as he caught one dusky nubbin between his lips.

"Milord," she gasped.

He leaned harder against her, pressing her down to the mattress and sliding his upper body over hers. Lifting his knee, he swung his left leg over hers and drew his other leg onto the bed.

"No," she said and shifted her hands to his shoulders.

He lifted his head. "What?" he asked, stunned by her reversal.

"Undress," she said. "Your buckle is cutting into my stomach."

He hadn't thought about being fully clothed. Hell, he hadn't even removed his coat. Before he took another breath, he catapulted himself from the bed and began to strip as though his clothing was aflame. As he did, she sat up—bracing her body on her elbows—to watch him.

The coat went in one direction, the waistcoat in another. He fumbled with the belt behind which he tucked his gun until it was undone then jerked the shirt from the waistband of his britches and pulled it over his head. His hands got caught in the sleeves to make him growl with frustration. The shirt went sailing as he put his hands to the buttons of his fly.

"I would think it best to take off your boots before you go much further," she advised.

He looked down at his boots, groaned then glanced over at her only to stop in mid-action. She was reclining there with her breasts fully exposed, her legs apart with the hem of her petticoat resting mid-thigh. She looked wanton and...

He let out a shuddery breath.

She looked ready.

That spurred him into action and he hurried over to the table, pulled out a chair and sat down heavily to yank off his boots.

"There is no hurry, milord," she said and he heard the humor in her voice.

"Aye, there is," he replied through clenched teeth. He dropped the first boot, had trouble pulling off the other and released a long stream of curses in his native Gaelic.

"I don't believe I want to know what you just said," she told him.

"Nay, you don't," he agreed and flung the offending boot across the room. His stockings came next then he shot up from the chair and made quick work of the buttons of his fly.

"You have a very nice chest," she said. "As dark and curly as your hair is, though, I would have expected a rich thatch of hair on your chest."

Her off-handed insult brought his head up. "Is that a deal breaker, milady?" he demanded.

"No," she said and wiggled her toes. "Merely an observation."

He narrowed his eyes for he had something hiding behind the opened V of his britches that he was itching for her to observe. Hooking his thumbs into the waistband, he pushed the britches down his hips. As his cock sprang free, he watched her eyes widen.

"Oh my," she said, lips parting.

"Aye," he said with what he realized was a touch of pride.

She was staring avidly at his shaft as though afraid to look away.

"It doesn't bite," he said with a laugh.

Slowly she tore her gaze from his cock to look him in the eye. "I had no idea," she said in a near whisper.

He came toward her much as he would have a wild filly he wished to tame. No sudden or menacing moves. As he neared the bed, she once again lowered her eyes to his manhood. Once he was beside the bed, he made no attempt to join her. Her chest was heaving as nerves took over her breath. At the moment she put out her tongue to lick her lips, his cock pulsed and her eyes widened even more and her mouth dropped open.

"It is…" Her lips moved but she couldn't seem to find the words she wanted to say.

"A part of me, milady," he said quietly. "Not some alien appendage intent on doing you harm. God designed it to give pleasure, not pain. To create life, not produce death."

"P…pleasure?" she repeated and lifted her gaze to his.

"The greatest of pleasures, milady," he said. He extended his palm to her. "Give me your hand."

She hesitated for a second or two then shifted her weight so she could take her left hand from the mattress. It shook as she reached for his hand—expecting to slip her fingers into his palm—but he took gentle hold of her wrist, stepped closer to the bed and brought her hand toward his cock.

"Touch it, Althea," he said. "Wrap your fingers around it. You will see it is nothing more than flesh."

Tucking her bottom lip between her teeth, she reached for him. The moment her palm made contact, she drew in a shuddery breath. "The flesh is soft," she said then closed her fingers around his girth. Surprise shifted over her face. "Yet hard as steel beneath."

It was the hardest thing he'd ever done to stand there and let her caress him, run her hand up and down his length, test the texture of the head as she ran her thumb over it. His knees felt weak and his blood was running lava-hot through his veins.

"What is this liquid at the tip?"

"Semen," he said in a choked voice. "The seed of life."

He watched her frown. "Your seed," she said then it was almost as though a candle had been lit for she slowly took her hand away. "Seed that would get me with child." She turned frightened eyes to him. "I am not ready yet for a child, Highwayman."

"Then when the time comes, I will not spend my seed within you," he said. He put a hand to his heart. "On my honor, I will not."

She seemed to be considering his words. "That would work?"

"For centuries that is all that has been used by many couples," he replied. "I cannot swear it works every time but it is my understanding that it does most times."

"It is the chance we take," she said. "It will not matter once we are wed."

"What?" he asked.

"We will marry eventually," she stated.

"Milady, I have no inclination to marry," he told her. "You know what I am. You know—"

"I know you are of the peerage," she interrupted.

The breath caught in his throat. "The peerage?" he echoed.

"Your speech is too precise, milord. Your bearing too noble for you to be anything but an aristocrat. I have heard it said your skill with a rapier is unequaled. Such skill is taught by a fencing master, and a man of lower lineage would not have access to such an instructor."

"Mayhap I am the boyhood friend of a noble," he countered. "And learned alongside him."

"Mayhap, but unlikely," she said.

He couldn't help but think what a ridiculous conversation this was. There she reclined upon his friend's bed with her breasts and calves uncovered. There he stood with nothing save the air clothing him and his cock now at half-staff. For want of something to do, he looked around him.

"For what are you searching, milord?" she asked.

A way out, he thought. He wasn't sure this was a good idea. As much as he wanted her—and God knew he wanted her—he knew marriage to him would not be to any woman's benefit. If anything, it could very well ruin that woman's life. He was a wanted man with a very high bounty on his head. He risked his neck every day of his life and had no plan to stop doing so. Not for wealth from the gold or the trinkets he gathered from the rich, pompous men and snooty women he robbed but for what that wealth could do. It could buy another week of living for those who needed to make it through another day.

She patted the bed beside her. "Your lady is waiting for you, Highwayman. Will you not join her?"

What if he got her pregnant? he thought. The stigma of bearing the child of an infamous outlaw would ruin her socially. Not even his father's immense wealth and position with the Crown would stop tongues from wagging and those of her class from ostracizing her. Could he really deal her such a desperate hand?

No, he thought. He had no intention of sliding past those creamy thighs no matter how much he wanted to.

"Milord, something tells me you are having second thoughts about speaking to me," she said and he saw merry glints moving through her gaze. "If that is the case, mayhap I should put forth my argument."

As bold as any doxy he'd ever encountered, she reached out and took possession of what she so obviously was determined to have. He had no choice but to put knee to mattress else have her pull the very root from his body.

"Milady, I beg you to be gentler with it," he said, wincing. "It is not a wagon tongue."

She released him but pursed her lips. "Then instruct me on how I am to handle it, milord. I am not a mind reader and by the by, should you not divest me of the remainder of my clothing before you begin your rebuttal?" she asked. She slid her arms from under her and lay upon the covers, arched her hips in invitation for him to peel the chemise from beneath her.

"Milady, we must discuss this tendency you have to be so forward," he said sternly. "That is not the way an untried young lady behaves."

"Mayhap not, but it is the way a young woman who wishes to be bedded by a handsome rogue behaves," she replied then smiled. "Is it not?"

"I suppose—" he began.

"Either take what you so obviously want, milord, or put on your clothes and leave," she interrupted. She pursed her lips, frowned with her eyes narrowed and lifted her chin in challenge.

It was her cute little chin raised in the air and the way her lush lips were pressed tightly together that was his undoing. He sighed and gave in. He put his hands to the bunched bodice of the chemise and slid it down her abdomen and over her hips.

"Sweet Morrigunia," he whispered as the soft curls at the juncture of her thighs were revealed. He stilled, staring intently at the dark V that concealed her most private parts from him.

"Do you gain pleasure from torturing women, milord?" she asked with a burst of pique. "Take the bloody garment off me. Now."

He jerked his gaze from her groin to her face. She had one eyebrow arched in such a way it reminded him of the way his governess would glare at him when she was annoyed. For some reason that amused him.

"Milady," he said. "Has no one ever told you that expectation is half the fun of being taken?"

"I am not finding this fun, milord," she snapped. "I am finding it frustrating." Not giving him any more time, she sat up, lifted her rump from the mattress, batted his hands away then shoved the chemise down her thighs, kicking it from her legs as he stood there with one knee on the mattress and his hands up at his shoulders as though she held a pistol on him. She lay back down. "There. All done," she pronounced. "Nothing left to impede us."

Lips twitching, he raised his eyebrows—trying not to return his gaze to the curls between her creamy thighs. "You are at the ready, are you not, milady?" he teased.

"Overly ready, milord," she said. She held her arms out to him.

Those silken arms extended toward him pushed away any resistance he had left. He nodded in acceptance of what was going to be and swung his leg onto the bed. With infinite care but deliberate intent, he slid his body up hers, reveling in the way her eyes widened at the touch of their flesh meeting.

"Like that?" he inquired as he lifted his knee to press it lightly against the inside of her knee. Gently, he nudged her left leg to the side so he could settle his body where it needed to be.

She swallowed hard. "Aye," she said on a soft whisper. "Very much, milord." She shifted her other leg so he could position himself between her spread thighs.

"Good," he said. "Then you will love this."

Before she could ask what he meant, he slithered down in the bed until his lips were just above her navel. Her hastily sucked-in breath made him smile as he put his mouth to that sensitive indention.

"Declan," she hissed and her hands went to his head—her fingers spiking through his hair.

"Mm," he said against her navel and her entire body quivered. Giving her no time, extending no quarter, he flicked his tongue into the concave little hollow. Again she shuddered as her fingers tightened almost painfully in his hair. It took some doing to lift his head to look up at her for she was pressing his mouth to her body. He hoped he wouldn't have to speak, but that the way he gazed up at her would loosen her hold on him.

It did and she marginally relaxed, though her heels were digging into the mattress, her pelvis arched toward him.

He winked then lowered his mouth to that sweet spot just below her navel and midway to the beckoning curls that hid her nether lips from his sight. Pushing himself up so he could slide farther down the mattress, he kissed his way to the soft, spiky locks then turned his cheek to lay it upon her abdomen, lowering his hand to rest it upon her right hip and thigh.

"Milord?" she questioned.

"All in good time, milady," he replied. "All in good time."

He drew his hand down her side from the outside of her breast to her hip then continued its journey onto her thigh. Yet again she shivered under his touch and goose bumps popped up under the pads of his fingers.

Idly he stroked her from the crease of her thigh to her knee, turned his hand so the backs of his fingers made the return journey, then turned it again to run his nails to her knee the next time. He continued the enticing movement several times before easing his fingers closer to the inside of her thigh on the next upward stroke. He heard her sigh—almost purr—and blew his breath across her hip. She was smoothing his hair much as if he were a pet, and that nudged the wicked little devil inside him. He could not—would not—let her sink into contentment. He ran the backs of his fingers down her thigh and then slowly dragged his nails upward on the return trip. This time he did not stop at the crease of her thigh. Instead, he moved his hand over even more so he could rake his fingers upward through those silky curls.

As though she had been poked with a red-hot dagger she jumped as he pressed the base of his thumb to that place he knew she would feel it the most—her clit. He fanned that little nubbin and grinned as she cried out.

Lifting his head again, he looked up to see her staring down at him with her mouth open and eyes wide. He didn't think she was breathing and her face was infused with a dark blush. Slowly he smiled at her then shifted his hand so his thumb was paused at the dampness that had formed between her legs.

"Milord?" she asked—her voice quivering.

He didn't answer. Instead—watching her the entire time—he moved even lower in the bed, put his hands to the insides of her thighs, pushed them as far apart as he thought would be comfortable for her then eased his thumbs to the warm lips that bracketed the entrance to her body. Her lips formed a perfect O when he anchored her flesh then placed his mouth to the slick heat.

She arched her back from the bed and her hands left his head to slam down to the coverlet. He was grateful she grabbed handfuls of the material rather than his hair, for she twisted the cloth and pulled at it savagely. A soft, vibrating keen came from deep within her throat.

One long, slow lap of his tongue from one end of her slit to the other made her entire body shiver and at the moment he thrust that warmth into her she cried out. He heard the coverlet rip from her tight hold upon it. As he pressed into her sweet cavern he splayed his hands to either side of her groin then began to run the pads of his thumbs up and down the inner folds of her vagina. He probed deep with his tongue and felt the immediate clinches that signaled she was about to find out what pleasure truly was.

"Milord," she screamed as her inner muscles vibrated. Her hands left the bed to grab his head as he flicked his tongue against her clit to intensify the sensation she was experiencing.

Strong little waves rippled through her then with one final flutter, they ceased. She was panting and when he lifted his head to see her face, her neck was arched against the pillow, eyes squeezed shut and her mouth open wide. He saw a vein throbbing in her neck. She said something unintelligible then stiffened as the release undulated through her cunt.

He had lain with many women in his lifetime. From the first older woman who took him into her bed to make him a man until the milkmaid just three nights back who had nearly broken his cock with her acrobatic pelvis, he'd carved many a notch on his proverbial headboard.

But he'd never experienced a woman's first time. It was a revelation to him. Watching her shudder, dragging at the coverlet twisted in her hands as her hips squirmed, he took pride in knowing he had been the first man to introduce her to such pleasure. He smiled for she was making little purring sounds he'd never heard any other woman make.

He had satisfied her well, he thought. Initiated her into the art of lovemaking in such a way she would always have fond memories of this night and of him. He only wished he could finish what he started, but that couldn't happen.

She was the only virgin he had dared touch past a few squeezes of a tit or a rub of his palm between their legs as he kissed them. Fucking a virgin was tantamount to marrying the little miss and that he had no intention of ever doing. He cherished his bachelorhood too much for that.

And then there was his profession…

She heaved a great sigh.

He lifted his head to watch her body melt into the mattress. With her thighs splayed wide, her breasts rising and falling rapidly, she looked far more wanton than any chit he'd ever tupped.

He slid up beside her, took her into his arms to hold her against him. "You enjoyed that?"

She pressed her face into his shoulders. "Aye, milord, but…"

Turning his face down to her, he arched a brow. "But?"

Her hand came up to his chest, her index finger to the tuft of hair between his breastbones. She coiled the curl around her finger. "Is that all there is to it?"

"No," he said. "If you were any other woman, I would take you fully."

"Put your manhood inside me, you mean." She wanted clarification.

"My cock into your cunt, aye," he said, wanting to shock her with the coarse language but his words seemed to have the opposite effect. Instead of recoiling, she pushed harder against him then lifted her leg to glide it between his thighs.

"What are you waiting for?" she asked.

That made him laugh. "Some other man to breach you, milady. I don't fuck virgins."

She shot up in the bed—her thigh pressing hard into his groin—and her beautiful face turned hard. "Wasn't that the point? To deflower me?"

"Not on my end," he said, lacing his hands behind his head. "You wanted to know what it felt like to have an orgasm and I more than fulfilled that desire."

"But you haven't done what I wanted you to do," she stated.

"I am not going to take your maidenhead, milady," he said.

"No?" she queried, eyes narrowed.

"No. That right is reserved for your husband and for him alone."

Her purr of a few moment before became a growl and she surprised the hell out of him by throwing herself on him, pushing his legs apart with her knees and slamming her mouth down upon his. The invasion of her tongue thrusting between his lips shocked him. She was writhing, grinding, wriggling against him in such a way his cock took immediate notice.

He tore his mouth from hers. "No," he said firmly and took hold of her upper arms to push her away. "We're not going to..."

"Yes, we are, milord," she said.

"No, hell, we aren't," he replied through clenched teeth. He had every intention of flipping her off him and scrambling from the bed.

That was until she reached down to enclose him in her fist.

"You, sir, are going to finish what you started," she said, squeezing him almost to the point of pain.

Some unchivalrous, nasty little part of his brain hissed at him to do just that. If ever a woman wanted to be fucked as badly as this one, he'd yet to encounter her. Even with her fisting him, sliding her palm up and down his rock-hard flesh, he tried to push her off him but she would not be denied. Her thumb moved over the slit of his cockhead and that was more than he could bear.

"Damn it, woman," he snarled between his gritted teeth. He tightened his hands on her arms then rolled until she was stretched out beneath him. Almost savagely he shoved her thighs apart and parked his hips atop hers. Trouble was: she still had a tight grip on his shaft.

He stared down into her challenging eyes.

"Let go," he said.

"Put it in me," she replied and shocked the hell out of him by trying to stuff his cock into her cunt.

"No," he said. Some other part of him—a part he didn't know he had—felt violated by her action.

"Put it in me or I will pull it from the root," she said, lifting her chin. Her fingers clamped down on him so tightly he yelped.

All right, he thought. If she wanted to be fucked that badly…

Letting go of her arms, he shot his hands down to her hips, slammed his palms under her ass and lifted her. He ground himself hard upon her, all but slithering his lower body across her arm as she held him.

"You want it?" he said. "Then let go."

He felt the pressure on his shaft loosen.

"You will take me fully?" she asked.

"Aye," he stated and rocked against her.

"You swear?" she queried.

"Aye, woman, I swear," he growled.

"On your honor as a gentleman?"

"Aye," he said with a downward snap of his head.

She stared at him for a moment then released him, dragging her hand from between them.

He pulled one hand from under her to take hold of his cock. "And if I get your pregnant, the onus will be on you, not me," he ground out.

"You said you would not spend your seed within me," she reminded him.

"I lied," he snapped.

Her eyes widened, her mouth dropped open and she tried to push him off her, but it was already too late. He had his cock at her entrance and at the moment he eased the head inside her, she bucked and impaled herself upon him.

"Damn it, woman," he hissed.

He'd had no intention of fully penetrating her. He'd had no intention of breaching her maidenhead. He'd meant to scare with the thought of him getting her with child but she had surprised him yet again. Apparently his impregnating her hadn't concerned her.

Now the point was moot.

She was panting as she stared up at him with eyes wide and mouth farther ajar. If he'd hurt her, she gave no indication of it. She seemed merely stunned.

And he knew why. He was not a small man. He filled her completely and to the base. He was stretching her, realizing he shouldn't move until she was fully accustomed to his shaft spiked within her lest he cause her pain. He watched her pupils dilate then she slowly closed her lips. She swallowed then her lips parted. She blinked.

"You are inside me," she whispered.

"Aye," he said. The urge to thrust was like a brand burning his shaft but he kept rigidly still.

"I can feel you touching my womb."

He knew that wasn't possible but didn't disagree. Her breathing was changing which meant she was becoming aroused again.

That was all the encouragement his shaft needed.

Slowly—with teeth grinding together—he began moving inside her. The moment she sucked in a breath he stopped, but then she shook her head.

"Don't," she pleaded. "Please don't stop. You have no idea how good that feels."

Oh, but he did, he thought as he started to move again. Drawing back slowly, easing forward. Drawing back a little more, then seating himself firmly again. That slow pull and push was making him pant, had brought sweat to his forehead. Pushing aside the need to pump like a madman to ease the ache in his shaft, he dug his toes into the mattress and rocked against her as he withdrew almost all the way out.

"Ah," she said—the word drawn out on a long sigh. Her eyes drifted closed.

He twisted his hips then pushed in to the hilt.

Her hands went to his shoulders, her nails digging lightly into his flesh.

"Lift your legs," he said and realized his voice was harsh, grating. Which made sense for his arms were shaking from trying to control himself.

"What?" she said, snapping her lids open.

"Lift your legs and wrap them around my hips," he instructed.

"Like this?" she asked and encircled him.

"Aye," he replied, clenching his molars together.

He couldn't maintain the stoic calm any longer. His shaft was burning with need. His balls felt so tight he thought they might explode. He clenched his fingers into her soft ass and began to thrust into her with more speed.

Sweat clung to his chest now, dripped from his temples. A fine sheen of moisture coated his upper lip and he swept his tongue over it. He increased the rhythm of his drives but held himself still for a second or two within her when the tip of his head touched her far wall.

He heard her moan, felt her tight walls clench around him. He pulled back until only the crown of his shaft was inside her. She moaned again and clawed at his shoulders. From that moment on, he was no longer in control. His cock was.

She was sufficiently slick and stretched that he felt he could thrust into her with more force and not hurt her. She needed; he needed it.

Gods how he needed it.

The bed beneath them squeaked as he thrust harder into her hot sheath. The iron headboard banged against the wall in time to his lunges. She was making that strange half purr/half growl sound that spurred him on. Her legs tightened around his waist. She arched her hips into his.

"Declan," she screamed, looking past his shoulder.

Stunned, he stopped moving. "What?" he asked, fear jumping up his throat.

But it was too late. Their releases came simultaneously and he could never remember that ever happening before, but that was the last thought he had before the cabin door crashed open. He turned his head just as the butt of the musket crashed against his temple.

Chapter Two

Standfield Hall, Oxmoor, several weeks earlier

Althea was bored beyond tears. Her cousin's engagement party was as bland and uninspiring at the girl herself. A masquerade ball? How simply droll.

The musicians? Mediocre at best. The food? Barely palatable. The company?

Snapping her fan open, she plied it vigorously while she surveyed the guests gathered in her father's ballroom. There were precious few among the throng who were gout- and arthritis-free. Few who didn't require the employment of a cane or a guiding hand upon the arm. Fewer still who still had all their teeth.

"Sweet Merciful Morrigunia," she said, rolling her eyes. Not even the Triune Goddess, Herself, would blame her for taking a cannon and blowing the crowd apart in a fiery explosion.

Her aunt's raucous laughter drew Althea's notice and she turned to glare at the woman. Not only did Aunt Millicent caw like a crow, the woman looked like a crow. All skinny arms and matchstick-thin legs. She had dyed her bushy mop of hair as black as that bird's wing.

"Ridiculous," Althea pronounced. She knew full well Aunt Millie's hair was really as snow-white as the porcelain tub in the guest room.

Stomping her foot, she swung around and headed for the opened Francachi doors to the balcony. If she remained one moment longer among her father's guests, she was sure to murder at least half of them. As she walked, her pale green ball gown made an angry rustling sound as it scraped against her silk stockings.

And that was another thing, she thought as she ignored the greeting of one of her father's cronies. Her garters were cutting into her thigh, her satin pumps were pinching her toes, and the gown's bodice was pressing all the air out of her lungs. Why had she ever agreed to wear the gown her aunt had brought back from her shopping trip to Ollainnis? Althea had hated the thing on sight and couldn't wait to tear it from her body.

Stepping out onto the deep balcony with its elaborate wrought-iron balustrade, she was relieved to find no one was lurking in the semi-darkness. Only light from candles glowing softly in milk-glass globes granted her the freedom to reach up to remove the dark green domino mask covering her eyes. The mask was an abomination and she hadn't wanted to wear the silly thing. It wasn't as if anyone at the party did not know who she was. At the age of twenty, she was the youngest person there. Her cousin Sara was closest in age; an old maid at twenty and six.

"Good thing Uncle Walter finally found a man willing to marry your scrawny ass," she mumbled. Thinking of Sara's aquiline nose, thin limbs, flat chest and beady black eyes, no one could doubt whose daughter she was.

Althea walked to the rail to look out over the moon-shot pond behind the manor. Jasmine filled the night air and she inhaled deeply to rid her nostrils of the myriad scents of perfume, hair pomade and sweaty bodies. She closed the fan, let it fall from the silk braid hanging at her wrist and leaned forward with her forearms braced against the cool top rail of the balustrade.

Behind her she heard a muted gasp go through those gathered in the ballroom. She turned but could see nothing beyond the doorway. Leaving the railing, she walked to the opening. Although the less-than-stellar musicians were sawing away on their instruments, all movement on the dance floor had ceased. The guests were as still as statues as they faced the archway that led into the ballroom.

Venturing onto the parquet floor, Althea tried to see around two gentlemen who were blocking her view.

"Who has arrived?" she asked.

Neither man turned to look at her. One was clutching his wineglass so tightly his knuckles had bled of color.

"The Duke of Arlington and his demon spawn," one of the men muttered.

The other gentleman—a captain of the Governmental Regiment—flicked imaginary lint from the sleeve of his bright red uniform jacket. "A man whose company no one should have to suffer," he added.

Intrigued by the disdain she heard in the captain's voice, she asked if he was acquainted with the duke's son, the Earl of Dungannon.

"Aye, milady," the man replied. "I had the misfortune of attending boarding school with Declan Farrell."

"More's the pity, Royce, old chap," his friend commiserated.

"Where is he?" Althea asked. She could see the duke across the way for he was a tall and imposing man with a shock of salt and pepper hair that melted into a rather hefty pair of muttonchops sideburns.

"The man in black," the captain said with a sniff. "Always in black." He shot his cuffs, straightened the front piece of his uniform jacket. "I do not believe he wears anything save black."

"Mayhap he is still in mourning," his friend suggested.

"His mother and brother have been in their graves nigh on ten years," the captain snapped. "How long does a man need to grieve?"

"For as long as the grief hurts," Althea said and walked away. For years she'd been hearing about the young Earl of Dungannon but she had never laid eyes on the black sheep of the Farrell family. What she knew of him had come primarily from the gossiping mouths of the kitchen staff. As she skirted the guests who were still staring at Duke Edward, she tried to remember what she'd heard of Declan Farrell.

Oldest son of the duke and the Duchess Kathleen, he had been with his mother and younger brother Eion on their way back from St. Andrews Academy, the boarding school from which Declan Farrell had graduated the day before. As fate would have it, the ship they were taking from Lanceister to Wexford had been capsized by a rogue wave. There were only two survivors—the earl and one of the cabin stewards. Both had repeatedly dived into the chilling, tumbling waters off the coast of Madragil in vain attempts to rescue the passengers and crew, but the water had been too cold and the waves too strong. All that could be done was for Declan Farrell to drag the young steward to safety when their efforts had failed. Pulling the steward onto the bank, the earl had slipped and his leg became caught in a crevice. The bone snapped—making it impossible for him to climb the steep, craggy cliffs behind them.

For over three days rescuer and rescued waited to be found. With no food, no way to light a fire, the earl was close to death by the time a passing fisherman spied them. However, it was too late for the young steward who had died from hypothermia a few hours before the rescue.

Heartsick over the loss of his mother and brother, guilty over not being able to save them, and for the steward's death, Declan Farrell had tried drowning himself in another way; by guzzling liquor until he knocked himself out. His father, the duke, had allowed that to continue for precisely one month before he intervened. At his father's insistence, and with the help of members of the Governmental Regiment, Declan Farrell had been inducted into the Royal Marines against his will.

That turned out to be a miscalculation on his father's part. What the duke thought would help his son only made matters worse. Brawls—drunken and not—as well as conduct unbecoming, the occasional absence without leave, and numerous infractions sent the duke into a murderous rage. But it wasn't until he learned his son had been in a duel with his commanding officer that the duke threw up his hands. Engaging in mortal combat over an affair with the commanding officer's wife was the last straw. Within a week of the duel—where he'd only wounded the lady's husband in the shoulder—the earl was cashiered out of the Regiment and sent home with a less than honorable discharge.

"Now the prodigal son is home," she said softly.

And apparently still creating havoc wherever he went.

She eased past a trio of old women who had their frizzled heads together.

"Rapscallion."

"Scoundrel."

"Rogue," the women labeled him.

Tragic hero, Althea thought as she finally had a clear sight of the Duke of Arlington.

But where was the earl? Althea wondered. The duke was engaged in conversation with Althea's father but his son was nowhere to be found. Looking around her, scanning the crowd, she saw no man dressed entirely in black. Most were dressed in unmanly pastel colors that washed out their pasty complexions and vied horribly with their coifed hairstyles.

Returning her attention to the duke, his cobalt blue eyes shifted to her and she realized she was not wearing her mask. Behind his apple-red mask his gaze was sharp, filled with speculation. She felt that scrutiny crawl over her like maggots and shivered. Althea was thankful he had not vied for her hand when he was looking for a replacement for his second wife. That lady had died in childbirth when Declan was busy courting disaster with the Royal Marines.

"Your daughter, Alastair?" she heard him ask her father.

"Aye, Your Grace," the Duke of Oxmoor replied then motioned her to his side for introductions.

If she had thought the Duke of Arlington's gaze was heated before he took her hand in his, she was overpowered by it when her flesh was touching his. The press of his lips as he brought her hand to his mouth made her acutely uncomfortable. It was all she could do not to snatch her hand back.

"Your Grace," she said. "Welcome to Standfield Hall."

The high-pitched skirl of a fiddle drowned out whatever the Duke of Arlington replied and gave her a reason to look toward the platform upon which the musicians were standing. The lively song they began to play was better than what had gone before it.

"Dance with me."

The words were whispered in her ear, causing her to jump. As a result, she jerked her hand from the duke's moist grip. Before she could turn to whomever had spoken to her, a strong arm circled her back and a firm hand was slipped into hers as she was led out onto the dance floor. Her captor spun her around to face him.

Him! Her gaze encountered a solid chest clothed in a black waistcoat lined with jet buttons. Heart pounding in her chest, she lifted her eyes to look up at him and was disappointed to find he was wearing a mask that hid most of his face from view. He was staring down at her but there was no warmth in his blue eyes. His lips were pressed together, a muscle flaring in his lean cheek as he waltzed her into the center of the dance floor. In the periphery of her vision she noticed no other dancers were gliding beside them. They were alone on the intricate pattern of the elegant parquetry.

He didn't speak to her but he kept his eyes locked on hers. The hand at the small of her back was steady. The hand holding hers felt like iron. His broad shoulders blocked most of the light from the chandeliers overhead as he spun her around the room. He was an excellent dancer—light on his feet and sure of his steps—and he smelled heavenly. Whatever cologne he wore was playing hell with her libido.

She cleared her throat, unnerved by his silence. "We have not been properly introduced, Your Grace," she said. "I am…"

"Lady Althea Standfield," he supplied. "I know who you are, milady."

"And am I to presume you are Lord Declan Farrell, Earl of Dungannon?" she inquired.

His lips twitched. "You presume correctly," he said.

"Thank you for rescuing me."

She realized she had said the wrong word the moment it left her lips and she knew why. He stopped in mid-step, released her then bowed. When he straightened, he offered her his arm.

"May I return you to your father?" he queried.

"Yes, please," she said, contrite over the mistake she had inadvertently made.

Head high, shoulders back, he escorted her across the room then bowed stiffly to her father before turning to her.

"Thank you for the dance, milady," he said. "It was highly enjoyable."

He bowed again then spun on his heel and marched away.

"Impertinent little brat," the Duke of Arlington said. "My apologies, Lady Althea."

That made her bristle, and she turned what she hoped was the coolest gaze she'd ever aimed at man directly at him.

"For what?" she asked. "He was a perfect gentleman." She inclined her head. "If you will excuse me?"

She gave no explanation for turning away. Her father's sputter of surprise made her smile. It would be up to him to apologize to the duke for her untimely departure.

Once more searching the room for the illusive Earl of Dungannon, she was discouraged to find him nowhere in sight. He had disappeared like a will-'o'-the wisp. Letting out an irritated breath, she reached out to swipe a glass of champagne from the tray of a passing servant. Bringing the rim of the crystal flute to her lips, she thought she saw a dark shadow slipping out the doors to the balcony.

Lifting her skirt with her free hand, she headed in that direction and found him right where she had been leaning earlier. He was standing with his hands curled around the top rail, his head back as he stared up at the stars.

"Are you are bored as am I?" he asked without looking around.

"Most likely more so," she replied, coming to stand beside him. She glanced up at his profile. The mask and the shadows on the balcony hid his face from her.

"I wasn't going to come," he said.

"Why did you?" she asked, taking another sip of the heady wine.

He shrugged. "It was more boring staying at Edgerton Manor, my late mother's family estate. I thought the ride over would clear my head, but the perfumes and colognes inside that room have clogged up my sinuses."

She giggled. "Mine, too."

"The elderly gentleman in the puce waistcoat smells like mothballs," he said.

"Lord Summerall," she told him. "I believe he bathes in them."

He grunted then lowered his head to look out over the pond. "Do you swim there?" he asked, nudging his chin toward the crescent-shaped expanse.

"I did when I was a child, but once I turned twelve my father would no longer allow it."

"A shame," he said. "It looks inviting." He braced his arms on the top rail much as she had done. "Especially on a night like tonight. It's sweltering."

She was keenly aware of him. He was a good head taller than her and quite fit if the cut of his jacket was any indication. She vehemently wished she could see his face—wondering if the features fit the deep, gravelly cadence of his voice. There was just a touch of a Chalean brogue his good manners and breeding couldn't disguise. She remembered his mother, Duchess Katherine Edgerton-Farrell, had been from Chale and had birthed both her sons in that lush green land.

"Want to take a moonlight dip?" he asked.

She wasn't sure she'd heard him correctly. "Beg pardon?" she asked.

He looked down at her and in the soft light of the moon, his eyes seem to glow. Though his face was shrouded in the shadows those blue orbs were like searchlights staring down at her.

She had to shake her head to clear her mind of the images of him wearing little more than his breeches. She could imagine spreading her hands over his naked chest, though she'd never touched any man—or boy—in such an intimate way.

"I didn't stutter," he said and before she knew what he was about, he vaulted over the railing and dropped to the ground below.

"Oh my gods," she gasped, leaning over the railing. Though it was only a drop of about ten feet, she couldn't believe he'd done something so reckless.

He was gone again, she thought as she searched the grounds below. Her heart was thudding in her chest as she looked for him among the shrubs and trees of the formal garden. He had not taken the fieldstone path that led down to the pond and with the deep shadows spread out across the far end of the lawn she could not see him. Naturally he would blend in with the night, considering his black apparel and dark hair.

What color was his hair? She wondered and why hadn't she noticed it? She thought perhaps dark chestnut but she wasn't sure.

She heard a splash and felt her mouth drop open.

"Oh, you didn't," she said aloud.

Far out in the pond she saw a white flash and knew it was his arm cutting through the water.

"Irresponsible, careless, rash and..." She smiled. "Wild."

No wonder there was so much gossip about him. He was unlike any man she'd ever met. He intrigued her with his mysterious manner and blatant male appeal. She longed to know the man behind the mask.

She sighed deeply. It was only a matter of time before her father found a man to take her off his hands. She was rapidly nearing her expiration date for marriageability. Older than most girls who were already well into nursing their second babes, she dreaded the day he would tell her he had found the right man for her.

"Older and wiser," she said, straining to hear any more splashes out on the pond. "With a pot belly and a receding hairline."

It was too much to ask he be young and vital and handsome.

As she knew Declan Farrell would be.

"Stop thinking about that man," she berated herself and turned away from the balcony. Instead, she thought of the man her cousin was going to marry and shuddered. If that was the best her aunt and uncle could come up with, it did not bode well for the man her father would pick for her.

* * * * *

When she came down the next morning to break her fast, her father was standing at the dining room window with his hands clutched behind his back. From the set of his shoulders she knew he was not happy.

"Good morning," she said.

His answer was a low grunt.

She went to the sideboard to fill her plate. "Is something wrong, Papa?" she inquired.

"Four of our guests were robbed on their way home last eve," he told her. "They say it was the same highwayman who stole the shipment of gold destined for the bank in Scranton."

"So, he struck again," she said, carrying her food to the table. "You predicted he would."

"Brazen thief," he grumbled. "I would like to be there when he is hanging from a gibbet."

"He's not waylaid any of our shipments, has he?" she asked.

"Not yet," her father answered. "But it is only a matter of time before he strikes at us."

"Our men are highly trained and proficient with their weapons," she commented. "Mayhap that is why he has left us alone."

"Mayhap," her father agreed.

"Have you eaten?"

"My stomach turned sour when I heard the news of the robberies," he replied. "How can one eat when one's neighbors have been violated so reprehensibly?"

"I'm sure they will catch him."

"Indeed they will," her father said with a growl.

"I'll venture to say we have nothing to worry about from this wicked highwayman," she told him.

"From your lips to the gods' ears," her father mumbled.

* * * * *

Arlington Castle

The hangover from hell was pushing against the inside of his skull demanding to be let out. Declan lay on his belly with one arm dangling over the edge of the mattress, his cheek in a cold pool of drool. When the drapery over his windows was thrown back and the brutal morning light speared into his face like a sharp pike, he whimpered like a little boy.

"Up with you," his father ordered. "If you can't handle the drink, don't partake of it, boy."

Another drape was pushed aside and more light flooded the room.

"Father, please," he pleaded. "Have some pity."

"Pity is reserved for those who deserve it. You, Declan James, do not. Up with you or before the gods I will fetch a bucket of iced water and toss it upon you."

Declan groaned. He labored his way up from the bed—his cheek bringing the sheet along with it for the material was stuck to him—then stilled. His arms were shaking and felt like jelly. His head was pounding brutally. His mouth tasted of something he'd prefer not to put a name to lest he puke, and his eyes refused to focus.

"What time did you stumble your way home to last eve?" his father demanded. The old man had come to stand beside the bed with his arms folded and his features set in stone.

"I don't know," Declan whispered.

"Where were you?"

"The inn," Declan muttered and managed to push himself up until he was in a partial sitting position. He ran a trembling hand through his hair.

"Which inn?" his father asked. "Where?"

Squinting from the bright light and the horrendous pain engulfing his head, Declan lifted his head to look up at his father. "What difference does it make?"

"Several of Duke Alastair's guests from that abysmal party last eve were robbed on their way home along the coach road. It was the same masked man who has been plaguing the district for some time now."

Declan swallowed against the rising bile threatening to erupt from his throat. It was all he could do to ease his legs—legs that seemed to weigh a hundred pounds each—over the side of the bed.

"What has that to do with where I was drinking?" he queried.

"What inn, Declan James?" his father repeated.

Declan cocked a shoulder. "The Briar's Hold," he replied as he tentatively put his feet on the floor that was rolling like the deck of a ship.

"Is that right? How convenient. An inn some forty miles from the scene of the robberies?" his father questioned. "And can anyone vouch for your being there?"

Alarm spread up Declan's spine and he forced himself to look his father in the eye. What he saw in that stern, unforgiving face made his blood run cold. He decided the best way to handle his father when the old bastard got that unbending look on his hard visage was to brazen it out.

"Why in the name of the Father God would I need anyone to vouch for me, sir?" he inquired.

A muscle in his father's cheek twitched then bunched. The unfathomable blue eyes sharpened. "You know perfectly well why," he answered. "Do you think me a fool, Declan?"

"No, sir."

"I'll have no more of this," his father told him. "No more riding out after the sun sets. I want you home where I can keep an eye on you."

"You are bestowing a curfew on me?" Declan asked, aghast at such a notion.

"Aye, that is precisely what I am doing. That is how you handle a recalcitrant boy such as yourself."

That rankled and Declan fumbled for a grip on the headboard to pull himself to his feet so he could square off with his father.

"I am a grown man, milord," he said. "I…"

"That is news to me," his father interrupted. He unfolded his arms and raised his hand to jab his index finger into Declan's shoulder. "No more of it, Declan. Do you hear me? I will not have you sullying my family's good name." He jabbed Declan again. "I will not have my only son swinging from the gallows." He narrowed his eyes. "Do you understand what I am saying to you?"

Declan was stunned that his father knew what he'd been about. Surprised, as well, for obviously the duke had no intention of informing the authorities that he suspected the infamous highwayman was none other than his heir.

"Do you?" the old man asked again and put more force behind a third jab.

"Aye," Declan said, wincing. He clung to the headboard like a monkey to a tree else he would have fallen, considering his head was spinning like a top.

"By the gods, boy," his father growled. "You positively reek." That said, the Duke of Arlington squared his shoulders, pivoted on his heel and left the room.

"Shit," Declan muttered as he eased down to the bed.

How the hell had his father found out? He thought he'd been so careful. His very life depended upon him keeping his secret. If his father knew, who else was privy to the real identity of the man the gazette was calling the Gypsy for the claret-red coat and Francachi cocked hat the highwayman wore.

Chances were good since his father knew, his father's personal assistant knew as well. The two were as thick as thieves.

That thought made him chuckle—which was a mistake. The hangover tapped on his skull to let him know the nausea had arrived and he barely had time to grab the chamber pot beside his bed before the hot bile made its appearance.

He was straining to get the last of the gods-awful liquid out of his system when he felt a cool rag laid to his forehead. He pried one eye open and was relieved to see a dainty ankle inside a soft kid slipper and the hem of a serviceable grey work gown. He knew who had come to take pity on him.

"Thank you, Meg," he whispered for his throat was raw from the puking.

"I've brought you a touch of the hair of the dog, milord," she told him. "Best you drink it down as quickly as you can." She held out a glass containing whiskey and a shiny yellow egg yolk.

"You are a veritable angel," he replied. His hand shook as he took the glass from her. He was grateful she kept the rag on his forehead even as she put her other hand to the back of his neck to hold his head as he tipped it back so he could drink the vile brew.

Even as his throat moved convulsively to get the whiskey down, his stomach threatened to push it back up again. When the slimy egg slid down his gullet, it took all his concentration not to hurl. Egad, the taste was the absolute worst, he thought.

"There now," Meg said. "You lay yourself back and let that do its job." She helped him to stretch out on the bed, lifted his legs onto the mattress for him. "And I'll close the curtains for you."

"No you won't," his father said from the doorway. "I told him to bathe. As soon as he can stand on his own and put one foot ahead of the other, I want him in the bathing chamber, young lady, even if it means you must apply the washcloth yourself."

Declan looked up at Meg and winked. The two of them had shared many a bath over the years.

"Bath, Meg," his father said. "Not tupping. Am I clear on the matter?"

"Aye, Your Grace," Meg said, dipping her head. "No tupping."

"If I come back and find you bare-assed in the tub with him, there will be consequences," his father warned.

"Aye, Your Grace," she replied. "My arse will stay covered."

"Make sure of it," his father said then was gone.

"Interfering old bastard," Declan grumbled.

"You are in no condition to tup me or any other woman," Meg said.

"Wanna bet?" he asked and reached out to put his hand on her breast. He kneaded the soft mound, ran his thumb over the fabric where he knew her nipple to be.

"Behave yourself," she said, pushing his hand away.

"You wouldn't like me if I were tame, Meggie my love."

"Best you get up and take that bath lest your father come after you again," she advised.

He let his arm drop as though it were a stone then floundered it around as though he couldn't control it. "Can't...seem...to...get...it...to...work," he said, taking his other hand to lift his wrist.

She put her hands on her hip. "You are such a wicked man," she said. She held out her hand. "Come on with you, then."

He grinned at her—the same grin he had practiced to perfection; the grin that could lift any skirt and pull down any bloomers—and took her hand. When she levered him from the bed, he wrapped his arms around her and nuzzled her neck.

"You smell like roses," he said, kissing the column of her neck.

"You smell like puke," she said and pushed him back. She fanned the air in front of her face. "And your breath could stop a raging bull in its tracks."

Laughing though his head was splitting, he kept one arm around her and walked with her to the bathing chamber, hanging back for her to walk through the door first. As she did, he swatted her ample rear, followed her in and kicked the door closed behind them.

* * * * *

Duke Edward sat at his desk with his elbows on the arms of the plush leather chair, his fingers steepled. He was worried about his son. Terrified the boy would get caught during one of his ridiculous escapades. The thought of his Katherine's child chained to a wall in a dank, dark dungeon cell—or worse yet, hanging from a scaffold—set waves of despair through his very soul. He loved his son although they did not have the best of relationships. Declan looked so much like his dear mother it was hard not to see her each time he looked into their son's eyes. Over the years he'd overlooked most of the predicaments, peccadilloes and delinquencies the boy had gotten himself into but this new venture was not to be borne.

"Highway robbery," he said with a growl.

"A very dangerous enterprise, indeed, Ned," his personal assistant, Lord James Giddens, pronounced.

"I'll not have it," the duke stated. "I'll have him committed to Baybridge before I see him hanged."

James shuddered. "That, I fear, would be a fate worse than death to a young man such as he."

"Better alive than moldering in his grave!" Edward snapped.

"True, but you know you will never be able to make him cease this rash behavior," James warned. "He has little to no care for his own safety and I'm sure he truly believes he is doing the right thing."

"Since when is robbery the right thing?" Edward demanded. "It is a crime, Jamie."

"Aye, it is. But he gives what he takes to those less fortunate. You must admit he is doing good with evil."

"If he would only get over this penchant for placing blame on himself, thinking he needs to atone for whatever perceived sin pesters him. That is from whence all this shit hails," Edward said. "He did all he could to save Kate and Eion. Had he died…" He hung his head, rested his forehead on the apex of his fingers. "If I had lost him…" He let out a hard breath then raised his head, fixed his friend with a hard stare. "I want a guard at his door and one under his window at all times. Another is to follow his ass everywhere he goes within the keep."

"Oh, he's going to like that," James said with a chuckle.

"I don't give a damn whether he likes it or not," Edward said. "I will put an end to his foolishness even if I have to open up my own dungeon and park his ass in there!"

* * * * *

Standfield Hall

Captain Royce Penry of His Majesty's Royal Marines straightened his jabot, tugged the bottom of his uniform jacket down smugly, cleared his throat and lifted his chin. He had come to Standfield Hall to call upon the Duke of Oxmoor's beautiful daughter. It was his intent to put forth his suit for the lady's hand. Lifting his own, he took hold of the large door knocker and rapped smartly three times before stepping back to await entry.

The massive oak portal opened slowly and an elderly butler appeared. Although he knew the servant recognized him, Penry gave the man his name.

"Captain Royce Penry to see His Grace," he announced.

The butler inclined his head and stepped back to allow Royce to enter. Doffing his Regimental pith helmet, he handed it to the butler.

"Right this way, milord," the butler said. He placed the helmet on the entry table and headed for the duke's drawing room.

Royce looked about. Oxmoor Hall was gaudy but would be a fit place to entertain his cronies once the duke and was out of the picture. Althea would inherit the palatial estate and—in essence—it would become his. He could envision himself ensconced in the elaborate office he had spied whilst at the party the evening before. His covert training with the Governmental Regiment had held him in good stead as he surreptitiously surveyed the kingdom he planned to make his own.

Leaving Royce in the elegantly appointed drawing room with its deep leather sofas and plush suede chairs, heavy oaken tables and sideboards and a tea table carved from elephant tusks, the butler left to inform his master that company had come to call.

Taking a seat in one of the rolled-arm chairs, Royce curled his hands around the chair arm and felt every inch the rich man he intended to be. Every painting upon the damask-covered walls. Every carved figurine made from scrimshaw. Every brass accoutrement, leather-bound book, and intricately carved humidor would belong to him. He swept his gaze about the room and settled it upon the cut crystal decanters of the very best liquor money could buy or prestige could demand. The amber color within the tallest decanter made his mouth water for a taste of what he knew must be a very well-aged Chalean brandy.

"To what do I owe the honor, Captain?"

Jumping at the sudden interruption in his contemplation of being a man to be envied, Royce got quickly to his feet. He bowed formally. "Good morning to you, Your Grace," he said.

"It has not been a good morning as yet," Lord Alastair snapped. "Why are you here? Have you caught that wretched thief?"

Royce felt heat rush to his cheeks and put up a hand to pretend to cough—in the hopes the duke would think that was the cause of his sudden blush.

"Sadly, not as yet, Your Grace, but we will," he said though he had reservations about that ever happening. The man they were after had proven to be a hell of a wily fox.

"He is making a fool of you," the duke said. He took a seat on the sofa, braced his arm upon the curved back and regarded Royce with an arched brow. "The reason for your visit?"

Royce felt the sweat gathering under his arms, in his palms, at the edge of his hairline but he forced a smile to his lips. He had to clear his throat of the sudden lump that had formed there.

"I have come to seek your blessing to court your daughter Althea," he stated in a rush.

The duke's eyebrow rose even higher. He said nothing for a moment then frowned. "Is this some sort of joke, Captain?" he asked. "A Regimental jest?"

"I was born to an influential family," Royce said. "Our ancestral home is at Norus Keep. My father is…"

"I know who your father is. I am familiar with your mother, as well. Norus belongs to her family as I recall. The Marquis and Marquesan are passing acquaintances."

"Then you know we are a proud heritage and I have much to offer your daughter in way of…"

"What is your title again?" the duke interrupted him.

"T…title?" he repeated.

"You are the youngest son, are you not?"

"I am, Your Grace. My title is Viscount Cumbria."

"A middling rank."

Royce dug his fingernails into the fabric on the chair arm. "One that has been borne by many a stalwart Penry male," he replied.

"My daughter deserves no lower than an earl," the duke told him. "I am leaning toward the Earl of Dungannon."

"Declan Farrell?" Royce asked. He felt his anger rising. "Surely you have heard the tales of his exploits, Your Grace. He received a dishonorable discharge from…"

"A *less than favorable* discharge," the duke corrected. "The lad lost his military career over some flighty female with a light skirt. Happens to the best of men."

"There were other infractions, Your Grace," Royce stated. "Insubordination, dereliction of duty among the more serious."

"A young man sowing his wild oats," the duke replied. "But such things mean nothing to me."

"Then what does, Your Grace?" Royce asked.

"Wealth and power and position within the realm. The Earl of Dungannon stands to inherit a vast estate, the lands of his father and those lands in Chale that were his mother's inheritance—not to mention Edgerton Manor, the shipping yards in Devonshire, Rexroat and Palmer. All of which will be passed on to Declan. As wealthy as his father is now, young Farrell will be doubly so when he comes into his own."

"And he will squander it all on women and drink within a year of taking it on," Royce predicted. "That is if he does not die in a duel with a jealous husband."

The duke got to his feet. "Thank you for your interest in my daughter, but I must decline your suit," he said. "Rivers will see you to the door."

"You are making a grave mistake, Your Grace," Royce said, pushing up from his chair. He clenched his teeth, spoke harshly through them. "I would make her a loving, protective husband. I am rising in rank within the Royal Marines. I will be Rear Admiral before I retire."

"I am sure you will try," the duke said. He turned his back and headed for the door. "Talk back to me in that tone of voice ever again and you'll be spending the remainder of your military career as a cabin boy."

The elderly butler appeared at the door. "If you would follow me, Captain?" he asked.

"I know the bloody fucking way out," Royce hissed. He strode to the door, pushed past the butler and left, pausing only long enough to grab his pith helmet from the entry table.

His mount sidestepped as Royce untied the reins at the hitching post and grabbed the pommel. He cursed at the animal then swung into the saddle. Not having a groomsman to assist him was just one more insult he knew the duke had handed him. Once seated, he looked up to see the woman he had been sure would be offered to him standing in a window on the second floor of the hall. She was smiling at him but even from that distance he could tell it was a more a smirk than a smile.

"You'll be mine," he said under his breath. He pulled brutally on the reins to turn the horse toward the oyster-shell driveway that led back to the main coast road. "When I put Declan Farrell in the ground."

Kicking the animal into motion, his fury was aimed at the man who had been his foil since boarding school.

* * * * *

Jack McGregor buckled his belt as he watched his wife, Fairling, slipping back into her gown. She was humming—as well she might since he'd tupped her more than well this afternoon. As he had before they rose this morn and as he had after breaking their fast, eating their noon meal and twice more as the sun lowered in the sky.

"You are a randy man, my husband," she remarked. "Sometimes I think it is a useless thing putting clothes on this body when all you do is take them off again."

"Then stay naked, wench," Jack told her. "I'll not gainsay you if you do."

Fairling snorted. She dodged the sweep of his arm when she passed him, swatting at his groping hand. "Stop," she ordered. "I've gotten nothing done today as it is."

"'Tis a Saturday. What needs doing that can't wait 'til Monday?" he asked.

"Why don't you go see Declan and pester him a while?" she replied. For the fifth time that day she leaned over the bed to arrange the covers.

"He went out again last night," Jack said with a frown.

His wife looked around at him. "Sooner or later he's going to get caught."

"That's what I'm afraid of."

"And they'll hang him, Jackie. Earl or not." She plumped his pillow, placed it neatly beside hers. "You should talk to him."

"When has that ever done any good, Fair?" he inquired. "He's as mule headed as they come."

"Then you'd best hope there's a guardian angel looking out for him, else you are going to lose your best mate," she predicted.

Jack nodded. He picked up his pipe, put the stem in his mouth to chew on it. Walking to the door of their small cabin, he opened the portal and looked out over the thick greensward beyond the shallow porch.

He'd known Declan Farrell all their lives. They were closer than the brothers neither of them had. Dec had lost his young brother while Jack had been saddled with eight sisters. It was enough to drive a poor boy to madness but it had given him a gentler side that few other men he knew had.

With the exception of Dec; his gentler side had come from a doting mother.

Bored with life around Arlington, Jack had followed his friend into the military. Though he was an enlisted man and Dec an officer, they had spent as much time together as they could without raising the question of fraternization—a major transgression in the Royal Marines. Many a time Jack had pulled his friend out of drunken brawls, houses of ill repute and away from dubious acquaintances. He had been there the dawn Dec had dueled over a woman who wasn't worth a tarnished button from Jack's boot. When Dec was cashiered out, Jack found a way to leave the military with him. It had taken some doing and a great deal of Dec's money but the two had returned to Arlington together.

Going out onto the porch, he took a seat in one of the two rocking chairs he had made for his woman and reached for the tobacco pouch he had left on the table between the chairs. Fairling would not allow him to smoke what she called his "foul weed" inside the confines of the cabin. Tamping tobacco into the bowl of the pipe, his thoughts were on Dec.

The evening before he had followed Dec from Standfield Hall. He was very good at shadowing his friend for he had been doing it for a long time with Dec being none the wiser. For some time he had suspected the highwayman they called the Gypsy was someone he knew. Now that he knew the man's true identity, Jack was beside himself with fear for his friend. That first time when he'd witnessed Dec galloping away with his prize, Jack had made sure he wasn't followed. Then he had gone home to his cabin to brood over what he had discovered, hoping Dec made it back to Arlington without incident. Every time since, his worry for his friend had increased.

He struck a match and once he got his pipe pulling as he liked, he lifted his bare feet and braced them on the edge of the porch rail, leaning back in the rocker as he stared out at the forest. What, he wondered, was he going to do about this new box of troubles Dec had unlocked?

It went deeper than the childish pranks they pulled together as boys. Deeper than the adolescent shit they'd engaged in before Dec was shipped off to St. Andrew's Academy. Much deeper still than the scrapes Dec had gotten himself into during his brief stint with the Royal Marines. These were dangerous waters his friend was wading into. Waters that could surely take his life.

"Did he see you last eve?" Fairling asked as she came to stand in the doorway.

"He never sees me," Jack replied.

"Are you going to talk to him?"

"For the time being, no. Talking would do absolutely no good. He'd just nod and look contrite then forget everything I said to him the minute I'm gone."

"Then what are you going to do?

Jack sighed heavily. "I wish to the gods I knew. For now, I'll keep following him, watch his back, and keep him safe. Intercede if need be. Maybe he'll get it out of his system then I can sleep of a night and not worry that he's lying face down on the highway with a musket ball in his chest or hanging from a gallows somewhere."

"What he needs is a good woman to take him in hand," Fairling stated.

"I'll not disagree with you, there," Jack replied. "She'll have to be a helluva woman, though."

"The gods help her," she said. "He'll give her a run for her money, he will."

Chapter Three

For three days Bess Arbra had been abed with a wicked cold that had brought her low. Chills, fever and a hacking cough kept her from her duties. Her father had seen to it. To him, her health was the most important thing in life. Even if it meant postponing his dream, he would see her well and fit before all else.

After working and saving his money for years to buy the old waystation at North End to turn it into an inn, he had delayed the opening until she was able to be there to reap the benefits.

Together they had remolded the waystation with their own hands. Hammering, thatching, painting and refinishing the tongue and groove floor, it was a labor of love. Exhausting and painful at times, but fulfilling. They could hardly wait to open the doors to their first customer.

Last eve, that customer had appeared.

And oh my, what a customer he had been. Stuck in her room at the Hound and Stag Inn she had been unable to greet him, usher him to a table, take his order and serve him. Her father had been the one to do that.

Waking to the sound of hoof beats clattering and crashing in the inn yard sometime around midnight, she'd thrown back the covers and gone to the window. She opened the shutters to peer out but all she could see was a handsome brute of a horse standing at the hitching post, one paw striking at the cobblestones. The rider had already dismounted and was tapping on the inn door. Even though she leaned out the casement window, she could not see him, though his deep voice could have raised the dead.

"Why is this door locked?" he shouted.

"We are not open yet, milord," she heard her father say. "I was just about to blow out the lights."

"Well, hell," the potential customer said. "And here I am in need of sustenance after a busy night."

His voice sent shivers down her spine to curl around her hips in search of their final destination in her lower belly.

"I've nothing to offer you but drink," her father said. "The kitchen isn't open and I'm no cook."

"And I'm not hungry," the stranger said. "'Tis sustenance of the liquid variety I'm in need of. I've plenty of coin and it's burning a hole in my pocket."

"Then come in," her father invited, chuckling.

She nearly fell out of the window trying desperately to put a face to that mesmerizing voice that held more than a touch of her native Chalean brogue. No doubt that was why her father had let him in.

Hastily wrapping her shawl around her, she went to her bedroom door and eased it open. The sound of male laughter drifted up to her. Her *da* was a gregarious man and him making a go of a public tavern was a given in her book. He never met a stranger. He made more friends than any man she'd ever known. It was his fun-loving personality and the compassion that was so easy to see in his big brown eyes. A big, soft bear of a man with arms the size of tree trunks, he was a gentle giant with a heart of gold.

Carefully making her way down from the top of the stairs, she was careful to step only on the planks she knew wouldn't creak. It wouldn't do to alert her da that she was out of bed and creeping about barefoot.

"The water was like ice," the stranger said. "The moment I hit it I knew I'd fucked up."

She blushed at the coarse language—language her da had warned her she would hear from time to time in the inn. Best get used to it now, she thought, as she pressed into the shadows midway down the stairs.

"Were there critters in there with you, lad?" her da asked.

"Something bit me on the leg," the stranger replied.

"Did you take a look at the bite?" There was true concern in her da's voice.

"Aye, but there wasn't anything there to be worried about. A bit of redness."

"Nevertheless, you might want to keep watch o'er it to be on the safe side, Declan."

"You may be right," the stranger agreed.

So, she thought, her father was already on a first-name basis with the stranger.

"Declan," she said quietly, testing the name on her tongue. It was a good Chalean name that meant "full of goodness" in her native tongue. She wondered if he was a good man. His easy laughter and the way he spoke said he was, but who could tell from just the sounds a man made?

Sitting down on the stairs, leaning against the wall with the shawl clutched tightly around her shoulders, she listened to her father and the man named Declan carrying on a conversation that lasted nearly to the rising of the sun. By the time their first customer scraped back his chair, he was fully three sheets to the wind. Despite her father urging him not to, the stranger stumbled his way out of the taproom. As he passed the stairs, he turned his head and looked up at her. She was fairly sure he'd known she was there all along.

With a gasp, she pressed back into the darker shadows so he could not see her face.

"Milady," he said, bowing—which almost cost him his balance. He had to scramble to catch the newel post to keep from pitching face down on the floor. "Oopsies."

It was that one silly word that caused her to lose her heart to him.

That and the good look she got at his incredibly handsome and manly face. Though she couldn't see them all that well, she could tell his eyes were a striking color of blue and the lopsided grin he bestowed upon her was so endearing it made her heart ache.

"I do believe I'm rather drunk, lass," he muttered.

"I do believe you are, too, milord," she surprised herself saying.

He swept his hand before him in a courtly gesture. "Then I shall take my leave until I am more fit company for you."

With that, he staggered to the door, fumbled it open and ventured out into the first rays of the morning light.

She turned and ran up the stairs to the landing, through her bedroom to the casement window. Leaning out, she could only see the top of his head as he clumsily mounted his steed. The horse seemed to understand its rider's condition for it stood still as after three attempts at getting his foot into the stirrup, the stranger finally managed to pull himself into the saddle.

"Home, James," she heard him say.

The horse bobbed its head, turned from the hitching post and with what looked like very delicate steps carried his master across the uneven cobblestones and away.

"Get back in that bed this instant."

Bess looked around—feeling the heat invading her cheeks—and made quick work of diving under the covers.

"Nosy miss," her father said. He came over to tuck the quilt securely around her.

"Our first paying customer," she said, hoping to mask her true reason for spying.

"I shouldn't have let the little bugger ride off but he was resolute, and with a man like that…" He shrugged, his words trailing off.

"A man like what, Papa?" she asked.

"Dangerous," her father replied. "And determined." He reached down to smooth the hair back from her forehead. "Now stay put." He leaned over, kissed her forehead then left her to think about the handsome stranger she had seen at the foot of their stairs.

She crawled under the covers and turned to her side, clasping her hands together under her pillow and drawing up her knees. It was how she slept each night. Her father had once joked it must have been how she slept in her mother's womb.

"'As your child will sleep in yours,'" he'd said.

That memory made her sigh heavily. A child was not something she had ever wanted. Her dreams were not of husband and family but of living her life on her own terms. Running the best inn in the country where the elite came to sup and wile away the hours. Taking lovers if she so wished. Being the mistress of a rich and powerful man but having his children?

"Not for me," she mumbled as she closed her eyes.

Before she and her father had come to buy the inn, she had taken precautions to make sure an unwanted pregnancy never happened.

"Better to be safe than sorry," she said with a yawn.

The image of the handsome stranger flashed across the darkness and she smiled. Mayhap he would be back. She drifted into sleep with his beguiling, lopsided grin chasing her down into the darkness.

* * * * *

A bath might have taken the stink off him but had done nothing to help the vicious hangover that was still plaguing him. Not even Meg's foul brew had put a dent in the armor that was squeezing his head like a vise. He'd gone straight from the bath back to bed and now that the sun was nearly down, he was hungry, thirsty and itching to be about his business. After dressing, he opened his room door and came up short.

"Good day, Your Grace," the burly servant said with a slight bow.

"What are you doing, Jasper?" Dec asked.

"Helping you to walk the straight and narrow or so's I've been told," Jasper Hawkins replied with a gap-toothed smile. His red bulbous nose was only marginally lighter than the mop of ginger hair atop his overlarge head.

"How exactly are you helping me to do that, Jasper?" Dec inquired through clenched teeth.

"I'm to accompany you wherever you go here in the keep."

Dec narrowed his eyes. "And beyond the keep?"

"There be two more men who'll be riding with you when you go beyond the walls of the keep."

"Oh, they will, will they?" Dec snarled.

"I was told to tell you there be guards outside your window, too," Jasper said then shook his head sadly. "You done went and made His Grace angry 'bout somethin' I'm reckoning. We was told not to let you out of our sight."

Dec dug his fingernails into his palm. "Do you know where my father is at the moment?"

"Not at the moment, no, milord. He rode out a while ago. Said he wouldn't be back for supper." Jasper leaned closer. "Bet he's seeing that Lady Gay?"

He opened his mouth to chastise the servant for gossiping but then realized with his father gone, he shouldn't have too much trouble slipping past his jailers. He forced a smile to his lips.

"Mayhap he is and let's hope she makes him happy," he told Jasper. He clapped Jasper on the shoulder. "Well, come along. I've got a helluva appetite. Have you eaten yet?"

* * * * *

Cook had always had a soft spot in her heart for the young earl. From the time he was a toddler she had made special treats for him. His favorite was a chocolate-covered coconut candy with pieces of chopped cherry and pecans mixed inside. It was her own invention she called tin soldier for she formed the confection inside a gingerbread man mold and piped it in edible silver paint. When she sat two of the treats in front of him after his meal, he did what he always did—slipped his arm around her waist and hugged her.

"You spoil me, Suz," he told her.

"If I don't, who will?" she asked and with years of loving him like a son and having that love returned, she reached out to smooth his curly hair. "You need a haircut, lad."

"Aye," he acknowledged. "I'll get one when I'm in Iomal tomorrow."

"Is that wise, milord? His Grace is on the warpath," she said, exchanging a look with Jasper who was sitting at the table with the young man. "Best you be staying closer to home for a while."

"I've business in Iomal," Dec stated. "Business that can't be put off."

"That's where they say the Gypsy has his hideout," Jasper said. He sopped up the last of the gravy from the roast beef on his plate and plopped the soggy bread into his mouth. "Hear tell the red coats are crawling all over the place."

Dec looked at him. "When did you hear that?"

"Just this morn," Jasper replied. "Man came by to tell His Grace about the robbery last eve. He said the red coats got a new captain and he's got spit in his eye 'bout catching the Gypsy."

"Did he give the name of the new man?"

"Penry, I believe is what he said," Jasper said, pushing his plate away now that it was bare of even a morsel of food.

"Royce Penry?" Dec wanted clarified.

"That sounds 'bout right."

"Shit," Dec said under his breath.

That was all he needed. He and Penry had hated one another since they were in short pants. Though they had been in separate regiments in His Majesty's Royal Marines, they had sparred together often at the inter-regimental maneuvers. Penry's commission as a second lieutenant was only a few months longer than Dec's. They had been pitted against one another in mock battles that Dec's regiment always won. The bad feelings between the two had grown in leaps and bounds. Penry had been the one to instigate many of the charges that had been brought against Declan and had testified before the Regimental Court when Dec was dismissed from service. Now that Penry was a captain with his own regiment, the man would be even more insufferable.

And posed a sharper danger to him. If Penry so much as suspected Dec was the Gypsy he would double his efforts in apprehending him and there would be no arrest. Penry would execute him on sight.

Troubled by this new development, Dec asked Cook to keep the tin soldiers safe for him.

"You'll not be having at least the one?" she asked, hurt showing on her lined face.

"I'll eat them both when I return," he said. He pushed his chair back, scowled when Jasper did the same. He turned narrowed eyes on the taller, heftier man. "Are you going to wipe my arse for me, too?"

Jasper's ruddy face turned darker but he bobbed his head. "If needs be, Your Grace."

"Stop that," Dec snapped. "Since when have you ever called me that?"

"Always a first time," Jasper replied.

Dec leaned in, kissed Cook on the cheek then mumbled, "Well, stop doing it."

With Jasper following close behind him, Dec left the kitchen where he preferred eating when he could and exited the door to the walkway that led to the stables. Out of sorts and striving to keep his temper in check, he didn't fail to notice the two men who fell in behind Jasper. Grinding his teeth, he increased his speed until he reached the stable.

"You want him saddled, Your Grace?" asked the stable boy who'd come running as soon as Dec approached him.

"Aye, Stevie. Thank you," Dec said and forced a smile to his lips. It wasn't the lad's fault he was being shadowed.

He knew once he was atop the stallion he could outrun the bloodhounds whose mounts were already saddled and waiting.

"Figured I'd be going out this eve, did you?" he snarled at the older of the two men.

"His Grace thought you would," the man replied.

"Think you can keep up with me?" he challenged.

"Aye, Your Grace," the man stated. "We know we can."

Smirking to himself, Dec leaned against a timber upright as the stable boy led the big black horse out of its stall. He'd helped at the birthing of the animal and had trained it himself. There were times he didn't need to give directions to the beast; it seemed to read his moods and anticipate what he wanted. Fleet of foot and strong, Warlock was a purebred Rysalian. His coat glistened in the sun with a bluish shimmer to the jet-black flanks. Standing at seventeen hands tall, the stallion was a hot-blooded brute but as loyal as the day was long. It whickered as soon as it caught sight of its owner.

Berating himself for not bringing a treat for the beast, Dec pushed away from the beam and went over to rub Warlock's head, smooth his hand down its neck, speaking softly to him in Chalean. The horse stood still as he was being saddled but there was a gleam in its black eyes that gave notice the beast was ready to run.

"Don't worry, boy. We'll lose them soon enough," he said in the language he had learned at his mother's knee. There wasn't a horse in his father's stable that could keep pace with the Rysalian stallion much less catch it.

Warlock bobbed its head as though it understood.

Once the animal was saddled, Dec vaulted into the saddle without warning and the horse needed no encouragement to leave the stable yard.

"Your Grace, wait," Dec heard one of the shadows yell after him as he and his partner scrambled to mount their steeds.

"Catch me if you can," he chuckled then drummed his heels against Warlock's belly.

Racing away from the keep with the warm wind pressing against his face, he urged the mount to stretch its legs and Warlock accommodated him with a long, fluid stride that quickly left his pursuers in the red clay dust billowing behind its hooves.

* * * * *

The road to Iomal wove a serpentine path through lush green hills and past a narrow silver-shot stream edged with cattails that undulated down to the bridge at Dead Man's Crossing. The bridge spanned the pitch-black waters of the Flint River and sat only a few hundred feet from a dark, forbidding limestone cave known by the locals as Black Chasm Hole—the opening to which was covered in dense vines. Beneath the graceful arch of the wooden bridge the river flowed briskly. It was rumored many a living thing had lost its life in the rapid current and deep waters that ran into the cave, and those who got trapped inside the fissure were never seen again, their bodies never recovered.

Slowing Warlock to a walk as he neared the bridge, Dec looked around him. He had long since lost his shadows but Jasper would have told them his intended destination, so he knew they would be coming to the bridge soon enough. Making sure there were no eyes spying on him, he clucked his tongue and urged the animal down the slippery bank and into the water.

He did not worry the steed would balk at entering the fast-moving water. They had made this trek many a time and the beast knew what most men didn't: the water looked deep and dangerous but at that point—about ten feet from the first plank of the bridge floor—the depth was less than a foot. Warlock moved into the current with barely a stiffening of its body and headed straight for the straggly vines draped over the cave's entrance. Sweeping aside the thick growth with his arm, ducking beneath the low-hung rim of the opening, Dec maneuvered his mount into the stygian darkness. Once inside, he began to count slowly. When he reached twenty, he halted the horse and stretched out his right hand to feel along the rough, craggy wall. He found the lantern he had placed there years before and plucked it from its niche. Shaking the lamp to see how much oil was left and making a mental note to bring more when next he came, he balanced the lantern on his pommel then reached into his pocket for a match. With a hiss light flared in the darkness to illuminate the eerie underground grotto. After adjusting the brightness to a softly muted glow, he held the lantern aloft and lightly drummed his heels against Warlock's sides.

Black Chasm Hole stretched far back into the gently rolling hillside beyond Iomal. It wound through a chamber adorned with stalactites and stalagmites, past a strange, eerie-green grotto then sloped gradually downward until it came to an intersection. Tugging the reins to the left, Dec moved his steed into the smaller of the two byways that intersected the main gallery. It was a tight squeeze, and considering Dec was claustrophobic, he was sweating profusely by the time a faint light shown about ten yards ahead. He had to force himself to extinguish the lantern when he spied the peg upon which he would leave it for his return trip.

"Almost there, boy," he said softly for sound carried within the cave system.

His words were as much for himself as they were for his mount. The swift flowing water made him uneasy. It brought back the bitter memories of slamming into the frigid, churning waters off the coast of Madragil. Of going under, clawing his way to the surface, turning around and around in the waves in a vain attempt to locate his mother and brother. Of diving into the dark maelstrom as the ship slowly sank—taking its passengers with it. Of screaming the two names that were the only lifeline he had to throw to them.

Of failing.

His mother. His brother. His father.

Himself.

He'd fought the waves for as long as he could before helping the only other survivor to the rocky shore. There he had sat—shivering and crying—never taking his eyes from the spot where the *Molly Celeste* had gone down. Staring mindlessly at the debris washing against the craggy cliffs and scattered amid the incoming tide.

It was the one task of utter importance he'd been handed, and he'd fallen short of what had been expected of him. His belief in himself had run aground just as surely as the ship had capsized beneath him.

A fitting metaphor for his life, he thought.

Ruined.

Defeated.

The water beneath Warlock's hooves was a vivid reminder of the disaster that was Declan Farrell.

Beneath the hooves of the steed the path began a steady incline. By the time rider and beast crested the rise, another cave entrance led them out into a thick copse of trees. Leaving the Black Chasm Hole behind, Dec turned Warlock to the west.

And ran right into Jackson McGregor.

* * * * *

"Where the hell did you come from?" Dec demanded, unnerved to find his boyhood friend in such a remote spot.

"Did you forget we found that cave together?" Jack asked. He was sitting with his arms folded over his chest, his hat pushed back on his thick, curly blond hair, one leg crossed over the pommel of his saddle.

"Are you following me?"

"I saw you leave the keep and thought I'd tag along. Figured since you made it a point to tell everyone where you weren't going, you'd come through the Hole." Jack grinned. "On your way to where, exactly?"

"None of your business," Dec snapped.

"Not familiar with that place. Rather anxious to see if for myself," Jack returned. He threw his leg over his horse's head, stuck the toe of his boot in the stirrup and took up the reins. "I'll follow your lead."

"Fuck you, McGregor," Dec told him. "I've business in Wixenstead and I don't need a babysitter."

"Oh, I know what you need, Farrell," Jack said. "But the sun is over the yardarm. Why don't we stop at the new inn between here and there and have a tankard or two."

Dec growled then kicked Warlock into a gallop. He had no need to turn around to see if Jack was following. He knew he would be racing right behind him.

Which complicated matters immensely.

A diplomatic courier would be taking the road to Wixenstead this eve. Under the fall of night when he did not believe he would be observed, the rider would be carrying important papers to the Royal Marine command post in Gilhaven. Among those papers would be the routes the tax collectors would be taking over the next few weeks. Included would be the number of outriders who would be accompanying each tax collector. The more outriders, the more valuable the cargo. It was imperative Dec get a look at what was inside the courier's pouch. Having Jack traipsing behind him was an impediment he did not need.

Coming out of the forest into a large open expanse of meadow, Dec ignored Jack when his friend pulled alongside him. He could feel Jack staring at him—no doubt grinning like a fool—and that set his temper rising and his nerves on edge. He had a job to do and having Jack following his every move would put a major crimp in his plans.

"What's the name of that new inn?" he asked, not bothering to look at Jack.

"The Hound and Stag," Jack supplied.

"The Hound and Stag," Dec said under his breath. He'd been there the evening before and drank himself into a stupor after he'd robbed four of the Duke of Oxmoor's uppity party guests. He winced thinking how he had roused the landlord so rudely yet the man had been cordial despite the inn not having opened as yet.

He also remembered the young woman who had been sitting on the stairs spying on them.

The landlord's wife? He wondered. Surely not, for he was no doubt in his fifties and she had appeared to be in her late teens.

Daughter? Ward? Most likely she was one or the other although...

She could be an indentured servant.

That thought made him frown.

"What brought that expression on?" Jack asked.

Dec turned to look at his friend. "What expression?"

"The one that said you got a good whiff of somebody's stinking turd," Jack replied.

"I'm riding beside a stinking turd," Dec groused. "Does that count?"

"You need to get your wick waxed," Jack told him. "And the sooner, the better. Fairling and I were discussing that just this..."

Dec sawed on the reins; Warlock protested with an irritated whinny. "I know gods-be-damned well you were not discussing my sex life with Fairling!"

Jack reined his mount, wheeled it around to face Dec. "She was the one who said you needed a woman to take you in hand."

"I have women who will take me in hand," he snapped. "And mouth."

"Who, Meg?" Jack said then blew a raspberry.

"I won't have it, McGregor," Dec yelled at him. "Do you hear me?"

"Partially deaf men five counties over from here heard you, Farrell," Jack replied. "Want to try for six counties?"

"Fuck. You," Dec said then sent Warlock into a gallop.

"I'm not the one you need to fuck," Jack shouted after him.

* * * * *

The door opened and Bess almost dropped the tray upon which were full tankards of ale that she was carrying.

It was him, she thought, stopping in mid-step to stare at the scowling man who came storming into the taproom. An equally handsome—yet jovially grinning—man trailed close behind him. Without so much as sparing her a glance, the dark-haired god strode over to a table in the corner, jerked the chair back and sat down with a loud grunt.

"That time of the month for him," the blond said, winking at her as he passed. "Two pints, if you will, milady."

"Right away, milord," she said and caught herself before she could bob a curtesy and spill the ale for a certainty.

Hurrying to deliver the five tankards to the men who were eyeing the newcomers with suspicion, she placed the drinks on their table.

"Who's the toff?" one of the men asked.

"I don't know, sir," she said though she remembered his first name was Declan.

"That ain't the duke's boy, is it?" another one asked quietly. "The Black Earl of Dungannon?"

"Well poke my boar and call him a sow if it ain't," a third man proclaimed. "Lord Declan Farrell, it is."

Bess slowly turned her own gaze to the two men in the corner and her infatuation with the dark-haired man got stronger even as her hopes of catching his eye plummeted. He looked to be in a hell of a sour mood if his clenched fist and pursed lips were any indication.

"Best not keep the likes of him waiting, Bessie," the first gentleman advised. "He's got the devil's own temper, they say, and he already looks outta sorts."

Since her father had gone into the storeroom to tap a new keg, Bess was the only one serving in the taproom. Slipping the tray beneath her arm, she wiped her hands on her apron and all but ran to the bar to fetch the pints that had been called for. As she poured the brew her heart was pounding brutally against her ribcage. She'd never seen a man as handsome as Lord Declan—not that she'd seen all that many good-looking men in her nineteen years—and his looks had surely bewitched her. She saw the blond man glance over at her and smiled tremulously at him as she poured the second pint. He smiled back then leaned in to say something to his companion.

Then Bess wished the floor beneath her slippers would open wide for the Earl turned his head to look at her, too, and as their gazes met, his blue eyes widened.

* * * * *

"Mother of the goddess," Dec whispered. The girl behind the bar had to be the one he'd seen on the stairs the night before but he had not gotten a look at her face. Now that he had, he felt as though someone had slammed a meaty fist into his gut. She was the most beautiful woman he'd ever seen. Her golden dark skin was flawless and it shone with vibrant health. There was a glow about her, an aura—as the gypsies called it—that drew him like iron filings to a magnet. He couldn't take his eyes from her. His fingertips itched to touch her sleek, glossy black hair. To roam over her caramel skin and trace the sweet curve of her spine. Drift across her belly and dip between her thighs. His mouth watered to taste her lips. The sight of those voluptuous lips did wicked things to his lower body. He ached with the need to ease his body over hers.

"Gorgeous, huh?" he heard Jack asked. "If I wasn't a married man…"

"Shut up," Dec ordered. He swung his head toward Jack. "I mean it. Not another gods-be-damned word about her."

Jack's mouth dropped open, his eyebrows shot up and he blinked.

Declan watched her as she came from around the bar and headed for his table. The soft grey cotton gown she wore did not do her lush figure justice. This was a woman who should be dressed in the finest Chrystallusian silk, the most elegant Ionarian satin trimmed with the best Chalean lace. Jewels should drape from her lovely, swan-like neck and around her slender wrists. Her thick ebony hair hung down her back in a loose braid but it should be spilled about her shoulders—the rich, shiny tresses caressing a man's bare body.

And her eyes, he thought as she reached the table, were as black as midnight and with a bright sheen that pulled him deep into their depths. He could happily drown in that sultry gaze.

"Two pints, Your Grace," she said, placing his tankard before him.

"What is your name, milady?" he asked. He was aware his gaze was devouring her and she knew it, as well. The smile that spread over her rosy lips made him ache.

"Elizabeth, Your Grace, but my da calls me Bess."

"You are from Chale," he said, thrilled by her Chalean brogue.

"Aye, milord," she acknowledged. "We are Crónórgan though some mistakenly think we are Black Chale." She put Jack's tankard on the table then turned her full gaze on Declan. "You, on the other hand, I would say are true Black Chalean with your dark hair and blue eyes. Am I right?"

"My mother was from Chale and I was born there," he said. "I have a fond spot for Chalean lasses."

Her smile widened. "That's good to hear."

"I was here last eve," he told her and saw Jack's stunned expression turn to something to which he couldn't put a name.

"I saw you," she said.

"I saw you, too," he told her. "Though you were hiding your beauty in the shadows."

She blushed at his compliment. How refreshing, he thought, for a woman to have modesty. Those he had known over the years—with the exception of his mother and Cook—did not know the meaning of the word.

"Thank you, Your Grace," she said. "Can I get you anything else?"

"What's on your menu tonight?" Jack asked.

Dec kicked him under the table.

"Ow," Jack yelped. He shot Dec a look Dec had no trouble understanding.

"We have mutton stew if you would care to try it," she said. "I made it myself and I'm told I am good cook."

"Then by all means, if your sweet hands made it, we'll take two bowls," Dec said.

She laughed and his entire world cantered off to one side. Birds sang in the trees. Rainbows appeared over pots of gold. Roses bloomed. Primal lust drove red-hot into his groin. It took him a moment to realize she had left the table.

"What the hell is wrong with you?" Jack hissed at him. "You damned near broke my leg."

"Go home," Dec ordered, not looking at him. When Jack didn't move, he turned his full attention on his friend. "Go home, McGregor. Now. This minute. This very second. Get up and go. Leave. Bye-bye. *Slán*."

Jack slumped back in his chair. "By the gods, you have gone 'round the bend."

Dec narrowed his eyes to emphasis his words. "That was an order from your earl, McGregor. Leave now."

"Are you going on the coach road tonight?" Jack countered.

"Am I what?" Dec asked, but he knew. He knew! Jack was privy to his secret as surely as he was sitting there glaring sternly at him.

"How did you get past me last eve to come here?" Jack demanded.

"What the hell are you talking about?" Dec growled. Had Jack seen him on the coach road?

"You may not give a gods-be-damn about your own foolhardy neck, Declan, but there are those of us who have great affection for you," Jack said. "The last thing we want is to have you taken from us as your mother and Eion were taken from you."

"I don't know what you're talking about," Dec said, trying to deflect the censure he saw building in his friend's blue eyes.

"You are not a stupid man," Jack snapped. "Please do not..." He stopped as Bess returned with two oversized bowls filled with steaming stew. He smiled up at her. "It smells heavenly, milady."

"Thank you, milord," she said, beaming. "I didn't bake the bread but I pledge to you it is very good. A lady down the way will be bringing it fresh to us each morn."

"I am sure it will be just what the doctor ordered," Jack said.

She bobbed a curtsy, gave Dec a look that set his blood to boiling then asked if she could get them anything else.

"I think we're good for now," Jack answered for them.

When she tucked her bottom lip between her teeth, Dec had to dig his fingernails into his palms to keep from groaning. One did not groan with lust while in the midst of a fierce argument with one's friend. It simply wasn't done.

With a saucy wink she was gone, making her way to a newcomer who had just entered the inn.

Jack leaned over the table, his voice low but insistent. "Please do not take me for a stupid man, either." He finished what he had been about to say before Bess interrupted him. "I know precisely what you are about and if you don't cease, you are going to get yourself killed or worse."

"What's worse than getting myself killed?" Dec snapped as he reached for the salt.

"Hanging, drawing and quartering?" Jack countered. "Tarred and feathered then hanged, drawn and quartered? At the very least being branded a thief then clapped in irons and chained naked to a slimy dungeon wall for the remainder of what will surely be a very short life amid the rabidly insatiable rats prowling the Labyrinth Prison?"

"You make it all sound like such fun," Dec mumbled.

Jack snaked out a hand and grabbed hold of Dec's wrist, preventing him from bringing the spoonful of stew to his lips. "Jest if you will but it isn't funny, Declan. I am worried about you."

"Don't," Dec said. "I am perfectly capable of doing what I have set out to do." He tried to pull his hand back, but Jack kept possession of it. "Will you rein it in? Someone needs to help those who cannot help themselves. It might as well be me."

"Since you could not help your mother, Eion or the cabin steward from the *Molly Celeste*?"

Dec flinched but held Jack's angry stare. "Give me some credit for not being a reckless fool, Jackson," he asked. "I am careful."

"Who else knows?" Jack queried. "Other than your father and probably Lord Jamie?"

"Why would you think…?"

"Jasper wasn't trailing you for no reason, you idjut. Those two galloping like the wind after you when you left the keep had been sicced on you by your father. You know I know that's the way of it." He tightened his grip on Dec's wrist. "Who else knows?"

"Other than you and I assume Fairling?" Dec hissed. "No one."

"Are you sure?"

"Aye, I'm sure. I would know if…"

"You didn't know I was privy to your lunacy," Jack reminded him.

"I knew you would be eventually," Dec said. "As nosy as you are." He jerked his arm from Jack's hold.

"At least you admit it is lunacy on your part," Jack snapped.

"Eat your gods-be-damned stew and for the love of the gods let me eat mine."

Jack pursed his lips. He grabbed up his spoon and filled it, brought it to his mouth then gasped as the scalding meat burned his tongue.

"Serves you right," Dec told him.

"Bastard."

"Asshole," Dec returned.

They ate in silence—relishing every spoonful of the delicious stew. Big chunks of mutton swam in a thick, rich gravy alongside carrots, potatoes, turnips, parsnips, rutabagas, celery and wedges of succulent onions. It was hearty faire—peasant faire—expertly prepared. The hot, crusty bread to sop up the gravy was like manna from the heavens.

"A girl who looks like that and cooks like this should…"

"What did I say?" Dec snapped. "Did I tell you not to speak of her?"

Jack frowned. "Be left alone," he finished.

Dec went absolutely still. He lowered his voice almost to a whisper. "What did you say?"

"Obviously she knows who you are and is setting her cap for you," Jack told him. "You want a good case of the clap?"

Fury lanced through Dec so rapidly it made his head swim. He was about to get to his feet when a heavy hand landed on his shoulder. Before he could shrug it off, a voice he had hated for a good many years cut through his anger.

"Fancy meeting you here, Farrell, old chap."

Swinging his gaze up to a face he could have gone the rest of his life without seeing up close, he rolled his shoulder to rid it of the man's grip.

"Penry," he said through clenched teeth.

"Still hobnobbing with the underlings, I see," Royce said, flicking a disdainful glance over Jack.

"Still being a horse's ass, I see," Dec replied.

"What are you doing here?" Royce inquired.

"I know you were several levels behind me at the academy but even you should be able to realize I am having my supper with a good friend," Dec told him. He smiled nastily. "Or is that assumption above your mental capabilities–as so many, many things are?"

Penry's face turned hard as stone. His muddy brown eyes glittered with rage at the insult but he maintained his correct military bearing, though his tight voice betrayed the emotions roiling through him.

"Be careful what you say to me, Farrell. I am the commandant of the garrison at Gilhaven." He raised his chin. "I am Captain Penry now."

"That and a copper penny won't get you much," Dec quipped.

"I am the law here!"

"And that's supposed to intimidate me?" Dec questioned.

"It should put the fear of the gods in you," Royce snapped.

"Well, it doesn't," Dec said. He leaned back in his chair and tilted his head to one side. "Put on quite a bit of weight, haven't you?" He surveyed his nemesis stem to stern. "You've actually got a gut beginning to flop over your belt."

Penry opened his mouth but the words never left his lips. He looked past Dec to where Bess was coming into the taproom from the kitchen. The man's eyes turned hot and speculative. "Well, now what do we have here?" he asked. "A very pretty woman of color."

"Go anywhere near her and I'll carve your heart from your chest," Dec told him.

His enemy slowly lowered his gaze to Dec. "Are you threatening a Regimental Captain, Farrell?" he asked in a deadly tone. "Do you dare?"

"I don't make threats, Penry. I make promises and I keep them."

Aware Penry's hand had moved toward the hilt of the sword sheathed at his side and that he himself was not armed, Dec laid his hand over the knife beside his plate. He knew he could plunge the utensil into Penry's chest before the man ever drew his weapon.

Penry knew it as well. He let his hand fall to his side. "This isn't over," he said.

"It is if you keep well away from the lady," Dec stated.

"And if I don't?" Royce demanded.

"Then you'll suffer the consequences of yet another of your stupid mistakes," Dec replied. "You've never won a battle against me, Penry, and you aren't going to do so now."

"I could have you arrested for…"

"For what?" Dec interrupted him. "Telling a toy soldier he has no authority over me?"

"You may well be surprised at the extent of the authority I have over you, Farrell."

"Aye, well having the authority and being man enough to execute it are two entirely different things, old man," Dec said. He folded his arms over his chest. "You want to make a run at me? Go ahead. I'll be waiting."

"When I do, you'll never see me coming," Penry snapped then swiveled on his heel and marched out of the taproom. The air in the room changed immediately, the charge gone.

"You do know what you just did, don't you?" Jack asked softly.

"Reinforced his hatred of me?" Dec said. He picked up the napkin that Bess had left beside his plate and wiped his lips. "Tweaked his pointed nose?"

"No, you just gave him leverage over you," Jack stated. "You showed him a weakness he's been searching for since we were boys."

"What the hell are you talking about?"

"You let Penry know you are interested in that girl."

Bess came over to their table, a worried look on her face. "Is something wrong, Your Grace?" she asked.

"Nothing a heavy boulder rolling over that fool who just left here wouldn't cure," Dec joked.

"Who is he?"

"He is a captain in the Royal Marines," Jack answered for him. "The new commandant of the command post in Gilhaven. I'm surprised he wasn't wearing full Regimental regalia."

Dec snorted but his gaze and his full attention was steady on the beautiful woman standing beside him.

"They must have sent him here to catch the Gypsy," Bess said. "I will pray every night he fails at his job."

"You and me both," Jack mumbled.

"Do you think your father would allow you to take a walk with me, milady?" Dec inquired.

A look of triumph passed quickly over Bess's face a moment before the smile returned to her lovely face.

"I believe milady is working," Jack said.

"After the taproom has closed, of course," Dec amended.

"That will be well after midnight, I imagine," Jack stated.

Dec turned his eyes to his friend. "It never fails to amaze me how you come up with such needless information."

"Milady has spent the day working," Jack reminded him. "I'm sure she's tired. This is, after all, the first day the inn has been open. I would think you would have a care for her health. She sounds as though she's getting over a cold."

"I do have a care for her health," Dec said. "I'm not asking her to run pell-mell across the meadow with me, McGregor."

"Let it go, Declan," Jack warned. "I believe you said you had business in Iomal."

"Best you leave now, milord," she told him. "And be careful as you ride out. The highwayman strikes around these parts regular like. You wouldn't want to fall prey to him."

Those words almost made Dec laugh. He felt the eyes of the landlord on him and looked that way. Patrick Arbra held his gaze for a long time and a tremor of concern wiggled its way down Dec's back. There was no doubt in his mind the man was aware of who— and what—he was. How many more people were to be privy to the secret? Was he giving himself away so easily?

"We should go," Jack suggested then in a lower, more forceful voice. "Now."

Although he didn't think the landlord would betray him unless Dec hurt his daughter in some way, he thought it best to follow Jack's suggestion. He nodded, got to his feet, reached into his pocket for money to pay for the meal then went to the door. Every eye was on them as Jack retrieved his hat from the rack on the wall beside the portal.

"Ride safely, Your Grace," Patrick told him.

He nodded and opened the door. Once outside in the darkness, he turned his face to the full moon threading its way through the clouds.

"All I wanted to do was talk to her," he told Jack.

"You wanted more than that and well you know it," Jack snapped. "Mount up and let's get the hell out of here before someone goes looking for that gods-be-damned bounty they put on your head." He went to his horse and snatched the reins from the hitching post.

"Bounty?" Dec queried. "They've posted a bounty?"

Jack swung into the saddle. "Surely you knew that was going to happen. It's a hefty one at that."

"How much?"

"One hundred gold pieces," Jack told him.

"That's all?" he asked as he mounted Warlock.

"Wait a while," Jack snarled. "Rob a few more stagecoaches and the price will be sure to go up."

"What is your problem, McGregor?"

"You were going to tup that girl," Jack accused. "As sure as I'm sitting atop this horse, you were going to do what you do best."

"Weren't you the one who told me I needed to get tupped?" Dec asked. "Don't you think that's talking out of both sides of your mouth, McGregor?"

"You're drunk. The hell with you," Jack said and kicked his mount into motion.

Dec sat there on his horse until Jack was a hundred or so yards away then sighed deeply. He had three choices as he saw it. He could either go after Jack to ride home with him, cut across country to Wixenstead to waylay the diplomatic courier or stay where he was in the hope Bess would come outside at some point so he could talk to her.

There was a fourth choice. He could rent a room for the night. The Hound and Stag was more than a tavern. There were rooms above the taproom. He would be close to Bess and that was something he wanted more than anything. The ache in his groin needed seeing to.

Jack had accused him of being drunk but he'd not touched one drop of the pint she had brought him. He was stone-cold sober—a rare condition for him. He was completely in control of his thoughts and actions although his mind was teeming with things he wanted to do with her.

He squinted but could no longer see Jack in the shadows of the night or hear the sound of his horse's hoofbeats.

It was an hour's ride to Iomal. Two hours back to the keep. Half an hour to Wixenstead.

He looked up at the window above his head and was just in time to see a head pull back from the opening. He smiled. She was watching him. He walked Warlock over to the spot directly under her window, pulled his whip from where it was looped around his pommel, rose up in the stirrups and tapped the whip handle on the shutter.

"Go home, milord," she said.

"Come to the window," he countered.

He waited for what seemed like forever then she appeared framed in the window opening. The light behind her made a halo around her sleek hair.

Somewhere in the darkness there came a creaking sound. He snapped his head around and saw the stable-wicket—a small gate—moving. In the opening between the edge of the gate and the jamb, he saw the hostler peering at him.

"'Tis only Tim," Bess told him. "He is feebleminded."

"Does he usually spy on you?" he asked, tearing his gaze from the moon-faced man.

"He calls himself watching over me," she said. "You should go, milord. The roads are not safe at night."

He sighed. "Still trying to get rid of me. You are going to give me a complex, milady."

"Naught good will come of this, milord," she said.

"How do you know?" he asked.

"Because I do," she said. She stepped back and pulled the shutters over the window, shutting him out.

"Bess," he hissed but she did not answer. Instead, the light went out in her room.

Warlock pawed the ground—anxious to run—and whinnied softly.

"Aye," he said on a long sigh. "That's exactly how I feel." He wheeled the beast away from the inn.

* * * * *

Bess pressed her back against the wall beside the shuttered window and smiled. Her heart was racing beneath the bodice of her gown. She put a hand to her chest, took a deep breath and shivered.

"His eyes," she said. "He has the most beautiful eyes."

Eyes that sparkled as they looked at her.

He was interested. By the sweet gods, he was as interested in her as she was in him and that thrilled her so completely it made her knees weak.

She stayed where she was until she could no longer hear the thud of his horse's hooves. Releasing a long, slow, shuddering breath, she began to untie the laces of her bodice. With the parting of the fabric, she imagined his fingers on the ties and closed her eyes to savor the fantasy. In her mind, she could picture his eyes glowing hot with desire as he slowly peeled the bodice from her shoulders.

Would he smile as the gown slipped down her back, past her hips, gliding over her thighs to pool at her feet? Would his gaze travel slowly, heatedly over her chemise before he tugged it up her body to pull it over her head? Would he then enclose her in his strong arms and bring her—naked and aching—to his hard chest? Lower his head to kiss the tender, sensitive spot where her neck met her shoulder?

"Declan," she whispered as she stepped out of her gown then dragged the chemise over her upper body, tossed it to the chair by the window.

Naked, she ran her hands down her sides, her hips and onto her thighs—imagining his hands instead of her own.

"Good night, Bess," her father called out as he passed her room.

She jerked her hands from where they had gone and felt the blood heating her cheeks.

"Good night, Da," she called out.

She stayed where she was until she heard his door close then she went to her bed, threw the covers back and crawled atop them. She drew her knees up, encircled them with her arms and tried to calm the raging desire that was sending prickles over her skin.

"Behave yourself, Elizabeth," she snapped.

She was no virginal lass whose fevered dreams had yet to be put to the test. There had been the vicar's son who had enticed her into a closet at the vicarage just before her sixteenth birthday. They'd fumbled with each other's clothing and the culmination had been anything but satisfying. It had been unpleasant, a bit painful and somewhat embarrassing.

Her next encounter had been much better. The blacksmith's son was older, more experienced and had actually wanted her to enjoy herself.

She had.

Many times over with him.

And there had been the chandler's nephew. More handsome than adept, at least he had been respectful of her. Their brief liaison had lasted until her father had purchased the inn and they'd moved. Until the blue-eyed Adonis had walked into the inn, she'd not seen anyone she'd even deign to give the time of day—much less free rein of her body.

But Declan?

"I want you," she whispered. "And you want me."

Smiling to herself, she straightened her legs and slid down in the bed. For a moment she just lay there staring at the ceiling.

"You want me and you will have me," she said as she moved her hand to the juncture of her thighs.

* * * * *

"Stand and deliver!"

The courier nearly tumbled from his horse at the thick Chalean brogue that broke the stillness of the night. In the moonlight his face was as pale as a sheet and his eyes two large black sunken pools. "I've n…no money on me," he stammered.

"'Tis not money I'm after," Dec told him. He had his pistol aimed at the man's head. "I want the pouch you are carrying inside your coat."

Fear made the courier's lips tremble, but to give him his due, he tried to brazen it out.

"I don't know what you mean," he said.

Dec cocked the pistol. "Last chance," he stated. "Toss me the pouch or die like a dog on the highway. Either way, I'll be taking that pouch."

There was a moment when he thought the man might go for the pistol in his belt but he must have thought better of it. Instead, he fumbled inside his coat for the leather pouch. It shook as he pulled it out.

"Toss it over."

"You won't shoot me after I do?"

"I have no reason to unless you think to run," Dec answered. "You run, I'll send you to hell."

The pouch came sailing at him and he caught it easily, stuffed it behind his belt then dug into his pocket for his trademark silver dollar.

"Never let it be said I left you with nothing."

He flipped the coin at the courier but the man was so terrified, he put his hands to his face thinking he was about to be shot. The coin fell to the ground with a hollow thud.

Smiling to himself behind the handkerchief, Declan rode away to the sound of the courier losing his supper in the dirt.

A mile down the coach road, he turned Warlock into the trees and took off his coat, turning it inside out so the claret color was now the lining. He pulled the kerchief from his face and stuffed it into the pocket of his britches. The Francachi cocked hat was carefully folded and placed in his saddlebag. There was nothing to identify him as the Gypsy save the black beast he rode, and there wasn't a militiaman alive who could outride the Rysalian. If he came upon a patrol—and he knew they were blundering about nearby—he could easily outrun them in the darkness. He knew the countryside better than any of the soldiers billeted at Gilhaven.

But to be on the safe side, he meandered his way back to the hidden entrance to Black Chasm Hole through the dense forest, backtracked a couple of times, stopped and listened for any sound that would warn him he was being followed. Satisfied he had not been seen and there was no one tailing him, he headed for the cave.

Chapter Four

Royce could not stop thinking of the woman he had seen at the Hound and Stag Inn. She had been lovely beyond words with a dewy dark complexion that spoke of good hygiene and vitality. Although generally he preferred green-eyed pale blondes he would make an exception in this wench's case. The soft curves that hinted at full breasts and hips made for a man to ride. Full, ripe-plum-colored lips concealed strong white teeth and her eyes. By the gods a man could drown in those long-lashed stygian orbs.

As he sat as his desk he had to rearrange himself in his uniform britches. His thoughts were decidedly wicked and that pleased him. It had been a few weeks since he'd taken a woman to his bed and done things to her that pleased him greatly. Rarely did he keep a wench for more than a week or two before moving on to the next but he could see himself taking longer with—what was her name again?

"Bess," he said. "Her name is Bess." He snorted. "Common name for a common whore."

He had learned all he could about the landlord and his black-eyed daughter—wondering how people of color could afford an inn. They had come to Serenia from Chale six months earlier. Arbra had used an inheritance from his uncle—his white uncle—to buy the old waystation. He and Bess had done every bit of the remodeling that had turned a once-decrepit hole in the wall into a fairly comfortable inn. Despite his Chalean heritage, Arbra had done well for himself.

"Go anywhere near her and I'll carve your heart from your chest," Farrell had warned.

"As if I am afraid of the likes of you," Royce said aloud.

He leaned back in the chair with his hand still on his aching cock, absentmindedly rubbing the tumescence beneath the britches.

"So you want her, do you, Farrell?" he asked. "Well, we'll just see about that."

Sometimes at night he lay awake thinking of all the ways he would like to hurt Declan Farrell. Visions of stringing the bastard up naked by his wrists and lashing his back—and chest—until every last scream and drop of blood had been wrenched for Farrell's body never failed to arouse him. He refused to think about why masturbating to thoughts of the man's torn and disfigured frame was far more enjoyable than tupping a female. It was not as though he had sexual feelings for the fool.

Far from it.

His hatred was what had sustained him through boarding school, and the day he stood in the dock to testify to the infractions that had tossed Farrell out of the Royal Marines, was now a day of celebration for him, marking the occasion each year with a toast of a fine Chrystallusian plum brandy.

"I despise you," he said. "I loathe you."

He realized his hand had somehow found its way inside his britches and his fingers were wrapped tightly around the head of his shaft. For a moment shame washed over him but the feeling was too pleasurable to let die.

With Declan's handsome face and strong, sculpted body fixed firmly in his mind's eye, he tightened his grip and his speed, leaned his head back and gave in to the pleasure.

* * * * *

The lecture went on and on and on until Dec thought he would lose his mind. To be treated like a teenage boy who had overshot his curfew was humiliating. To have James Giddens sitting there listening in as his father read him what was in essence a writ of house arrest was adding insult to injury. He drowned out most of what his father was hurling at him but what made it through his self-induced deafness brought him upright in his chair.

"And you will accept the invitation and be there this night!"

"Where?" he asked.

His father threw his hands ups. "You have not heard one bloody word I have said, have you, boy?"

"Aye, milord, I did," Dec lied.

The duke came to stand over him. He put his beefy hands on the arms of Dec's chair and leaned down until he was almost nose to nose with his son. "Then what exactly did I say?"

"You were scolding me for having outmaneuvered the babysitters I did not need," Dec replied. "You warned me that what I was doing was dangerous and a potential embarrassment to the family. You…"

"Embarrassment?" his father said quietly then turned his head to look at Lord James. "Did you hear him, Jamie? An embarrassment, he calls it."

"I did hear him, Your Grace," James said with a twitch of his lips. "Shameless. Utterly shameless."

Dec shot his father's personal assistant a narrowed look that was completely lost on the man who also happened to be his godfather.

"Don't look at him. Look at me," his father demanded and once Dec had returned his attention to him, the duke lowered his voice. "You want to hang, boy? Is that what you really want?"

"No, milord," Dec said.

"Well that is where your little escapades are taking you. Was it you who robbed the courier last eve?" Before Dec could lie and deny that it was, his father took one hand from the chair arm and held it up to silence him. "I know it was so don't bother spinning some tale that says you were between the thighs of some whore in Wixenstead."

Dec felt his ears burning at those words, but his father still hadn't answered the question that was pushing nausea up his throat.

"Where am I to be going this eve, Father?" he asked.

"He wasn't listening," his father said to Jamie. "I knew he wasn't." He straightened, crossed his arms over his chest. "You, my recalcitrant son, will be dining at the invitation of the Duke of Oxmoor. You will be discussing with him your betrothal to his daughter Lady Althea Standfield."

A cold chill flowed through Dec. "Betrothal?" he whispered.

"Aye, betrothal. It is high time you married and settled down, gave me a grandson or two, a few granddaughters to spoil. Vacated your debauched life and left your immoral ways behind. Grew up and became a responsible adult male. You cannot—nor will I allow you to—continue living without consequence for your actions."

"I have only met the lady the once," Dec protested, stalling for time as he tried to think of a way out of his predicament. "How do you expect me to say vows to a woman I don't even know?"

"I did not meet my lady-wife until our wedding day," Lord Jamie put it.

"Aye, and look how well that turned out," Dec threw at him and knew a moment of satisfaction when Jamie's face turned red.

"There will be no more discussion of it, Declan James," his father stated. "You will be taken over to Standfield Hall this evening and you will accept the lady's hand in Joining."

Like hell he would, Dec thought. He clamped his mouth shut. There was no way he was going to be forced into marrying a woman he barely knew.

Or any woman at all for that matter. Even as he tried to picture Lady Althea's face, Bess's intruded to push her out of his mind's eye.

"Lest you think you will run from this, let me disabuse you of that notion," his father continued. "There will be two guards at your door and two under your window. You will not be allowed to ride to Standfield Hall this eve; you will be taken there in my coach with four guards accompanying you and Jasper Burrows sitting with you in the coach to make sure you don't *accidentally* fall out and scramble away."

"I only did that the one time," Dec grumbled, "and I was ten if memory serves."

"I would put nothing past you," his father told him.

"Gave us a merry chase if my memory serves," Jamie said with a chuckle.

"And got his backside tanned for the effort," his father put in.

"A bit too big for tanning, now, Ned," Jamie remarked.

"He thinks so," his father said, "but that ain't necessarily the case."

"You realize what you are doing is enslavement," Dec accused. "Forcing me into bondage to the Duke of Oxmoor. Selling me to the highest bidder."

"Oh, for the love of the gods, Declan. Grow up," his father snapped. "Did you truly believe you could go blithely through life debauching young women, drinking yourself into oblivion and robbing His Majesty's coffers without there ever being a reckoning?

Well, mister, let me assure you that you can't and the Day of Atonement has arrived."

"Lady Althea is a beautiful young woman," Jamie injected. "Quite an accomplished pianist I'm told. She is the only child of the duke and will inherit a very sizeable estate."

"Second only to my own," his father stressed.

"With your holdings and hers combined, you will be a force with which to reckon," Jamie pointed out. "Think of the good you could do—legally I might add—for those you are striving to help by nefarious means at present."

"And without the threat of jail or the gallows hanging over your head."

"Not Jasper," Dec said. He knew when he was outnumbered and beaten. All he could hope for was to salvage a shred of control. Perhaps with the right man beside him he could think of a way out of this sorry mess.

"Beg pardon?" his father asked.

"I'll not have Jasper babysitting me. Call for McGregor. Let him…"

"Absolutely not," his father snapped. "You and Jackson McGregor have been the bane of my life from the time the two of you learned to crawl. Instead of stopping you from diving out of the coach, he would hold the door open for you to do so." He shook his head. "No, Jasper it will be."

"Father, please…"

"You are going and that is final. Get your arse to your chambers and stay there until it is time for you to leave," his father ordered then pointed a rigid finger at him. "And you had best be dressed in your most sophisticated attire or I will have you dressed appropriately. Is that clear?"

"Perfectly," Dec said, grinding his teeth.

"You may leave," his father granted with a wave of his hand.

Pushing up from the chair, Dec bowed slightly to Lord James, a bit deeper to his father, and then hurried from the room.

"That boy will be the death of me yet," he heard his father say as he gained the stairs.

* * * * *

Standfield Hall, Oxmoor

"I apologize for my daughter's absence," Duke Alastair said as he poured a snifter of Chalean brandy for his guest. "Women's problems, it seems."

Dec winced. He didn't want to—need to—know the chit was having her monthlies. He took the proffered snifter. "I am sorry she is under the weather," he said as politely as he could manage.

"Aye, well, a man gets accustomed to such things," the duke said on a long sigh. "They are, after all, the weaker sex." He took a seat across from Dec, crossed his leg at the knee and relaxed. "So, Declan. Tell me why I should allow you to marry my daughter."

It was on the tip of his tongue to tell the pompous old fool that he shouldn't allow him to marry his precious daughter. That no man should allow him to marry his daughter. He wasn't marriage material.

"Lord Declan?" the duke pressed.

"My apologies, Your Grace," Dec said, "but I seem to have an eyelash in my eye." He set his snifter down on the table beside him. "May I make use of your facility?"

"Of course," the duke said. He pointed to a door off to the left. "Through there."

Dec stood and walked over to the indicated portal. He closed the door behind him then slumped against it. His entire body was one massive lump of despair. He was being forced into doing something he truly did not want to do and knew he would regret his entire life if he allowed it to happen. Having the responsibility of anyone other than himself scared the hell out of him. Taking a lady to wife, being accountable for her safety?

"No," he said, shaking his head. "I will not do it."

But how, exactly, was he going to avoid his father's command?

He looked around the small room but there was no window. No way out save the way in which he'd entered. He looked down the hole of the privy seat and a part of him wished he could flush himself down the tube. It was an odorous affair, but if it had been possible it would have been a way out. What was a little offal when your life was rapidly imploding around you?

"Is everything all right, Lord Declan?" the duke called to him.

"I'll be out in a moment, Your Grace," he said with a groan and a slump of his shoulders. This whole thing had given him a headache.

Nerves, he thought. Nerves and the feeling of being trapped. His claustrophobia apparently wasn't confined to closed-in places but extended to having no way out of an untenable situation.

He levered away from the door, hung his head, sighed so heavily it made the center of his chest hurt, and then turned to open the portal. The duke was lighting a cheroot as he trudged back to his seat and sat down.

"Your Grace," he began, "I am sure there a hundred men of the peerage who would pay a king's ransom for the honor of marrying your daughter."

"I had one speak to me just yesterday," the duke said. "I believe you know him. The Viscount Cumbria?"

Dec's head came up. "Royce Penry?" he asked.

"One and the same," the duke replied and frowned. "I, of course, turned him down." He took a puff of his cheroot then looked at the glowing tip. "He is not without a small measure of wealth but I have it on good authority he is an unbending and rather obnoxious fellow. He most certainly did not endear himself to me yestermorn." He shrugged. "Wasn't happy that I sent him packing with his tail tucked between his legs."

"You were most wise in not accepting his suit," Dec said. "I have known him all our lives and he can be a cruel, demanding dictator at times. The sort of a man I would not want to see with my daughter if I had one."

"My sentiments precisely," the duke agreed. He looked Dec in the eye. "From all accounts I have had of you, you are the exact opposite of Captain Penry."

"I have my faults, Your Grace, but cruelty is not one of them," Dec replied. He put his fingertips to his right temple where a faint pain had begun to throb.

"I would think not given the sweet disposition of your lovely mother, may she rest in peace."

At the mention of his mother, Dec felt the room squeezing in on him. What, he wondered, would she make of this? Would she have sided with his father or would she have gently insisted her husband allow their son to make his own life choices?

He was pulled out of his reverie but the duke's next words.

"Althea can be a handful," the older man said. "She needs a strong man who will not give into her every demand. One who is capable of telling her no." He reached over to flick the ash from the end of his cheroot into a crystal dish. "I realize she is a bit older than most girls who have been married now for a while and have been graced with children. I fear I have spoiled her unbearably by now forcing the question of marriage upon her but I believe the time has come that she takes a husband."

Dec cleared his throat. "I met her at your niece's engagement party the other evening," he said. "She is a lovely young woman and will make some man a very happy fellow."

"Aye and isn't it grand that you will be that happy fellow?" the duke queried.

"Your Grace…" he began and the vicious pain that rocketed through his head nearly toppled him from his chair. He reached up to press the base of his palm over his right eye as the nausea hit almost simultaneously.

"Is something wrong?" the duke asked, his voice seeming to come from several rooms away.

"Migraine," Dec whispered.

The duke got out of his chair and came over to Dec's. "Tell me what you need, son."

"Home," Dec told him. "I need to go home."

Nearly fifteen years of suffering the ailment had taught him a dark room, a dose of tenerse and a cold rag were the only things that were going to get him through the next twelve hours or so.

"Why not stay here?" the duke inquired. "Surely the ride home will be absolute agony for you."

"Home. Please, I just want to go home," Dec repeated and was ashamed of the pleading in his voice.

"Of course," the duke said. "I will get my men to help you to your carriage."

Left alone in the duke's elegant drawing room, Dec prayed he would not spew the hot bile that was pushing at his gullet. The scent of the cheroot was making his stomach roil.

"Up you go," Jasper said, slipping his meaty arms behind Dec's back and under his knees.

He would have protested being carried out of Standfield Hall like a child, but the pain had become nearly intolerable, crushing his skull, pounding fiercely. Every jolt of Jasper's footsteps sent fresh spasms of anguish rippling from his temple to the top of his neck.

"Would you happen to have any tenerse, Your Grace?" Jasper asked as he carried Dec out into the cool night air.

"Garrett, fetch the tenerse," the duke ordered.

The squeal of the coach door being opened sent another sharp pain through Dec's head and he gagged.

"Easy does it, milord," Jasper said. He handed Dec off into the arms of some other man who smelled of wood smoke and that man laid him down gently on the plush velour seat.

The coach tilted as the smoky-smelling gent left and Dec put his arm over his eyes to shut out the glare from the torchlights shining in through the glass windows of the coach.

"The tenerse," someone said.

"Much obliged," Jasper answered then the coach tilted again as the big man got in. He knelt beside Dec then gently put his calloused palm under Dec's head to lift it. "Here, milord. Have a sip of this."

Cool glass touched his lips. The scent of wild cherries invaded his nostrils. The taste of the liquid was ghastly—as it always was— and it immediately numbed his tongue.

"Has he had these headaches long?" the duke inquired.

"Since he was a lad," Jasper replied.

"My late wife suffered from them," the duke told him. "I know how bad they can be."

"We'll get him home and to bed and he'll be right as rain, won't you, milord?" Jasper asked, smoothing the hair back from Dec's forehead.

The tenerse was a powerful drug that in combination with a variety of other liquids could cure—or cause—a plethora of reactions. Mixed with vinegar it was used as a mild analgesic. With water, an instant hangover cure. Diluted with milk it caused uncontrollable sexual arousal. On its own, it was an extremely potent narcotic that did not simply lull the recipient into sleep but shoved him there. Within seconds of the drug flowing down his throat, Dec was falling into unconsciousness.

* * * * *

"Well, I must say that was one way to get out of signing a nuptial contract with Standfield," Jamie joked as he stared down at Dec. The young man was out cold on his bed.

"You think he was faking it?" Edward asked.

"Jasper says not and I'm inclined to believe him. It's been a while since the lad has had one of his headaches. What with all the tension of late and this ultimatum of yours, it's not improbable."

The duke looked around at the man who had been his best friend since they were boys. "You think I'm being unreasonable in this, Jamie?"

"I did not say that," Jamie answered. "I am inclined to agree with you he needs to settle down, but picking his bride for him? You know how I feel about that."

"Just because you got a raw deal does not mean Declan will," Edward snapped. "By all accounts the lady in question is quite a catch."

"I've no doubt she is," Jamie acknowledged. "But I think you should let Dec pick the woman he wants to spend his life with. Trust me; I know of what I speak when I say the wrong woman could make his remaining years on this earth a living hell. Better to pick your own poison than have one poured down your throat."

"The hell with you," Edward mumbled. "I'm trying everything I can to make sure he *has* remaining years on this earth."

"I understand, Ned, but could you not be a bit gentler and a little less tyrannical in going about it?" He reached out to lay his hand on his friend's shoulder. "You know you can catch more flies with honey than vinegar."

"He is such a stubborn little bastard," Edward said on a long release of breath. "Always has been. His mother spoiled him."

"No more so than did you," Jamie reminded him. "Especially when he came home after his rescue." He squeezed Edward's shoulder. "He was inconsolable, feeling such tremendous guilt. You began to cater to his every whim—no matter how ridiculous it seemed. That is when the problems with him truly began."

"Aye," Edward said, spiking a hand through his hair. "I remember it all too well."

"Then think on that when you are tempted to command him instead of urge him." He removed his hand from his friend's shoulder and put his palm to his heart. "I believe marriage to Lady

Althea is in his best interests—just as do you—but don't force him into it. He will hate you for it if the marriage is a disaster."

Looking down at his beloved son, Edward Farrell felt a gentle presence lurking in the room. Declan looked so much like his mother with his curly chestnut hair and pale blue eyes. He had her coloring and her smile, her oftentimes silly sense of humor. Most of all, he had her sense of social justice and responsibility.

"Responsibility," he said.

"Eh?" Jamie inquired.

"He feels it is his responsibility to help those less fortunate than himself. I know he blames himself for being unable to save Kathleen and Eion but it goes deeper than that. Kate always taught him to stand up for those who could not stand up for themselves, to protect those who needed it. He is only doing what he feels is right, but—gods-be-damn it—his way could get him hanged."

"Then let us find another way for him to go about it," Jamie suggested.

Edward nodded. "Aye, that is a sensible proposal."

"I am a sensible man," Jamie replied, and at his friend's snort, Jamie looked offended. "Well, I am."

"I'll believe that when Diabolusian warthogs learn to fly," Edward said with a grunt.

* * * * *

Tenerse was such a vicious drug, he thought as he tried to swim his way out of the undulant current that tried to keep him under its control. Every time he thought he had reached the surface of consciousness, the drug pulled him down into its shimmering depths once more. He knew he'd been dreaming—and that his dream wasn't a good one—but he couldn't seem to grasp any part of it other than a sense of impending danger.

He tried moving his fingers but they seemed incapable of action. Likewise his feet. His head no longer hurt yet it felt packed full of cotton batting, his hearing muted to such a degree he could hear his heartbeat loudly in his ears.

A nagging irritation, he thought.

Hands touched him and he fought to open his eyes but they refused to obey. At least the hands were gentle and the cool cloth laid upon his forehead soothing.

"You poor man."

It was Meg's voice. Her soft hands stroking his cheek. If he knew her—and he knew her better than any man ever had—that gentle hand of hers wasn't going to remain on his face. It was going to slide under the covers and…

All right, it was already there. Her fingers flexed around him.

"Are you awake, Deckie?" she whispered. "Do you feel me holding you?"

She began stroking him until he felt the hard erection straining between his thighs. Her thumb eased over his slit and he mentally groaned. Why she did things like this when he was helpless to prevent it had always puzzled him. When he'd asked her why she molested him in that way, told her he neither liked it nor appreciated the violation, she would simply smile. He supposed it was the power she wielded over him when he was unable to resist.

Truth was, he lied when he said he didn't like it. He enjoyed the hell out of it, but his manly ego would not let him admit to taking pleasure in being sexually misused.

Struggling to push aside the lethargy, to pry his lids apart, he heard himself moan and her hand stilled for a heartbeat or two.

"Are you awake?" she repeated. "Aye, I think you are but you can't move just yet. Good. Then let's get right down to the root, eh?"

There was satisfaction in her voice as well as touch of laughter. That rankled and made him angry, but that anger whirled away when she tossed the covers back and put her mouth over his straining flesh.

Merciful Morrigunia, he thought as her lips closed around him. The woman could suck the silver plating off a doorknob. Her tongue was like a serpent coiling around and around the head of his cock—striking at the slit then gliding down to the base of his shaft. The graze of her teeth along the sensitive underside of the head sent spirals of intense pleasure up his cock to spread through his groin and thighs.

"Mm," Meg said and she began bobbing her head up and down.

The release was coming. By the gods, it was coming fast. He felt his fingers twitch. He managed to crook them so he could grab hold of the sheet beneath his hips. His arms, his legs, his scalp tingled. When her speed and the force of her mouth upon him increased exponentially the breath caught in his throat and…

He let go.

Jet after jet shot from his hard as a rock cock. He could hear her lapping at it, feel her tongue tugging at him, her lips compressing as she milked him of every last drop. With the last surge of cum he succeeded in snapping his eyes open. All he could see was the punched tin ceiling tiles above him. Dragging his gaze downward, he saw her head between his legs. As if she sensed he was watching her, she lifted her head and looked up at him.

"Good morn to you, milord," she said and grinned. Her mouth was slick with his seed and she ran her tongue around her lips.

He knew he wouldn't be able to speak even if he was capable of prizing his lips apart, so he just lay there and looked at her with the bottom sheet still clutched savagely in his hands.

"Headache gone now?" she asked, straightening up. "Both of them?" She pulled the covers over his nakedness, lifted his arms in succession to place them atop the duvet. "I'll get you a cup of coffee, then."

He tracked her with his eyes as she left the bed and walked to the door. As he knew she would, she turned to look back at him. Her audacious wink was her calling card just as the highwayman's was the leaving of a silver dollar at the scene of a robbery.

After she'd gone, he drew in a long breath, tried to move and still couldn't flex any muscles save those in his hands. The drug took a long time to wear off when it wasn't measured properly. The long draught of it Jasper had poured down his throat certainly hadn't been measured. It was going to be a few minutes yet before he could move his arms and legs and at least an hour before he could hoist himself out of bed. Even then his legs would be like rubber.

The door opened but it wasn't Meg who entered. It was Jack McGregor—which was a surprise.

"Still encased in cement?" Jack asked. He'd had a lot of experience with the aftereffects of tenerse on Dec. Dec knew he didn't expect an answer. He came to the bed and sat down on the edge.

He grunted to let Jack know he still couldn't speak.

"I can wait," Jack stated.

He grunted again in acknowledgement.

"Lord James told me where you were last eve."

A growl followed the grunt.

"Aye, well, you could do worse than the lovely Lady Althea," Jack told him.

The muscles in his face were loosening and that allowed Dec to narrow his eyes at his friend.

"Well, you could," Jack said. "If it's any consolation, I approve of the duke's choice of mate for you."

That didn't warrant even a snort so he just glared at his friend.

"He's going to make you do it, Dec," Jack warned. "You know it as well as I do. Might as well accept it and get on with your life. Marriage ain't such a bad deal, you know."

He rolled his eyes.

"You think that now but having a beautiful woman in your bed to wake up to of a morn is better than a sharp jab in the eye with a stick."

Only marginally so, Dec thought.

"Of course, my guess is the Lady Althea will curb your habit of tupping every maid who crosses your path, but I could be wrong. She might not give a Diabolusian warthog's ass whether you stray or not. Hell, she might even be inclined to do so herself."

Now that required a growl and the one he imparted upon McGregor had the strength to break the seal on his lips.

"Fuck you," he hissed.

"Don't want the little woman screwing around on you?" Jack asked with a merry grin. "Can't say I blame you. But what's fair for the gander is fair for the goose, am I right?"

"Dick smack," Dec called him.

Jack laughed. "That's the Declan Farrell we know and love."

Meg took that moment to come in with a tray. Her amble hips moved like two pigs fighting in a burlap sack and her big breasts jiggled when she saw Jack.

"Have a nice ride over, did you, Jackie?" she asked.

"Nice enough," Jack replied.

"Want another before you go?"

Jack shook his head. "I don't think Fairling would like that, Meggie."

"What Fair don't know won't hurt you," Meg replied.

"Go away," Dec told her.

Meg shrugged. "You know where to find me if you want that ride, Jackie-boy."

When she was gone, Jack looked around at him. "Did she blow you again?"

"What do you think?" Dec grumbled. He found he could move his arms and legs a bit.

"I think that's a very nice way for a man to wake up each morn," Jack said. "Wish Fairling felt the same way."

"Doesn't have a taste for it," Dec replied.

"I can't believe you said that," Jack chastised.

"Help me sit up," Dec asked, ignoring the annoyed look on Jack's face.

"So," Jack said as he twisted so he could push his arms under Dec's and heft him up against the headboard, "what now?"

"I've got to piss."

Jack jerked his hands back, held them up to his shoulders. "Don't expect me to aim it for you."

"Just help me swing my legs off the gods-be-damned bed, McGregor. I can piss in the pot if you will hold it for me."

Jack snorted. "And let you splash me with your piss?" He shook his head. "I'll get you to your feet and you can do it standing up with me well away from your lousy aim."

"Bitch, bitch, bitch," Dec said. "Is that all you can do, McGregor?"

Jack took his legs and swung them over the side of the bed then bent down to loop his arm behind Dec's back to lever him to his feet. "Hold on to the bedpost," he ordered.

"Like I don't have sense enough to do that," Dec mumbled.

Jack released him as soon as Dec had a grip on the headboard then squatted down to retrieve the chamber pot. He pushed it in front of his friend then did as he said he would—stepped out of range.

"So," he asked. "What are you going to do about the Lady Althea?"

"I've not the faintest idea," Dec said. His head was swimming again and his stomach queasy. He eyed the cup of coffee Meg had put on his bedside table but it held no appeal. The greasy film floating over it made the nausea worse.

"You need more tenerse?"

"No, I need a new head," Dec said. He massaged his cock until the urine began to flow and he sighed with relief. Sometimes the tenerse had the nasty habit of preventing him from pissing.

Jack walked to the window and opened it. He glanced down, nodded at the two guards who looked up at him. "Not that you are in any condition to repel the wall but should you think to do so, I would advise against it. Lucas Pratt and his baby brother Micah as positioned beneath your windows."

"Aye, Father said he was going to post men there to keep me in check," Dec groused. "Two guards at the door, as well."

"Well, he did what he said he'd do. Not only two at your door but two on each end of the landing to make sure you don't take to the steps," Jack informed him.

"The gods-be-damn it," Dec said. He shook his cock then sat down heavily on the bed. "He might as well geld me while he's at it."

"According to Lord James, the duke wants grandchildren. I seriously doubt gelding is on his agenda," Jack said.

Easing down to lay on his back with his legs dangling over the edge of the bed, Dec threw an arm over his eyes. "Doesn't matter than I don't want brats clinging to my legs, though, does it?" He pounded his free fist on the mattress. "Or a wife to provide them to me. A woman I've got to watch every minute to make sure she's safe."

Jack left the window to come over to the bed. He reached down and hoisted his friend's legs up and swept them around so he could lie more comfortably. "You've sown so many wild oats in your day how do you know you don't have a veritable army of brats causing mischief in the kingdom?"

"I would know," Dec said. "Their mothers would be pounding on the doors of the keep with one hand while the other was extended for their due."

"I suppose you're right," Jack agreed.

"You tell me what I should do," Dec said.

"Marry the woman and go about your business as usual," Jack said. "Do your duty as your father decrees it and when he dies, do whatever the fuck you want to do about your lady-wife. Divorce her if you like. What else do you want?"

"Bess," Dec stunned himself by saying. He dropped his arm behind his head and stared at the ceiling.

"Who the hell is...?" Jack started to ask then apparently realized who his friend meant. He sat down upon the mattress again. "I doubt her father would allow you to take her as your mistress, Declan."

"What if I asked for her hand?"

Jack shrugged. "Unless it is attached to her arm, what good is it?"

Dec glared at him. "You know perfectly well what I meant. This isn't a joke, McGregor."

"Mayhap not, but it is sheer folly," Jack said.

"It isn't unheard of," Dec said. "Nor is there a law against it. If the tables were reversed, aye, there is, but a male has leeway a female doesn't. He can marry a commoner then elevate her to the peerage by the union. It can be done."

"Not when you are the son of the Duke of Arlington, it isn't. There's also the matter of her being a woman of color. Social gatherings would be difficult for her."

"No one would dare say a word to her," Dec snapped.

"Not to your face, at any rate," Jack replied. You aren't being serious about this, are you?"

Dec shrugged. "We'll see."

"You might as well get that ridiculous notion out of your head," Jack told him. "Your father would have you committed to Baybridge for even suggesting such a thing."

"He doesn't have to know. We can elope then quietly divorce a month or so later. I would give her a nice settlement, find her another husband if she wants one."

"And what about you?" Jack pressed.

"I'd be off the marriage market and a social pariah for a while. Besides, I can't get her out of my mind," Dec said.

"Aye, because you haven't had her and know you shouldn't," Jack tossed back at him. "For once in your gods-be-damned life, think with the head atop your shoulders instead of the one between your legs."

Imparting that less-than-wanted wisdom, Jack stomped over to the door, jerked it open and slammed it shut behind his departure.

"Ill-mannered boor," Declan grumbled.

As Declan lay there staring, he had never felt so hopeless. It ranked close to when he'd been unable to save his mother and brother or the young steward. He couldn't help but equate that heartbreaking failure to the failure of living his own life the way he wanted to live it.

He was being forced into doing something he didn't want to do, and that not only rankled, it stung his ego. It hurt his pride. He was no toddler in short pants to be ordered about. He was a man—full grown and capable of handling his own affairs.

He loved his father and Jamie and Jack. They were his family. He respected all three more than he could put to voice and he knew they had his best interests at heart, but none of them could see past the duty he was being forced to uphold.

A duty he didn't want. Didn't need.

And wasn't sure he could fulfill.

All his life his father had instilled him the tenets of duty and honor and honesty. Loyalty and respect and compassion. Duty to king and country and family. Honor to his father. Loyalty to his friends. Honesty in all undertakings. Respect and compassion for those less fortunate than himself. He had been brought up to be a good man. An honorable man. A man who would take care of his people and see to the welfare of the tenants and villagers under his protection. Cruelty and avarice had never been part of his genetic makeup and never would be.

So why was he being forced to do something that so went against the very grain of his soul? He knew if he didn't find a way out of his predicament, he would be forced to marry the Duke of Oxmoor's daughter.

He turned to his side to stare at the wall. There was a pattern in the wood that looked like a grinning bear and he smiled, tracing it with his fingertip.

"I just want to be happy," he said to the image. "As happy as my parents were together." He dragged his fingertip down the wall. "With Lady Althea?"

He sighed deeply and returned to his back and his perusal of the ceiling.

She was a pretty enough chit, he thought. Not as lovely as Bess and she would most certainly not be as sensual. If happiness was to be found with her, it would be a sedate, proper thing. Sex would be under the covers with the lights out. There would be the missionary position and nothing else—and then only on certain nights, no doubt.

If he was lucky.

But with Bess?

He sensed the sultriness simply in the way she walked. The way her hips swiveled, her eyes flashed.

Fire and ice, he thought. That was the difference between the two women.

There was no choice. He'd made up his mind and that was all there was to it. He couldn't be forced to marry one woman if he was married to another. The first woman wouldn't want him if he was divorced from the second. That was a social faux pas among their kind—second only in sinfulness to being a divorced woman.

He realized he was going to need to play his part very carefully so no one would suspect his plans. If his father wanted to believe him a petulant, recalcitrant little shit, he'd play the part. That apparently was how they saw him.

He grinned maliciously.

And what a petulant little bastard he was going to give them.

* * * * *

One part of Althea was relieved she had been indisposed with her monthlies when the Earl of Dungannon had been ordered to dance attendance on her father. Another part was heartsick at not having the chance to see what the man looked like. The night of the engagement party his face had been hidden behind the camouflage of the domino mask, but those vivid blue eyes within the black silk fabric had appeared in her dreams every night since.

"I suppose he is handsome enough," her father had replied to her demand to know if he was handsome or not. "I imagine you would think so." He rustled the newspaper in his hands without looking at her. "The maids certainly giggled enough over him."

"You should have insisted on him staying with us if he was in such pain, Papa," she said.

"I did not want to press him," her father replied. "He did not seem particularly pleased with the arrangement his father and I have made."

Althea looked up from her needlepoint. "In what way do you mean?" she asked.

A heavy sigh came from her father and he lowered the paper to look her in the eye. "He does not want to marry you, daughter, but he will. His father and I have agreed to the match and that is the way it will be."

"Not marry me?" she said, putting the needlepoint on the table beside her. "Why ever would he not? Did he say he found me lacking in some way?"

"Not at all. He simple does not wish to marry—you or anyone else. Or so his father tells me. But that is neither here nor there. He will do as he is told. Edward is at his wit's end with the boy's randy behavior toward females in general and wishes for him to settle down." He raised the paper again, snapped it then sniffed. "Thus he will be forced to do just that."

Althea's thoughts went to all the things she'd heard about Lord Declan Farrell's randy behavior toward females. That was one of the things that so intrigued her about him. It was rumor he'd thrust his blade into the soft sheaths of many a maiden and married woman alike and that each of them sang his praises afterwards.

"He is a swordsman of high degree," Lady Bertrice Cumberbatch and whispered. "His sword is much in demand, if you get my meaning."

Althea wanted to see that sword in action. She wanted to duel with him—his thrusts to her parries. She wanted to feel that strong body pressing her down, holding her captive as he pressed his point.

Heat washed up her neck and over her face as she thought of what that point would feel like piercing the maidenhead that had become a true burden to her. She ached wanting to know the pleasure nearly every woman of her acquaintance had already experienced. Shifting in her seat, pressing her thighs together, she tried to will away the strange feeling that persisted on plaguing her from time to time. That heaviness, that—itch—that simply would not go away.

And there was the way her womb jumped when she saw a handsome man with a well-built form walk past. The strong flutter than came and went when she caught sight of a laborer's bare chest as he went about his business around the estate.

"What ails you, daughter?" her father inquired and she jumped as she swung her gaze to him.

"Monthlies," she said and hopped up from her chair.

"Oh, for the love of the gods," her father grumbled. He waved his hand at her. "Go."

She curtsied then all but ran from the library. Her heart was pounding, her palms were sweating and that heavy feeling had settled once more in the pit of her belly. Climbing the stairs, she pressed one hand just above the heaviness.

"What is wrong with me?" she asked.

You need a man between your legs, an inner voice whispered to her. Strong arms to hold you against a broad chest. Firm lips to claim your own. A sword to be sheathed inside you.

By the time she reached her bedchamber, she was covered in sweat and trembling. She ran to the window, threw it open and stuck her hot face into a cool mist of rain. The moisture helped to ease the flames glowing in her cheeks but did nothing to still the disquiet lower down her body. Nor did seeing the stable boy gathering forkfuls of hay from the mound—his shirt plastered to a very enticing body. When he glanced up at her with the fork thrust into the hay, she trembled.

He smiled and leaned on the pitchfork as he stared at her.

She licked her lips—wondering what his would taste like. How the sculpted muscles that undulated beneath the wet shirt would feel against her palms. How tight those brawny arms would hold her.

His smile widened, became knowing and he began to slide his hand slowly up and down the handle of the pitchfork in a suggestive way.

Althea stumbled away from the window, turned then looked wildly about her.

She had to have him.

Declan Farrell.

She must have him whether he was willing or not.

If it was the last thing she ever did, she would claim that man as her own.

Chapter Five

Bess heard the horses clattering on the cobblestones and looked to her father. "Four," she said.

"Only three," he replied with a grin.

It was a little game they played, trying to guess the number of visitors to the inn.

The laughter of several men, the ominous crack of thunder in the distance, the squeak of the stable door opening as horses were led inside out of the bad weather was a good indication there would be more than a few coins spent at the Hound and Stag this late afternoon.

"Soldiers," her father said.

She nodded. They were part of the company that was trying to bring to justice the highwayman known as the Gypsy. For the last two days regular patrols had passed the inn on a daily basis beginning around six of the clock. The thief usually struck around the midnight hour so having the troops out and about trying to catch him in the act was becoming routine.

The door opened and in walked the one man Bess had hoped would not grace their establishment with his presence yet again. Each time he did, she felt as though she should take a bath after his departure for his greedy stare made her feel dirty.

"Captain Penry," her father greeted the man, his voice a touch less than was polite.

"Arbra," the captain replied. His hot stare shot to Bess. "Milady."

Bess forced herself to curtsey to the man, though what she really wanted to do was slap the smirk from his sharp face. She had to be careful not to get too close to him for she feared sooner or later he was going to put his hand to her. The thought of him touching her sent shudders of distaste down her spine. She dared not slap him out of fear of what he might do. He had the look of a man to whom revenge was a way of life. He could put the inn off-limits to his men, close them down entirely if he liked.

"You won," her father said of the four men who had entered. After removing their oilskins, the three soldiers accompanying their captain took a table near the bar and the captain walked to his usual haunt in the far corner. The words were barely out of her father's mouth when the striking of hooves to stone was heard again.

"A busy day for us," Bess told him.

"Would appear so. I'll see to the captain. You see to his men."

Their eyes met and she smiled her gratitude. Her father knew how she felt about the commandant of the Royal Marines.

"Ale all around," the sergeant of the group told her. "And for me, whatever you have cooking that smells so good."

"Beef barley soup and soda bread," she informed him.

"I'll have that, as well," one of the other men said and the third nodded in agreement.

Going over to the bar, she drew three ales and clutching them in her hand started back to their table when the door opened again. She glanced at the newcomers—a smile on her face that froze in place as soon as she saw who had entered the taproom.

He was alone this time, as he had been the first night he had come to the inn. His black coat and britches were soaked, his boots muddy and the brim of his cavalier hat rained water from it as he removed it. The only thing dry about him appeared to be his dark hair.

"Well, look what the cat dragged in," Penry said from across the room. "A drowned rat, it seems."

"Bess," he said as though he hadn't heard the captain's rude remark. "Would you happen to have an available room for the night?"

"Of course, Your Grace," she said. "Let me serve the men and I will take you to it."

"Much obliged," he said, shivering. He ran the sleeve of his coat under his dripping nose then sneezed.

"Mayhap you'll catch your death of cold, Farrell, and put an end to your wretched existence."

From the corner of her eye, Bess saw the earl turn his attention to the captain but he said nothing to the insult. He was removing his leather gloves, stuffing them inside his sodden coat as he held the other man's mocking glower.

"This way, Your Grace," Bess said. She cast a passing glance at her father and saw him frowning.

The earl followed her to the stairs and the heavy tread of his boots on the steps told her he was bone-tired. Looking around at him, it made her heart ache to see his shoulders slumped, his head down.

She led him to the room across the hall from her own, opened the door and stepped aside. "In here, Your Grace."

He leveled his gaze on her. "Don't do that," he said quietly. "I hate that gods-be-damned title. Call me Declan or don't call me anything."

His words shocked her. It had been her experience in life that those of the peerage took umbrage if they were not addressed properly, given their due in their station of life. All she could do was nod her acceptance of his request although she wasn't sure she could oblige him.

He placed his hat on the bureau by the door as he entered the room. She watched him look about him.

"It's very nice, Bess," he told her. He put his hands to the front of his coat to pull it off but had to stop as he sneezed twice in succession.

"You should get out of those wet clothes, milord," she said. "If you do not mind wearing some of my father's I could clean and dry yours and get them back to you by morning."

He nodded and sneezed yet again.

"Undress then get in bed. I will be right back with the clothing and then I will get you a hot toddy to hopefully ward off a cold," she said and softly closed the door behind her.

On the way to her father's room she marveled at her boldness. She put a hand to her cheek. How dare she order the earl about as though he were a commoner? He had every right to chastise her for her forwardness, but she did not believe he would. Unlike the uppity captain in the taproom below, the earl had a layer of kindness to him that showed in his remarkable blue eyes. A gentleness that was just as appealing to her as his handsome face.

She went into her father's bureau and pulled out a pair of britches, a long-sleeve shirt, and a pair of soft woolen socks. She did not think the earl would appreciate wearing another man's underpants so she refrained from adding them to the other things. Hurrying back to his room, she tapped lightly upon the panel.

"Come."

She entered to find him stretched out in the bed with the covers pulled all the way up to his chin and he was shivering, his teeth chattering.

"Oh, milord," she groaned and hurried to the bed. She placed the clothing on the straight back chair beside it and dared to put her palm to his forehead. He was burning up.

"Do you want another quilt before I go?"

"Aye."

Hurrying across to her room, she jerked her own quilt from her bed and ran back into the hall. She spread it over him, shocking herself again when she pushed the damp hair out of his eyes.

"I am going to make that toddy," she said firmly.

"T…thank you."

She turned to go and ran right into a hard chest.

"I was wondering what was taking you so long. Is anything amiss?"

She stepped back, her eyes going up to the unkind dark orbs of the captain. His thin lips were pressed tightly together as he stared down at her.

"His Grace is sick," she said. "I need to make him a toddy."

The captain switched his hard stare to the earl and his upper lip curled. "Is he now?" he asked in a hateful tone. "You have my sympathy, Farrell."

"Go to hell," the earl told him.

"Shall I take you with me?" the captain inquired.

"Get out of my room, Penry," the earl snapped and sat up, pushing the quilt from his bare chest.

"Or what?"

"Or I will toss you out the gods-be-damned window," came the warning.

"May I be of assistance, Captain?"

Bess turned to find her father standing in the doorway, his face as hard and set as the earl's.

"You really shouldn't allow your daughter to be alone in a bedchamber with the likes of him," Penry stated. "You need to take better care of her reputation and virtue."

"Get out," the earl shouted.

The captain snorted. He turned from the bed, pushed past her father and stomped down the stairs.

"Help him get dressed, Papa," Bess said, avoiding her father's eyes as she followed the captain out of the room.

"The man's a reprobate," the captain told her, glancing up at her as they went down the stairs.

"He's been nothing but a gentleman to me," she replied.

"Give him time," the odious man said with a snort. "He'll show you his true colors."

She lowered her head as she stepped off the last stair and hurried to the kitchen. She wanted nothing more than to be upstairs caring for the earl but she'd not missed the look her father had shot her.

As she set about making the toddy, all she could think about was Declan stretched out in the bed. Her body tingled with wanting to crawl beneath the covers with him to warm him, to enfold him in her arms and hold him against her.

By the gods, she wanted him so badly it made her teeth ache. She knew it would happen—it had to—but what then? Could she entice him with more than just her body? Could she win his heart? Could she make him fall in love with her? Ask her to be his mistress?

"If only I could," she said as she poured a large amount of whiskey into the tankard then added a dollop of butter.

Every maiden dreamed of her white knight swooping down on his prancing mount to sweep her into his arms and carry her away to a life of luxury and ease. She was certainly no different. Her dreams had always been filled with gallant suitors wearing the finery of gentlemen. She fantasied of living in mansions filled with servants and all the trappings of wealth.

What would it be like to be the mistress of a man like Declan Farrell? Or his wife?

That thought made her hand shake as she reached for the tin of whole cloves. Where had such an idea come from? She wondered. She had gone from thinking of herself as a mistress—something she hadn't ever wanted—to thinking of herself as a wife, something even more foreign to her thinking.

She took several cloves from the tin and dropped them into the tankard. "Could I really win him if I tried hard enough?" she mumbled, putting the tin back and taking another tin with ginger root in it from the shelf.

Cutting a small piece off the ginger root, she paused with it over the rim of the tankard.

"He's interested," she said. "Definitely interested and I would love him as no other woman ever has or could."

She dropped the root into the tankard then plucked the honey pot from the counter to add a few spoonfuls to the brew before adding the hot water from the kettle.

She'd always heard the way to a man's heart was through his stomach, but she suspected Declan Farrell needed more than just nourishment of his body. She sensed he needed nourishment of his soul and encouragement, and she intended to see he got both.

*   *   *   *   *

Dec was chilled to the bone—which was odd since it was July and the weather had been hot as hell. He eyed the shirt on the chair and reached for it.

"Allow me, Your Grace," the landlord said.

"I hate being a bother," Dec told him.

"You aren't," the man replied. He picked up the shirt, shook it out then handed it to Dec.

Slipping his arms into the sleeves of the soft shirt, he looked over at the sodden mess his wet clothing was making on the floor.

"Never mind your clothing, Your Grace. I will see to it."

"Declan."

The landlord smiled. "Declan," he repeated.

"Patrick, wasn't it?"

"Paddy to my friends."

"Dec to mine."

The man's smile widened. "And are we to be friends, then, Dec?"

"I hope so."

Paddy nodded. "So do I." He reached for the britches. "Want these?"

"Aye," Dec said. "My arse is freezing."

Politely looking away as his guest threw the covers aside and lowered his legs to the floor, Paddy walked over to the wet clothing. "You should not go about unarmed," he said. "Especially with the likes of Captain Penry and his men lurking about."

"My pistol and rapier got lost when I fell," Dec said, stuffing his legs into the britches.

Paddy looked around—turned back quickly for Dec had not pulled the britches up his thighs. "Where did you fall?"

"In the gods-be-damned river," Dec said. He left the top button of the britches undone then scrambled back under the cover, trying to keep his teeth from clicking together. "Rather I was tossed in there when my mount shied from a clump of debris that touched his leg."

"Were you hurt?" Paddy inquired. He picked up the clothing and turned to face Dec.

"My pride more than my body although I've got a nasty bruise on my hip where I landed on a rock."

The fall had happened as he was walking his horse down into the river to the cave. The Rysalian was skittish when it came to anything touching its legs, and as soon as the floating debris swirled around it, the horse reared. Dec had tumbled from its back, hitting the rocks underneath the water. His sword got caught between the rocks and he was forced to unbuckle his baldric and leave it. Cursing, he stumbled to get up, fell again—his pistol falling out of his waistband—and had to scramble like mad to catch the reins of his mount before Warlock turned and fled back up the slippery incline to get out of the swirling water. As quickly as he could he pulled the horse into the Black Chasm Hole and kept him still and quiet as the riders chasing them thundered over the bridge.

Then the hoof beats had stopped.

"He can't have gone far," he heard Jasper shout. *"Span out. Check the trees."*

"How 'bout the cave?" someone asked.

"He has better sense than to go in there," Jasper replied.

Apparently not, Dec though. For nearly twenty minutes he stood hip-deep in the waters rushing past his legs with his hands clamped around Warlock's muzzle to keep it from making a sound. In the dark with seven riders passing over and back across the bridge, shouting to one another he realized just how dangerous his situation was. The waters were rapidly rising, frothing through the cave from the torrential rains that had begun the moment he had fled the keep. He didn't have that long to get through the cave to the far opening. Fear that the waters would continue to rise and drown both him and his horse was very real. Thankfully the gods had been with him and he had gotten them both out just moments before a thunderous wave of water came barreling toward them to completely fill the cave entrance.

"Thank the gods you weren't hurt any worse," Paddy said. "Is there anything I can get for you? If I know Bess, she's already brewing you up one of her gods-awful hot toddies."

"Bad?"

"The absolute worst," Paddy replied. "But they work. Just gulp it down as quickly as you can. That's the trick." He started to leave then stopped. "She'll probably want to rub your chest with camphor."

"I don't think…"

"Let her," Paddy said. He looked Dec in the eye. "Trust my daughter to know what's best for you." He smiled slightly. "And her."

* * * * *

Angrily, Royce drummed his fingers on the top of the table as he stared at the door leading into the kitchen. He forced himself to sit still when every instinct in his body screamed at him to go in there and speak to her. He did not want her anywhere near Declan Farrell, but he didn't see how he could prevent it. The bastard was a guest in her father's establishment and she was the only servant. With Farrell upstairs in one of their rooms, he posed a problem that had to be met head-on.

"Rain's slowing down, Captain," Sergeant Breslyn said. "When do you want to ride out?"

"When I am good and gods-be-damned ready," Royce snapped. "I will let you know when I am."

"Aye, sir," Breslyn acknowledged.

He saw his men putting their heads together—no doubt gossiping about him—but he didn't care. All he cared about was the woman, who at that moment, left the kitchen and turned toward the stairs. He was halfway out of his seat when her father met her at the first step. They looked his way and he sat back down.

"Damn him to hell," Royce said under his breath for the landlord was coming toward him.

"May I get you a refill on your ale, Captain?" the man asked—politely enough, although there was no warmth whatsoever in his black eyes.

"No," Royce replied then threw in a "thank you" simply because that was what one did and not because he meant it.

"Please feel free to stay as long as you like," the man told him. "This weather is good only for fish."

Royce nodded. "I hope you took to heart what I said about your guest upstairs," he couldn't prevent himself from saying.

"Concerning?"

He leaned forward in his chair with his hands clasped together atop the table. "Declan Farrell was cashiered out of the regiment for conduct unbecoming," he stated. "He is a rogue, a miscreant, a libertine of the highest order. It is not safe for a young woman to be left alone with him."

"I trust my daughter, Captain," the man stated. "If she thought His Grace presented a danger to her, she would have told me."

"Yet she's up there with him again," Royce said, wincing at the bitterness in his tone.

"She took up a toddy to stave off a cold. She'll be down soon."

"If not, I will fetch her down myself," Royce declared.

"Thank you, but that won't be necessary. I am fully capable of taking care of my daughter, Captain," the man said. "Have no fear on that account."

That said, the bastard turned and walked away, stopping at the table where his men were lounging.

Grinding his molars, Royce decided he had all the authority he needed to go up the stairs and question the landlord—as well as his daughter—about whether or not they suspected one of their patrons of being the thief he was after. He placed his palms on the tabletop to push himself up at the same moment the door opened and seven men came trooping in from the rain. He recognized one of them and sat back down again.

"Welcome, gentlemen," the landlord said, beaming at the new arrivals. "Sit wherever you like."

"We're looking for His Grace, the Earl of Dungannon," Jasper Burrows, Duke Edward's warden stated. He looked about the room. "His horse in in your stable."

"May I ask who is inquiring about His Grace?" the landlord inquired.

"That's the duke's hound," Royce spoke up.

Jasper pivoted his eyes toward the speaker then scowled. He turned his gaze back to the landlord. "I am Burrows, His Grace's warden at Arlington. Where is the earl?"

"Upstairs," the landlord replied. "He has rented a room for the night."

"He'll not be staying the night," Jasper said. He reached into his pocket. "How much does he owe you?"

"And why pray tell won't he be staying, Burrows?" Royce inquired. "Did his daddy send you to fetch his wayward little boy?"

"The earl is suffering from chills and fever," the landlord explained. "He is in bed."

"With the landlord's daughter taking a gods-be-damned long time to fetch the bastard a hot toddy," Royce stated.

Every eye turned toward the ceiling.

"Oh," Jasper said. He put his hand up and coughed. "I see. Then I will wait until she comes down before going up to speak with His Grace."

"If you would like me to go up…" the landlord began but the big man in front of him was shaking his head.

"I'll wait," he said and motioned the men with him to seat themselves. "I'll take a pint if you please, landlord."

"Patrick," the man replied, extending his hand.

"Jasper," Burrows provided.

"Why are you after him, Burrows?" Royce inquired, leaning back in his chair. "What's he done now?"

"His father has business with him," the big man replied.

"So he sent you and six other men to bring him to heel?" He folded his arms over his chest. "Interesting."

Completely forgetting about the landlord's daughter taking far too long to do what she had gone to do, Royce began to realize there was more to the matter of Burrows being sent to find Farrell than met the eye. If the man hadn't done something to piss off his father, then mayhap he was in trouble that required protection.

"Trouble of what sort?" he mumbled under his breath.

A potential abduction for ransom? That happened all too frequently among the peerage. An irate husband coming after Farrell with a loaded pistol or sharpened rapier? That wasn't entirely beyond the realm of possibility.

Or was it more serious than either of those?

It certainly bore some investigation, he thought.

* * * * *

Bess took the cup from her patient and set it on the bedside table. "I have also brought a pot of camphor, milord."

"To slather all over my chest," he said with a grimace.

"It does help to keep the more dangerous symptoms from developing," she told him.

"My mother swore by it," he said.

"Would you like me to…?"

"Might as well," he said, cutting her off. He lowered the covers and sat forward to pull her father's shirt over his head.

She reached into the pocket of her apron for the small crockery jar filled with the oil. She unscrewed the lid and when she looked up again, he was naked from the waist up.

"My back, too?" he asked, looking up at her.

She dropped the lid, couldn't seem to find her voice for she was staring at thick, hard muscles that were stacked up and down his chest, upper arms that were bulging with muscles. The little patch of hair between his breastbones drew her eye like a magnet.

"Milady?" he pressed.

"Aye?" she whispered.

He reached out to shackle her wrist, causing her to jump. His strong hand was clamped lightly around her flesh and his eyes were boring into hers when she tore her scrutiny from his chest.

"Do you want to rub that gods-awful smelling stuff on my back as well?" he asked and she wondered if he was aware his fingers were caressing her wrist.

"I should," she answered, staring into those wicked blue eyes.

"There are a lot of things you should do," he said huskily and his hand moved up her arm to her elbow then down again—his palm sliding over her skin.

"Things I would love to do, milord," she said.

He tugged on her hand and she had no choice but to sit down on the bed beside him or fall across his bare chest.

"Declan," he reminded her.

"Mayhap this isn't the right time," she said.

"And who decides whether it is or not?" he asked and lifted his free hand to cup the side of her face. "You? Me?" When she didn't answer, he slid his hand along her cheek then behind her neck to pull her toward him

"No," she said and pushed him away.

He blinked. "No?"

She put her hand to his forehead. "You are burning up. I'll not have it said you caught your death of cold at the Hound and Stag," she told him. "'T'would be bad for business."

His lips parted. He looked as though he was about to say something, thought better of it and slowly lay back down.

"Thank you," she said. She poured a portion of the oil in her palm, set the jar on the bedside table then rubbed her hands together to warm the oil. As she did, she happened to glance down and saw the tenting under the coverlet.

Slowly she lifted her gaze to his.

They stared at one another for a long time.

She put her oily palms to his chest.

He growled low in his throat.

She started rubbing the oil into his skin.

"Milady, you have no idea what you are..." he began then stopped. He squeezed his eyes closed. Sweat was glistening on his forehead.

"I know it's terrible, but it is good for you," she assured him.

"So good for me," he said under his breath.

He shivered and his eyes popped open. There was such heat in them, such intensity, she stopped moving her hand.

"Come away with me," he said in that throaty tone that did such delicious things to her body.

"What?" she gasped.

"Leave this place and come away with me," he told her. He took her wrist in his hand once more. "We can sail to Ionary, to Virago, Oceania. Anywhere. I will find a priest to marry us and..."

She snatched her hand out of his grip. "A priest? Marry?" she asked. "What are you saying?"

"I'm saying we could get married." He reached for her hand again but she jumped up from the bed and put a good ten feet between them.

"It's the fever talking," she stated. "The fever has taken hold of your mind and…"

"I know precisely what I'm saying, Bess," he said. "From the moment I saw you, I wanted you."

"Aye, that may be, for I want you, too, but to tempt me with marriage just to have your way with me is cruel," she snapped. "And unnecessary."

"Will you just listen to me?" he asked, throwing the covers aside. He started toward her just as the door opened and her father appeared.

"There are men below who have been sent to find you, Dec," he said. "The one named Jasper is insisting on speaking to you."

"Bloody hell," Dec cursed.

"Bess, you need to go downstairs," Paddy said.

"I asked her to come away with me, Paddy."

Her father nodded. "Understandable given the situation you find yourself in," he replied.

Bess saw her patient's forehead crease.

"Jasper told you?" Dec asked.

"No, it was a man named Micah," Paddy replied. "I overheard him talking to one of the soldiers. He told him it was the reason they had been chasing you."

"Chasing?" Bess asked, turning back to Dec. "What did you do?"

"It's what I won't do," Dec replied.

"What does that mean?" Bess asked.

"It means his father wants him to marry a woman he doesn't want to marry," her father said. "So he thinks by running away with you he can get out of it. Once he is safely out of the country, he'll leave you high and dry."

"I'd never do that. Why do people always think the worst of me?" Dec asked.

"Perhaps it is the reputation you have nurtured, milord," Paddy replied. He came further into the room, lowered his voice. "You and I both know you are a dangerous man. A man who lives a perilous life. I wouldn't be much of a father if I allowed my daughter to tie herself to such a man."

"Papa..."

"Go below and see to our guests," her father ordered. When she hesitated, he pinned her with a stern look. "Now, Elizabeth."

* * * * *

Dec was feeling lightheaded and his knees were threatening to give out on him so he backed up to the bed and sat down.

"Is the woman to whom you are engaged that terrible a catch?" Paddy inquired.

"First of all, I am not engaged to her," Dec stated.

"That is not what I heard."

"You heard wrong."

"No, he did not," Jasper said. He had come in at some point and was leaning against the doorjamb.

"I am not engaged to that woman," Dec denied.

"Then how do you explain the banns being posted on the front doors of the churches in Oxmoor and Arlington?" Jasper queried.

That was a blow Dec had not been expecting. Maybe a right cross or left hook from Patrick Arbra's meaty fists but not the hit Jasper had thrown. He thought he might well lose the hot toddy he'd drank.

"When was that done?"

"This morn. The dukes' signatures are on the papers along with their seals," Jasper replied. "As soon as Duke Edward found out you had managed to flee the keep, he had his horse saddled and he rode over to Oxmoor to seal the deal."

"This can't be happening," Dec groaned. He ran his arm over his sweating face.

"You look awful, milord," Jasper said. "Why don't you lie down? It's started up raining again and I can't take you back in this condition."

"Just as well 'cause I have no intention of going back with you," Dec mumbled.

"Then we'll be staying until the weather is clear," Jasper said. "And this time, there'll not only be men outside your door and under your window, I'll have one up on the gods-be-damned roof, too."

"Wasn't expecting that, were you?" Dec said as he climbed under the covers. He grimaced as the sheet stuck to the oil on his chest.

"Climbing down the wall, aye, but not up it and across the roof," Jasper replied with a shake of his head. "'Twas a right dangerous thing you did."

"I'm a dangerous man, ain't I, Paddy?" Dec mumbled.

"Would appear more so than I originally thought," Paddy agreed.

"Mayhap I should bring a cot in and sleep in the room with you to make sure the danger is past this night," Jasper suggested and Dec saw him wink at the landlord.

"Mayhap you would like to look for other employment if you try that shit," Dec told him.

"We should let him rest," Paddy said. "I don't believe he'll be going anywhere tonight."

Jasper nodded then pointed a finger at Dec. "Best you get plenty rest. You're gonna need it when you get back to Arlington."

Dec stuck his hand out from under the cover to extend a rude reply.

* * * * *

He had a raging cold the next morning. When Bess brought him in a light meal of coffee and oatmeal he frowned at it for he had no appetite. One look at the grey lumpy mess in the bowl and his gut rebelled.

"Nope," he said, shaking his head. He put the bowl on the bedside table.

She put her hands on her hips. "Why not?" she demanded.

"Starve a cold and feed a fever," he told her.

"Nice try, but it is feed a cold and starve a fever," she corrected and promptly laid her palm to his forehead. "And you have no fever thanks to the toddy."

They were alone in his room although he half expected Jasper to walk in at any moment. He had to make his move before he did. He reached up, hooked an arm around her waist and brought her down to the bed—his lips to her ear.

"I need you to go to the stable and let my horse out the back way," he said. "Just whack him on the arse and say 'the cave.' Make sure no one sees you doing it."

She pulled back to give him a perplexed look. "Why would you want your horse to…?"

"Just do it for me, Bess, and fetch me my clothes while you're at it," he insisted.

"They're still damp," she said.

"Doesn't matter. I need them and I need my father's men to see you bringing them up to me. Will you do that?" He searched her eyes. "Please?"

She pursed her lips. "Anything else you need me to do?"

"Does your father have a horse?"

"We both do," she said.

"Then I'll need to borrow yours. I'll return it tonight."

"Tonight?" she repeated.

"Can you leave the side door unlocked?"

"For what purpose?"

"For me to come inside when I return your nag," he said. "That is if you don't mind sharing your room with me for a day or two."

Her lips parted and her eyes widened. "Without Papa finding out? I don't know if…"

"I'll be as quiet as a church mouse. He won't know I'm here." He put up his hand and crossed his heart. "I swear it."

"Are you him?" she asked.

"Him?"

"I washed your clothes, milord," she said. "It would have been hard not to notice the claret velvet lining of your coat or the fact that it can be turned inside out and worn that way."

"Many a coat has a velvet lining, milady," he stated.

"With a black silk handkerchief stuffed in the pocket alongside a tell-tale silver dollar that is the Gypsy's trademark?" she challenged. She narrowed her eyes. "I'll ask again: are you him?"

Dec shook his head. "It would be folly for me to admit such a thing to you. Dangerous, as well."

"You think I would betray you to the soldiers?"

"Dangerous for you, milady. You could be held as an accomplice," he replied.

"Papa knows who you are," she said. "He found your coat hanging on the line in the kitchen and pulled it down, turned it inside out so the lining wouldn't be seen lest that nasty Penry or one of his men happen to come in."

"Bess, this is something we should not be talking about," he said, eyeing the door lest someone be listening.

"Your secret is safe with me," she told him. "With us. What you are doing is a godsend to many a poor family. No one would ever betray you to Penry."

A light tap at the door prevented him from warning her not to be discussing her suspicions of him even with her father.

"Come," he snapped and gritted his teeth when Jasper entered.

"Sun is shining and it's nice and warm out," Jasper declared. "You need to get dressed, milord, and let's be heading home. The men are eating and as soon as they're done we'll be saddling up."

Dec looked at Bess, scrunched his forehead in pleading and hoped she understood the gesture. Her long sigh told him she had.

"I will fetch your clothes, milord," she told him. She winked at him before she left.

"A right comely lass," Jasper said, watching her go. "A fine cook, too."

"Am I to be a prisoner at the keep until the Joining day?" Dec asked, not liking the way Jasper had looked at Bess.

"I imagine that might well be the way of it," Jasper replied.

Dec flinched. If I have anything to say about it there won't be a gods-be-damned wedding, he thought.

The sound of the stable door squeaking open made him tense. If that was Bess slipping into the stable to do as he'd asked, he prayed no one was about to see her'.

"You need to eat that, milord," Jasper said, nudging his chin toward the oatmeal. "You're gonna need your strength."

The wicked, knowing grin that tugged at the beefy man's face made Dec want to put his fist through it, but he nodded and reached for the bowl. He brought it to him, dug the spoon into the glop and lifted it to his mouth. It was all he could do to shovel it into his mouth but when he did, the taste was an unexpected treat. Maple syrup underscored the pleasant taste of well-cooked oats.

"See what I mean about her cooking?" Jasper asked. "The lass can even make mush right tasty."

He all but inhaled the oatmeal as Jasper stood there beaming at him then held the bowl out to him. "I need more of that," he said.

"Be my pleasure," Jasper said. "You're too pale by far." He took the bowl and was whistling as he skipped down the stairs.

"You'll be whistling out the other side of your mouth in a few minutes," he said under his breath. He grinned at the guards who were peeking in the door at him and told them to shut the portal.

A few minutes later, Jasper opened the door, stepped back to let Bess enter the room ahead of him then brought the second bowl of oatmeal to Dec.

"Your clothes are a bit damp," she told him as she laid them carefully at the foot of the bed.

"They'll dry on the ride," Dec said. He took the bowl from Jasper and toasted her with it. "Really good goop, wench."

She laughed. "I'll leave you to gum it, then, milord."

"Leave me to eat in peace this time, Jasper," Dec said. "I'll get dressed when I'm finished."

"Need any help just yell," Jasper told him. "The guards will look in on you."

Dec nodded and shoved a big spoonful of oatmeal in his mouth, smiling around it as he chewed.

The door closed and he was up faster than a musket ball. He ripped off the shirt and pants, tossed them to the bed then donned his breeches, shirt and coat as quickly as he could. Fetching his boots, he pulled them on, looked for his hat, retrieved it then went back to the window. He opened it, peered out, nodded to the two guards standing below then ducked his head back in. He dropped to the floor, stretched out and rolled under the bed, pulling the covers down to hide him from sight. After adjusting the covers on the other side of the bed, he lay there with what he knew was a nasty grin.

* * * * *

"Where the hell did he go?"

Jasper's loud voice echoed through the room.

He lay there listening to the stomping of feet—one heavy pair right by his head as Jasper hurried to the window.

"How the fuck did he get past you?" he yelled down to the men below.

"Who?" one of the men called back.

"The earl," Jasper bellowed. "Who the fuck else were you supposed to be guarding?"

"Didn't come up here," someone else said, and Dec knew that had to be the man on the roof.

"Are you fucking sure?" Jasper barked.

"Aye, well, I think so. I had to take a piss but…"

"Get your arse down here and help us find him. Lucas, check the stables. If that big black bastard is gone, so is he," Jasper ordered.

Jasper ran from the room, hissing at the guards flanking the door to check every room in the inn.

He figured he had maybe five minutes before Jasper and the others rode out in search of him. Once they found Warlock gone, they would figure—as he intended for them to—that he had managed to get out of the inn, to his mount, and flee. As soon as he heard them galloping away, he would hurry downstairs, to the stable and take Bess's horse. He had no doubt Jasper would split the men up—half going east and the other half west to search for him. If that proved to be the case, he would head south toward Arlington. That would be the last place they would think he'd go.

* * * * *

Bess and Paddy stood in the doorway of the inn as Jasper Burrows and his men galloped out of the inn yard.

"Where is he?" Paddy asked.

"I truly don't know," she said.

"I saw you sneaking out to the stable and I saw what I reckon was his rider-less horse tearing out across the meadow. Did you set the horse free?"

"Aye, Da," she answered.

"Was he waiting out there?"

"I don't think he ever left," she said. "I think he's still inside."

"Most likely he is."

"He asked to take my horse," she told him.

"Then you'd best get it ready for him. I'm curious to know where in my inn he is hiding that all those men couldn't find him." He turned to go inside. "Be quick about it, Bess. If we're going to help him, we're going to do it the best way we know how."

"He is who we think he is, isn't he?" she asked softly.

"Aye, I'm afraid he is," her father replied.

Paddy knew there was nowhere below the stairs for the earl to hide. That meant he was somewhere in one of the rooms. He put his foot on the first step at the same time the young man appeared at the top of the stairs.

"Are they all gone?" he asked.

"Aye," Paddy answered. He put his hand on the newel post. "Where were you hiding?"

Dec smiled as he came down the stairs. "Under the bed."

"Under the...?" Paddy grunted. "That would have been the first place I would have looked."

"Jasper doesn't have much of an imagination," Dec told him. "Do you have a pistol I can borrow?"

Paddy frowned. "Aye, I suppose you should have one. It's under the bar." He went to fetch it. He bent over, retrieved the pistol and a box of shells, pushed them across the bar to Declan. "It kicks to the right so you'll need to adjust your aim."

"Much obliged," Declan said, sticking the pistol into his waistband. He put out his hand. "Thank you for not telling them I was still here."

Paddy took his hand. "I had no idea that you were." He covered their clasped hands with his other one. "You are merely postponing the inevitable, son."

"I have no intention of being forced into a marriage I don't want," Dec said then eased his hand from Paddy's. "Would you do it if it were you?"

"Like you, I was given no choice. Mine was an arranged marriage, but I learned to love my wife with all my heart," Paddy said. "The day she died—the day Elizabeth was born—was both the worst and best day of my life. We never know what fate has in store for us. It could be the lady in question is the love of your life. How do you know?"

The door to the inn flew open and Bess stood framed on the threshold. Her eyes were wide. "The soldiers are coming up the lane."

"Go," Paddy said. "If they see you and run into Jasper, they will tell him."

Dec rushed past him, Bess moved out of his way to let him leave but as he came abreast of her, he swept out his arm, jerked her to him and kissed her hard.

"There is no time for that," Paddy said sternly. "And you're going to give her your bloody cold."

"Meet in the stable at nine of the clock tomorrow evening," Dec said.

"She'll do no such thing, now go!" Paddy insisted.

Bess stumbled as Dec released her. He ran from the inn and into the stables.

"Nothing good will come of the two of you meeting," Paddy told her as Dec raced out of the stables and in the opposite direction of the advancing soldiers. "It is a dangerous game he plays."

* * * * *

Bess kept glancing at the tall floor clock that sat at the end of the taproom. As the hands moved closer to nine, her father became more watchful—seeming to never take his eyes from her. He would not allow her to go into the kitchen or alone or into the main hallway. He kept her in his sight at all times

But he did not see her unlock the side door before they left the kitchen after cleaning up for the night. As she climbed the stairs, the clock struck midnight and the hoofbeats of the horse of their last customer faded away.

"Do not leave your room," her father told her. "I want your word of honor that you will stay in your room until it is time to get up tomorrow morn."

She nodded obediently for she knew what he did not. At some point the side door would open and a silent figure would slip into the kitchen. A dark shadow would quietly climb the stairs, enter her room and spend the night.

In her arms—if the gods were willing.

"I will hear you swear to me, Elizabeth," her father insisted. "Swear to me you will not leave your room 'til morn."

They had reached the landed.

"I swear it, Papa," she said, walking to her room.

"It may be a bit stuffy in your room this eve. I have locked the shutters on your windows," he told her.

"Why?"

"You know why," he said. He gave her one last look then entered his room and closed the door.

She stood with her hand on the latch for a long while—her eyes glued to the darkness that rippled down the stairs. She wondered where he was at that moment. Was he close by? Was he waiting until the lights were out in her father's room?

A sudden thought shuddered through her mind and she reached out to take hold of the door jamb.

What if his father's men had found him? What if her horse stumbled, fell and threw him? What if he were lying in a ditch—hurt, in pain or worse?

Fast on the heels of those thoughts were images of him robbing a stage. Of a musket firing. Of a musket ball hitting him. Of him tumbling from his own horse onto the highway. Of blood spreading over the crisp white of his jabot. Of him whispering her name then taking one last breath.

"Stop it," she hissed.

"Why aren't you in your room, Elizabeth?" her father asked through the closed door of his room.

"I'm going," she muttered. Could the man see through walls?

She went into her room, closed the door then leaned against it. Her heart was racing because of her horrible thoughts. She could barely draw breath for the lump lodged in her throat.

"Go about your business as though it were an ordinary night," she said and put her hands to the buttons of her gown.

He would come. She had to believe he would.

And she would be waiting for him.

Her dreams—and his freedom—depended on them being together.

* * * * *

There had been within the papers he had stolen from the diplomatic courier a notation that a certain government operative would be traveling under cover of night on his way to the palace in Boreas. There would be something of value on that man's person and Dec was determined to take it. As he'd lain awake the night before sweating the fever from his body, he had gone over the plan he'd devised to do just that. Though he ached from the cold that made his nose run, eyes water, and tonsils ache, he was at the point in the man's journey where an ambush would work best.

He'd left Bess's mare tucked safely in a copse of trees two miles away and was sitting bareback astride Warlock as he waited impatiently for the bastard to ride by. Not for the first time did he regret having left his saddle behind at the stable or remembering to remove the one from Bess's mare. His rump was going to be sore come morning.

"Stop bitching," he told his inner voice.

The pistol was primed—the three revolving barrels of the flintlock resting on his thigh. He caressed the trigger, anxious to be finished with his business and on his way back to the inn.

Warlock shifted beneath him—a warning that another horse was nearby. Putting aside his longing for the sensual body of the landlord's black-eyed daughter, he tugged the black silk kerchief into place over the lower portion of his face, pulled down the brim of his cocked hat and when he saw the rider coming, moved his mount out from the shadows of the rowan trees under which he'd been sitting.

Out into a strong ray of moonlight that lit the purple moor.

"Stand and deliver," he told the startled rider.

* * * * *

At two of the clock, moving as quietly as one of the grey clouds passing overhead, he led Bess's mare to the stable and tied her beside the trough. He led his own beast into the shadows at the side of the inn. Looking up, he saw a faint light in her window and knew she was waiting for him.

Opening the lid to the wooden box that held kindling, he laid the rapier he had taken from the man he had robbed earlier and the pistol he'd borrowed from Paddy inside. They would be safe there and he could not risk them making any noise as he entered the inn.

Easing the door latch up, he gently opened the side door and with much practice, skirted the edge and moved silently into the kitchen. Just as carefully he closed the door behind him and stood listening.

Not a sound came from the inn save the tick-tick-tick of the great clock and the now and then soft pop of settling timbers, yet he remained where he was until he was satisfied there was no one waiting for him below stairs. Quietly, he eased to the floor, sat down and pulled off his boots. When he stood—boots in hand—he walked to the kitchen, moved swiftly through the taproom to the stairs. With infinite care, he put his hand on the rail, one foot on the far side of the first step and pulled himself up. He put his other foot on the opposite far side of the second step and moved up the stairs—careful to balance his weight only on the strongest part of each stair so there would be no squeaking beneath his weight. Once he gained the landing, he stood still again and listened. The rhythmic cadence of a man's snore told him Paddy was fast asleep. Stealthily he made his way to Bess's door, found it open a crack and soundlessly pushed it open slowly.

She was sitting up in bed with the lamp beside her only a dim glow. Her hair was unbound—flowing around her shoulders—and as black as midnight against the snow-white gown she wore. Her welcoming smile made his heart race.

He returned her smile, bent down to place his boots just inside the room. He closed the door gently behind him and with extra care ran the barrel of the lock through the hasp. With the door secure, he turned to face her and peeled off his coat as he walked toward the bed.

As quiet as he was being, as silent as the room was, he heard her shuddery breath as he removed his coat then laid it aside. He undid his jabot, tossed it aside then pulled the tail of fine linen shirt from the waistband of his pants. Even in the near darkness he could see the hot gleam in her beautiful eyes as he worked the buttons through his fingers.

Her lips parted as the sides of his shirt separated and he shrugged it from his shoulders. He let it fall behind him to the floor. He put his hand to the belt he used to hold his gun, pulled the leather from the tang then slipped the buckle.

In the faint light he watched her tongue curl over her bottom lip and had to tamp down the groan that threatened to leave his throat. His cock was hard as stone behind the fall front of his breeches. It was straining at the fabric and literally sprang free when he undid the two buttons of the front.

A gasp brought his head up—both of them—and he put a hasty finger to his lips and gave her a low shush.

Her eyes were wide as saucers as she stared at him and he grinned. He knew what had surprised her. He had been told by every woman he'd ever bedded that he was larger than any man with whom they'd ever slept. It was a source of vanity for him as it would be to every other man graced with such an organ. That he'd been taught well how to ply it was another source of pride.

Shouldn't be.

But it was.

Unbuttoning the waistband of his breeches, he kept his attention riveted to hers. Hers was directed at his crotch. He pushed the breeches down his hips and stepped out of them then peeled off his stockings.

Naked—his shaft leading the way—he went to the bed. One knee to the mattress was as far as he got before she reached out to take hold of him.

No shy miss was his tavern wench as she all but pulled him onto the bed with her by his very root.

"Mine," she whispered as he fell atop her.

"Yours," he whispered back. He wanted to kiss her, needed to kiss her, *ached* to kiss her, but her father's words to him intruded. He had no desire to give her his cold.

Her hand was wrapped around his straining cock. This—he thought with a wide inner grin—was going to be one hell of a ride.

Chapter Six

Edward looked up to see his son come strolling into the dining room as though nothing had happened. He paused with a forkful of eggs almost to his parted lips.

"Good morn, Father," Dec said as he went to the sideboard and took a plate from the stack. "Lord Jamie."

Jamie brought his napkin to his lips to hide a grin. "Good morn, godson," he muttered.

"Where the hell have you been?" Edward demanded, letting the fork drop to his plate with a heavy thunk.

"Outrunning your posse," Dec replied. "Are they back yet?"

"No, they most certainly are not," his father bellowed. "They are still out looking for your arse."

"Well, I am going to park my arse in a chair and partake of this wonderful-smelling repast," Dec told him as he took a seat.

"The banns were posted yesterday," Edward stated.

"So they tell me," Dec replied. "But you can unpost them, Father. I have no intention of marrying the Standfield chit or any other woman you think to foist off on me."

"I'd rethink your words, Dec," Jamie said softly. "He's been like a bear with a sore paw since you managed to outwit your guards." He chuckled. "How did you hoist yourself up the bloody castle wall?"

Dec looked him in the eye. "I'll never tell. I might want to do it again."

"You most certainly will not be doing it again," his father snarled. "You'll be lucky if I don't clap you irons in my dungeon."

"That threat is getting old," Dec said with a sigh. "Do try to find another that will at least attempt to put the fear of the gods in me."

"Oh," Jamie said. "Not a smart thing to say, son."

"Put that fork down, now," Edward bellowed.

Dec sighed and did as he was told. He leaned back in his chair. "All right," he said. "Let me have it, Father. All of it. Don't hold anything back."

"You are going to marry the Lady Althea whether you like it or not," Edward told him. "Alastair and I have put our signatures and seals to the banns and they will be read every Sunday from now until the end of August. At that time, there will be a wedding at Standfield Hall. You and your new wife will honeymoon at your mother's estate in Chale with a full complement of my men there to make sure you do not leave."

"Do not escape, you mean," Dec said, a muscle bunching in his cheek.

"Take it however you like," Edward replied.

"And until then?" Dec questioned. "Am I to be a prisoner again in my own home?"

"The gods damn you, boy," Edward hissed. "You..." He choked on his anger and started to cough.

"What your father was going to say is if you do your duty as you are honor bound to do, he will not restrict you to the keep," Jamie said.

"My duty?"

"Your father and the Lady Althea's father have given their words, their pledges—if you will—as members of the King's Council to join their two families together." He gave Dec a steady look. "They also sent the contract for the two of you to be Joined to be ratified by the High Council."

Dec's eyes widened. "They did what?"

Jamie gave him a commiserating look. "That contract was approved and sanctioned by the king himself. The decree came from Boreas Keep at dawn this morn."

"And is irrevocable," Edward managed to sputter. "Balk at the marriage now and you will go to jail for breach of contract."

"Breach of contract?" Declan repeated. He hadn't counted on that. That put a fly in the ointment.

"Aye, and I'm told you've been prattling on about marrying a chit you chanced upon at some sordid inn," Edward stated. "Let me disabuse you of that ridiculous notion. Should you do something so idiotic as marry another woman, you will still be in breach of the contract and you will *still* go to jail. Are we clear?"

Dec felt the rug being pulled out from under him with every word his father spoke.

"You like screwing her? Fine. Do so until you come down with the clap. You want to play the brigand, Declan James?" Edward queried. "Fine again. Be about your business; I will not try to stop you." He pointed his finger at his son. "But hear this. If you do not go through with this marriage, I will turn you in to the Royal Marines myself."

"You don't mean that," Dec whispered.

"Not for being the infamous thief the entire country is talking about but for dereliction of duty, breach of contract, dishonorable behavior, and any gods-be-damned thing else I can think of to have you put away. I promise you, you will spend the next year or two behind bars. That will give you ample time to contemplate just how foolish you were to defy me."

"You're going to blackmail me?"

"Call it what you will. If you want any freedom at all, you had best think twice about not going through the Joining."

"If you are thinking of running, Dec," Jamie put in. "It would be best that you don't. Your father has pledged Jack McGregor as your ancillary if you flee. Your punishment will become his punishment. Since he is a commoner, he will spend the rest of his life paying for your mistake."

"Jack has nothing to do with…"

"Run and he pays," Edward stated. "It's as simple as that. You want to put your friend in jail then—by all means—run."

* * * * *

If there was one thing Dec had learned over the years since he'd been spared the same fate as those who had been on the *Molly Celeste* with him that fateful day, it was that life goes on after it kicks you in the teeth.

People are born, grow up, marry, perhaps conceive and bear a child then die. It was a cycle that rolled along from century to century like a juggernaut. No matter how many people died, that many more were brought into the world to continue the circle of life.

What was one man's life compared to the millions that had come before him and would come after him?

Slamming the door to his room, he stood just inside the chamber and wanted to scream at the top of his lungs at the injustice that was being forced on him. The chains that were slowly but surely constricting him until he thought he would suffocate from lack of air. Tearing at his jabot, he ripped it from his neck in an effort to fill his lungs. He found himself gasping, unable to breathe. He was drowning—not from water but an absence of oxygen.

Drowning, he thought as he dropped to his knees, clawing at his constricting throat. Drowning should have been his fate all along. He should have died alongside his mother and brother. Gone down with the ship as they had.

Tears filled his eyes as he rocked back and forth. He'd never felt as helpless as he had that day. He had failed those who had loved him, depended on him. Failed the very woman who had conceived him, borne him and raised him to manhood. Failed the little brother who had looked up to him, trusted him, believed in him.

Now here he was helpless again. His failure coming back to make him atone for a multitude of sins he had committed in his life. Mayhap jail was where he belonged, he thought. At least there he could not fail those who still loved him.

Shoulders slumping, he buried his face in his hands. The low keening that came from his throat shamed him but it helped to alleviate some of the sense of suffocating. Scraping his hands down his face he dropped them to his thighs and dug his fingers into his flesh.

He'd tried so hard, he thought, to make up for having failed his mother and Eion. To be a good and dutiful son. But the screams of the dying echoed in his thoughts and the flailing hands going under for the third time played before his eyes day and night. He couldn't cope. Didn't know how. Drinking helped ease the pain, but it only served to bring out the worst in him. The scrapes with the constabulary began soon after his mother's funeral and continued on until his father forced him into the Royal Marines. He hadn't wanted to go. The military wasn't for him and he'd tried to tell his father that', but the Duke of Arlington refused to listen.

And Dec had been right. He hated the military and the military hated him. He'd gotten into even more trouble under the iron first of his commanding officers and rebellion was the only way he had to handle how helpless he felt at being ordered around like a puppet. The military treated him like a mindless dummy. He was perfectly capable of doing what needed to be done without having his face shoved into it. Nothing they expected of him had any real consequence anyway. It was all meaningless drilling and saluting and clicking of the heels. Ordered to toady to men who were one step up from the moronic irked him like an ingrown toenail.

He had failed dismally at the only real obligation he'd ever been given—that of saving his mother and brother—so nothing the military demanded of him was important. Being unable to protect those who had been placed in his charge had been a hard blow to his manhood. To his ego. His self-esteem. That failure had crippled him in ways he knew would never heal. It turned him cold and numb inside and left him with a burgeoning rebellious streak that bordered on the suicidal for a long time. All the military managed to do was bring out the stubborn, reckless part of his nature. He hated being away from Arlington Hall and the harder the officers pushed him, the more recalcitrant he became.

When he was sent home in disgrace, his father had shunned him for weeks. The old man's silent treatment was no only condemnation, but an indictment of all that was broken inside Declan.

He hadn't felt wanted or needed.

Until the day he'd been out riding and had seen a family of four being evicted from the hovel that was all they had in the world. The displacement of that family mirrored the way he felt about his own life: he had no more control over it than the poor family had of theirs. He understood well the helplessness, hopelessness, and futility of it.

That was when he decided to even the playing field for those who could not enter the game themselves. At least this was one wrong he could right. As the privileged son of the Duke of Arlington he was privy to information that could be used to target those who would stomp their boot upon the necks of the less fortunate—those they felt were beneath them anyway. He had access to baronial homes and castles, entre into a world where wealth and prestige could be turned into an asset to help the poor rather than extend the prosperity of the rich.

Thus the Gypsy had been brought to life and the highwayman had saved many a family from starving, from having their land confiscated for lack of the money to pay their taxes. He was bringing good to those who desperately needed it.

And still did.

He lifted his head and looked across the sumptuous room that had been his since he was a toddler. His father's words rang in his ears.

"You want to play the brigand, Declan James? Fine. Be about your business; I will not try to stop you."

There were those who truly needed him. Had come to count on him. There wasn't a single soul he had helped who knew the real identity of their savior but they blessed him nonetheless. They appreciated what he was doing for them. He was not failing them.

But to continue to do so, he had to be unrestricted, free to come and go as he needed to.

"If you want any freedom at all, you had best think twice about not going through the Joining."

The face of Althea Standfield passed through his mind's eye and he pushed up from the floor. He walked to the window to look out.

They were there again—the guards. He supposed there would be two more on the roof and though they hadn't been there when he'd come upstairs, he was sure as hell they would be outside his door now.

Trapped. Unable to leave. Watched day and night. He might as well be in prison.

Jamie's words came at him like a slap.

"If you are thinking of running, Dec. It would be best that you don't. Your father has pledged Jack McGregor as your ancillary if you flee. Your punishment will become his punishment. Since he is a commoner, he will spend the rest of his life paying for your mistake."

Jack.

His best friend. The man who had always had his back. The man who would take a musket ball for him.

A man he desperately needed to talk to at that moment.

Clenching his teeth, he turned from the window and strode to his door. He flung it open and—surprise!—there were two burly men lounging across the hall. They straightened as soon as he left his room and fell in behind him as he walked.

Down the stairs and to his father's study where he knew the man would be at this time of morn. He didn't bother to knock but opened the door and entered. His father looked up in surprise then frowned.

"What is it, Declan?"

"I want to talk to Jack," Dec told him.

"For what purpose?"

Dec walked to his father's desk and leaned his weight on his balled fists on the desktop. "If you want me to prostitute myself to the Standfields then send for Jack. Let me talk to him."

"Again," his father said, putting aside the document he had been reading. "For what purpose?"

"What harm is there in allowing him to talk to young McGregor?" Jamie asked from behind him.

Dec glanced around and was somewhat relieved to see support on the face of his father's trusted confidante.

"Send a messenger, then," Edward ordered. He narrowed his eyes. "But if it is your intention to cook up some wild scheme to get you out of doing your duty, remember who will pay for that scheme."

Dec nodded—not trusting himself to speak—and pivoted on his heel. As he passed Lord Jamie he did not miss the compassion in the older man's eyes.

* * * * *

"What are you going to do?" Jack asked.

They were sitting on the rim of the formal fountain in the garden with six—not two, but *six*—men within tracking distance, watching Dec's every move.

"Does it seem to you as though I have a choice?" Dec countered. He would not tell Jack about the threat to his freedom. There was no reason for Jack to know because Dec had no intention of letting his friend be punished for something that was none of his doing.

"I guess not."

"I was told the marriage has been tentatively set for the fifteenth of September. A request for a visiting priest from the abbey to come celebrate the Joining has been sent," Dec told him. "That should give

Standfield time to invite as many pompous asses as he has in his address book."

"I know this isn't what you want…"

"Hell no it isn't what I want," Dec snapped.

"But it may turn out to be a good thing for you, Dec."

"How?" Dec demanded. "How can being tied hand and foot to a woman I've only met once be a good thing? To have the responsibility of her?"

"Is she an ogre?" Jack queried.

Dec shrugged. "She's comely enough."

"I've heard she's a raving beauty," Jack said.

"Beauty is in the eye of the beholder," Dec quoted.

"I've also heard she has a sweet temperament and goes weekly to the village to help feed the hungry."

Dec frowned at him. "So what?"

"That tells me she has a kind and giving spirit." Jack nudged him with his boot. "Do you think her father orders her to do that?"

Dec snorted, rolled his eyes.

"I have also heard she's…"

"Has a halo and wings and strums on a harp while singing hymns," Dec snarled as he hopped off the fountain edge.

"Got a wicked sense of humor."

Putting his hands on his hips, Dec stared out across his ancestral lands and shook his head. "You've asked about her."

"Learned all I could," Jack admitted. "I wanted to know who it was we were up against."

"It's going to be me up against her," Dec mumbled. "Every day and night for the entirety of my fucking life."

"What I have learned has been nothing but good things. She is nothing like her father and seems to be an accommodating person. Mayhap if you are faithful to her…"

"Fidelity is not on the menu," Dec stated. "I may be forced to service her but I will take my pleasure where I find it. I won't allow her to emasculate me. I'll sleep with whomever I please."

Jack scowled. "Like the tavern wench?"

"Her name is Bess," Dec hissed.

"You're not going to listen to reason, are you?" Jack asked.

"Are we friends?" Dec queried.

"Of course."

"Then be my friend and don't give me the same shit everyone else is dishing out," Dec told him. "It's coming from every side of me, Jack, and I don't know how much more I can take without being buried under it."

Jack stared at him for a long moment then nodded. "If you want my advice, you can ask for it. Otherwise, I'll not give it."

Dec put his hand on his friend's shoulder. "Just be there for me. That's all I ask."

* * * * *

When he left his bedroom later that evening, the guards were gone. Neither had they been under his window.

All because he had prostrated himself before his father, swallowed his pride and extended his wrists for the virtual shackles that were being placed there.

"As long as Jack is not dragged into this, I will do what you want," he had told his father.

"You will do your duty?"

"I will do whatever you think must be done," he'd agreed.

"One mistake, Declan, and McGregor will pay for it," his father warned.

"I understand. As long as I'm the good little neutered sycophant everything will be right as rain in Serenia," he'd said.

"All I ask is that you be careful," his father said, and he could have sworn there was moisture in the old man's eyes.

No one stopped him at the stable when he went in to fetch Warlock. No one looked askance at him as he saddled the horse himself. Not one servant stood in his way as he mounted the beast and rode out. None of his father's men followed though he couldn't shake the notion that he was being watched. If he was, whoever was tracking him was very good at his job.

He rode to the bridge at Dead Man's Crossing and sat there for a long while watching the waters swirling under the wood and stone structure. His gaze shifted to the cave but there was no reason for him to venture inside, so he nudged Warlock. The Rysalian continued on across the bridge, their shadows gliding across the moonlit planks.

He had a tax collector to intercept in Waterford, a small town five miles north of Wixenstead. According to the papers he had taken from the courier, taxes were being collected the past two days in the riverside berg and the collector would be leaving on the morrow for Boreas Keep. Tonight, he would be staying at the Piper's Horn, a seedy tavern with two rooms to let on the top floor of its ramshackle building. There would be two redcoats to guard the collector's take and they would have use of the second pigsty of a room. Chances were good all three would be well into their cups by ten of the clock and in bed by the stroke of eleven. He felt sure none of them would pose a threat.

As Warlock trotted along the coach road, Dec's thoughts were on the kind of man it took to earn his way as a tax collector. Universally hated, such a man was shunned by the villagers even as they feared him. It was a cesspit job that only men who could not seem to find other gainful employment took. Sometimes the bastard was a craven coward but there was the rare bird who was a sadist at heart and enjoyed watching the suffering of others. Listening to their tearful pleas.

That could well be the man at the Piper's Horn.

He hoped so for he was in the foulest of moods and itching for a fight. His fists itched to break teeth, shatter a jaw or two. He fervently hoped one—or all three—would try to keep him taking back the money they had taken from the poor people of Waterford.

It wasn't customary for him to venture into a village or town to do his thieving. He was, after all, a highwayman and the coach road was his usual haunt. But of late, the good Captain Penry had forbidden tax collectors and messengers, couriers, envoys, and government officials from traveling after sundown. Those who traveled about in their personal coaches had been warned to stay off the coach road until the Gypsy was brought to ground. Because of the new restrictions, he was having to take his business to the taverns and inns where such individuals might stay. It was a nuisance more than anything and it doubled the chances of him being caught. Considering the frame of mind he was in, he relished the danger such an enterprise posed.

Waterford was one of those towns that had absolutely nothing going for it. It sat beside the river like a dead, decaying toad on a hump of land what smelled of sulfur. There were no street lamps for there was no street. Mud comprised the thoroughfare that ran through the center of town. Only three windows among the dozen or so structures glowed with light. Most of those who lived in Waterford worked in the mine at Cumberland and had to be up well before dawn to make the two-mile trek—mostly on foot for horses were an expense many of the villagers could not afford.

"Yet along comes the king's tax collector to take what little they do have," Dec said quietly as he sat beneath the spreading limbs of a live oak and stared at the nearly dark town.

At the far end of the thoroughfare, the dilapidated tavern sat beside a stable that had seen better days. At the end nearest to where he sat were the meeting hall and another nondescript building he knew to be the undertaker's abode. The rest of the constructions were where the miners lived: identical one-room shacks with roofs badly in need of new thatching and chimneys that were cracked and missing stones. All of it was a sad commentary on the harsh life these people were forced to live.

As he watched a light was extinguished in the last miner's shack—leaving only two lights left burning in the tavern. He set Warlock into motion, keeping the animal at a slow walk that took them behind the row of shacks on his right. The stench was overpowering and he pulled up his kerchief more to block the odor than hide his face.

This night he was dressed all in black for the claret velvet coat would have stood out like a red flag in the bright moonlight. Although he doubted any of the miners would raise the alarm if they saw him, he didn't need one of the redcoats to be out and about and catch sight of him. Gone, too, was the cocked hat with its snowy white plume and in its place a simple black tricorne minus of any adornment. No pistol was stuffed into his belt and no rapier hung from a scabbard at his waist. He carried a single black obsidian dagger that he had purchased in Necroman after leaving the Royal Marines.

Skirting the edge of the stable where he knew the redcoats and tax collector's horses would be, he walked his own steed to the copse of trees behind the tavern, threw a leg over Warlock's head and dropped quietly to the ground. The heels of his knee-high boots sank into the mud and he bit back a curse that came rushing to his throat.

He stayed where he was and took in the position of everything surrounding the back of the tavern. There was a privy off to one side. Two rows of unfinished boards had been placed atop the mud as a walkway from the back of the tavern to the outhouse. Another row of boards led to a chicken coop and a fenced area where a scrawny goat lay atop a hay mound. A covered well was between the tavern and a lean-to under which cords of wood was haphazardly tossed.

When the last light went out in the tavern, he moved as quietly and quickly as he could through the slush of the mud. With every footstep there was a sucking sound that made him grind his teeth but there was nothing to be done about it. Just as he reached the well, the door to the tavern opened and a man stepped out carrying a lantern.

Ducking down behind the well, he watched the man walking down the rows of boards that led to the privy. From the way the man was dressed, Dec knew it was the tax collector. Though the clothing was not fashionable by any stretch of the imagination, it did look clean, if worn. With his hair pulled back in a queue, it was hard to tell the bastard's age but the most important thing was that he was unarmed.

The man reached the privy and opened the lopsided door to enter. He hung the lantern on a hook just inside the structure then closed the door behind him.

Dec eased up to a standing position then made his way to the door of the tavern. He listened for any sound from within but there was only silence. In one quick move, he drew his dagger, opened the door and slipped inside. He pressed his back to the wall to await the return of the tax collector.

* * * * *

Althea sat at her window and glared at the moon. It looked so happy sitting up there—without a single care—while her world was rapidly falling apart.

"He doesn't want to marry you," her father had told her when she had come down to break her fast. "But his father and I have taken the matter out of his hands. The banns have been posted, a contract has been signed by Edward and I, and the Joining will be in mid-September."

She had stared at him with horror turning her backbone to ice. "You are *making* him marry me?" she asked.

"You are not getting any younger, Althea," her father reminded her. "In trying to find the right husband for you..."

"The right *wealthy* husband," she corrected him.

"It would be remiss of me not to find you a husband who has the wherewithal to provide for you as well—if not better—than have I," he said. "The combined Standfield and Farrell estates will make you the wealthiest woman in Serenia." He smiled smugly. "Even wealthier than the queen."

"You know full well I don't care anything about wealth, Papa," she told him. "I want the man I marry to love me. To be in love with me. By forcing Lord Declan into having me against his will, you will quite effectively make sure that never happens."

"Posh," her father said with a snort. "Love is overrated and it is not necessary to have a good marriage. The uniting of two illustrious families with impeccable bloodlines is far more advantageous for you than having a man moon over you."

"Moon over me," she said to that. "As though I should be ashamed to want a man who would do so."

She thought back to the night of her cousin's party and the man with whom she had danced. He had been most pleasant, witty and she had enjoyed spending time—as short as it was—with him. His leap over the balcony and plunge into the pond told her he had a carefree reckless side to him that would be fun to get to know. She had been attracted to him right from the start and when the prospect of marriage to him had first been mentioned, she had been thrilled. Then when she'd learned he didn't want to marry her, she'd been hurt and a bit offended that he had not been as taken with her charms as she had been with his allure. He might not want her but she wanted him.

Fiercely. From that first night they had danced together.

And she meant to have him.

But not this way. Not made to take her to wife despite having strong feelings against the union. That did not bode well for a happy lifetime together. That was simply a recipe for disaster.

Apparently, though, it was out of both his hands and hers now. The banns had been posted. The entire county, district and country would know of their engagement. It would be impossible for him to back out if his father and her father held the proverbial pistol to his handsome head.

"Damn and double damn," she said with a stomp of her foot.

Turning from the window she went to her desk, pulled out the chair and sat down. Reaching for a sheet of paper and her quill, she dipped the nib into the ink pot and put pen to page.

* * * * *

He heard the tax collector returning from the privy and tightened his grip on the handle of the dagger. He was calm, clear-headed and centered.

The door opened, the wash of the lantern's glow spreading over the floor and up the far wall followed by the man's shadow. Mumbling to himself, the man closed the door behind him, turned and took two steps before Dec hooked his left arm around his throat and pressed the tip of the dagger over his heart.

"Cry out and it will be the last thing you do," he hissed in the man's ear.

The man had gone as still as a statue with his left hand holding the lantern and his right arm clamped closed to his body by Dec's biceps.

"Is the tax money in your room?"

"Aye."

"How many guards are with you?"

"Two."

"Are they in their room?"

"I believe so."

The man's voice was steadier than Dec thought it would be. He was close to Dec's size though a bit taller.

"We're going to walk over to the table and you're going to set the lantern atop it."

"If you're the one they call the Gypsy, you can have the gods-be-damned tax money. You will make better use of it than the king's men will. The people here are as dirt poor as any I've ever seen— even the wretched natives in Barter Town."

There was something in the way the man spoke, the cadence of his voice, his accent that made the hair stir on Dec's neck. But when he mentioned Barter Town, a tingle ran down his spine. "Who are you?" he asked.

"The name is Daniel Rees and unless the gods were so fucked up they created two of you—and by the gods I hope not—you are Declan Farrell."

Dec drew in a quick breath and stepped back, pulling his arm and the blade from the man in front of him who turned slowly to face him.

And it was a face Dec knew well but hadn't seen in over ten years. A face belonging to a dead man.

"Sweet Merciful Morrigunia," Dec whispered. He pulled down the kerchief. "It is you."

"In the rather worse for wear flesh," Daniel replied.

"We thought you were dead," Dec told him.

"Apparently the gods weren't finished with me." He went over to the table and placed the lantern atop then turned, spread his arms. "Come here, you little bastard, and give us a hug."

Dec looked down at his dagger then quickly sheathed it at his thigh. He hurried to the man who had saved his life more than once and wrapped his arms around him. Tears pricked behind his eyes, for Danny Rees was a ghost from his past that had meant as much to him as Jack did.

"You've put on weight," Daniel said then eased back from the embrace. Hands on Dec's upper arms, he looked him over. "Filled out right nicely though. That skinny little brat I knew from the Royal Marines could have slipped through the eye of a needle."

"What happened to you?" Dec asked him. "We looked all night for your…"

"My body?" Daniel finished for him. He shrugged. "I got caught up in some debris far down the river—snagged me as I shot past. My arm was broken and it got hooked around a tree branch."

"Why didn't you come back to camp? At least let us know you survived the fall."

"After what those bastards tried to do to me, do you think I wanted to go another round with them?" Daniel inquired. "Fuck that. I like my dangly right where it hangs."

Heavy footsteps walking across the floor above them drew their eyes to the ceiling.

"That's the guards," Daniel said. "I think they're coming back downstairs." He swung his head about the room. "You need to hide, Dec."

"I need to put them out of commission," Dec replied. "They're probably on their way to the privy."

"I'll take one; you take the other," Daniel suggested, reaching for a couple of empty wine bottles sitting on the table. He kept one and tossed the other to Dec.

Dec grinned as he caught the bottle. "Works for me."

Slipping quickly over to the door that led to the taproom, Dec took the left side and Daniel took the right, putting their backs to the wall.

"Who else is in the tavern?" Dec whispered.

"Just the blowsy old battleax who owns it."

The sound of the guards arguing as they came down the stairs all but drowned out Dec's next question.

"Where is she?"

Daniel jerked a thumb twice toward the ceiling and Dec nodded. They tensed for the guards were almost on them, their voices floating down the stairwell.

"And I say if you beat her every now and again, she'll…"

The first man came through the door, took two steps into the kitchen and went down with an oomph when Daniel brought the wine bottle down on the back of his head. The guard dropped like a rock and the man behind him stumbled over him. That man had just a moment of stunned surprise before Dec swung the bottle in his hand and cracked the guard in the temple. He, too, slid to the floor atop his companion.

"Smooth as Chalean cream," Daniel said and he and Dec slapped palms together.

"Just like old times," Dec replied.

"I'll get the strongbox with the tax money," Daniel said. "You stay here and watch them. Smack 'em again if they need it."

Dec nodded as his old friend stepped over the two prone men and jogged lightly up the stairs. He didn't have long to wait for Daniel was back with a small wooden box sealed with a padlock.

"Where's your nag?" he asked. He put the strongbox on the table beside the lantern

"Back in the trees."

"All right, you take the money and get the hell out of here."

"What about you?" Dec asked.

"You need to pop me, too. Make it look like a robbery."

Dec shook his head. "I'm not going to hit you with the gods-be-damned wine bottle, Danny."

"If I don't have a goose egg to match theirs when they wake up, they're gonna know I helped you," Daniel said. His smile turned pleading. "As piss-poor as this fucking job is, I need it, Dec. I can't afford to go back to prison so just fucking hit me with the bottle and be done with it."

"Prison?" Dec queried. "You were in…?"

"Hit me with the bottle and go before they wake up," Daniel hissed.

"Wait. Where are you living?"

"Groversner's Point," Daniel snapped. "The cottage with the green door. Now shut up and do what I told you for once in your stubborn life."

As much as he hated to do it, Dec saw the wisdom in Daniel's plan. He exhaled heavily then swung the wine bottle again. It clanked against Daniel's temple, his friend's eyes rolled up in his head and he started to fall. Dec grabbed him before he could and laid him gently on the floor.

"I'm sorry, my friend," he whispered.

He started to pick up the strongbox but his gaze went to the floor beside the door. There was one pair of muddy footprints leading from the back door to where he and Daniel had taken out the guards. As sure as the gods made little green plums, the second man was going to remember there being two men in the kitchen.

With a growl, he hurried to the back door, went outside, stomped around in the mud again then tracked it back into the kitchen to stand in the same spot Daniel had been standing. He turned, picked up the strongbox, took one last look at Daniel then hurried away.

* * * * *

Declan was sound asleep the next morning when there was a light tap at his door. He groaned, pulled the pillow over his head. It had been well after dawn when he'd gotten to bed and it felt as though he'd barely closed his eyes. When the tap came again he cursed.

"Come," he snapped.

The door eased open and Iverson, his father's manservant, poked his head into the room. "I have a missive for you, Your Grace," the man said.

His head still under the pillow, Dec growled before telling the servant to put it on his desk.

"Milady wishes a reply, Your Grace. Her man awaits below."

He lifted one side of the pillow from his face. "Milady who?"

"Standfield, Your Grace," Iverson reported.

"Shit," Dec hissed. He tossed the pillow aside then held out his hand. "Give it here."

"Aye, Your Grace."

"And stop staying that, gods-be-damn it," he ordered.

Iverson's lips tightened. The man was a stickler for propriety, rules and regulations and anything—Dec firmly believed—that smacked of subservience. The white-haired gentleman brought the note from Althea Standfield to the bed. He handed it over then stood there with his hands behind his back.

Dec looked up. "What?" he asked.

"I am to take your reply to her man, Your…" Iverson frowned. "Milord."

"Can I at least read the gods-be-damned thing before I give her my reply?" Dec queried.

"Of course, milord," Iverson agreed. He raised his eyes and looked at the wall beyond.

Dec glared at him. "In fucking private?" he snapped.

Iverson's stony face turned beet red but he bowed slightly. "Of course, milord," he replied and did a precise military about-face before striding regally to the door and leaving the room.

"Uptight walking stick," Dec mumbled. He pushed himself up to lean his back against the headboard. He ran his thumb under the bright blue wax that was imprinted with the Standfield crest and opened the missive. The elegant, flowing handwriting was quite beautiful with its curlicues and delicate strokes. Her words, however, were not at all what he had been expecting. There was nothing flowery or mincing about them.

Milord, she began.

It has been made clear to me that you do not want this marriage. I am told you have been pushed into it, coerced and quite possibly threatened. For that, I apologize. I wanted to assure you I have had nothing to do with the thrusting of this onerous task upon you. I am as much a pawn in this game as are you and have even less say in the matter than you do. No matter how I feel about the situation, I understand your reluctance to wed a woman you do not know.

If I had the wherewithal to flee my father's rule and the obligations of this Joining, trust me, I would and this union would not be consecrated. However, females of our class have no control over their future. That is especially so for those of us in the upper echelons of wealth. Our fate is in the hands of our male kinsmen.

Were it possible for me to buy my way out of this Joining that you find so burdensome I would do so, but I have not a copper to my name. I am totally at the mercy of my father—and soon—yourself.

I have but one request of you and will never presume to ask anything further. If you would be so kind to provide my man with your answer I would be extremely grateful.

Here is my request. All you need do is reply either yay or nay.

Will you swear on your honor as a gentleman and a peer of the Court of King Valdric that you will not hold this ill-fated union against me nor seek to punish me for a matter well beyond my control? Your answer will go a long ways in helping to settle the fear that is growing in my soul.

With respect,

Lady Althea Marie Standfield

He read the missive again then dropped his hands to his lap as he continued to stare at it. Apparently milady was as disheartened and unhappy about their coming nuptials as he was.

If I had the wherewithal to flee my father's rule and the obligations of this Joining, trust me, I would and this union would not be consecrated....Were it possible for me to buy my way out of this Joining that you find so burdensome I would do so but I have not a copper to my name.

He raised his head and turned his face to the window where a sliver of light was peeking through the closed draperies. Thoughts were tumbling through his head like water over the rocks at Dead Man's Crossing.

If I had the wherewithal to flee.

He realized he had to think more on this. Throwing the covers aside, he left the bed and walked to the door, opened it—knowing he'd find Iverson on the other side.

"Tell her man that my answer is yay."

"Very good, milord," Iverson said with another bow.

Dec closed the door and headed for the armoire. He needed to talk to Jack—and to Bess—about the plan that was slowly taking shape in his mind. As he dressed and the plan began to have structure, he realized there was something he needed to have his father do and the outcome of that had him grinding his teeth.

* * * * *

"A dowry?" Edward inquired. "You want a *dowry?*"

"One hundred thousand *denestras*," Dec stated. "Surely that is a mere drop in the bucket for a man of Duke Alastair's presumed wealth."

"But there was no mention of him providing a dowry for Lady Althea in the marriage contract he and I signed. Now you want me to go to him and demand he pay you to take his daughter off his hands?"

"Precisely so," Dec replied. "I believe I should make something off the deal."

"Why?" Edward asked, narrowing his eyes at his son. "What do you intend to do with the money?"

"Call it a bribe to make sure I treat his daughter with the respect and honor she is due."

"You will do so with or without compensation," Edward snapped.

"I've not asked you for even one concession in this, Father," Dec reminded him. "You are holding Jack's fate over my head and I am being sold into sexual slavery. I don't think asking for a few measly *denestras* is too much to ask."

"Sexual slavery?" Edward repeated. "For the love of the gods, Dec, how could you say such an odious thing?"

"All right, how about putting me out to stud?" Dec queried, playing his part of petulant brat to the fullest of his abilities.

Edward winced. "Please stop," he asked.

"A bit embarrassing to think you're forcing your only son into a loveless marriage with a woman he doesn't even know and expecting him to lay with her X amount of times to produce X amount of offspring?"

"Enough," Edward told him.

"Then ask for the dowry," Dec said. "Tell him I'm being intractable and obstinate and if he does not pay me, I'll hold my breath until I turn blue."

"And you would do it, childish little bastard that you are," Edward grumbled.

"I want that money by the end of the day tomorrow," Dec said.

"Now you are being absurd," Edward snapped. "One does not have that kind of money lying about the keep."

"He can get it from his bank in Iomal," Dec said. "Tell him to send a courier to fetch it."

"Why the rush?" Edward demanded. "For what are you going to use this money?"

Dec looked to the ceiling. "Someone saw me along the coach road the night the government courier was robbed of his diplomatic pouch. He says he'll go to the redcoats and turn me in if I don't pay him to keep quiet."

Edward gasped. "You are being blackmailed?"

"You mean by someone other than you?"

"Declan…" his father warned.

"Aye."

"By someone who believes you are the…" Edward clamped his lips together.

"Precisely," Dec acknowledged. "He'd have a hard time proving it but considering the hatred Royce Penry has for me, he'll sic his inquisitors on me until I confess."

"What is to prevent this man from continuing to demand money from you, Declan?" Edward questioned. "Blackmailers are the scum of the earth. They have no honor."

"He has cheated the wrong people and needs the money to buy quick passage to Chrystallus. If I don't give it to him, he'll turn me in for the bounty. If we pay him we would never see him again."

"You only have his word that is so," Edward reminded him. "He could come back for more money at a later date. Keep his knowledge hanging over your head for years."

"Give me credit for having some common sense, Father," Dec snapped. "I've checked him out thoroughly. My life depended on it."

Edward paced his study—his eyes tracking back and forth across the rich Rysalian carpet as he contemplated his son's words.

"We should pay the money," Dec nudged him. "Standfield is the reason my mind wasn't entirely on what I was doing that night. If I had not been distracted…"

"All right," Edward told him. "I will ask for the dowry but he may decline to pay it since it was never mentioned in the contract."

"But…"

Edward held his hand up. "If he doesn't pay, I will. We can't have the threat of your identity being exposed lurking out there."

Dec's forehead. "Thank you, Father."

"You can thank me by doing what is right and taking the request to the man himself."

That set the boy back on his heels, Edward thought. There was sudden disquiet in Dec's blue eyes and a decided tinge of pink at his cheeks.

"Me?"

"You are in need of the money and you should state your case to Alastair. Either way, the money will be available to you to pay the blackmailer. An added bonus will be that you get to see Lady Althea, perhaps spend some time with her."

"Oh, aye, her," Dec said. He ran his palms down his thighs.

"Aye, *her*," Edward said. "Your future wife?"

"It can't be today," Dec said.

"Might I inquire why not?" Edward asked.

"I have business in Wixenstead," his son replied. "Business I cannot put aside."

Edward scowled. "At the Hound and Stag Inn, no doubt." When his son's eyebrows shot up, Edward pursed his lips. "I know all about the girl, Declan James. Jasper informed me of her." He shook a finger at his son. "Get her pregnant and there will be hell to pay. Do you understand me?"

"I have no intention of getting her or any other woman with child, Father," Dec declared.

"I should hope not. At any rate, I expect you to be here first thing tomorrow morn so you can make the trip to Standfield Hall."

"Aye, milord," Dec replied. He bowed slightly then excused himself.

Edward went to his desk to pen a note to the Duke of Oxmoor.

* * * * *

Lying in Bess's soft arms with his cheek pillowed on her breast, he twirled a long lock of her sable hair around and around his index finger.

"Do you think it will work?" he asked her.

"I think it is a good plan," she said. "Whether it will work or not depends on what she will do with the news."

"You read the note," he said. "Did I somehow misunderstand her words? Did she not say had she the money to leave, she would?"

"Aye, she did, but if you give her the dowry—which is a lot of money, Declan—can you be sure she will flee as she suggests she will?"

He brought the lock of hair to his face and fanned it across his lips. "She doesn't want this marriage any more than I do."

"She didn't say that," she said, drawing the words out.

"She didn't say she did," he countered.

"No, she didn't," Bess agreed. She was raking her fingers through his hair, looking down at him. "But my guess is she does but wrote you what she did to save face."

"So do you have another suggestion?" he asked. "If so, tell me for I need to leave by eleven of the clock if I am to make it to Belvedere Glen by midnight."

"Who are you after tonight?" she inquired.

"There are five very well-heeled young gents who have a regular card game the first Friday of each month at a cottage just beyond the Glen. One or two of them will be riding back to Wixenstead. I intend to relieve them of their winnings."

She leaned down to kiss his brow. "How do you know which ones will be the winners?"

"The ones who always win," he said. He craned his head to look up at her. "The ones who have a nasty habit of pilfering money from the local widow's trust to fund their games."

"Ah," she said. "Vengeance is mine, sayeth Declan Farrell."

"You think they should get away with cheating those poor women?" he queried.

"No and I am proud of you for stepping in. All I ask is that you be careful," she replied.

"I'm always careful, wench," he said with snort.

He scooted down in the bed beside her until he could kiss her naked belly. Dip his tongue into the deep indention. Looking up at her through his eyelashes, he grinned, wagged his brows and moved lower still, sliding his hands under her rump. He nuzzled the soft hair at the apex of her thighs then flicked his tongue across the tender little nub there.

"Aye," she moaned, her fingers threading through his hair.

He moaned against her core and she writhed beneath him. Her reaction to his lovemaking did strange things to his heart as much as it pleasured his body. She was fast becoming an addiction to him.

One he had no intention of ever breaking.

Stabbing his tongue lightly into her cunt, he locked his lips around her nether folds and probed deeper. The taste of her was like nectar to him—warm cream that exploded upon his taste buds as he lapped at her body's offering.

"I love you," he heard her whisper.

He paused with his tongue pressed as deep as he could probe inside her. Something extraordinary shifted through him as what she'd said sunk into his mind. He really didn't want her—or any woman for that matter—to love him.

How many times had he heard those three words from women lying beneath him and knew they didn't really mean it? He wondered. A dozen? Two dozen? A hundred? He'd had so many women in his twenty-four years that he had lost count. He wasn't a man to mark his conquests with a notch on the bedpost.

Slowly he lifted his head to look up at her. She was staring down at him with a soft, gentle look he had never seen on any other woman's face. There was desire there, yes, but there was something else that bespoke her truthful feelings and that scared—and worried—him.

"I do," she said. She smoothed the hair back from his eyes. "I truly do love you, Declan. With all my heart."

"Then why did you tell me no when I asked you to marry me?"

"You know why," she told him.

And he did.

He desired her. Wanted her. Lusted after her. Cherished her. He was quite fond of her, but in his heart he knew he didn't love her. What was more, she knew it, too.

"Bess..."

"You don't have to say anything."

"I would marry you tonight," he stated.

"And be in prison by the end of the week," she said, shaking her head. "Even though I love you, Declan, I will not be the reason you are arrested. I would do anything else for you, but not that." She smiled sadly. "I would give my life for you."

A shiver of cold dread slithered down his spine and he pushed up from between her legs, moved to her side.

"Don't say that," he said. "Don't ever say that."

She blinked—her eyes wounded as her eyebrows drew together. "That I love you?" she asked and he heard a tremor in her voice.

"No," he said, shaking his head adamantly. "That you would die for me."

"I would," she insisted.

"Don't," he said. "Never, ever say that."

Her wounded look turned a bit amused although the pain did not leave her dark eyes. "Are you superstitious, my Gypsy?" she asked.

"Just don't say it again," he commanded. "Promise me, Bess. Promise me you won't."

"All right," she said yet he knew she was humoring him. He could see it in the way her gaze roamed over his face. He knew there was worry stamped on his features for it was thundering in his heart. "I won't."

"You swear?" he demanded.

"I swear."

* * * * *

Declan couldn't shake the uneasiness that had been plaguing him ever since he left the inn. Her words had scared the hell out of him and he couldn't stop them from reverberating through his mind. The thought of anyone dying for him filled him with such terror it made his hands shake, brought bitter bile to his throat.

Warlock whinnied softly. The beast sensed other horses coming toward them. It would be the two Baxley brothers whose pockets would be filled with their ill-gotten gains at the gaming table.

Absentmindedly, he pulled the kerchief over his nose, adjusted the wide brim of his cocked hat and drew the pistol from his belt.

He shouldn't be doing this, he thought. His mind wasn't completely on what he was about to do.

And there was that niggling feeling that pricked at his senses and scraped a wickedly sharp nail down his spine that warned him he was being watched. Though he had spied no one lurking nearby and he did not sense a troop of redcoats or even a scout spying upon him, the feeling would not go away. He shifted his shoulders against the sensation as the sounds of hoofbeats reached his ears.

"Here we go," he said to Warlock.

The Rysalian bobbed its head and moved quietly from beneath the camouflage of oaks under which his rider had placed him.

"Did you see his face when I laid down those two aces?" Brad Baxley asked—punctuating the question with a whoop of glee.

"He never learns," his twin brother Chad replied. "Like a lamb to the..." He stopped when he saw the dark figure that suddenly appeared in the middle of the coach road.

"Stand and deliver," the Declan stated, his pistol pointed toward them.

"The Gypsy," Brad said in a loud whisper. "Do you believe this?"

"I want your winnings, boys," the highwayman told them. "Every last gold piece you took from Lawrence Grant and Stanley Pell."

It was Chad who drew his own pistol and fired before his brother could take action. The lead ball fell well short of its intended target but Brad's did not. His aim was truer, calmer than his twin and the lead that spat from the end of his three-barrel pistol grazed Dec's cheek. Before Baxley could fire again, a shot rang out from somewhere in the forest off to Dec's right and the pistol went flying from Brad's hand.

"Don't shoot!" Chad shouted. "Don't shoot!" He threw his gun to the ground and slammed both hands into the pockets of his coat. He pulled out two coin purses and dropped them as well. He snapped his head toward his brother. "Give them your money, Brad."

"I will do no such…" Brad began but another shot came from the other side of the road and hit the dirt beside the hoof of the young man's horse. "All right," he cursed then reached inside his own coat for his winnings.

The assistance of whoever was lurking about in the trees had stunned Dec. He had seen what his intended victims had not: a dark rider moving quickly and quietly across the road behind the Baxley's to fire the second shot—making it seem there was more than two assailants.

He cursed his inattention but pointed his pistol at the young man he thought the one who considered himself in charge. "Get off your horse, Bradley and pick up the gold." When Baxley did not readily comply, Dec cocked his pistol.

Baxley growled but swung down from his mount. He picked up his own fat purse then went over to retrieve his brother's. He came toward Dec with a brutal look that might have alarmed lesser men.

"This isn't over, Gypsy," Baxley said.

Dec took the purses from him, stuffed them into his pocket, cast a quick look to the far side of the road—surprised to see the rider had disappeared—then lowered his gaze to Baxley.

"I have left a note at the parsonage in Belvedere Glen to apprise the authorities of your penchant for raiding the widow's fund. That bank is now closed to you and if I know Constable Wayne—and I know him quite well—he will be coming to question the two of you tomorrow morn," he told the Baxley twins.

"You're going to regret doing that," Brad hissed.

"Run along, little boy," Dec said. "Before I decide to return the favor of your shot and put a nice long groove down that peach-fuzz face of yours."

"Brad, mount up," Chad pleaded. "He means it."

"It's not over," Brad said, but it was all brag and Dec—as well as both the brothers—knew it.

He watched the surly young man vault into the saddle and viciously kick his mount into motion. His twin hastened down the road behind him—neither turning to look back.

"Are you still there?" Dec called out.

There was no answer.

Someone had saved his life this night but he had no idea who.

* * * * *

"The little bastard might not have hit him but I couldn't take the chance," Jack told Fairling as he climbed into bed beside her. "I wasn't going to sit there and let anything happen to the idjut."

"Are you sure he didn't see you?"

"No and he wouldn't have recognized the horse. I didn't take Spirit," he replied, referring to his white stallion.

"What horse did you take?"

"A roan I borrowed from the duke's stable," Jack said with a grin as he nestled his wife in his arms.

"It's a good thing you were there," Fairling said though he could hear the fear in her soft voice.

"I was careful," he told her.

"He wasn't," she reminded him.

"No," Jack said, staring into the darkness. "He wasn't and that scares the shit out of me."

* * * * *

The next morning, Dec dressed in his best waistcoat and breeches and presented himself to his father who was just sitting down to break his fast. He had not slept all night—replaying the scene on the coach road in his mind over and over again.

His father glanced up, down then up again. "What happened to your face?"

Dec put his fingers to the place where the iron ball had burned his cheek. "Cut myself shaving," he replied."

"Looks more like a rash to me. Will you join me for the morning meal?" his father inquired.

"I'm not hungry," Dec told him.

And he wasn't. Not only did he have a sour stomach for having to make the trek to Standfield Hall to make his request for the dowry, he was troubled over what had nearly transpired the evening before.

"Understandable," his father said with a twitching of his lips.

"I am so happy you find this amusing, Father," Dec grumbled.

"What?" the duke inquired. "Taking you down a peg or two?"

"Humiliating me," Dec replied.

"Was it not you who wanted the dowry, Declan?" his father queried. "You who needs it?"

"Aye," Dec mumbled, hating feeling like a little boy caught with his hand in the cookie jar.

"Then go fetch it. Spend some time with your betrothed— mayhap have a spot of lunch with her and Alastair—then go pay off your blackmailer." He flexed his hand toward his son. "Off you go, then. You do have a busy day ahead of you."

Clenching his jaws to keep from saying something disrespectful, Dec inclined his head and turned away.

"And Declan?"

He looked around.

"Try not to fuck up anything else."

That hurt.

As he made his way out to the stable his father's words continued to lash at him. Those words added to the guilt he'd been carrying around all the years since the day the *Molly Celeste* went down. He didn't believe his father did it a' purpose or even realized he had said something to hurt him, but that was the case. It brought a sting to his eyes and an ache to his heart. That his father thought him a fuckup was a bitter pill to swallow.

"You want the big boy saddled, Your Grace?" George, the stable master inquired.

"Aye," Dec mumbled. He spied Jack at the blacksmith's and nodded to him, wondering what his friend was doing. Jack farmed the land Dec had insisted be given to him when they'd returned home from the military, but he spent as much time hanging around Arlington Castle as he did as his cabin.

Jack lifted a hand in greeting then turned back to the man with whom he was speaking. When George led Warlock out into the stable yard, he didn't even look toward Dec. He appeared to be deep in conversation with the smithy.

A bit curious why his friend was all but ignoring him, Dec pulled himself wearily into the saddle and drummed his heels to put Warlock into motion. He rode out of the bailey and across the drawbridge with a heavy heart and a lump the size of Virago lodged in his throat. He was going to the last place he wanted to be, talking to people with whom he really had no desire to spend time.

* * * * *

Althea barely glanced at the rider she saw galloping toward them. She looked down to adjust her lace gloves and was tugging them up her wrist when the man and his horse passed her carriage. She was out of sorts for her father was sending her on an errand she had no desire to undertake. Though she had pleaded to be spared the trip to Warrington Keep, he had insisted. She hated traveling so early in the morn and it would be in the heat of the day by the time she arrived there. The August sun would be sweltering.

What she wouldn't give to go down to the pond, strip down to her chemise and dive into the cool, dark waters. Better yet, strip down to nothing and dive in as her intended had the night of her cousin's party. That he had done that might be wishful thinking on her part, but she doubted he had kept on his underpants when he went into the water.

"Wish I'd been a wee froglet sitting on one of the lily pads and seen that," she muttered as she lifted her head and turned to look at the passing scenery.

She'd like to see him period, she thought. He'd answered her note to him with a simple Aye—and that had been a relief of sorts—but she would have thought he would have presented himself to her by now.

"Ah well, all this is an abomination to him," she said. "Just as I am an abomination, apparently."

She snapped open her fan to ply what breeze there was to her already heating face. Perspiration was already forming at her hairline and between her breasts.

It wasn't just the trip to Warrington Keep that had her irritated. It was the fact that she would be expected to spend a few days with her late mother's cousins, the Earl and Countess of Warrington. She loathed the pair of them for they were the most obnoxious imbeciles she had ever had the misfortune of encountering. In twenty years of life she had never met a man and woman more insufferable and intolerable to be around. The earl gave new meaning to pompous ass and the countess was the very epitome of pretension.

"A miserable four days," she said. The mere thought of spending time at Warrington Keep was enough to make her want to pull her hair out. "Four long, hateful days of sheer boredom and trying to keep from screaming at the two fools."

The woman sitting across from her opened her eyes and sat up. "Did you say something, milady?"

Althea shifted her attention to the woman her father had hired the day before to be her traveling companion. A woman who had promptly fallen asleep as soon as the carriage cleared the barbican of the keep.

"Just talking to myself, Teresa Anne," she replied. She didn't like the horse-faced old hen and suspected Teresa Anne Mullavey didn't like her in return.

"They say such soliloquies are the first sign of a slipping mind," Teresa Anne said with a sniff.

"Who are they?" Althea asked but the women merely blinked at her. She waved her hand. "Never mind. I don't really care to know."

"I do hope we don't run into that wicked highwayman," Teresa Anne said.

"He only strikes at night and we will be at our destination long before then," Althea told her although she wished that wasn't the case. She would love to have the infamous Gypsy waylay them. What a grand adventure that would be.

* * * * *

"Your father sent me a note to inform me you were coming to speak with me," Lord Alastair said as he motioned Dec to have a seat.

"That was good of him," Dec said, annoyed that his father had not informed that was the case.

"He didn't say why, though," the Duke of Oxmoor stated.

"Ah," Dec thought. Naturally not.

"I must apologize, again, for my daughter. She left this morn for a brief visit with her cousins, the Earl and Countess of Warrington. I say, my boy. Do you know them?"

Dec refrained from rolling his eyes at the thought of the earl. "Aye, I have had the opportunity to make their acquaintances."

"Very astute businessman, the earl," Lord Alastair said.

"Quite," Dec agreed but had to bite his tongue to keep from guffawing at the ridiculousness of the statement.

"So," his host said. "To what do I owe the honor of your visit, Declan?"

Dec shifted in his seat. He was acutely uncomfortable and the formal morning wear that he was sporting made him feel as though he was encased in an Iron Maiden. His jabot was strangling him so he ran his index finger behind it to loosen the constriction.

"Come now," Lord Alastair said with a merry grin. "It can't be as bad as all that. You look positively green."

Girding his courage, Dec lifted his chin. "My father was remiss in including certain items in the marriage contract you and he signed," he said.

"Remiss?" his host repeated. "In what matter, Lord Declan?"

He swallowed then spat the answer out as though it was about to choke him. "The dowry."

Lord Alastair stared at him—no facial expression at all upon his moon-shaped face. When he spoke, the words fell from his mouth like heavy stones. "The dowry," he echoed.

"Aye, Your Grace," Dec said. "Lady Althea's dowry."

"With the merging of two such vast estates as mine and your father's, it was deemed unnecessary to provide a dowry," Lord Alastair said, his eyes narrowed.

"It is an ancient custom in Serenia, Your Grace, and is expected and demanded as a condition to an agreement of Joining among men of our position," Dec pointed out.

"Pray do not think to lecture me on the legalities of Joining agreements, young man," Lord Alastair snapped. "I studied law at the same academy from which you graduated."

"Then you know a dowry is a binding form of protection for the wife against the possibility of ill treatment by her husband and his family," Dec reminded him.

Lord Alastair shot to his feet. "Is it your intention to abuse my daughter, Farrell?" he demanded. "I did not think you the sort to do such a thing."

"And I am not," Dec said calmly. "The dowry is simply a protection for Lady Althea. Failure to provide…"

"Yes, yes, yes," Lord Alastair snarled. "I am well aware the Joining can be called off if a dowry is asked for and not provided."

"It is a protection for her," Dec repeated, feeling like the lowest kind of heel. "Nothing more."

Lord Alastair lifted his chin, looked down his long nose at Dec. "How thoughtful of you to demand it, then, eh?" A muscle tightened in his cheek. Flexed again before he spoke. "How remiss of me not to pay you to take my daughter off my hands."

Dec flinched. The man was glaring at him as though he was a loathsome thing slithering over his boot.

"You shall have your gods-be-damned dowry you greedy little bastard," his host told. "Now get the hell out of my sight. Accepting a grasping reprobate such as you as a son-in-law will surely prove to be the worst decision I have ever made."

Dec got slowly to his feet. He bowed formally then fled the room as nobly as he could despite the burning in his cheeks and the sour taste threatening to choke him. Once outside, he swung into the saddle feeling even worse than he had when he'd dismounted.

"It is for Althea," he said under his breath.

And was the only way he knew to prevent the farce of a marriage neither of them wanted.

Chapter Seven

"I need the cabin for one day and night only," Dec told Jack. They were sitting on the porch in the rockers as the sun dipped down behind the tall aspens.

"And just where the hell are Fairling and I supposed to go?"

"To the Hound and Stag," Dec said. "I've paid for the room for two days."

"What reason am I to give her?" Jack inquired.

"Tell her you are taking her on a holiday," Dec replied.

"To the Hound and Stag?" Jack queried then snorted. "Some fucking holiday."

"I need to bring Althea here to give her the money so she will leave and the Joining will be a moot point."

Jack shook his head. "That is going to backfire on you as sure as shit. She'll take that money and still demand you marry her."

"You have a nasty opinion of women in general, don't you?" Dec threw at him. "You don't like Bess and you don't trust Althea. Is there any woman for whom you have respect?"

"My wife," Jack said. "And my mother. The rest of them?" He shrugged. "They are suspect. You know as well as I that most of them are a greedy, grasping lot intent on snaring unsuspecting men into lifetimes of sheer misery."

"Good thing for you I'm not like that, eh, Jackson?" Fairling asked as she appeared in the doorway. She gave him a hard look then looked at Dec. "Are you staying for supper?"

"No, I've got business tonight," Dec replied.

"Aye, well we know what kind of business that is," Fairling said.

"Since you seem to have been eavesdropping on our conversation and know far more than you should about my business, did you hear the part about vacating the cabin for a day?" Dec asked her.

"I heard. My instincts tell me the same thing Jack's are telling him. This is going to backfire on you but you might as well learn your lesson now and get it over with." She cocked a shoulder. "You can have the cabin for as long as you need it."

* * * * *

Royce Penry finished reading the latest report concerning another robbery committed by the Gypsy the evening before then tossed the paper to his desk with a growl of frustration. His attention went to another report and held. It was a complaint filed by twin brothers who had been waylaid two evenings previous. He leaned back in his chair, steepled his fingers and considered what he'd just learned.

"Three of them," he said aloud. "Three highwaymen plying the coach road near Belvedere Glen that night."

It made no sense.

He swiveled his chair around so he could look at the map of Serenia on the wall behind his desk. There were flag-topped pins stuck in the places where the Gypsy had struck. Four pins near Iomal, three at Farmington, three at Hubbard, half a dozen around Springdale and twice that many near Wixenstead.

Wixenstead was his preferred stomping grounds and Belvedere Glen wasn't that far from the Hound and Stag Inn where he suspected the thief made frequent visits.

But was he gathering information there—for many a coach driver spent time at the new inn—or was he there to see the landlord's beautiful daughter?

"And to warn other men from going near her," Royce said through his teeth.

He knew—he *knew*—Declan Farrell was the highwayman. If he'd been asked to testify how he knew he wouldn't be able to, but in his gut the knowledge of the thief's identity was a surety. The thing was: how was he to prove it? How was he to catch a shadow that had managed to slip past all his patrols? To bring to justice a man as slippery as an eel?

If he sent troops north, he struck to the west. If he split his troops to the south and east, he would strike the west yet again. There was no rhyme or reason to where he did his thieving though Royce knew the courier list he had stolen gave him the locations where he needed to strike. Picking the site where he would hit next was proving to be impossible.

"If only I had enough men to patrol the area as it should be patrolled," he grumbled.

The bastard was no longer attacking government officials, couriers and the rich. Now he was stealing from the general populace. Why the sudden change? Why the Baxley brothers? He wondered.

"I wounded the son of a bitch," one of the young men had insisted. He streaked a finger up his cheek. "Right here. Nearly took his head off and would have if his accomplices hadn't fired at me."

That raised the question why he had suddenly taken on accomplices when he had used none in the past.

"I wounded the son of a bitch."

What he needed to do was take a ride up to Arlington Castle and see if Declan Farrell had a gunshot wound to the face. If he did, that would be grounds for bringing him in for questioning. If he didn't, he could still set a man to watching him.

"Which I should have done as soon as I took over command of the troops," he said.

Sooner or later, the bastard would make a slip.

"And then I will have him."

His decision made, he got up from the desk, called to his Sergeant-at-Arms to saddle his horse. He had business with his old adversary.

* * * * *

"She is visiting her cousins," Edward told Jamie. "I believe after Alastair read my note informing him Declan would be coming to see him, he sent her away for a while."

Jamie brought the two snifters of Chalean brandy over to two chairs in which he and his friend were sitting. "For what purpose?"

"So she would not be there to know she was being sold as chattel," Edward surmised.

"Would she not have expected a dowry to be presented to your family, Ned?" Jamie queried.

"Most likely she assumed it was part of the contract. I didn't know how my son was going to handle the demand for the dowry and that is why I informed Standfield to expect some amount of hostility on Declan's part."

"But you didn't tell him Dec was on his way there to ask for a dowry."

"No," Edward replied.

"May I ask why not?"

"Frankly, I wanted to know what Alastair's reaction was going to be. He handled it as I would have," Edward said, taking a sip of the potent, fiery brew.

"Which was?"

"Hostility of his own," Edward told him. "He all but threw Declan out of Standfield Hall."

"Why would you instigate something like that, Ned? It will not bode well for a peaceful union between the houses of Standfield and Farrell," Jamie said.

"It was never going to be a calm union, anyway, Jamie. Not with Declan so dead set against it." He stretched out his legs, crossed them at the ankles. "Best to know the lay of the land before going in with pistols blazing."

Jamie took a seat, leaning forward to gain his friend's complete attention. "Why do you do things to that boy that you know will cause him problems?"

"That boy, as you call him, causes his own problems," Edward said. He waved a hand toward the window. "He's out there playing a dangerous game of cat and mouse with the Royal Marines nipping at his heels. He allows some miscreant to figure out his identity and blackmail him. He demands money from his future father-in-law so he can pay that blackmailer and he is tupping some little tavern wench and is going to get her pregnant sure as shit," he snorted. "That boy has never grown up. I am trying to make a man of him and failing miserably at it."

"Mayhap if you showed him a measure of love, a modicum of respect you might make some headway," Jamie told him. "Instead of throwing every mistake he has made in his face; you are not helping the situation. He already believes you blame him for Kathleen's and Eion's deaths. That you wish he had died instead of them."

"That is not true," Edward snapped. "I have never blamed him and I don't want my son dead. I am doing all that I can to protect him. Jack McGregor is…" He stopped, clamping his mouth shut.

Jamie narrowed his eyes. "Jack McGregor is doing what?"

Edward tossed off the remainder of his brandy, winced then slammed the snifter on the table beside him. "We are doing everything we can to protect his foolish ass. McGregor follows him every night Declan goes out to do his thieving. I suspect there was real trouble last eve and that's how Declan came by that red mark on his cheek. I have seen enough lead grazes to recognize one when I see it. Someone shot at him and could very well have killed him. I believe Jack was there and might well have saved Declan." He clenched his teeth. "Again."

Jamie sat back. "Again?" he questioned.

"Aye," Edward said. "Had McGregor not intervened, Declan would have been tarred and feathered then castrated as the man my son saved from that very same fate."

"What man?"

"A priest named Daniel Rees," Edward answered. "He was the chaplain of Declan's regiment when he was serving in Diabolusia."

"Why have you never mentioned this to me?" Jamie queried.

"I wanted to forget I knew anything about it. That my son's name had even been linked with that of a sodomite."

Jamie winced. "One man falling in love with another is not degeneracy, Ned," he told Edward.

"That is your opinion," Edward snapped. "Not mine."

"Tell me what happened?"

"One of the soldiers discovered this Rees and a young native man having sex. He reported it to his sergeant who took the matter to their commanding officer."

"The same commanding officer who tried to get Declan court martialed for sleeping with his wife?"

"One and the same," Edward replied. "Captain Bertram Brooks."

"Go on."

"Sodomy is frowned upon within the Governmental Regiments. There is no law against it but those who engage in that unnatural act are severely disciplined by their fellow soldiers. Generally they are taken out in the wild, stripped naked and severely lashed before being castrated."

"By the gods," Jamie said, shuddering. "That is barbaric."

"Declan and McGregor had made friends with Rees. From what I learned the three of them were inseparable. I'm sure after it was discovered the priest was a sodomite, there were those who whispered that my son and McGregor could be as well."

"Anyone who knows Declan knows gods-be-damned well that isn't true," Jamie stated.

"It was while they were camped on a high promontory overlooking the Balsazin River that Rees was abducted by a group of five soldiers. It is my belief Brooks encouraged his men to punish Rees but no one can prove it. One of the natives who was the troop's guide came to Declan to tell him he had seen his friend being dragged into the forest."

"Did Dec know about the priest's feelings for those of his own sex?"

"I imagine he did but I doubt it mattered to him," Edward replied with a grunt. "A lot of his friends over the years have been suspect."

"In your eyes," Jamie muttered. "What happened then? I assume Declan went after his friend."

"He and McGregor. They got there in the nick of time. The soldiers had already lashed Rees and by then had him naked on the ground and were about to cut off his cock. Dec and the other boy jumped the soldiers and fought with them, giving Rees time to get to his feet. Instead of joining in the fight, the coward ran. Unfortunately for him instead of running to safety he ran right over a fucking cliff and into the raging river below."

"He died?"

"I assume so. His body was never found."

"Another friend lost that the boy could not save," Jamie said sadly.

* * * * *

On the fourth morning after his ill-fated meeting with the Duke of Oxmoor in regard to the dowry of Lady Althea, Declan stared down at the chest of gold coin that had been delivered to Arlington Castle only an hour before. He had waged a silent battle with himself over whether or not to rob the men who were bringing the dowry to him but decided it didn't matter. The gold was going to wind up in the hands of Althea Standfield either way. Within the hour, it would be on its way to Jack's cabin where it would be hidden until he brought the fair lady there to present it to her.

He had learned through a spy he had planted at Standfield Hall that the lady was on her way home from her brief visit to her cousins, the Earl and Countess of Warrington. The coach would take them from Warrington's keep to Wexford, the county seat of Oxmoor where they would meet with the duke for the noon meal. He intended to intercept them before that happened.

When he left his father's keep he was careful to make sure no one followed him. Satisfied no one was, he made his way across country to the Chappendale Forest. He would then keep watch for the coach on the windblown cliffs overlooking the Mid-Boreal Sea. As soon as he heard it approaching, he would ride down to the forest edge and out into the center of the coach road to block their passage.

He didn't have long to wait before the sound of the hooves galloping toward him broke the late afternoon quiet. He pulled the kerchief over the lower part of his face, tugged the brim of his hat down to shield his eyes and pulled the pistol from his belt. The coach was almost upon him when he directed Warlock into its path.

"Whoa," the driver shouted, sawing on the reins.

The guard sitting atop the high box raised his musket but Dec make quick work of halting the man from using it. He sent a musket ball scorching across the guard's wrist.

"The next shot will find its target," he told the man and the guard tossed his weapon to the ground.

"Down," he commanded the driver and guard and both men were quick to obey. "Now start walking back the way you came."

"Aye, milord," the driver said and the men started walking quickly away from the coach.

Laughing to himself, he threw his leg over Warlock's head and slid to the ground. He called to the earl to throw out his weapon.

After an argument with his wife, the earl submitted. "I've three ladies herein," he protested.

Dec advanced on the coach. "Aye, I know." He opened the door. "Ladies, if you please?"

The countess disembarked first. She gave him a hateful glower when she took his gloved hand then lifted her chin. "You are a detestable young man," she told him, snatching her hand back as though he had contaminated her in some way.

"So I have been told on numerous occasions, Your Grace," he acknowledged.

Next came one of the homeliest women he'd ever had the misfortune to lay eyes upon. Her face was long and sharp, her nostrils wide in an overly large nose and her eyes were as mean as a viper's. When he put out his hand to help her down, she knocked it away.

"Don't you dare touch me, you ruffian," she warned him.

Alighting with a grunt of annoyance, the earl shot him a worried look. "Take whatever you like and let us be on our way," he said. "There's no need for more violence."

"I believe there is one more person in the coach," Dec replied. "Milady, will you join us?"

When she stepped down from the carriage, he was taken back to the night of the masquerade ball—the first and only time he had ever seen or spoken to her.

"Lady Standfield," he greeted her.

"You are mistaken," the Countess snapped. "The lady beside me is—"

"This lady's maid," he stated. "Your ruse might have worked for others but not for me."

"I am at a disadvantage, milord," Althea spoke up. "And you are?"

"Alas," he said. "It would be unwise for me to provide my true identity to you, milady."

"Then what shall I call you?"

"What I am," he replied. "The Highwayman."

She smiled and he was struck by her beauty. "Indeed, and I suppose you are here to abduct me for ransom."

"That is my intent, aye," he agreed.

"Take whatever you want but you shall not abscond with the Lady Standfield," the earl snapped. "The entire might of the Governmental Regiment will descend upon you."

"The entire might of the Governmental Regiment has been after me for months now, Your Grace. I have no doubt they'll come after me for many more but they won't find me nor will they ever catch me."

"You are that sure of yourself?" Althea asked.

"I am, milady."

Her smile turned speculative. "Yes, I believe you are."

He turned to the earl.

"Now, if you will, Your Grace, I will have your coin and your wife's jewelry as well as the borrowed ones Lady Althea's maid is wearing. You may place in them in Her Grace's reticle."

"Do you want mine as well?" Althea inquired, putting a hand to the crucifix around her neck.

"What I want from you, milady, will be taken in private," he whispered to her.

She drew in a quick breath as those words had shocked her, yet her pretty eyes gleamed with challenge.

He told the earl he and the two women standing beside him could leave. It wasn't a surprise to him that the earl would protest, demanding who would be driving the coach. Neither did it surprise him that the homely woman stated she was capable of taking the horses in hand. He averted his eyes when she hiked up her skirt and climbed to the driver's seat.

Sweeping Althea into his arms, he carried her to his horse and swung her on its back. With Warlock's reins in his hand, he walked the beast to the coach where the earl was handing his wife inside. The older man glanced back at him with a touch of fear.

"Never let it be said I left you with nothing, Your Grace," he said, tossing a silver dollar to the startled man.

He swung up behind Althea, gathered her into his arms, sighed as she leaned back against him then drummed his heels against Warlock's side. Jack's cabin was an hour's ride to the west but with the soft, perfumed body of a beautiful woman wrapped in his arms, the journey would not be so boring for a change.

* * * * *

Declan woke with a brutal headache lodged in the back of his skull. Groaning, he tried to turn over to his side but couldn't. Everything shifted around him as though he was caught in a whirlwind. That intensified the pain in his head and brought instant nausea racing up his throat so he stopped trying to move. Bringing up a shaking hand, he touched his temple and felt something sticky there.

Blood, he thought. Gingerly he explored the area, felt a gash where his hair melded into his temple. The spot was tender to the touch and wondered if he'd fallen. If he had a concussion. He shivered.

He was cold, lying flat on his back on a hard slab of some kind and the air around him smelled of piss and vomit and shit. It took some doing but he finally managed to pry his eyes open. When he did, he saw a low stone ceiling stretching out above him.

"Where the hell am I?" he mumbled and tried once more to turn over.

That didn't work any better the second time than it had the first. His world skittered away and blackness edged his vision like the smoldering edges of a piece of paper on fire.

Off in the distance he heard the clank of a metal door and approaching footsteps. He couldn't seem to get his eyes to focus as he slowly turned his head toward the sound.

And caught sight of the vertical iron bars extending from the floor to the ceiling.

Jail, he thought. The gods-be-damn it, he was in jail. But how the hell had he gotten there? He tried to think, to remember but the pain in his head was so acute it pushed away memories before they could fully form. One thing was for sure, he felt helpless and confused.

And trapped.

What had happened to him? Obviously he had been arrested but when? Where? And how had he wound up in this ice-cold cell?

The footsteps were drawing closer—echoing off the stone walls to drive the agony deeper into his brain. When they stopped at his cell he tried to get his eyes to cooperate, to make out the blurry images behind the bars.

"I see you're awake, Farrell."

He knew the voice but couldn't place it. Couldn't put either a name or a face to the clipped, arrogant tone.

The skirl of the cell door opening was like someone had taken a steel spike and driven it through his head from ear to ear.

"Get him up."

Scuffling footsteps and the blurred silhouettes of two men leaned over him. They grabbed hold of his upper arms and levered him to his feet but his legs proved to be no more cooperative than his eyes. They folded under him but the men didn't seem to notice. They jerked him around and began dragging him between them—his head lolling on his chest for he was in such pain he couldn't lift it.

That was when he noticed he was naked as his bare toes scraped along the rough stone. No wonder he was cold, he thought.

Then fear washed over him in waves.

What the hell was he doing lying naked in a jail cell? That thought didn't last long for his shins met the sharp edges of a set of steps.

"Damn it, that hurts," he yelped but the only response to his protest was a nasty laugh from the man who had spoken to him.

He tried to get his legs to work rather than be scratched bloody on the jagged steps. It took some effort but he was finally able to stumble along between his captors. When they neared the top of the darkened stairwell a bright light suddenly flared to blind him. He snapped his head to one side and squeezed his eyes shut but the sudden motion turned his pain to exquisite agony and he groaned.

"In there," the man ordered the ones holding him.

He was propelled into a room and whipped around so fast he blacked out—his world tumbling down into utter darkness.

When he woke, his chin resting on his chest, the first thing he saw when he opened his eyes was his naked cock lying between his spread thighs. His arms were tied behind him so tightly his fingers were numb and his ankles were strapped to the legs of a hard, straight-backed wooden chair.

Cautiously he lifted his head—giving his eyes time to adjust to the movement—and realized he was alone in a small, bare room lit by four torches set into each corner. He tried once more to remember what had happened to put him there but nothing stayed in his mind long enough for him to grasp it. Images formed then skittered away before he could identify them.

He knew he was hurt. How badly, he couldn't tell. His head was one solid band of pure torment that throbbed with the heat of his heart. His ears were ringing so loudly it blotted out much of anything else. The nausea bubbling in his throat was a misery unto itself. What was worse, he couldn't seem to recall what his name was.

"Concussion," he whispered. "I have a concussion."

Either he'd fallen and cracked his head open or someone had done it for him. He was leaning more to the latter.

And he'd done something to land him in jail. What that could be he had no idea. Mayhap if he had some idea of who he was…

What had the man called him?

Trying to think hurt, but it seemed vital that he remember that name. He remembered the voice. The sound of it. The ugly cadence and sneering of the words. Why couldn't he remember the gods-be-damned name?

Apparently whoever had smacked him had knocked who he was and what he knew completely out of his brain.

He had no idea how long he had been sitting in the room. Reason told him it had to be hours for his arse was as numb as his hands. Thirst had reared its insistent head. The cold had settled into his limbs and he shivered with each intake of breath—his teeth clicking together. Miserable was a kind choice of words to describe how he felt.

Calling out didn't seem like much of an option. Something told him it wouldn't bring anyone to his aid. Obviously he was being left alone as either punishment or to give him time to build up a healthy dose of fear at what was going to happen to him. He thought mayhap it was both.

By the time a door opened behind him he was ready to do or say anything he had to in order to get warm and have something to quench the savage thirst torturing him.

* * * * *

Lady Althea glared at the man sitting across the desk from her. So far she had refused to answer his questions for the ones he had posed to her would spell certain doom for Declan Farrell. Each query put to her by the odious Captain Penry was like another knot being coiled into the noose the brute wished to drop around Declan's neck.

"Your silence leads me to believe you are in league with Farrell," Penry said. He reached out to lay his hand on the chest his men had confiscated from the cabin. "These ill-gotten gains might well send you to the gallows beside him."

She rolled her eyes. His threats were becoming monotonous. Although she could have told him the chest sitting atop his desk bore the seal of the Bank of Wexford and was marked with the number one—which signified the bank's principal depositor—she said nothing. Why Declan had monies she was sure belonged to her father was a mystery but she had no reason to believe he had stolen it.

"I need to know…"

"I demand you send for both the Duke of Oxmoor and the Duke of Arlington," she interrupted him. "And posthaste, for delay will cost you dearly, Penry."

"And I demand you answer my questions, milady," Penry snapped. "You were found in the company of a known highwayman who…"

"Known by whom?" she countered.

"The evidence…"

"What evidence?" she asked, turning the tables on him to throw the questions at him like rocks.

"This evidence," he said, slapping his hand on the chest. "Over one hundred thousand dollars' worth of evidence!"

"Can you read, Penry?" she asked and had the satisfaction of watching his face turn red.

"I most certainly can," he declared.

"Do you see the seal on the chest?"

He glanced at the chest.

"That seal belongs to the Bank of Wexford, the county seat of Oxmoor. Do you see the number one etched into the wood?"

His brows drew together.

"That signifies the premier depositor of the Bank of Wexford. Do you know who the premier depositor of the Bank of Wexford is, Penry?"

"You will address me by my rank when you are…."

"Do. You. Know. Who. The. Premier. Depositor. Is. Penry?" she said, snapping each word like a bullwhip.

"I assume it is the Duke of Oxmoor," Penry replied with a twist of his lips.

"You aren't as stupid as you look," she said. "As the daughter of the Earl of Oxmoor, I am included in the designation as premier depositor. What belongs to my father belongs to me. Ergo, that chest belongs to me. It is not ill-gotten gains, it is my dowry."

She thought that sounded about right. She'd had time to contemplate why Declan had the chest at his friend's cabin. All the way to the garrison at Gilhaven she had tried to make sense of the situation then it finally dawned on her. She had made reference in her note to Declan that had she the money at her disposal she would flee the country and there would be no wedding. Obviously he had insisted upon a dowry from her father with the intention of giving it to her.

"How do you explain the graze mark on his cheek?" Penry demanded.

Snapped back to the horrid man before her she had no answer nor would she have provided it if she had. Anything she said about Declan could well be used against him and that was to be avoided at all cost. So, she simply stared at him as she did when he posed any question to her.

He rifled through the papers on his desk, found one and held it out to her. "Read this," he ordered.

She raised her chin and one eyebrow at his command but made no move to take the paper from him.

"Fine," he said and read it for her. "The brothers Baxley of Belvedere Glen were accosted on the road home two evenings past by a masked man. One of the brothers managed to get off a shot, striking the robber on the left side of his face. He..."

"How does he know he hit the robber?" she asked.

"What?"

"You say he was masked? How does this Baxley person— whoever he is—know he hit the man? Did the robber remove his mask at that point?"

Penry was grinding his teeth as he stared at her and the paper in his hand was quaking.

"How long was this supposed injury? One inch? Two? Five? Where exactly on the robber's cheek did..."

"Enough!" Penry shouted at the top of his lungs. "Do you think this is a game, woman?"

"Do you think to intimidate me, *man*?" she threw back at him. "I assure you, better men than you have tried and failed." She narrowed her eyes. "I demand you send for the Duke of Oxmoor and the Duke of Arlington as well as their legal representatives."

With a snarl, Penry skirted his desk and stomped to the door. He jerked it open then slammed it behind him.

"Ill-mannered boor," she said.

Though her hands were as steady as her voice, inside she was shivering as with the ague. She was terrified. Not for herself but for Declan. She had no idea where he was or what they were doing to him. If he was all right or how much damage the brutal hit from the soldier's musket to the side of his head had done. She had demanded to see him but Penry had refused—telling her Declan Farrell was under arrest.

That they had found the chest was easily explained. There was no other supposed loot discovered in the cabin though the soldiers had torn it apart in their searching. What could not be so easily explained was the claret velvet coat, Francachi cocked hat and the silver dollar that had been found in the pocket of Declan's doeskin pants.

On that long coach ride with Declan lying naked and unconscious in the floor of the coach with Penry's muddy boot on his hip, she had time to spin a web of lies that would explain it all, but until she spoke with her father or Declan's, his solicitor, she would keep her fabrications to herself. One slip could drop that noose over the head of the man she loved.

That realization—that she loved him—had also come as the coach bumped along the rocky coach road. He looked so defenseless with his wrists and ankles bound with rope, the wound to the side of his head oozing blood. She was terrified he wouldn't wake up—couldn't wake up—and kept her eyes locked on him the entire time. Penry had babbled on and on and on but not once did she take her attention from Declan. She wanted to make sure he was breathing.

She heard Penry yelling at some hapless man and dug her fingernails into the fabric of her gown. That the horrible man—as well as four of his guards—had seen her sprawled naked beneath Declan infuriated her. It did not shame her but it made her angry enough that, had she a dagger at hand, she would have lunged it into the bastard's black heart. His knowing smirk as he stared at her, his eyes slowly moving up and down her before she could grab the quilt to cover herself, was the evilest thing she'd ever experienced. He was a pervert and had proved himself no gentleman for he had stood there watching her dress though he had sent his men from the room with an unconscious Declan pulled behind them.

If it was the last thing she did, she would have her revenge on Royce Penry.

* * * * *

The vicious slap that slammed against his cheek woke Declan and snapped his head sharply to the side.

"Where did you get the money?" the man who hit him shouted.

"What money?" Declan asked.

Another slap split his lip.

"The money in the chest," the man said through clenched teeth. He reached out and took hold of Declan's chin in a painful grip. "And the mark on your cheek. How did you get it?"

"Mayhap when you hit me with whatever the hell you hit me with," Declan replied.

The man tightened his grip so brutally Declan could taste blood as the inside of his mouth was ground against his molars.

"You best watch what you say to me, Farrell," he warned. "I have the authority to have you tortured."

Declan doubted that. If he did, he would have already put that savagery into motion. Now that he could focus his eyes he realized the man was wearing a military uniform. He also now had at least half a name to call himself.

"I know you're the Gypsy," the man stated. "I know you robbed the Earl and Countess of Warrington and made off with the earl's cousin Lady Althea Standfield. She is sitting in a cell awaiting questioning."

He had no idea who the Earl of Warrington was—much less his wife—or the Lady Standfield and he was pretty gods-be-damned sure he wasn't a Gypsy though, in that, he could be wrong.

"You are going to hang, Declan Farrell," the man told him. "On the gallows at Tyrnebee."

Well, now he had two names to call himself. He rather liked the names. They fit well together, had a bold flare to them but he still had absolutely no idea who he was.

"Captain?"

The man released his jaw and spun around. "What the fuck do you want?"

"The Dukes of Arlington and Oxmoor are here, sir," the man said.

"Who the fuck told them he was here?"

"They did not say, sir. They are demanding to see you immediately and sir? They have their solicitors with them as well as the local magistrate."

Declan watched the color blanch out of his inquisitor's face.

"Where are they now?"

"I showed them to the quartermaster's office for I did not think you would want them taken to yours."

Some color crept back into the man's cheeks.

"Good thinking. No, I do not want them near her until I have had a chance to see what they know of this matter." He looked down at Declan and snarled. "Take this one back to his cell and give him some prison garb to wear." He glanced at Dec's feet. "And find him a pair of boots."

"Should I also send the medical officer in to see to his head wound, sir?"

Once again color fled his persecutor's high cheekbones.

"Aye, that would be best."

"Kinda hard to cover up whatever the hell it was you did to me," Declan said and was rewarded with a backhand slap that rattled his teeth.

"I told you to be careful of how you speak to me," the man barked. He turned to the guard. "Get him the fuck out of here before I strangle him and be done with it."

Declan watched him storm off as though the hounds of hell were after him. Had the bastard been a cur, his tail would have been quivering under his belly. He chuckled despite the blood dripping from a torn lip and the headache that was still ripping his skull apart.

The guard knelt down to untie Dec's ankles. When he went behind the chair and began untying the ropes binding Dec's wrists, Dec wished he had some use of his arms. He would have liked nothing better than to beat the shit out of the guard and escape but since he didn't know where he was, it was probably just as well he stayed put.

"So," he said as the ropes came undone and his arms fell uselessly to his side. "The Duke of Arlington is here, huh?"

That name rang a bell, but why it should he didn't know.

"Your father isn't going to be able to save you from the executioner, Farrell," the guard snapped.

My father? Dec thought. By the gods, that couldn't be true. There was no way he could be the son of a duke unless…

"I'm a bastard," he said to himself.

"One that's going to be swinging from a rope if Captain Penry has anything to say about it," the guard told him.

So that was the name of the sadistic bastard who had hit him. It was good to know. That name seemed to mean something to him, too, but whatever it was, the pain in his head was keeping him from latching on to it.

The guard took hold of his arm and propelled him to his feet. He pulled him toward the door where another guard was standing. That guard took hold of his other arm and between them they marched him along a short corridor then down that wretched flight of rugged stairs.

* * * * *

"I demand to see my daughter," Lord Alastair Standfield snarled as soon as Royce walked into the quartermaster's office. "Right this bloody instant, Penry."

"I have a few questions for you before…" Royce began, but a rather hefty man in a dark gold brocade waistcoat stepped forward.

"I am Magistrate Jenkins of Gilhaven," the man said. "I am here to insure Lord Alastair and Lord Edward are reunited with their progeny. There will be no questioning of either of them until that matter has been settled."

"There are certain questions I must insist be answered before I will allow that," Royce stated.

"You will *allow*?" Lord Edward asked. "*You* will allow? Why you pompous little martinet. Do you know to whom it is you speak?"

"With due respect, Your Grace," another man Royce assumed was the Duke of Arlington's solicitor intervened. "Let us hear the questions. You are not required to answer them but it might be to your benefit to know what it is the captain wants."

"I want to know about a chest of money that was confiscated from…"

"A chest containing one hundred thousand gold pieces?" Lord Alastair interrupted. "That would be my daughter's dowry which I gave to Lord Declan."

"Monies that belong legally to my son, the Earl of Dungannon," Lord Edward stressed.

That answer hit Royce like a wet mackerel, but he continued on.

"There is the matter of a graze along Farrell's..."

"That is Lord Declan to you, Captain Penry," the magistrate reminded him. "He is above you in rank among the peerage."

Grinding his teeth, Royce bobbed his head curtly. "The matter of the graze..."

"A mishap with his razor," Lord Edward stated.

Royce clenched his hands into fists at his side. "Your Grace, your son told you a boldface lie if he told you it was..."

"I went to my son's room to confront him over a matter that is not pertinent to the matter we are here to discuss. I was angry with him and I yelled at him. His razor slipped. I will testify in court that I saw that razor scrape down Declan's cheek."

Royce held the duke's stony stare. There was no way he could accuse the man of perjuring himself but he knew Lord Edward was lying through his teeth.

"Anything else you need explained?" Lord Edward's solicitor asked.

Royce smiled. "How do you explain the claret red velvet coat and cocked hat we found among your son's possessions at the cabin where we took him into custody? That is the clothing worn by the highwayman known as the Gypsy."

"I own a claret red velvet coat," the magistrate said. "As well as a cocked hat. Does having them in my armoire make me a candidate to be the Gypsy?"

"I, too, own a claret red velvet coat," Lord Alastair said. "Haven't worn the thing in years but it was—at one time—the height of fashion."

"Many men wear cocked hats, Captain Penry," Lord Alastair's solicitor said.

"And do they all have a silver dollar in the pocket of their coat?" Penry threw at them.

Lord Edward reached into his pocket and pulled a handful of silver dollars. "Are these what you mean?" He rattled the money in his palm. "If so, I would venture to say Lord Alastair has a few in his pocket as well."

"I do," Lord Alastair confirmed. He narrowed his eyes. "Now, I demand to see my daughter."

"And I, my son," Lord Edward stated.

* * * * *

The guards shoved him into his cell and slammed the door shut behind him. They turned away and headed back to the stairs.

"What about the clothes?" he asked, wrapping his tingling hands around the iron bars. When they didn't answer but continued walking, he shouting at them. "Hey! What about the clothes he told you to give me?" He pulled on the bars. "And the fucking boots?"

Freezing in the frigid cell, he snugged his arms around him and laid his aching head against the cold bars. At least that helped the headache but did nothing for his raging thirst.

Furious, he didn't even consider what he was about to do until he slammed his forehead as hard as he could into the bar and the pain took the very breath from his lungs. He staggered back, lost his footing and plummeted to the floor. The back of his head hit the stone and stars fell from the heavens.

* * * * *

She'd lied to Royce Penry and Lord Edward knew she had. Her father, the solicitors and—she suspected—the magistrate also knew she had. Penry certainly knew, but he dared not accuse her of doing so. What had precipitated her lie had begun with her defending Declan.

"If you have harmed one hair on my son's head, I will have you stripped of your rank," Lord Edward stated.

"I have not laid a hand to him," Penry said. "If he tells you otherwise, it will be a lie. As you know, there has been bad blood between your son and myself for decades. Declan would do anything to discredit me."

"So when he walks through that door, he will be in good health?" Lord Edward wanted clarified.

"Nothing has happened to your son, Your Grace," Penry lied.

Althea cleared her throat. "That is not quite true, Your Grace. While it is true Penry did not put hands to Declan—at least within my sight—one of his men hit Declan in the head with the butt of his musket," she said. "The blow rendered him unconscious."

Lord Edward turned a brutal glower to Penry. "Why was that necessary? Was he attempting to evade arrest?"

"He was about to flee when we entered…"

"That is a bald-faced lie. Declan was lying atop me, Your Grace," Althea interrupted. She glanced at her father then away. "We were in the process of making love and he would not have—could not have run—because he was naked and…" She lowered her head. "He was inside me at the time."

Lord Alastair made a choking sound and shot up from his chair. He strode to the window and stood there with his back to the room, one hand covering his mouth.

Declan's father stared at her with his lips parted and his eyes stunned. That was when she told her lie…

She squared her shoulders and lifted her head. "We have been lovers for quite some time. On those nights Penry states he was not at Arlington and supposedly out and about the countryside robbing people, he was with me. Lying with me."

"Merciful Alel," her father whined.

"Milady, do you know the penalty for perjury?" Penry broke in.

"Milady is not under oath," the magistrate reminded him.

"Mayhap she should be," Penry snapped. "She is giving testimony that Farrell was with her on the nights the highwayman struck. I will have her swear that what she is saying is the truth."

"Do you have proof that she isn't?" Lord Edward's solicitor inquired.

"I have the sworn testimony of the brothers Baxley that Farrell robbed them at pistol point," Penry stated.

"They named him specifically?" the solicitor asked. "If so, I would like to see that affidavit."

"As would I," Lord Edward said.

"Will they swear without doubt that it was the Duke of Dungannon who robbed them?" the Magistrate queried.

Penry was saved from answering by a firm knock at the door. "Come," he barked.

A pale and somewhat dazed Declan Farrell was brought into the room by a guard.

"Mother of the gods!" Lord Edward's solicitor exclaimed.

Althea got slowly to her feet. The man she would have moved heaven and earth to protect, to keep out of jail was dressed in the shapeless dingy grey and tattered shirt and loose pants of a convict. The right side of his face was black and blue from his temple to the edge of his jaw from the blow he'd taken. There was a clear imprint of the butt of the musket on his discolored flesh. The hair on that side of his head was matted with blood and a deep gash bracketed the curve of his right eye socket.

"You son of a bitch," Lord Edward snarled. "I will see you pay for this, Penry."

Declan leveled his gaze on a pitcher and glass that set on a table by the window. "May I…" He cleared his throat. "May I have some water, please?"

Lord Alastair jumped into action and grabbed the pitcher.

"Where are his clothes?" Lord Edward's solicitor demanded.

"They left them at the cabin," Althea said. "He was dumped in the floor of the coach as he was when they burst in on us."

"Naked?" the magistrate asked with a gasp.

"Aye, milord," she replied. "And was that way the entire journey here."

Lord Alastair brought him a cup of water. Dec lifted the cup and downed the liquid in two gulps then held the cup toward Lord Alastair. "More please."

"And have you starved him, too?" Lord Edward asked. He put a hand on his son's shoulder. "When was the last time you ate?"

"I don't know," Declan answered. He took the refreshed cup and downed it just as fast.

"Your Grace, I think you should take your son home now," the magistrate said. "Let him bathe and put on decent clothing." He shot Penry an angry look. "Feed him and see to that wound."

"We will discuss filing a formal complaint with the Governmental Regiment," Lord Edward's solicitor stated.

"As will we," Lord Alastair's man echoed.

"A complaint accusing me of what?" Penry demanded. "Apprehending a man I know to be…"

"Watch what you say, Penry," Lord Edward warned. "You had already made an enemy of my son and now you have made a life-long enemy of me."

"And me," Lord Alastair declared. "The very thought of you seeing my daughter naked..." He pointed a finger at Penry. "This matter will reach the ears of the king, trust me."

"He is guilty," Penry said. "As guilty as he is standing there. He is the highwayman!"

"And you are a fool," Lord Edward told him. He took hold of Declan's arm and led him to the door.

It bothered Althea that Declan allowed himself to be ushered about as though he had no say in the matter. He looked confused, ill and was definitely not behaving like the man she had encountered at the engagement party and certainly not the one who had made her his at the cabin. The docility disturbed her—as did the way his hand shook as he set the cup he was holding down on a shelf before being led from Penry's office. She hurried behind him, shaking off her father's outstretched hand.

"Declan?" she asked. "Darling, are you feeling well?"

He turned to look at her. "No," he said then his eyes rolled up in his head. He would have pitched to the floor had his father not caught him.

Chapter Eight

The concussion kept him in his bed for six days.

On the fourth day, his head was still hurting. On the fifth, he woke to a flash of memories that passed through his mind with such speed it made him physically ill. Like a dizzying dream they danced rapidly from scene to scene. Everything came back in a rush: who he was, what he'd done, who he'd done it with. Faces crowded one after another in his mind's eye until he dug the heels of his hands against his eyes in an effort to stop them.

He saw Jack, Jamie, his father frowning at him, pointing fingers.

He saw Bess walking up the stairs, her rear end swaying like a willow tree.

He saw Althea lying beside him, his arms wrapped around her.

He saw Penry's fist coming at his face.

Along with the memories came emotions that tripped over themselves as they slammed into him. He had trouble sitting up for the room wanted to whirl away from him. He had to find his father. He had questions that needed answering. At the top of that list of questions was why he felt he needed so desperately to see Althea. Why he was so anxious to talk to her. Why he was worried about her.

It took him half an hour to get to his feet and dressed without feeling as though he was going to pitch to the floor in a heap. Hand against the wall for support, he took the stairs as slowly as a toddler just learning to walk. The smell of the breakfast meal drew him to the dining room where he found his father and Jamie reading the morning paper.

"Well, look who's among the living," Jamie quipped, laying the paper aside. "How do you feel, son?"

"I need to see Althea," he said. He wobbled his way to the table and took hold of the chair back with both hands. His arms were trembling and his knees felt weak.

"You deflowered that girl in a filthy cabin in the middle of the woods," his father accused without looking up at him. He shook his paper.

"Fairling McGregor is an excellent housekeeper and there is no room in this keep better kept that her one-room cabin," Declan told him. He staggered and gripped the chair harder.

"Sit down before you fall down, Dec," Jamie said. "You want some coffee?"

"Aye," Dec said. He pulled the chair out and slumped into it. His head was hurting again but the dizziness was passing. His stomach rumbled at the smell of bacon and eggs.

Ever-present Iverson brought a cup of coffee to the table and set it down. "Nice to see you up, Your Grace," he said softly.

"Thank you," Dec replied. He took a sip, winced at the heat then looked at his father. "About Althea…"

"You should never have treated that girl like a common trollop," his father stated.

"That girl has a name," Declan reminded him. "Her name is…"

"I know her name," his father said. "I also know she lied before two solicitors, a magistrate, a military commandant—not to mention both her father and yours—to keep you from going to prison. That makes her an accomplice. If you are caught, she will be arrested for her complicity in the matter."

That explained part of the reason he was worried about her.

"And just in case I need to remind you, Penry would have hanged you at the garrison if he could have gotten away with it."

"No, you don't have to remind me. My ears are still ringing from his slaps."

His father's eyebrows shot up. "What slaps?"

"It doesn't matter."

"The hell it doesn't!" the duke snapped. He crumpled his paper and tossed it to the floor.

"Edward," Jamie said quietly then shook his head.

"I need to talk to her, Father," he said.

"You are going to marry that girl."

"Aye, I will," Dec replied. "But I need to talk to her first."

"Tomorrow mayhap. McGregor will accompany you," his father stated firmly. "That is not open to debate."

"Fine," Declan said, overjoyed at the news. "Send for him."

"He will go everywhere with you from now on. There will be no other chance of Penry catching you."

"I'd like to know how he found me in the first place," Declan said.

"He had a man watching you. He trailed you to McGregor's cabin but lost you when you left. He went back to the cabin, broke in and found the chest of gold. They figured you'd go back there and you did."

"Careless," Declan said.

"Aye, well that carelessness nearly cost you your freedom. Were it not for Althea, you would be in that garrison jail awaiting transfer to the gallows."

"Where is the dowry?"

"In my safe," his father replied. "At Lady Althea's insistence."

"She told us why you wanted it," Jamie said softly.

Dec set the coffee cup down. "What did she say?"

"She told us about the bloody note she wrote to you," his father said with a snort. "Nice try, Declan James, but she has no intention of fleeing the country with her father's money. It wasn't an offer she was making to skip out on the Joining but rather a way of trying to save face for you rejecting her."

Dec winced, felt the shame of it all the way to his soul. "Does Lord Alastair know she…?"

"No," his father interrupted. "Nor will he." He pushed his chair back, pointed a finger at Dec. "Don't lie to me again, Declan. There never was a blackmailer and that is a relief to my mind."

With that, his father pushed away from the table, spun on his heel and marched out of the room.

"On a happier note," Jamie said, "Your lady-wife-to-be has given you alibies for every night the Gypsy struck."

"What?" Dec asked, frowning.

"She told Penry that you and she have been lovers for quite a while now and that on those nights the two of you were in loving embraces in that cabin where Penry found you."

* * * * *

Two days later he and Jack were riding to Standfield Hall so Dec could speak to Althea. The day was overcast with a brisk wind whipping at their coats. Warlock was in the mood to run but Declan kept a close rein on the rambunctious nature of the stallion.

"He's as antsy as I am," Declan remarked.

"I hope you've got better sense than to give him his head," Jack grumbled. "A tumble might well finish killing off what little brain you have left."

Declan chuckled at Jack's peevish tone. "I'll try to restrain myself and Warlock."

"What are you going to do about Bess?" Jack inquired.

"I asked her to marry me and she turned me down—even when I told her about getting a divorce later."

"Good thing she did else you'd be in breach of that gods-be-damned contract and you know what would happen then," Jack reminded him.

"Aye, I know. She's content to be my mistress."

"Oh, for the love of the gods, Declan," Jack hissed and reined his mount. When Declan twisted around in his saddle and halted Warlock, Jack shot him an angry look. "You know gods-be-damned well that's not going to continue once you marry Lady Althea."

"I know," Declan said. He clucked his tongue and Warlock took that as permission to run.

"Declan, damn you!" he heard Jack shout.

The wind felt good rushing against his face. It pushed all thoughts of both women out of his mind for the length of time it took to crest the hill overlooking Standfield Hall. The moment the manor house came into view, something strange happened to him. He felt different than he had the last three times he'd been in Althea's home. There was no sense of dread hanging over his head as he urged Warlock down the incline of the hill. It was the same feeling he'd had when he'd regained his memory: a deep, overwhelming desire to be with Althea. To thank her for saving his life. For saving him from prison. For giving him alibies for the times he'd been out on the coach road as the Gypsy. To beg her pardon for making her a fallen woman. Yet the guilt of that didn't sting as sharply as he thought it should. Perhaps abasing himself before her would help to purge him of some of that regret.

But speaking to her was not to be.

"The duke and Lady Althea are not in attendance at this time," the servant said with a sniff.

"When will they return?" Declan asked, feeling more disappointed than he could understand.

"I am sure they will be back in time for the Joining," the servant said then firmly closed the door.

"Are you shitting me?" Jack asked and would have pounded on the door had Declan not stopped him.

"I'll just leave a note," he told Jack.

"You think the bastard will give it to her?"

Declan chewed on his lip. "Mayhap not." He turned from the door. "I can see I've got my work cut out for me."

"What work is that?" Jack asked as he went down the steps with Declan.

"Repairing my reputation with her. She really doesn't deserve a man like me. She deserves a man who is whole in body and mind, and right now? That isn't me."

* * * * *

On the ride back, Declan was quiet. Jack seemed to sense he didn't want to talk just yet and kept the silence between them. When they reached Dead Man's Crossing, Declan pulled Warlock to a halt.

"What's the matter?" Jack asked.

Declan stared down into the swirling waters, his brain working feverishly.

"Dec?" Jack pressed.

"I have to marry her and—in good conscience—I need to," he said.

"That's a given, isn't it?"

He continued to stare at the water.

"They've moved the wedding up by two weeks in case..." He heaved a long sigh. "In case I got her with child."

"That's a strong possibility," Jack conceded.

"What we need to do is intercept that priest and replace him with someone else."

"Replace him with who?" Jack asked.

"Daniel Rees," Declan said, shifting his attention to the entrance to Black Chasm Cave.

"Daniel was defrocked," Jack said. "He can't legally perform a Joining."

"Aye, that's the key word, McGregor: legally."

Jack shook his head. "I'm not following. What am I missing?"

"Althea deserves to get married. No one outside you and Fairling and the people who were in Penry's office that day know that I took her maidenhead, ruined her. None of them—and that includes Penry—would dare reveal what they know. Althea would be ruined socially as well as morally."

"I understand that, but that still doesn't explain why you would want to have a man who is not entitled to bless your Joining…" Jack stopped and he sucked in a deep breath. "You are going to pretend to marry her?"

"Aye but no one but you and I will know the marriage isn't legal. No one knows Danny. He's never visited Arlington and there is no one from our old regiment who will be attending the ceremony."

"I fail to see how this helps anything, Dec. Why begin your marriage with a lie? Live with her in sin even though she might never know that. Is that fair to her?"

"Just listen," Declan said. He swung his leg over Warlock's head and dropped to the ground. He walked over to where he usually took the horse down into the river to cross over to the cave. "What if after the Joining, I die?"

"Die?" Jack asked, his eyes wide. "What the hell are you talking about?"

"We'll have a fight," he said. "I'll storm out of the house. With any luck at all it will be raining—hopefully storming—and I will ride out into the night never to be seen again."

"And just how the hell are you going to do that?" He got down from his horse and walked over to where Dec was standing.

Declan pointed to the cave. "I'll have fallen into the river and gotten sucked into the cave. As so many others before me, my body will never be found. Althea will be a widow—a very wealthy widow—who will be free to eventually marry a man who will love her as she should be loved."

"Where will you really be then?" Jack asked.

"I will leave Serenia," Declan said. "Change my name—since I will be free to do so considering the Joining to Althea wasn't legal in the first place—and no one will ever hear from me again."

"Not even me?" Jack asked, hurt rife in his voice.

"Especially not you," Declan said. He reached out a hand to lay it on Jack's shoulder. "I love you like a brother. You know that, Jackson, but I have to leave. Althea needs someone she can trust, can count on. She deserves a man who doesn't ruin everything he touches. Sooner or later I'll fuck up. I always do and what if she got hurt because of something I did? Something I didn't do or I didn't do right? What if—the gods forbid—I prove unable to protect her?" He shook his head. "No, I'm doing this more for her than me. She doesn't deserve a man like me and I sure as hell don't deserve a good woman like her. There's another godsend to me leaving. The highwayman will have been put to rest. I've got one more silver dollar to give away and then I'll retire."

"Who are you going to rob?"

"There will be an envoy taking foreclosure notices to Boreas tomorrow night. All the paperwork for the king's men to steal the property from over two dozen farmers will be in his pouch. I want that pouch."

"Declan, I don't know. Penry has men tailing you. There are two of them behind us now."

"I know. I saw them the moment they fell in behind us, but there isn't a tracker I can't dodge. I know the countryside better than any of Penry's men."

"You tweak his tail, Dec. The man isn't going to rest until he catches you. Think about that. The rest of your plan I can go along with. I'll do whatever I can to help you disappear but just forget about the envoy. Don't push your luck."

Declan blew a raspberry. "Stop being an old maid," he told Jack. "I know what I'm about. I'm very good at what I do."

"Mistakes happen, Dec. You've made a few in the last month. Another one could cost you your life."

"You want to help? Here's what you can do. Ride over to Groversner's Point. You should be there by morning. Danny lives in the cottage with the green door. Ask him to do this for me and tell him our slate will be wiped clean if he does."

"Oh, he'll do it," Jack said. "I've no doubt of that. What then?"

"Take him to Arlington, but hide him somewhere so no one will see him. When the time comes, it'll be up to you and him to intercept the real priest. Tell him there was a change of plan. I'll give you money to pay him for his time so he won't raise a stink."

"All right," Jack agreed.

"I doubt Danny still has his robes. You may have to pilfer those from a church."

"And thus make sure I'll be going to hell alongside you," Jack grumbled.

"We'll jump through the fire together, my friend," Declan replied with a laugh. "Have a merry old time with Old Scratch."

"What about the men tailing you now?"

"We need to split up. You go east; I'll head west. They'll pay no attention to your leaving. I'll lead them to the Hound and Stag where I'll be spending the night with Bess."

"Where will I be?"

"You come the long away around from East Plain. That way leads you to the back of the stable. I'll leave Warlock at the hitching post in front of the tavern. He needs to be in plain sight. Leave Spirit out behind the stable for me. Slip around the side of the inn and hide by the woodshed. A little after midnight, come around the side of the inn and mount Warlock. Head for Groversner's Point. They'll think you're me and follow you. If you can't lose them, you don't have a hair on your balls."

"Oh, I can ditch them," Jack said. "You'd better hope they take the bait and follow me."

* * * * *

She paused in mid-plait as she heard the pounding of hoofbeats along the coach road and looked to the casement window. It was just past ten of the clock and she had been expecting him.

Her father had gone to bed early with a toothache—had taken a touch of laudanum to help him sleep—so he would not hear the steed's hooves clattering over the cobblestone pathway. There was no one—save perhaps Tim, the hostler—who might be privy to the late-night caller and Tim would never tell.

At least she didn't think he would.

Heart pounding, hands twisting at the waist of her white lawn nightgown, she waited for the clops of the hooves to slow then stop just below her window. With two low, single notes the whistle came then a tap on her shuttered window brought heat to her cheeks. She swallowed nervously then walked slowly to the portal. Hand trembling, she reached for the latch and pushed open the shutter.

He was waiting there on his midnight black steed. In the light of the moon sailing overhead she saw his merry blue eyes twinkling. She put a hand to her throat as he doffed his cocked hat and swept it elegantly to the side.

"Good eve to you, Lady Bess," he said.

"Good eve to you, milord," she replied quietly.

"All is locked and barred, I see," he commented.

"Indeed," she said. "As it should be at this time of night."

"Is everything locked and barred?" he queried.

She felt the heat deepen on her face and neck and she began fiddling with her braid. "Mayhap there may be a side door that I forgot to latch," she told him.

His roguish grin sent waves of hunger rippling through her body. When he threw his doeskin-clad leg over the horse's head and dropped lithely to the ground, she felt her heart speed up.

"Mayhap I should check to make sure if you did or not?" he asked.

"That would be prudent," she said huskily and the blood in her ears began to pound.

He winked at her then looped the reins of his horse over the hitching post. He moved so quickly, so stealthily—as befitted his stock and trade—to the corner of the inn. The last she saw of him was the tail of his claret velvet waistcoat.

Heat pooling low in her belly, dampness gathering at her core, she turned away from the window to lock her gaze on the door. Faintly she heard the creak of a stair tread then a soft rattle as the latch to her door was lifted. Moisture flooded her mouth as the door opened quietly.

He stood framed in the doorway. He looked so elegant despite his ride down the coach road and over the moors.

Her avid attention traveled slowly down him from bare head to booted toe. There did not appear to be any dust on his black leather boots. The lace jabot at his throat was crisp and pristine. The dark red velvet waistcoat fit him perfectly—stretched across broad shoulders and tapered to a trim waist. Brown doeskin britches clung sensually to his thighs. He stood there with hat in hand, hip cocked and that grin that could melt the chastity belt off any maiden. She was dying to ask him why he had bruises on his face but never had the chance. The hat went sailing across the room and he started toward her.

"Oh," she whispered. That predatory look, that swaggering walk turned her blood to molten lava.

"Come here, wench," he said as he reached her.

He swept a brawny arm around her waist and pulled her to him. His arm like steel, his chest like iron—the gold buttons of his coat pressing against her breasts—sent wave after wave of desire racing through her body. She put her arms around his neck as he lowered his mouth to hers.

Soft, firm lips that tasted of sweet wine claimed her own. A wet, hot tongue pressed for admittance and as it met hers, her knees weakened. She heard the low growl of amusement that came from his throat and knew he was perfectly aware of what he was doing to her. His mouth left hers.

"Ah, Bess, you turn me inside out, m'darling," he whispered against her lips.

With all her heart she loved this reckless rogue who plied his trade upon the coach road. Robbing the rich and galloping away with redcoats in hot pursuit.

She saw his eyes wander to her bed and smiled. "Are you cold, milord?" she asked.

His smile could have lit the darkest night. "Are you up to warming me if I am?"

She lowered her arms and reached down to take his hand. "All I can do is try, milord," she answered.

"That's all a man can ask for, wench," he said with a wink.

"Tim was lurking about," he said as she put her hands to his jabot to pull it from his neck. "I saw him peering at me from the stable."

"He's always lurking about," she said. "He's harmless." She pushed the dark red coat from his shoulders and he allowed it to fall to the floor.

"I'm not so sure," he said as her fingers went to the buttons of his waistcoat. "I don't particularly like the way he watches you."

She ran the buttons on the brocade waistcoat then peeled it from his chest. "He watches everyone, Declan." She would have folded it but he plucked it from her hands and tossed it over his shoulder.

"You are so careless of your clothing, milord," she said with a tsk.

He shrugged and took a seat on the edge of her bed to pull off his boots. She shook her head then dropped to her knees to do it for him. The thigh-high boots were a gleaming black, expensive Spanish leather and they fit him almost like a second skin. She had to tug forcefully on the heel of the boot to pull it from his foot. When she had both standing side by side next to her narrow bed, his stockings stuffed inside them, she used the tall poster beside her to rise. She motioned for him to stand. He obediently obeyed—his lips twitching with amusement.

"I should hire you as my valet, wench," he said.

"You could not afford me, milord," she teased.

He stood still as her hands lowered to his belt. She drew the pistol from it and turned to lay it on the bedside table. It was heavy and she hated the sight of it, but the weapon kept him safe for her and that was all that mattered. When she turned back to him, he was unbuckling his belt—his gaze steady on her and as hot as a crucible.

"I've waited all week for this night," he said in his low, husky brogue. He swept his scrutiny down her body. "I can almost see through that nightdress."

She smiled and batted his hands away as he started to unbutton his britches. "Let me unwrap my present, milord," she said with a toss of her head.

"Unwrap away, wench," he agreed. "We'll play with whatever pops out."

Heat flooded her cheeks and she felt it all the way to her bare toes. When she risked a look at his face, his eyes were twinkling with promise.

Once she'd tugged the fine white shirt from his britches, he raised his arms and she pulled it over his head. With as little care as he had shown, she tossed it aside.

"You're learning," he said with a grunt.

Before her was a broad chest—bare except for a small patch between his chiseled pectorals. Ripples of muscles advanced down that rock-hard chest to fan out over a flat belly and flow into twin ridges just above his hips. She had no name for those two muscles but the sight of them made her womb clench.

She swallowed hard, took a deep breath then slid her hands beneath the waistband of his britches and began to push them down his lean hips. The garment didn't go far before his cock sprang free and—as it always did—the sight of that thick, long shaft filled her with red-hot desire.

"He's eager tonight, milord," she managed to say.

"He's been waiting for your kiss, milady," he said. His voice was low, raspy and his words caused his cock to pulse. As she watched, a pearly drop appeared in the slit of the broad mushroom head.

Bending over, she slid the britches down his legs and he braced his hand on her shoulder as he lifted his feet free of the garment. When she straightened he reached for the laces at the neck of her nightdress and slowly untied them. All the while, his heated blue gaze was locked on her eyes.

"I have such need for you, wench," he said.

That was more than evident to her. He was close enough for her to feel the tip of his cock pressing against her body.

The laces undone, he pushed her nightdress over her shoulders and it fell from her arms, rippled down her body to pool at her feet. Before she could take another breath, he snaked his arms around her, put his hands to her rump and lifted her. She wrapped her legs around his waist, her arms around his neck and kissed him. He took three steps to her bed, turned and drew her down with him to the narrow mattress.

From their very first night together she had known he would always be a gentle—and thorough—lover. He always put her pleasure before his own and this night was no different. His hard body covered hers, his delicious weight pressing her into the covers, and he smoothly eased her thighs apart with his hips. His lips moved to her chin, her neck, the sensitive sweep of flesh between neck and shoulder and then he was gliding down her. The moment his mouth closed over her straining nipple, she arched toward him. His low chuckle vibrated against that turgid peak to send chills down her sides.

His mouth and cock hot as the fires of an inferno, he trailed kisses, nibbles and grazes from nipple to nipple then down her belly to make it quiver. He planted a tender kiss on the hair of her mound then eased her lips apart with his thumbs, his shoulders resting on her mid-thighs. The wet firmness of his tongue sweeping along her core brought her hips from the mattress and another chuckle from deep in his throat. She threaded her fingers through his dark chestnut curls and anchored his head between her thighs. He was doing things to her body—as he always did—that would bring her so much pleasure she wondered how she could survive it without coming apart at the seams. She knew he would not cease until that first, tantalizing orgasm shook her to her foundation. Then, and only then, would he slide up her body to take possession.

Flesh to flesh.

Heat to heat.

Wet to wet.

A tidal wave of sheer pleasure undulated inside her and swept her up in the crest. She rode it—soft cries she barely recognized coming from the very depths of her—until she sank beneath the surface of the release and floated there.

His smile was slow and wicked as he began to crawl up her body.

Flesh to flesh.

Heat to heat.

Wet to wet.

He slanted his mouth over hers.

Breath to breath.

Hot cock to slick pussy.

Thrust to arching.

Going deep. Claiming. Pulsing.

One slow push. Retreat. Another slow invasion then slower retreat.

He stilled with his elbows elevating him above her. His eyes fused with hers and she watched the muscle in his jaw clench.

One quick thrust and a quicker retreat then the pistoning inside her began. His eyes never left hers. One last hard, deep penetration then he held himself steady as jet after jet of cum shot into her core. She felt the kicking of his shaft with each discharge. When he was depleted, he lowered himself gently atop her, turned his cheek upon her shoulder and lay there breathing shallowly.

She twined her arms around him and began to hum an old lullaby. It always soothed him, eased him into sleep. Within moments he was snoring lightly with his breath fanning the cusp of her shoulder.

* * * * *

She watched him buckling his belt—chewing on her lip as he drew on his waistcoat. It was nearly four of the clock and dawn was rapidly approaching.

"Don't go tonight," she said.

He looked around. "Beg pardon?"

She threw the covers back, swung her legs from the bed and padded over to him. "I don't want you to go."

"I'll be back," he told her. "Before morning light."

She put a staying hand on his arm. "Don't go, Declan. For me. Please?" she pleaded.

He took her chin in his hand. "Where is this coming from?" he asked.

"I dreamed—" She tucked her lip between her teeth. "I saw you lying on the road in a pool of blood," she told him.

"Nothing's going to happen to me." He tugged on her chin. "Nothing ever happens to me, wench. I have the fastest steed in Serenia and he always shows the redcoats the dust from his hooves. Beside, there's a prize to be had tonight. There are very important papers that should not reach the king's men. Those papers are worth their weight in gold. I'll be back before the dawning. I promise you this will be the last time. My last ride as the highwayman."

"And your last time coming to me?" she asked, her heart aching at the surprised look he gave her.

He released her chin and turned to gather up his coat. "Why do you ask that?" he hedged.

She shrugged. It was more a feeling than anything he'd done and said. His lovemaking had been more intense this time 'round, but it had carried with it a touch of melancholy she could not dismiss.

"When is the wedding to be?" she asked.

He cocked a shoulder. "A few weeks."

She nodded. She knew he would not—could not—be deterred now. He had that glint of determination she recognized all too well in his blue eyes. He was going through with the Joining.

"I'll be back tomorrow," he said.

She would be his alibi tomorrow should the redcoats come marching. She would swear on her life he'd been with her the entire night. But she knew their days of making love in her bed would cease with the coming of the new day.

"You'll be careful?" she asked.

He tucked the pistol behind his belt. The sight of that lethal weapon disturbed her.

"I'm always careful, Bess," he said with just a touch of exasperation. "It's hard to catch a man riding full-out in the dark of night."

"What if they come after you in the light of day?" she countered.

"Well, if they press me during the day, it may be night before I can come to you. But keep watch in the moonlight, wench. I will return."

He started to fetch his hat but stopped. Turning back to her, he held out his arms.

She went to him, pressed her cheek against his solid chest, wrapping her arms around his waist. It was all she could do not to sob.

"I wish you wouldn't go this time," she mumbled against his chest.

"I'm not going to let them catch me. I'll be back before the dawning," he said. "Now, come. Give me a kiss."

Reluctantly she raised her head and he tilted his head to the side to take her mouth.

With a heavy heart and belly filled with fear, she watched him leave. She opened the casement shutter, squinting against the first bright rays of the dawn. He appeared beneath her window but did not look up at her. He untied his mount then vaulted easily into the saddle. He lifted his head then rose up in the stirrups, extending his hand to her. She took it for a moment—never wanting to let it go. He gave her a broad wink, puckered his lips to blow her a kiss then pulled his hand from hers. He wheeled the stallion away from the inn, dug his boot heels into the side of the horse and the animal sprang forward.

From the corner of her eye she saw movement by the stable and turned her head in that direction. Tim, the hostler, was staring up at her with a look that chilled her blood. His slow, decayed-tooth grin made the hair stand up on her arms before she stepped back and hastily closed the shutter.

* * * * *

As Declan rode toward the spot where he would stop the envoy, he thought of the clandestine group of spies he had cultivated over the past four years. Men, women—and the occasional young boy—kept their eyes and ears open for any tidbit that might be of help to the Gypsy. None of them knew his true identity but they wanted to help. Through things he overheard the spies, gleaned from the keep or from the taverns and inns he frequented, he kept a close account of everything he learned. A written note here, a written note there, a whisper in the ear of a known gossip and those he chose to help him left their information in various secret spots where he would retrieve it. Always he left a silver dollar in that spot for his informant.

"Why a silver dollar?" Bess had asked him.

"It's my way of paying them back for the risk they take," he'd told her.

"And the ones you leave with those you rob?"

"These men and women take every last copper from the peasants, leaving them with nothing. It is a reminder that no one should be left with nothing."

This would be his last ride. He had one more silver dollar to hand out. That would be his last act as the Gypsy.

And his goodbye to his black-eyed Bess.

Jack's horse was not as nimble of foot as Warlock and the beast wasn't any happier about him riding it as he was doing. The jarring gait when he was accustomed to the smooth glide of his own mount had given him a headache. It was a relief to reach the point where he had chosen to intercept the envoy. Urging the horse into an overgrown hedge of cherry laurel bushes, he kept tight control of the reins for Spirit was a nervous beast—skittish and a bit on the stubborn side.

In the distance he heard the pounding of hooves. The envoy was right on time. He figured it was just a little past three of the clock and the man would be tired. Irritable. Wary of the dark shadows stretching across the road. He had learned all he could about Silas Caits, but what he hadn't been able to discover was whether or not the man was given to fits of retaliation. If that was the case, he might put up more of a fight than expected. He wanted this last mission to go without a hitch. He hadn't really hurt anyone yet and didn't intend to but that had largely been luck, he thought. He prayed that luck would hold just one more time.

* * * * *

Bess looked in on her father and found him snoring soundly. His tooth had gotten worse during the day and he had taken more laudanum when he went to bed. The drug had worked all too well. She doubted if a cannon going off near his ear would wake him. As she eased his door closed just in case, she thought she heard a noise downstairs. She stilled with a hand on the door latch and listened but there was no repeat of the noise.

"The wind," she murmured. She was afraid a storm was brewing to the west.

Which made it both safer and at the same time more dangerous for Declan. With that new worry wriggled through her mind she turned toward her room. The noise came again.

Was he back already? She thought. Had he been hurt?

Fearing that was the case, that something had gone horribly wrong, she hurried down the stairs.

"Declan?" she called out.

The taproom was dark but she saw the shadow standing at the far end of the bar.

"Declan?" she said, uneasy when he didn't answer.

Before she could reach for the lantern by the doorway, a hand slapped across her mouth and a strong arm slid around her waist to pin her to a hard, thick chest. She reached up to pry the fingers from her mouth—digging her nails into leather that tasted of horse sweat and musket oil.

A match hissed. Light flared in front of the dark shadow and then she saw the face of the man holding the match. The glow from the flame cast his hawkish features into a death mask. Her heart jumped in her throat as she realized who he was.

Then she saw the other men who had been hiding in the shadows. Four of them. Six in all. The dull red of their coats looked like dried blood in the flare of the match.

"Take her upstairs."

That voice that sent chills down her spine roused her in a furious attempt to break free of her captor. His arm was a steel band around her waist and though she kicked out at his shins with her heels, the soft kid slippers she wore made no impression on him at all. He hoisted her from the floor, turned and began carrying her—on his hip—up the staircase. The sound of muffled footsteps followed behind them.

* * * * *

"It would be best if you came and stayed close to us," Jack told Daniel Rees after they'd spent an hour reminiscing about their time in the Royal Marines together. As a cleric assigned to the military, Danny had trained alongside the men, though he would never have been able to fire a pistol at a living being if his life depended upon it.

"Where would I stay?" Danny asked.

"Well, I have a barn that I could make very comfortable for you," Jack said, looking around. The hovel in which he'd found his old friend was a hell of a lot worse than the barn on Jack's land.

"It doesn't take much to make me comfortable as you can see," Daniel admitted. The straw-filled bed, a single table and a rickety chair were the only furniture in the small cottage. "I got used to a monk's cell at the Abbey."

"We can do much better than this for you, Danny," Jack told him.

"Your wife won't mind?" Danny asked.

"You're my friend. Why would she mind?"

"Some women do," Danny replied, looking away. "When they hear my story."

"Fairling isn't like other women. She'll welcome you to our home as she would any other friend. Have no worries of that." Jack lifted the cup of bitter coffee his host had poured for him. "Besides, if she has no problem with the infamous highwayman visiting us, I doubt she'll bat an eye at a defrocked priest."

"I worry about him," Danny said. "I could scarce believe me ears when he spoke to me that night."

"Aye, well, I worry about him, too. He swears this is the last time."

"I fervently pray it is," Danny said quietly. He sat forward on his bed for he had given Jack the only chair. "Mayhap we should ride to Wixenstead instead of going on to Arlington."

Jack gave him a long look. "Why? I am to meet him back at the keep," Jack said.

"He's not going to the keep. He can't get there," Danny said. "Don't ask me how I know but he's in trouble, Jack. I have a sick feeling. Right here," Danny replied, putting a hand to his gut.

"You think he needs us," Jack said.

"Aye, I do."

Jack got to his feet. "Then what are we waiting for?"

* * * * *

The envoy pulled up short just as he came round a bend in the road. He would have turned and galloped away had Declan not fired a warning shot over his head.

"Quarter!" the man shrieked, throwing his hands into the air. "Quarter." His horse shied sideways then whinnied loudly. "I've a wife and four boys. Don't shoot me."

"Throw down the pouch and you can ride away," Dec told him as he walked Spirit closer to the envoy. He looked around them for once more he had a tingling feeling down the center of his back. He knew it wasn't Jack who might be spying on him. Jack was forty miles to the west.

"Aye," the man agreed and peeled the strap of the pouch from his shoulder then threw the leather bag to the ground.

"Are you traveling alone?" Declan asked.

The man betrayed himself by cutting his eyes to the left. "Aye, Gypsy, I am."

That tingle became a shock down his spine. He leveled the pistol at the man's heart. "I'll ask you again. Are you traveling alone?" He cocked the pistol.

Once more the man looked away and Declan knew. With a curse, he kicked Spirit in the ribcage and bent low over his saddle as the horse sprang forward. The iron ball that had been aimed at his head sailed past him and he thought he had felt it kissing the queue at the base of his neck. More shots rang out but he beat at the horse's flanks with his whip, silently begging the animal's forgiveness for spurring him on in such a cruel way. But he had to outdistance the troops he could hear shouting as they thundered after him.

His life depended on it.

* * * * *

Penry laughed at her as he dragged her by the arm to the casement window. He threw wide the shutter and the moonlight lit the darkened room.

"That's the direction from whence he'll come," he told her, his hand brutally tight just above her elbow. "He'll not know we're here until the first lead ball hits him."

"I don't know who you mean," she said.

"I am going to tie you to the bedpost so you will have a front-row seat to the final act," he said as though she hadn't spoken. "I'll need to gag you to prevent you from warning him though."

"Milord, I have no idea who you..."

He shook her hard enough to make her teeth rattle.

"Farrell!" he shouted in her face, spittle flying. "Your lover. The bastard who fucks your diseased cunt when he comes here after his robberies."

One of the redcoats came into the room from having gone to check on her father.

"The old man is trussed up like a feast goose," he reported. "Didn't move one muscle as I tied him. He's dead to the world."

"Good to know," Penry snapped. He shoved her against the post. "Tie her," he ordered his man.

She tried to run but the same redcoat that had manhandled her to her room caught her and dragged her—kicking and screaming—back to the bed. While the other four men laughed, he made quick work of tying her hands behind her back, looping the end of the rope around the upright.

"Tim," she yelled. "Tim, help me!"

"If you mean the dimwitted sot in the stable, he'll be of no use to you," Penry said with a chuckle. "He is out cold in the straw." He grinned nastily. "If he didn't die from the blow."

"Tim," she tried again.

"Gag the bitch," Penry snapped.

She tried to bite the hand of the ruffian who pulled out his dirty handkerchief, whipping it around and around between his hands to turn it into a roll then forced it between her teeth. Though she struggled, and behind the gag called him every filthy name she had ever heard from the tavern-goers, it only made him and the other men laugh.

"I want two of you at that window," Penry said. "He'll be here before sunrise so be sharp. Let him get just inside the inn yard before you shoot him."

Bess whined at the words. Twisting and turning her hands behind her she could feel them bleeding as the ropes bit into her flesh.

"Stop that," Penry ordered. He grabbed a musket from one of the men and shoved it between her and the robes that bound her to the bed. The barrel of the weapon gouged into her back, the muzzle pressing painfully into her shoulder blades.

"That musket has a hair trigger, bitch. Keep struggling and you might blow yourself to kingdom come," Penry sneered.

She gaped at him and stilled but his words wound through her head like a lifeline playing out from the shore to a drowning man. Slowly she turned her eyes back to the window and the narrow roadway that led from the brow of the hill to the inn yard.

There would be no help for him. He would come riding down the road. Riding to his death. He was coming to see her. To take her to that mystical place he called Oceania. He loved her and wanted her with him and because he did he would die for love of her.

"Just in case you are wondering," Penry said. "I've stationed men out of sight all around the inn. He'll not escape what is coming to him." When she hissed at him, he chortled and walked from the room as though he were the most important man in the kingdom. He motioned the other three redcoats to follow him.

"This ain't nothing but an execution," one of the men at the window said after his captain had left the room. "We don't know for a fact the earl is the Gypsy."

"Ain't up to you to make the call," the other man said. "Cap'n wants the earl dead and it's our orders to see it done."

"What if he's innocent?"

"Innocent men die all the time."

"It will be murder, Jonas. Pure and simple. The man deserves a trial."

Jonas stroked the barrel of his musket. "This here is the trial, the judge, the jury and the executioner all rolled into one. What the fuck do you care about what happens to a toff anyways, Belk?"

"Just ain't right is all," Belk said. He glanced at Bess.

She pleaded with him with her eyes and he looked ashamed, worried, but he shrugged and turned his gaze from her. Despite his reservations, she knew he would do nothing to stop what was coming. It would be up to her to do what she could. She stretched her fingers toward the trigger, trying to hook the tip of one finger through the trigger guard. Her flingers kept slipping away from the metal for they were slick with her blood.

* * * * *

Dawn came and went and the man Penry knew was the highwayman did not come. By the striking of the clock at noon, he still had not shown. Cursing, he stomped around the taproom where his men were swilling down pints of ale. He should have said something to them, ordered them away from the liquor, but at that point he didn't care about anything other than watching Declan Farrell die.

"Where is the bastard?" he snarled. He'd made dozens of trips up the stairs to the bedchamber of the woman who had given herself to Farrell—and by doing so forever earned his contempt—but the road down from the hill remained empty of riders.

The landlord was still tied to his own bed and the whore was lashed securely to hers. When last he visited her bedchamber, she was nodding but came awake as soon as he entered. The look she gave him suggested Farrell had made a fool of him. It was a look of gloating he wished he could slap from her beautiful, deceitful face.

"I will get him," he told her. "As the gods are my witnesses I will see him in the ground."

She lifted her chin, her eyes locked on his.

He glared back at her—hating her even as he admired her delicate peasant beauty. For a fleeting moment or two he had contemplated using her as he had scores of other women beneath his station, but that had passed quickly enough. What he wanted most was to hurt her in such a way that it would utterly destroy Farrell. It was obvious the man had feelings for the chit. Mayhap he even loved her, though how a man of his station could lower his standards to such a degree was beyond his comprehension.

The main objective was to hurt Farrell, to kill him. To erase his very existence.

"He will come," he said. "And when he does, he will die like the dog he is."

Pivoting on his heel, he left the room with his fists doubled and a wild ache in his belly.

* * * * *

They'd chased him for miles and now he was far from the Hound and Stag with a lathered horse and fury raging through him like none he'd ever known. Not only had he failed to gain the papers that would save the cottages of the people, failing those good people he had tried to protect, he was being harried across three counties. Ran to ground like a stag.

"Not good," he said as he led Spirit into a cave. The animal needed rest. He needed sleep and something to stop the rolling hunger pains eating at him—two things he wasn't going to get any time soon.

He had to get back to the Hound and Stag. Jack would be coming to Arlington tonight on Warlock and that set a blazing fear burning its way through his very soul. Penry was behind this. He had to be and Declan would bet the last silver dollar in his pocket that the bastard had another trap set for him. If that trap was being staged near Arlington Castle, the redcoats could mistake Jack for him. Claret velvet coat and cocked hat aside, they'd arrest Jack and take him to Gilhaven for questioning and that he could not allow.

He squatted down beside Spirit and hung his head. He was tired, hungry, and so was the horse. They'd almost caught him when he stopped to let the animal have a drink of water at a creek a few miles back. He had been moments away from turning his pistols on the four men chasing him and bringing them down. That was not what he wanted to do. Violence was something he'd tried hard to avoid. Killing? Well, killing was out of the question unless it came to his life or the fate of the man facing him or threatening those he loved.

Staying in the cave as long as he dared, he walked to the entrance and looked out, scouting the area around him. He listened carefully to the sounds of the forest that told him no one was close by. The birds were singing, the squirrels chattering at one another. A few yards away, a fawn minced its way delicately through the ferns. There was nothing about to cause the animals concern. He hoped in his weariness and state of mind that he wasn't misreading the signs. He turned from the entrance and went back to gather up Spirit's reins. Leading the beast out of the cave, he once more stood still and cocked an ear to the early afternoon air. Reaching into his vest pocket, he pulled out his grandfather's watch, opened it.

"Two o'clock," he said softly. "Five hours before moonrise."

Looking up, he realized the sky was gunmetal grey. He had sensed a storm coming the day before, but apparently it had stalled somewhere to the west. Now it was easing eastward again. The air had a heavy feel to it and the winds were picking up again. With them came a bit of a chill, which was never good at this time of year. As he watched the clouds shifting and swirling above him, he knew the conditions were forming for a potentially bad storm to come whirling down from the heavens.

After leading Spirit down a slight incline he stopped yet again and listened. Hearing nothing but a far-off rumble of thunder, he swung up into the saddle but kept the animal still. Once more he surveyed the land around him before setting the beast into motion. Walking him slowly to the ridge that looked over the valley below; he breathed a sigh of relief when he saw his pursuers, galloping toward the road that led north to Beaverton. He smiled and turned Spirit eastward.

* * * * *

Jack and Danny had reached the outskirts of Belvedere Glenn. The Hound and Stag was only an hour's ride due south.

"You think he'll still be there?" Danny asked as they stopped to rest their mounts.

Jack pulled out his pocket watch. "It's half past two," he replied as he returned the watch to his coat. "He told me he would get back to the inn at dawn. He may still be sleeping."

"He always was the lazy sort," Danny said with a snort.

"Hasn't changed," Jack told him.

"Why does that not surprise me?"

"From what he told me of his plans, he intends to wait until nightfall to leave. He will need to stay hidden in her room until then and hope Penry and his men don't come looking for him."

"By the gods I despise that man," Danny said.

"As do I."

"What then?"

"He'll head straight to the keep to pick up Warlock."

"Why didn't he just ask you to return his horse to the inn and leave from there?" Danny queried.

"It isn't safe. Penry's men have been watching the area around the inn."

"He rode there last eve," Danny reminded him.

"Aye, but that was night. This is day. He's afraid a redcoat troop might spy me and follow me back there. They'll be looking for this big black. Under the cover of night Warlock is hard to keep in sight. In the daylight, he stands out like a sore thumb."

"Makes sense," Danny acknowledged. "But I can't shake this uneasy feeling, Jackie. I think I should go to the inn, check things out." He frowned. "Make sure he's there."

"Unless he got caught, he'll be there," Jack replied.

"All right," Danny said. "You stay here and I'll go check out things at the inn. If he is there, I'll try to speak to him. At the very least, I'll ask the girl to tell him we're nearby should he need us."

* * * * *

Bess was bone tired and though the guard with the conscience had brought her back some bread and cold meat when he took his last break, her stomach was rumbling. At one point Penry had untied her and allowed her to use the chamber pot. Despite the humiliation of him standing there watching her every move, she had been grateful to relieve her bladder. Now she was tied to the bedpost again and the gag was back firmly in place, the musket lashed beside her. This time the muzzle was pressed against her breast. Penry himself had pulled the bonds tight and his meanness had opened the gouges on her wrist to set the blood oozing again. The only good thing to come of it was that she was able to wedge her finger inside the trigger guard. The tip of her finger was resting on the trigger.

The clock below began chiming.

"Four o'clock," Penry said with a growl when the chiming stopped. He was standing at the casement window with the two guards who were hunkered down with their muskets pointed toward the road.

"Mayhap he returned to Arlington, sir," Belk, the guard with a conscience suggested.

"Did I ask for your opinion, soldier?" Penry shouted.

"No, sir," Belk said.

"Then shut your mouth and keep watch in the road!"

Thunder boomed loudly across the firmament and a few splatters of rain hit like iron shot on the cobblestones.

"Fuck," Penry hissed.

Behind her gag Bess smiled. Anything that irritated Penry was a good thing in her estimation. He was already on edge, nervous, chewing on his thumbnail as though it were a carrot. Annoyances, frustrations and time moving like molasses were adding to the man's miseries.

"I think I see him," Jonas said.

Bess snapped her head up and as soon as she saw the rider cresting the hill she tensed. Her fingertip was on the trigger but she had to wait until he was closer. So there would be no doubt that he would hear the warning shot and turn back.

"That's not him," she heard Penry said with a snort. "Wrong color horse and the man is thicker set than Farrell." He kicked at the chair beside the window. "Nothing more than a fucking farmer coming to wet his whistle."

Penry stripped off his uniform coat and cravat, tossed them onto Bess's bed. As she watched he ran out of the room and she heard him inside her father's bedchamber. When he ran past her door, he was tying an apron around his waist.

"Get out of sight," she heard him shout to the men waiting below in the taproom.

She turned her attention back to the window where the two guards had withdrawn their muskets from the edge of the casement. Both were pressed back so they could not be seen from below. From that distance she could tell the rider coming along the road wasn't Declan but she couldn't make out his features. She didn't believe it was his friend Jack. She prayed that it wasn't for she believed Penry was going to try to pass himself off as the landlord. Yet if the man was a regular patron he would see right through the ruse. Chances were good if he did come to the tavern often, he would also recognize Penry as a Royal Marine. It said much for the frazzled state of mind of her captor that he was willing to risk being found out.

The rider had reached the stable. She saw him glance toward the door that had been swinging back and forth in the brisk wind. Tim had not shown himself all day and she was worried about him. She said a silent prayer that the soldiers had not killed him.

"That's sure not Farrell," Jonas said. "Does he look familiar to you?"

Belk eased up so he could see out the window. "No," he said.

"Looks familiar to me," Jonas mumbled.

"You've most likely seen him about," Belk told him.

"Aye, probably so."

Bess could no longer see the man who had ridden up for he had stopped at the hitching post. She listened to hear the door to the inn open.

"Good day to you, sir." Penry's voice was overly jovial. "Welcome to the Hound and Stag."

It was her father's customary greeting to new customers and a part of Bess was disappointed that the rider would not think anything amiss.

"What can I get for you this fine day?"

She glanced at the window. Rain was beginning to fall. Lightning flared close by and the rumble of thunder shook the glass in the window. It was another indication of Penry's nervousness that he did not alter her father's words to fit the weather—which was what Patrick Arbra would have done.

"A pint would go a long way in making the day better," the stranger replied.

There was a pause then Penry's voice showed his fluster. "Aye, well, so it would. So it would."

"Nice place you have here. You run it by yourself?"

"Ah, no. My daughter usually helps but she's not here today."

"If she's like my missus," the stranger said. "She's out shopping. Is that where your daughter is?"

A warning bell went off in Bess's head. That was a strange question to ask and she hoped Penry was too on edge to realize it.

"Aye, that's exactly where she is. Up to Wixenstead at the market," Penry replied.

"Bad day for that, eh?" the man inquired. "Hope she makes it back safely."

"She's a good head on her shoulders," Penry said. "If the weather turns bad, she'll stay with friends there."

Who that might be Bess had no idea since she knew no one in Wixenstead.

"Say, I'm looking for a fellow who might have passed through here on occasion. He offered me a job on his estate but I went and misplaced the card he gave me. I'm in sore need of work so I'm hoping you might know him."

"I am new to these parts," Penry told him. "We just opened the inn this month."

"His name is Farrell," the stranger said. "Lord Declan Farrell. Ever heard tell of him?"

"Not that I recall, but a lot of men come through here," Penry replied and it was hard to miss the hostility on his voice.

"Handsome fellow," the man told him. "Black hair, blue eyes. About my height but slimmer. Rides a black Rysalian."

"Doesn't ring a bell," Penry lied.

"Ah, well, didn't hurt to ask, I reckon."

"You might head over Belvedere Glenn way," Penry suggested. "Ask the innkeeper there."

"I'll do just that," the stranger said. "Much obliged for the recommendation."

"My pleasure. Can I pour you another?"

"Nope," the stranger answered. "One's my limit afore the sun sets."

"That won't be long now," Penry said. "Looks like I might not be having many customers tonight. Might as well close up, I'm thinking."

A heavy roll of thunder shook the inn to punctuate Penry's words.

"Not good weather even for ducks," the stranger said then laughed. "Thanks for your hospitality."

Penry must have walked him to the door for as soon as she heard the crunch of the stranger's boots on the cobblestones under her window, the door to the inn shut and the latch was thrown.

She couldn't help but wonder if Declan had sent the man to the inn because he knew something was wrong. She prayed that was the case and he would not fall for the trap that lay in waiting for him.

Chapter Nine

"Something is gods-be-damned wrong at that inn," Danny told Jack when he found him at the inn in Belvedere Glenn.

"What do you mean?" Jack asked.

Outside it was raining so hard he could not see out the window. The gusty wind was howling like a banshee around the eaves as Danny began telling him what had transpired at the Hound and Stag.

"I recognized him as soon as I entered the room," Danny said.

"Who?"

"That cocksucker Royce Penry," Danny said with a sneer. "Pretending he was the landlord. Even if I hadn't known who he was, I'd have known he wasn't a publican. His hands are lily-white and his speech far more refined than any tavern keeper I've ever met. Not to mention he kept turning his eyes up to the ceiling like he expected someone to come running down the stairs."

"You think Declan is there?"

"No," Danny replied. "I sensed more men lurking about though I didn't see them. I wanted to go into the stable, but had no good reason to do so. I think I saw a man with a musket jump back when I looked that way. I believe Penry has set a trap for our friend."

"One he'll be riding right into," Jack said. He pushed up from the table. "We need to get there to stop him."

* * * * *

The deluge had soaked him to the skin. Wet velvet—clammy and cold wet velvet—was not pleasant sticking to the flesh of his arms. He wished he had his own saddlebags for at least there was an oilskin in them.

Rain ran down the back of his collar and he shivered. The only time he'd been more miserable had been in the prison at Gilhaven. He nudged Spirit under a tree to block some of the rain. Sitting there atop the beast he was more than a little apprehensive. He had lost his trackers but he feared there would be more lurking about the hills around Wixenstead.

Though there was forest around him, there were no abandoned cabins, no caves, nowhere for him to get in out of the downpour. Nowhere to hide. The sun was almost below the horizon and he was still miles from the Hound and Stag. He knew Bess would be worried about him for he was over twelve hours late in returning to her. Jack would be worried, as well, for he should have been back to Arlington by now to fetch Warlock.

With every breath he took he cursed Royce Penry. He'd never had the urge to commit murder, but for Penry he could make an exception. The man had been the bane of his existence in Diabolusia and was even more of a problem now. Penry wanted to catch him as badly as he wanted Penry to fail.

At anything and everything the gods-be-damned bastard did.

But especially at catching the Gypsy.

* * * * *

Lightning was cracking almost continuously above the inn. The fiery stitching seemed to be getting closer and closer to the stable. Jonas and Belk had been forced to shut the window for the rain was streaming in, blinding them. Their inability to see the road had Penry hissing and cursing like a madman as he paced the dark room, tugging at his hair.

"Should pass over soon now, Cap'n," Jonas made the mistake of saying and was rewarded by a backhand blow from Penry that split the guard's lip and broke his nose.

Bess was to the point of exhaustion as she slumped against the bonds holding her. She had lost count of how many long hours she'd been lashed to the bedpost. Her day-long ordeal had weakened her to the point her legs were giving out under her. At least her father was stretched out upon his bed—wrists and ankles tied—but she didn't think he was faring any better than her. No one had gone in to check on him since Belk had insisted on letting the poor man up to relieve himself. That had been at least five hours ago.

Groaning as she flexed her fingers to keep them from going numb, she tried not to notice the way Penry was staring at her with each pass across the room. The fury on his face, the utter evil in his eyes alarmed her.

"He is going to die this night," he had told her over and over again until she wanted to scream.

Two thoughts were warring inside her head. One was the agonizing fear that Declan had been caught. The second—even more unbearable—was that he was lying dead on the coach road.

Almost as quickly as it had begun, the rain ceased.

"Open the window," Penry snapped. "Now! Open the windows."

Jonas was trying to stop the blood from oozing from his nose so it was Belk who opened the latch and pulled the glass panels inside.

Bess was watching him and saw him stiffen.

And she knew. She knew.

She craned her neck to look around Jonas. At that moment, the moon came out from behind the sodden clouds. Her heart skipped a beat for a rider was coming over the brow of the hill.

It was him. There was no doubt in her mind that it was and her heart broke. With every last ounce of strength she had left, she hooked her fingertip firmly on the trigger and kept her eyes locked on the horse and rider galloping down the road.

* * * * *

Timothy Saur had been waiting all day. None of the soldiers had come to the stable to see if he was alive or dead. He knew they had forgotten about him. They did not know he was watching from the open stable door or that he had a musket of his own.

Or that he knew how to use it and use it well.

The world thought Tim Saur was simple-minded but that was not the case. Circumstances had made him what he was now. He had been to war and when he returned, he was not the same green lad who had been taken prisoner by the Diabolusians—tortured so badly he lost contact with the world around him.

He rarely spoke. When he did, it was generally only one or two words at a time. The reason for that was obvious to anyone who could look him in the face—though few could or did. His features had been horribly mangled by his captors—scarred, ravaged. One eye drooped—as did that side of his face, twisting his mouth to one side. His body had fared no better for it had been whipped and torn and burned until there was nothing left save madness in his pale blue eyes. What had once been a thick crop of dark blond hair now more closely resembled moldy hay. Timothy Saur had been all but destroyed.

So he kept to himself—mostly because of the way he looked, but also because he was wary of those he did not know. He slept in the barn to be near the horses he loved for they accepted him as he was. He moved about the inn yard as stealthily and silent as a ghost—sometimes appearing out of nowhere to frighten the guests. Actions that only solidified people's opinions of his mental capabilities.

When he came to the inn as Patrick Arbra and his daughter were renovating it, he had mumbled a request for a job. "Need work," he'd stated.

The man he asked did not hesitate.

"How are you with horses?"

"Good," Tim replied. "Horses love Tim."

Arbra named a wage, told him they would provide him with three meals a day.

"Do you have a place to stay?" Bess had asked.

Tim had pointed to the stable. "There," he said. "Stay there."

"You sure?" her father had inquired.

Tim had nodded. "Stay with horses."

Though he had not been long at the Hound and Stag he had come to have great respect for Patrick Arbra and had developed a strong affection for the man's lovely daughter. He followed her with his eyes everywhere she went. Not in a lewd way, he thought, but in a protective way. He knew his smile made her uneasy—and perhaps it was a touch menacing—but that could not be helped. The muscles of his face had been so badly damaged during the hours he had been in the trained hands of the Diabolusian interrogators.

When the handsome man on the ebony stallion had ridden into the inn, Tim thought he bore a strong resemblance to a young lieutenant he had known in the hellish high desert of Diabolusia. He'd stared hard at the visitor—trying to discover if they were one and the same. That young man—only a year or so older than Tim—had been kind, a joy to be around and the men had respected him.

Not their commanding officer who was a sadistic bastard with a wife whose legs parted for any man who gave her the time of day.

Tim included.

Once he had been a young man the ladies had chased. He'd had no trouble finding bed partners. The captain's lady had been the last woman Tim had tupped. He knew with the way he looked now, she would be the last ever.

Lightning flared, but the rain seemed to have moved on. That was good, he thought, as he braced the musket on his shoulder and sighted down the barrel. One shot was all he had in the weapon. One shot was all it would take. With one eye squeezed shut he tracked the rider coming toward the inn. Above and behind him he knew the two guards at the casement window were doing the same.

He had no idea how good they were but he knew how good he was. He'd been the best sharpshooter in his company. He never missed what he aimed at and he intended to fire his weapon before they could. He began to gently squeeze the trigger.

* * * * *

Declan had one thought only as he neared the inn. It was barely ten of the clock but there wasn't a light showing in any of the windows. The rain had stopped and he could see the establishment clearly. He smiled when he saw Bess's window was open. She was waiting for him.

* * * * *

The pounding of the hooves coming toward the inn was faint at first but Bess heard it. She could see the rider in the moonlight and her heart ached for him. He was almost within range of the muskets aimed at him. Only a few yards more, she thought. Once he passed under the stone archway that led to the short path up to the paved cobblestone courtyard of the inn, it would be too late for him to turn back.

Now, she thought and with one final whisper of his name, she pulled the trigger.

* * * * *

He was almost to the stone archway when he heard the bark of a firing musket and sawed on the reins. The horse's back hooves dug into the mud to slow it down. When the second shot came—hitting the left side of the archway near his head—he wheeled Spirit around and kicked him into motion, riding as though the devil were on heels back the way he had come as two more shots rang out in the darkness.

* * * * *

Tim lowered the musket and slowly turned his head toward the casement window and smiled the terrible grin he knew frightened those who saw it. The bastards had missed their target but he hadn't. He'd clipped the stone archway at the exact point and at the exact moment he had intended. He'd intended the shot to warn away the handsome visitor and it had achieved its purpose.

It was the first shot—coming a scant second before his own—that puzzled him.

* * * * *

Everything seemed to be moving in slow motion.

Musket smoking in his hands, Belk slowly lowered his weapon. He doubted the man kneeling beside him at the window even realized another shot had been fired in the bedchamber where they were hiding. Instead, Jonas was cursing vilely at having missed his target.

Three shots from the bedchamber and one from the stable—all coming within seconds of one another. Two hitting their targets and two missing.

Already knowing what he was going to find, Belk turned away from the window to look behind him.

Her chin was resting on her chest. The long black braid hanging over her left shoulder was glistening from the blood that was pulsing from the side of her breast.

"After him!" his captain shouted. "Catch him!"

Jonas jumped up, turned and staggered back when he saw the blood cascading down the young woman's skirt.

"Go after him, Belk!" Penry bellowed. "Jonas, stay. I have need of you."

Belk knew there was nothing he could do for the young woman. She had given her life to save the man she loved and he could not fault her for that. The blame lay entirely on his captain. He knew when he mounted his horse, neither Penry nor anyone else in the Royal Marines would ever see him again.

Downstairs the other soldiers had heard Penry's command and were running from the inn. The sound of galloping horses thundering up the road to the hill told Belk the men hiding behind the inn were already riding after the Gypsy.

He took one last look at the woman slumped over the musket, shook his head and followed Jonas from the room—cursing Royce Penry for the craven bastard he was.

* * * * *

"What do you need me to do, sir?" Jonas asked, avoiding looking at the girl.

"We will need a grave," Penry said. "Out behind the inn."

Jonas knew the kind of man he was. He'd never had illusions about himself. He was a womanizer, a thief, a murderer—a lot of things—but for a reason he couldn't explain, what the captain was asking him to do was shameful.

"Without a funeral, sir?" he inquired. "That don't seem right."

Penry pulled the pistol from his holster and leveled it at him. "Dig the fucking grave, soldier," he bellowed.

There was madness in the captain's eyes. He had no doubt the man would shoot him.

"Aye, sir," Jonas agreed and hurried to carry out the order.

* * * * *

After the solider left the room, Royce sat down on the chair by the window and started to shake. His attention was riveted on the red droplets falling from the hem of Bess' skirt. He could not seem to pull himself free from the abyss into which he had fallen. Hands curled palms up in his lap, sweat gathering under his armpits, he felt the gorge rising in his throat. He knew—beyond a shadow of a doubt—that he would be held accountable for the young woman's death. A civilian. He would be stripped of his command, quite possibly demoted. At the very least he would suffer a severe reprimand that would insure he never rose any higher in rank.

An absolute catastrophe for a man of his position and ambitions.

He tore his gaze from the blood to look down at his trembling hands.

"Calamity," he whispered. "Sheer calamity."

And all because of Declan Farrell.

When he heard the soft moan, he nearly jumped out of his skin.

* * * * *

Bess was in so much pain she could barely draw breath. Sheer agony was burning through the left side of her body—along her ribcage and up her breast. Every beat of her heart seemed to pulse right where the pain was located.

"Wench?" she heard someone whisper and tried to raise her head.

She couldn't. She was too weak, dizzy, and she couldn't raise her arms. It felt as though she was hanging from a peg on the wall with her legs of no use to her.

"Wench?" the voice asked again—closer this time.

A hand touched her right shoulder and she flinched. When she did, the hand was snatched back and a low whimper filled the room.

"You're not dead?"

A booted foot appeared in the periphery of her vision then a cool palm was placed to her forehead.

"By the gods, you're alive. Thank the gods, you are alive."

There seemed to be great relief in the voice.

A hand slid down her face to cup her chin gently. Slowly her head was lifted until she could look into the eyes of the person standing beside her.

Penry, she thought and recoiled at his touch.

"Milady, let me," he said and removed his hand.

She had no idea what he wanted her to allow but as soon as he let go of her chin, it sank to her chest. She groaned.

"Merciful Alel," he said as he untied the gag that was wedged between her lips, tugging too forcefully so that he pulled her hair in the bargain.

Mouth free, she ran her dry tongue over the seams of her lips and tasted blood.

"W…water," she pleaded, her voice nothing more than a rasp.

"Of course," he agreed and the boot disappeared from her vision. She heard him running down the stairs and wondered why he just didn't send one of his men.

The men kneeling at the casement to murder Declan.

As that thought shifted through her mind, she sucked in a rough breath for memory came back to her in a flash of muzzle fire. Swinging her eyes to the left, she saw the blood coating her bodice. The shot had not killed her but she was hurt badly. She could feel the cold wetness of the blood sticking to her flesh and caught a glimpse of the pool beside her foot.

Had she succeeded in warning him? Had the shot made him turn away from the inn?

Or was he—even now—lying down in the mud beyond the inn?

Penry came rushing into the room and up to her. With infinite care he lifted her head with one hand and placed a tumbler to her lips.

"Drink, milady," he said.

The water was cool and tasted so sweet. She was parched—her mouth as dry as tinder—and the liquid flowed wonderfully down her throat.

"Not too much," he said.

A gallon would not be enough, she thought as she swallowed greedily. When he took away the tumbler she wanted to hiss at him and would have had she the energy.

"I must get you to our physician," he said, putting aside the tumbler.

She felt his hands fumbling with the knots that bound her hands and when the robe loosened and blood began to flow into her numb fingers, she cried out.

"Sorry," he said. "I'm sorry."

He was being too accommodating by half, she thought and wondered why. Even as he caught her sagging body into his arms and tenderly lifted her to lie on the bed, she feared he would revert to kind and hurt her more.

She could do nothing to prevent him from ripping her gown down the side to inspect her wound.

"Good," he said and she wished with all her being she could slit his throat. "Good, it's no longer bleeding." His fingers slid over her naked side and chest.

"Don't," she groaned.

"The ball singed a nasty path up your side then pierced your breast. Went through this fleshy part here." He looked up at the ceiling and pointed. "And landed up there." He smiled cheerfully. "You will need stitching but I don't believe you will lose any more blood. Not a physician, of course, but that's what I believe."

"Leave me," she begged.

"Wagon," he said. He leaned over her. "Is there a wagon in the stable?"

"Aye," she whispered, not really catching his meaning.

"I shall fetch it."

"My father?" she managed to mumble, but he had already turned away and was thundering down the stairs.

She lay there unable to move because of the agony pulsing in her side. The minutes dragged by. With every breath she felt herself growing weaker. It seemed like hours since he had left her. Hours in which to worry about the fate of the man she loved.

"Declan," she said, tears filling her eyes.

Had he gotten away? Was he safe? Did he know she had been hurt? Would he come after her if Penry took her to the garrison at Gilhaven?

She was fearful that he would and if so, he would be arrested on sight.

Struggling to get up, she realized it was useless and closed her eyes. Either she'd lost too much blood or the muscles on that side of her body had been damaged beyond repair. Mayhap she was dying and that was why movement was beyond her.

A sound at the door made her open her eyes. She was surprised to see Tim, the hostler standing in the doorway.

"Hurt?" he asked, his lax face filled with concern.

"Declan," she said on a sigh.

"Got away," Tim said. He came into the room and she realized he was carrying a musket. He propped it against the wall, came to the bed. There were tears falling down his cheek.

"My father?" she asked and watched his eyes narrow. "In his room."

He nodded and turned to leave. As he did, Penry hit him in the side of the head with his pistol. Tim fell against the bed then slid down it.

"Bastard," she whispered.

"You'll think differently when I get you to the garrison," he said. Stepping over Tim, he thrust his pistol into his holster, scooped her into his arms and lifted her from the bed.

"He'll kill you," she said as he carried her through the doorway.

"Not if I get him first," Penry said.

It was agony being carried down the stairs. Unable to thwart him in any way she had no choice but to lie in his despicable arms and be taken to the wagon he had brought to the front of the inn. To give him his due, he had padded the bed with straw and blankets and laid her down as gently as he could.

"Captain?"

He turned, drew his pistol and fired.

"No," she gasped, thinking it was Tim he had shot. It took all her waning strength to turn her head to see who had been shot. When she saw one of the men who had been kneeling at her casement standing in the doorway of the inn with a hand to his chest, she was relieved it wasn't Tim.

"I just wanted to tell you…" the man began then dropped to the ground. She knew he was dead.

Penry stood there for a moment then nodded. He leaned down, hoisted the dead man to his shoulder.

"I'll be right back," he told her in a conversational tone.

She watched him carry the soldier around the corner of the inn and disappear.

He was gone again for what felt like forever. By then she was fading in and out of consciousness and wasn't altogether sure she understood him when he climbed into the wagon seat and took up the reins.

"He'll never know," he said, clucking his tongue and snapping the reins. "He'll believe 'tis you in the grave."

He looked around at her and smiled and she realized he was now wearing the coat of the man he'd killed instead of his own.

"Can't take you to the garrison, but there is bound to be a healer somewhere between here and Norus. I'll find him and we'll get you patched up."

His words made no sense to her and her exhaustion would not hold; she closed her eyes and slipped into the darkness.

* * * * *

Jack and Daniel arrive at the Hound and Stag around one in the morning. It had been an arduous journey for them. Because of the deluge, riverbanks had overflowed and many of the roads had become impassable. Twice it had been necessary for them to backtrack rather than risk being caught in swiftly moving waters the depths of which they could not judge in the darkness. It had been a frustrating trip but as soon as they saw the glow of lights at the inn, they hastened their mounts. Warlock knew precisely where he was going and sped up—leaving Daniel and his roan behind.

Mud sucked brutally at the hooves of the mount until it cleared the archway then left the road to clatter over the cobblestones. Jack noticed two twin ruts leading away from the point where mud met stone but paid scant attention to it. He returned his attention to the inn and the lack of any horse tied to the hitching post. One glance at the stable and he wondered why the door was standing open.

"Something's not right," he told Daniel when his friend caught up with him.

"Too quiet," Daniel agreed.

They reached the hitching post and both men dismounted quickly. The door to the inn was also standing open and on the threshold was a dull puddle of congealing blood. A quick exchange of worried looks and the men bolted through the door and into the inn.

"Declan?" Jack shouted. He rushed into the taproom, found it empty then spun around and raced for the stairs.

"It feels empty," Daniel said as he sprinted up the stairs behind him.

Jack entered the first door he came to and knew the room must belong to the landlord. It had the feel of a masculine presence.

"The bed," Daniel said from behind him.

When Jack saw the ropes laying upon rumpled covers, his heart skipped a beat. He spun around and shoved Daniel out of his way.

"Declan," he yelled again.

The next two rooms—one that Declan had occupied when he was ill—were empty, clean and neat but the fourth room he stumbled into bore the overpowering stench of spent blood. He came up short when he saw the pool of crimson staining the floorboards at the foot of the bed and the musket lying in the blood.

"Someone was tied there," Daniel said softly. He bent over to retrieve a handkerchief. "Gagged as well."

Jack knew who that must have been. He turned his gaze from the blood to the window where the mullioned panels lay open to the night air.

"They tied her to the bed, gagged her to keep her from crying out to him. Tied a musket besides her thinking it would scare her into not trying to escape." He walked to the window. "They were waiting for him," he said.

Daniel removed his hat and ran a hand through his thick black hair. He was staring at the blood on the floor. "Do you think they got him?"

"No."

Both men twisted around—their hands going to their pistols—but thankfully Jack recognized the landlord. He put his free hand on Daniel's arm and told him who the man was.

"She warned him in time," the landlord said. "They galloped after him but I doubt they caught him."

"They?" Jack queried. "You mean Penry?"

The landlord nodded. His face was gray, his eyes haunted. "And he'd better pray to the gods Declan Farrell gets to him before I do."

Jack swallowed, hating to ask. "Bess?"

The landlord's lips quivered and a single tear slid slowly down his ashen cheek. "They buried her behind the inn. Like garbage. Without benefit of words or a coffin." He whimpered then reached up to swipe at his face as more tears fell. "We are Chalean. She'll spend eternity in…" He broke down, his shoulders shaking.

Jack looked to Daniel.

"We Chales cannot exhume a body once it has been laid in the soil," Daniel explained. "That is one of our religious tenets."

The thought of Declan's love denied a casket, lying beneath the mud filled Jack with an anger so intense it tinged the periphery of his vision red. "We should ride to Wixenstead. Get the priest…"

Daniel exhaled loudly—cutting off his friend—then walked over to the older man. He put a hand on the landlord's shoulder. "I am an ordained priest," he said. "I can say the words over her."

Jack stared at his friend but kept his mouth shut.

"Would you, milord?" the landlord asked.

"It would be my honor, sir," Daniel replied. "Declan is an old friend and to send his lady to make peace with the Wind would be a blessing for me."

Jack and Daniel followed the grieving man down the stairs and out the side door of the inn. He led them back among the trees. There was a dark silhouette sitting hunched by a fresh mound of dirt.

"Who is that?" Daniel asked, hand going to his pistol once more.

"Tim, my hostler," the landlord said. "He was the last to speak to her." He looked around at Jack. "She asked after him."

Jack did not need to ask whom he meant.

Daniel stopped walking, put out a hand to stop Jack. "We need to find him before he hears what's happened."

"He'll go insane when he finds out," Jack said under his breath. "He's lost yet another person dear to him."

"I would, too, if I were him."

"He'll be too distraught to think rationally, Danny. They'll kill him."

"If they haven't already."

"Not him," the man huddled by the grave said. He was rocking back and forth on his heels, his arms wrapped around him. "Not our lieutenant."

Jack walked to the grave so he could get a look at the man squatting there. "Do we know you?" he asked.

The man nodded without looking up. "Used to."

Jack glanced around at Daniel, who shrugged.

"Tim was a soldier," the landlord said.

Jack hunkered down across the grave from the rocking man. He craned his head to look up into the man's face but the shadows hid the features.

"He was your lieutenant, too?" Daniel asked as he came to stand behind Jack.

"Knew him," the man said. He raised his head to look at Jack. "Knew you."

"Mother of the gods," Daniel whispered. "It's Corporal Saur."

Jack was so astonished he fell back, plopping his ass in the mud. His mouth had popped open the moment he recognized the tortured face of the man across from him and he couldn't make it work to speak.

"You know Tim?" the landlord inquired.

"Know me," Tim agreed, nodding.

Danny squatted down beside Jack then put out his hand. "Good to see you, corporal," he said.

Tim wiped his palm on his pants then took Daniel's hand. "Father Daniel," he greeted then looked away—his eyes going to the mound of dirt.

Jack still couldn't find his voice. He knew he must look like a catfish with his lips opening and closing without any sound issuing from his throat, but he was too astounded.

Timothy Saur had barely been alive when last he'd seen him, not expected to last the night after two weeks of brutal torture at the hands of their enemies. The boy's face had been destroyed, his body crippled by the horrible things that had been done to him. Shell-shocked, mute and as skinny as a rail, it was a miracle he had survived.

"Loved her," Tim said.

Daniel squeezed Tim's hand. "I'm sure you did, son."

"Hurts bad."

"I know," Daniel said.

Jack scrambled to his feet and walked quickly from the grave. There was too much sadness there, too many memories rearing their ugly heads to prod him. He heard someone coming behind him and knew it was Daniel.

"We've got to find him," Jack said, his voice breaking. "Before it's too late."

Chapter Ten

Declan finally lost his pursuers as the first rays of the sun began to spread across the eastern horizon. Tired beyond measure and so hungry he was lightheaded, he stopped on the outskirts of Jost to take off his coat and turn it inside out, button it so the claret color would not show. The cocked hat he stuffed into the saddlebags and secreted Spirit behind the blacksmith shop in a coral with two other nags. He thought for a moment about unsaddling the beast but a niggling voice in the back of his mind urged him not to.

There were few shops in Jost, but the tavern was open—as many taverns near a mining town always were—and it was to that establishment he headed. Knowing he looked the worse for wear was probably just as well. His hair was tousled and escaping the band that he used to tie it at the nape of his neck. His boots were caked with mud and there were dirty streaks on his hands and most likely his face as well. He would look the part of the drunkard he was going to pretend to be.

Stumbling into the inn, mumbling to himself, he wove his way to the bar and plopped his elbows on the top.

"Ale," he demanded in a slurred voice.

The man behind the bar who was the only one in the tavern came over to give him the stink eye.

"You got coin?" he asked.

Declan reached into his pocket for that last silver dollar and thought better of it. A man such as he was supposed to be would not have money of that amount.

And that was the only money he had.

He pulled his empty hand out of his pocket and grinned stupidly.

The barman snorted. "Go on with you," he snapped. "No money, no ale."

"I'll sweep your floors for a piece of bread," Declan told him.

"Don't need sweeping. Off with you, I said."

Weaving as he stood there to drive home the point he was a drunken derelict, Declan turned and braced his elbows on the bar as he looked around the room, He swung his head in an arch toward the barman.

"I'll wash your windows for an apple."

The man started to say something but then thought better of it. "Down on your luck, eh?" he asked instead.

"Woman threw me out," Declan said. He blew a raspberry. "Mean witch, she is."

"Aye, most of them are," the man said.

"Wipe the tables for a bite of anythin' to eat," Declan said, putting a whine into his voice.

Before the barman could respond to that, two men came through the door. Declan tensed for they were soldiers and both were armed. He turned away from them, lowered his head lest they recognize him.

"Ale," one of them said while the other hooked a foot around a chair leg and pulled it from the table.

The barman nodded and reached for two tankards. He drew the ale then carried it over to the table where both men were sitting.

"Long night, lads?" he asked.

"Aye," the one who had ordered the ale replied. "Chasing the Gypsy, we were."

"Almost caught him, too," the other one said. He took a long swing of the ale.

"Where was this?" the barman asked, folding his arms over his brawny chest.

"Out toward Wixenstead. Didn't catch him but we got his woman."

Declan flinched, molded his hands around the edge of the bar top. He squeezed his eyes shut, clenched his teeth.

"Had him an accomplice, eh?" the barman inquired.

"*Had* being the right word to use," the soldier said.

Declan slowly opened his eyes.

"Arrested her, did you?"

He lifted his head to look into the mirror over the bar—breathing stilled to hear the answer.

"Didn't get the chance. She blew her bloody head off to warn him, the slut."

He watched the blood drain from his face; his eyes went dead in the gleam of the lantern light.

"She's dead then?" the barman asked.

"As a fucking doornail," the soldier replied and laughed.

"Good riddance to a whoring collaborator," the other put in. "May she roast in hell."

Neither of the men sitting at the table had paid any attention to him when they came in. They didn't even look his way until he growled—low and mean deep in his throat.

"What's your problem?" one of them demanded.

He slowly reached up to unbutton his coat. His blood was pounding so fiercely in his ears he didn't hear anything else. Coat undone, he peeled it back, crossed his hands in front of him, took hold of the grips on the three-shot pistols stuck into the waistband of his pants then slowly turned. He saw their eyes widen as he brought up the pistols and pointed them. Watched as one soldier shot to his feet and went for his own weapon. That weapon never left its holster. Declan fired each of his pistols just once, but despite the terrible quaking inside his soul, his aim was true. Both iron balls went right between the soldiers' eyes.

For the first time in his life he had killed a man.

Nay, he thought. He had killed two and there was at least one more he would put down before the day was o'er.

The barman threw his hands up, backed away. "I want no trouble with you, milord," he said but Declan ignored him. He jammed the pistols in his waistband and headed for the door. When he passed the place where the two soldiers lay on their backs staring at what was beyond this world, he stopped, leaned over and pulled the rapier from the baldric of one of the dead men. With the blade clenched tightly in his hand he left the barman staring after him.

Running as fast as he could, he collided hard with the corral gate, ignored the pain then pushed it open. He ran to Spirit and swung himself onto the beast's broad back with a gasp. He was sure he'd broken a rib or two on the gate but he didn't give a gods-damn. Rapier in hand, he kicked the horse in the sides and sent it racing through the opening in the fence just as the sun chased the night away.

* * * * *

Hoping and praying Declan had not found out about Bess, Daniel and Jack began searching the areas Jack thought him most likely to have gone to ground. From having tracked him more times than he cared to remember, he had some idea where Declan would go. Which road or trail he would take. By the time he reached Jost, the sun was up and there was a crowd milling around in front of the tavern.

"That doesn't look good," Daniel said.

Riding up to the tavern, Jack called to group of men. "Something happen here?" he asked.

One man turned around. "The Gypsy was here," the man said with a broad grin. "Sent two troopers to their reward, he did."

Jack flinched. "He killed a man?"

"Kilt two of 'em," the man replied.

"Were they trying to arrest him?" Daniel queried.

"Might have been on their minds after they told him his woman was dead, but that was most likely the last things they thought afore he shot 'em 'tween the eyes," the man told him with a wink.

"He knows," Jack said with a groan.

"And he'll be going after Penry," Daniel stated.

* * * * *

Althea had been nervous since waking at first light but had no idea why. She had been pacing the battlements of her father's keep, her eyes turned to the west for hours now. The heavy downpour of the night before had put a slight chill to the morning air and she pulled her shawl closer around her. An image of Declan drifted across her mind's eye to send a shudder through her. It rippled from her head to her toes to chill her even more.

"Something has happened to you," she said. She leaned against the stone barrier. "I know it. I feel it."

It was the same feeling she'd had when she'd been locked in Penry's office at Gilhaven—beside herself with worry wondering what they were doing to the man she loved.

He was the Gypsy. There was no denying that. A part of her was shocked and dismayed, but another part was wildly thrilled at knowing he was such a dangerous and reckless outlaw. A criminal.

It was thrilling. Most certainly immoral.

Which made it all the more exhilarating.

The man she was going to marry was the stuff of legends. Tales were being told of him. Ballads were being written. He robbed from the rich and gave to the poor. How romantic was that?

As excited as she was at having such a man for her husband, she was filled with growing anxiety.

"You need to find something to occupy your mind," she mumbled. "Else you are going to go crazy imagining all manner of evil has befallen him."

The image of him wounded, hurt, lying on the coach road with no one to help him passed through her mind.

"Watch over him, *Mo Regina*," she prayed to the Triune Goddess, Morrigunia. "Keep him out of harm's way and bring him home safely to me."

Home. Arlington Castle would be their home once they were Joined.

That was where she needed to be, she thought. If he was hurt, that would be where he would go.

With that belief firmly in her mind, she left the battlements at a fast walk, picking up speed as she skipped down the steps to the great hall below. She called to the first servant she saw to run to the stables and have a horse and carriage saddled for her.

"Where are you going?" her father asked, sticking his head out of his study.

"To Arlington," she said. "Declan needs me."

Her father frowned as she hurried past him to take the stairs up to their living quarters.

"You have received word from him?" her father called after her.

"Aye, Papa," she lied. "And I must hurry."

She didn't know why but haste was of the utmost importance. She had to get to Declan as quickly as she could.

* * * * *

Streaking across the moors, cursing Royce Penry with every breath he took, Declan knew he had lost all reason, but he didn't care. He refused to picture Bess lying dead at the Hound and Stag, her lifeblood draining away. He pushed all thoughts of how she might have taken her life to save his out of his mind and instead filled it with the brutal, evil vengeance he had planned for the man responsible for her death. Every ounce of savagery that had been lurking in his genetic makeup had come roaring to the surface. He had no remorse for killing the two soldiers in Jost. They had deserved to die if for no other reason than they had spoken ill of her. Had cursed her and labeled her with ugly words that were not true. For that and that alone, they had forfeited their lives. His only regret was that he could not resurrect them and kill them yet again.

He knew he wasn't right in the head. He knew he was letting his temper control him. None of that mattered. He had a blood fever that tinged the world around him crimson red. The fever running through his body was scalding everything it touched. Fury had driven deep into what soul he had left and mercy was no longer a concept to him.

They would not be expecting him to come after them. He had some notion where Penry's troops were likely to be. Not a one of them was safe. He had four shots left between the two pistols and generally the squads were six-man teams. With certainty, he knew he could take down four of the men with the pistols; he was just that good a shot. The other two would meet their deaths by his sword hand. The thought of slashing and hacking his way through muscle, cartilage and bone—blood spraying high into the air—was almost orgasmic. Declan's bloodlust was high. He intended to keep it at that level until he could stand over Penry's mutilated body and piss in the bastard's dying face.

Lips peeled back from his teeth, jaw locked, his hand tight around the grip of the blade, he pushed Spirit as hard as he could across the purple moors and onto the coach road that led to Arlington Castle for that was where he knew Penry would have sent his men to arrest him.

* * * * *

Jack and Daniel were riding equally hard toward the same destination. They had learned in Pierpont that Penry had dispatched eight of his men to Declan's ancestral home before leading the rest of his troop to the Hound and Stag to ambush him. Four miles from Dead Man's Crossing they realized they were being followed by a lone rider who was pouring on the speed, coming on strong.

"Saur," Daniel shouted against the wind lashing their faces and saw Jack nod.

Just before they reached the bridge, Saur galloped up beside them. Single file, they thundered across the wide expanse then went flying three abreast toward Arlington Castle.

* * * * *

In the small town of Richter's Creek, the local sheriff and his deputy stood over the body of a man each had known since they were toddlers. It was the same man who had delivered the both of them and who—in his dotage—was long retired from the healing profession. Outside the doorway of the healer's cottage two local farmers were looking in.

"Who would have done this?" Matthew Kimble, the sheriff asked as he stared down at the dead man.

"Someone I'd like to catch and hang from the tallest tree," his deputy Andy Pine said between tight jaws.

They looked around at the young boy who had come to tell them of his grisly discovery. The boy—around twelve or thirteen—was panting heavily from his all-out run to the find the sheriff.

"Did you see anyone lurking about?" Kimble asked.

"Man. With. A. Wagon," the boy wheezed. "Woman."

"A man and woman driving a wagon?" Kimble wanted clarified.

The boy shook his head. "Soldier driving." He struggled to catch his breath. "Woman in the back of the wagon."

"Soldier?" Pine queried and reached out to grab the boy by the shoulder. "Are you sure, Randy?"

Looking up at his older brother, the boy nodded. "Wearing a uniform. It had one chevron on the sleeve."

"That signifies a private," Kimble said. "But why would he kill Healer Fisk?" Pine asked. He winced as his gaze went to the deep gash that had severed the old man's throat.

"Good question," Kimble replied. He squatted down in front of the boy. "Did you see the soldier enter Healer Fisk's house?"

Breathing more normally, the boy said, "I saw him coming out with the woman in his arms. She didn't look like she was awake and there was blood on her dress."

Kimble swept his attention over the bloody gauzes, basin filled with red-tinged water and instruments that had obviously been used to stitch a wound. He turned to Pine. "Obviously he brought the woman here to get patched up."

"Looks that way," Pine agreed.

Kimble got to his feet. "He's not going to be traveling fast in a wagon. We should have no trouble following the tracks," Kimble stated. He looked around at the men lurking in the doorway. "Brendon, mount up and ride to Gilhaven. We have no authority on a Governmental Regiment reservation but we can inform the local magistrate of what has happened. Mayhap he can send word higher up the chain of command for someone to look into this."

Brent turned to go.

"And Brent?" Kimble called out. "See if you can find out who the woman is."

"Aye, Sheriff," Brent agreed.

"It makes no sense for him to kill the healer," Pine said. "Why in the gods' names would he do that?"

"To keep Healer Fisk from telling anyone about the woman the bastard probably shot," Kimble said.

* * * * *

Althea sat in the back of her father's Landau with the leather top opened down the middle. It was beautiful day under the noon sky though clouds were gathering again in the west. As her driver cleared the rise just beyond Sadler's Mill and started the carriage down the incline, she had a magnificent view of the valley below. On the coach road she saw dust smoking behind a fleet rider. Had the beast beneath him been black she would have thought it to be Declan racing so wildly along the highway.

Movement to the west of the coach road made her look that way and she frowned. About a quarter mile ahead of the galloping rider, there was a group of redcoat riders winding their way along a twisting, turning forest trail. If they continued on the same trek, redcoats and rider would cross paths a quarter of a mile ahead.

A chill pebbled over her flesh. As surely as she sat there on the plush seat she knew the lone rider was Declan and that as soon as the troops saw him they would give chase. She got up to kneel in the facing seat and took hold of her driver's arm.

"How far are we from Arlington?" she queried.

"Two miles, Your Grace," he replied. "Mayhap a tad more."

"We must hurry, Danvers," she told him. "My husband's life may well be in danger!"

Snapping the reins to set the horses to a faster speed, the driver nodded to the east. "More riders, Your Grace," he said.

Althea twisted around in the seat and was disheartened to see three more riders converging on the scene.

"*Mo Regina*, please," she whispered. "Please don't let anything happen to Declan."

* * * * *

On the other side of the coach, streaking across the meadow, the three riders were advancing on the coach road.

"There he is," Jack shouted, pointing to the right.

"And there they are," Daniel yelled back.

"How many?" Jack demanded, casting a quick to the east.

"Eight," Tim replied.

All three men drew their pistols, drummed their heels hard against their mounts, and leaned forward in their saddles.

* * * * *

Barreling past a point where the forest dipped close to the coach road, Declan caught a flash of red up ahead a hundred feet or a little more and realized too late it was a squad of Royal Marines.

He brought the rapier down, thrust it between his thigh and the saddle to keep it safe then let go of Spirit's reins. He drew his pistols and cocked them, taking aim at the man leading the column. As soon as the man saw him, Declan pulled the trigger. The pistol bucked in his hand, the iron ball sped across the distance and hit the startled man squarely in the chest, knocking him from his horse.

* * * * *

Thundering down on the skirmish that was about to take place, Declan's three friends stared in horror as the first redcoat fell.

"Mother of the gods," Daniel shouted. "He drew first blood."

Tim groaned inwardly. Now they would have him for murder if not for being the Gypsy. There was only one thing they could do to save their friend and Jack voiced that assessment.

"Don't let any of them escape," Jack yelled.

"Not one," Tim whispered.

Taking careful aim from eighty yards away, Tim fired the first barrel of his flintlock and the shot went through the temple of the second man in line. He watched a third man fall before the remaining redcoats scattered among the trees.

With Declan firing at them from just south of the tree line and Daniel, Jack and Tim firing at them from the west, the troop quickly dismounted and ran for cover behind the closest tree trunk or rock they could find.

* * * * *

Althea could hear the gunfire and see the plumes of smoke wasting into the air. She saw the man she knew was her future husband wheel his horse around as the dirt beside the mount was kicked into the air from the shot coming at him from the trees.

"We don't dare get much closer, Your Grace," her driver shouted, sawing on the reins to slow the beasts.

"Do you have a weapon?" she asked.

"A coach pistol under the seat," he told her. "And one in my holster."

"Give me one of them," she ordered.

He snapped his head around to stare aghast at her. "Your Grace?" he questioned.

"Give me one of the gods-be-damned guns, Danvers," she snapped. "That's an order."

The driver pulled the gun from his holster and handed it behind him. She was glad to see it was a four-barrel flintlock—the very pistol her cousin Liam had taught her to use the summer before. Though she'd never killed anything and doubted she could, at least she could use the weapon to threaten one of the redcoats if necessary.

When the carriage rolled to a stop, Danvers secured the reins then bent over to retrieve the coach pistol from a box under the seat. He brought it out then glanced around at her.

"Are you sure about this, Your Grace?"

"We'll stay here unless we're needed," she said, standing up so she could see what was happening. They were at least one hundred yards from the action and the best effective range of a flintlock pistol was less than eighty yards. All they could do from that distance was divide the redcoats' attention.

* * * * *

The first ball hit him in the left shoulder, knocking the pistol from his hand. The second ripped into his right side. But it was the third that tore through his upper right thigh that hurt so badly he screamed with the agony as the iron ball went all the way through his flesh and into the side of his mount. The big horse screamed, as well, and went down—its rear legs buckling, neck thrashing. He barely had time to throw himself off the animal before it could crash to its side and pin him beneath it. Rolling away, he knew a moment of sheer panic before his forehead slammed into a large rock.

* * * * *

"No!" Jack bellowed. He leveled his pistol and fired twice in quick succession. The first shot missed but the second was true. It took down one of the redcoats that had a musket aimed at Declan's back.

To either side of him, Daniel and Tim were firing at the remaining four redcoats. His friends had no cover to hide behind as the soldiers did but were using their weapons to pin the bastards down as Jack raced toward Declan.

* * * * *

"Dear gods, no," Althea cried out when she saw Declan go down. She watched in horror as he rolled away from the fallen horse then lay still.

Before he could stop her, she had scrambled over the seat and was shoving Danvers out of her way as she grabbed up the reins. She popped them as hard as she could across the horses' rumps and the carriage lurched forward so forcefully the driver was pitched backward, tumbling over the seat and to the floorboard of the carriage.

"Haw," Althea shouted, snapping the reins and leaning forward as though that would make the steeds run faster. She saw one of the men who had come to Declan's aid galloping toward him while the other two kept firing into the tree line to keep the redcoats at bay.

* * * * *

As the carriage careened past them, Daniel looked around, startled by the movement. The burning sting of the iron ball pierced his belly and he looked down in surprise as blood began to mushroom from the blackened hole in his shirt.

"Get down," Tim shrieked at him but it was too late. A second ball dug its fiery way into his upper right chest.

He dropped to his knees—the jarring pain so intense it took his breath away. He had a vague impression of a man running toward him from the trees but that man went down as the side of his head exploded in a red mist.

As he began to pitch forward, he saw Tim reaching for his pistol. Tim had tossed both of his aside. There was only one shot left in his own gun but Saur was welcome to it.

"Make it count," he said before he hit the ground.

* * * * *

Jack used the remaining shot in his pistol to twist around in the saddle and send that iron ball right through the mouth of a yelling soldier as he ran toward Declan. He had no idea how many of the Royal Marines were left standing—or running as the case might be—but he was already jumping from Warlock's back to get to Declan's side.

His friend was as still as death with blood pouring from his wounds. The once-white lace at his throat was scarlet red and his head was lying in a crimson pool.

"Please gods, please," he begged as he ran to Declan and fell to his knees. "Please let him be alive."

242

* * * * *

His ammunition gone, Tim pulled the dagger from the sheath at his thigh and stared running pell-mell toward the remaining soldier who was loading his musket. Though it was hard for him to run—the agony so intense in his twisted legs—there was no way in hell he was going to allow the bastard to shoot either Declan or Jack. He was about twenty feet from his intended target. The soldier's musket was primed. He was bringing it up to his shoulder, sighting it.

Then there was a smart crack and the man lurched as though being pulled backward then pitched sideways to the ground.

Tim snapped his head in the direction from which the shot had come and was amazed to see a comely woman standing on the driver's seat of a carriage that sped past. She had her arm straight out in front of her and it was as steady as a rock. Slowly she turned her head toward him. The smile that stretched across her beautiful face would have scared far more people than his tortured one ever had.

"See to your friend," she ordered him before she hiked up her skirt and jumped to the ground.

"Damn," he muttered.

* * * * *

Daniel was dying. He knew he was and had accepted it. He'd managed to roll over to his back so he could look up at the blazing sun directly overhead. He tracked a hawk gliding along the thermals and felt at peace. Soon, he would be soaring with the other wispy spirits he could see flittering about the bright azure sky.

"Father Daniel," Tim said as he dropped down beside him.

"It's all right," Daniel told him. "Really, it is."

He started to cough and blood bubbled over his lips but he no longer felt the crippling, burning pain that had been eating at his gut.

Tim gently ran an arm under his head and lifted him.

"Listen," Daniel said, reaching up a shaking hand to grab the front of Tim's coat. "Take off my coat and take it over to Jack."

"What?" Tim asked; his mismatched eyes filled with tears.

"Take my coat and put it on Declan. Give his to me," Daniel said quietly but firmly. "Bring me his hat and his kerchief if it isn't in his coat."

"Father, please…" Tim began.

"Make them think it's me," Daniel said. He pulled with as much strength as he had left. "They have to believe I'm the Gypsy."

What he was asking seemed to be striking a chord in the younger man for Tim nodded.

"And tell him…" Daniel pulled Tim down closer to him. "Tell him I always loved him."

* * * * *

Tim felt as much as he saw the light leave Daniel Rees's body. The ex-priest's eyes stilled as he stared at what had been waiting in the Afterlife for him. There was a slight smile on his blood-streaked lips and a peacefulness to his features that said whatever it was he was seeing was good.

Choking off a sob, Tim cradled the dead man to his chest and hunkered there—rocking him as though he were a child.

They have to believe I'm the Gypsy.

That made sense to Tim. Father Daniel's final act was as unselfish as the man himself had always been. His good name had long since been taken from him so what was one more crime laid at his doorstep? In taking on the mantle—the claret velvet coat—of the highwayman, Declan Farrell was in the clear.

No greater love, Tim thought.

Slowly he turned his head so he could look to where Declan had fallen. None of it would matter much if Declan had not survived his wounds. He saw both Jack and the unknown woman kneeling beside Declan then watched as Jack ran his arms under Dec's back and knees and lifted him from the ground.

"Be alive," Tim said. "Please, be alive."

He watched Jack carry their friend to the carriage. The woman's driver leaned down to accept Declan's limp body then turn to lay him on one of the seats. Jack pulled himself into the driver's seat; the woman grabbed her skirts in one hand then held her other for her driver to hoist her into the back of the carriage.

"Wait," Tim shouted. He gently laid Daniel down then got clumsily to his feet. He thought Jack would leave him before he could do what Daniel had asked.

"Hurry up," Jack barked. "He's losing a lot of blood."

"His coat," Tim yelled back. "I need his coat and kerchief."

"His...?" Jack snarled but the woman in the back of the carriage with Declan must have understood for she said something to her driver and between them they began stripping the coat from Declan.

As he ran past the spot where Declan had fallen, he barely broke stride as he bent over to retrieve the cocked hat. He was only a few feet from the carriage when the woman tossed the coat to him. The tail of it was saturated with blood.

"I stuffed the kerchief into his pocket. Make sure you hide the other man's coat," she ordered him. The words were barely out of her mouth before Jack whipped the horses into motion.

As the carriage rattled up the coach road, Declan Farrell's black steed galloped in its wake.

Chapter Eleven

"The ball went through the upper part of his thigh and through a great portion of the muscle. I am not sure I will be able to save his leg," the healer told Lord Edward.

"You'd fucking better try," Edward snarled.

"Ned," Jamie said quietly. "He'll do everything he can for the lad."

"It will take months—perhaps as long as a year—for him to recover if I can, indeed, save the leg."

"You do what needs to be done," Edward told him. "Money is no object."

"I doubt money is of any concern to the man, Edward," Lord Alastair who—worried about his daughter—had arrived at Arlington Castle long before Althea.

They were all standing outside the room at Arlington Castle where Declan laid unconscious and in critical condition.

The front of Lady Althea Standfield's gown was bloodstained from the deep gash in Declan's head as Jack raced them to the keep. The healer had assured her head wounds bleed freely and that injury would not do in the man she loved.

Tim's clothing was likewise bloody. It had taken some doing to get Daniel's coat off him and put Declan's on. He'd tossed the hat to one side, made sure the kerchief was tied around Daniel's neck and that the silver dollar was still in the pocket of the velvet coat. A moment before he mounted his horse, a ghostly voice whispered in his ear.

Drag a soldier to the fallen horse. Take one of theirs with you.

The words had made perfect sense to Tim. All the mounts would be accounted for save the big black. Legends would crop up over the disappearance of the Gypsy's famed steed.

Jack had said nothing since arriving at the keep. He was pacing from one end of the corridor to the other. When anyone approached him, his set face and low growl warned them away.

"I would like you to send for the priest tonight," Althea told Lord Edward.

"No," Jack snapped. "He would not want that."

"Not to perform the Joining," Althea said. "But to bless him. Would you agree he needs all the help we can give him?"

"No wedding ceremony," Jack said. "The man is in mourning."

Althea nodded. "I understand he needs to grieve for his friend."

"Aye, for him, too," Jack stated, his eyes locked on her.

"There is someone else for whom he mourns?" Lord Alastair inquired.

"For her," Tim said quietly.

"Her?" Lord Alastair repeated then looked to his daughter. "To whom is he referring, Althea?"

"The young woman at the tavern?" Althea queried. She put a hand to her mouth. "She is dead?"

"She killed herself to warn him away from the inn," Jack told her, wondering how she knew of Bess. "They would have shot him down there and then had she not given her life to prevent it."

"Dear gods," Althea said. She turned her head toward the door behind which Declan lay. "The poor man." She shook her head. "He will blame himself."

"Always will," Tim stated.

Althea turned her gaze to the scarred man standing in the shadows. She had not recoiled at the sight of him—which had surprised the others. Instead, she looked him in the eyes when she spoke to him and had at one point put her hand on his arm to thank him for thinking of exchanging the coats.

"Father Daniel's idea," he had explained.

"The defrocked priest?" Lord Edward questioned.

"Aye, Your Grace," Jack replied.

"Thank the gods he was with you," Lord Jamie said.

"He gave up what was left of his name to protect your godson," Jack said, a muscle jumping in his jaw. "You should be thankful he was there to provide the means to throw the trail off Declan."

"And we are, McGregor," Lord Edward assured him.

"Declan will want his body brought here for burial," Jack said. "So do I."

"As do we all," Althea echoed.

"I'll send word to the garrison," Lord Jamie suggested. "I don't know that Penry will allow it but it's worth a try. He's going to be infuriated that Declan won't stand trial and be hanged for…"

"Did you not hear what I said, Lord James?" Jack all but shouted at him. "They were going to murder Declan at the Hound and Stag. There wasn't going to be a trial."

"And Penry will answer for that," Lord Edward said. "I will see to it."

Jack grabbed two handfuls of his hair, put his back to the wall and slid down it to drop to his ass. He lowered his head and made a soft keening sound that made everyone there feel a portion of his distress.

"As long as Penry is alive, he is going to pose a threat to Declan," Jack told them. "And in the condition he is now, Dec is defenseless against that crazed son of a bitch."

"Not so," Tim stated.

"Your friend is right," Althea agreed. "Everyone here will protect him until he is on his feet again."

"Twenty-four hours a day, seven days a week," Lord Jamie asserted. "Until he no longer needs us to shield him."

"And then?" her father asked. "What happens then?"

"Then Declan will go after Penry and kill him," Lord Edward replied.

* * * * *

Declan could feel someone looking at him but he would not open his eyes. It was only when he was sure he was alone that he cracked open his lids to stare silently at the ceiling.

He didn't move as much as a fraction of an inch for even the very breaths he took brought brutal pain to his body. His shoulder throbbed. His side ached. Those were discomforts with which he could live, but the excruciating torment undulating like a hungry viper through his thigh was slowly killing him.

He was incredibly weak, helpless, felt he had lost so much blood that—by rights—he should not be alive anyway. The fever that had come on even as he was being brought home to Arlington had nearly accomplished what the three iron balls that had ripped into his body had not. For over a week he had slept like the dead as poison ravaged his system and infection set in. Often he had awakened when either Jack or Jasper had plunged him into an ice water bath in an attempt to lower the raging fever. Water had been drizzled into his mouth along with a foul-tasting concoction the healer told him would help the infection. Dying pieces of his flesh had been cut from his thigh while Jack, Jasper, Tim and whatever servant was handy held him down. White-hot blades had been applied to his wounds to cauterize them.

The keep was often filled with his screams.

In between bouts of torture meant to heal him, he listened to Althea's soft voice singing to him, reciting poetry, recounting tales of the heroes of old in between her washing his face, arms and chest with cooling cloths. She told him of her childhood, her pets, her favorite horse, the parrot that could only say *pretty boy*.

When they thought him unconscious or asleep, he had listened to his father and godfather, Jack and Tim and Lord Alastair discussing his future.

Or lack thereof, he thought as he listened for the person who had been watching over him to close his bedchamber door softly behind their departure. Slowly he cracked his eyelids apart a tiny bit. Once he knew he was alone, he opened them all the way.

It was either sunset or sunrise. He had no way to tell. The drapes were drawn together but there was a crack between the panels where a pale red glow showed. Not that it mattered what time of day it was anyway. One second oozed into another then trickled into a minute then bled into an hour before pooling into another horrid day.

Just another bloody layer of hell compacting him.

They were expecting him to accept the horror of what had happened and get on with his life. To take his medicine, shut his mouth and swallow it—along with any hopes of the future he might have had.

He followed a crack in the ceiling that he saw every time he opened his eyes. The room was growing darker so it wouldn't be long before he couldn't see it. It would be much longer after that before someone came in to light the lantern beside his bed and Lord Jamie would park his ass in the chair by the bed and continue reading aloud the boring novel he had been forcing on his godson for several days now.

No doubt in the hope he would open his eyes and tell him stop.

Jamie was evil that way.

"We must keep his mind occupied," the healer had told his father. "I firmly believe even in unconsciousness he can hear us. We must anchor him here to our world and not let him slip into the next."

He sighed deeply although it hurt like hell to do so. He had no intention of shuffling off his mortal coil and following Bess into the Afterlife.

Not yet, anyway. He had to live if for no other purpose than to put Royce Penry in his grave.

A grave he intended to dig with his own two hands. He would stand over Penry and piss in the bastard's face. That was what had kept him from succumbing to his wounds on the trip back to Arlington. What kept him alive when the iron shots were removed and his thigh was cauterized? What kept him from giving in to the pain and the horrendous grief eating at his very soul? That once again he failed to protect someone under his care.

But first he had to regain his strength. He had to heal and he knew from what the healer said that was going to take many months of recuperating. Months more of physical therapy to regain the use of his leg.

If he ever did.

The fear of being a cripple for the rest of his life was a daunting thought. It scared him. Preventing him from sleeping—though he pretended to. He was exhausted from lack of the very sleep in which his watchers believed he was indulging.

So engrossed in staring at the ceiling, he didn't hear the door open and didn't realize he was no longer alone until she spoke.

"You're awake."

Startled, he jerked—snapping his eyes down to Meg's. The movement caused hideous pain to ripple through his thigh and he could not stop the whimper that shamed him.

"Here," she said and slid her soft, cool hand under his neck to lift his head from the pillow. She placed the vial to his lips. "Drink, Deckie."

He clamped his lips tightly together so she could not pour the drug into his mouth.

"You are hurting, sweeting," she said. "This will help."

It would do more harm than good, he thought, for it would stop the pain or—at the least—dim it to a manageable level but that wasn't what he wanted. He wanted to feel the pain. It was a constant reminder of what he had lost.

Who he had lost.

She had died for him. He'd overheard Jack talking and knew Danny had died for him, too. He would suffer for them. Atone for his inability to keep them safe.

"Deckie, please," Meg said. "I can't stand to see you hurting. Drink the tenerse, dearling."

He held her pleading gaze with an unblinking one of his own but kept his mouth firmly closed. Even when she leaned over and put her hand on his cock over the coverlet he kept as still as he could.

"I can ease you, milord," she said and he knew she meant well. She always did but her hand on his hurt deep in his soul. He started to open his mouth to ask her not to touch him but the door opened.

"Get your filthy hand off my husband!"

Meg jerked away from the bed, her head swinging around, the vial of tenerse clutched against her chest.

"What is that?" Althea asked, storming into the room. She held out her hand. "Let me see."

"Nothing to harm him, Your Grace," Meg said. She was trembling violently.

"Give it to me," Althea demanded.

Meg handed over the vial. Althea looked down at it then slowly up at her. "Tenerse?" she queried. "Is that what is in here?"

"Aye, Your Grace," Meg answered. "'Twouldn't hurt him. I'd never do nothing to hurt him."

"Get out," Althea ordered. "And stay out. If you come near my husband again, I will have you fired and you will find yourself unemployable in this country or any other."

Meg bobbed a hasty curtsy then ran from the room, sobbing.

Althea stared at the vial for a moment then slipped it into the pocket of her gown. She squared her shoulders then came to stand beside his bed.

"It's nice to see those pretty blue eyes looking up at me," she sat gingerly on the bed. "How are you feeling?"

He didn't want to talk. He just wanted to be left alone and he thought if he stared silently at her, gave no indication he was even listening, she'd leave.

"Don't do that, Declan," she said softly. She gently laid a hand on his arm. "Don't close yourself off to the world. There are a lot of people in it that love you."

He couldn't stand looking at her caring, understanding face or see the compassion in her eyes so he slowly closed his.

"All right," she said, rubbing his arm tenderly. "I won't press."

She rose from the bed and he had to bite his tongue from crying out for the slight motion—even as careful as she'd been—sent ripples of agony through his thigh.

"The healer will be in before retiring for the night. Mayhap you will talk to him if not to me," she said and he could hear the hurt in her voice.

She did not merit such treatment. She'd done nothing to cause the horrible ache that was flooding his soul. She'd been as innocent of the machinations their fathers had set into motion as had he. Bess had not given her life because of Althea. She deserved better.

He opened his eyes to watch her walk slowly to the door, her shoulders bowed.

"Thea?" he called out and the hopeful look that transformed her lovely face when she turned around, shamed him.

"Aye, my love?" she answered but stayed where she was.

His mouth was dry; his throat hurt but he got the words out. "Thank you."

"You are most welcome, Declan," she said. "If you need anything, want anything…"

He tried to smile—he truly did—but his face would not cooperate. Instead, he managed to lift his hand partially from the cover. "I'm hungry."

Her radiant smile put the sun to shame.

"I'll get you some broth," she said. "Straight away."

As she left she was humming to herself and for some reason that made him feel so ashamed. Her happiness over such a minor thing ate into his conscience like acid. He thought of what he had planned, the awful, treacherous deception he would have put her through with the fake wedding ceremony. The grief he would have handed to her with his phony death strategy. The hurt when she had no body to bury, no grave at which to mourn.

Aye, he felt lower than the slimy belly of a slug.

She had called him her husband on numerous occasions since that day she and Jack had brought him back to Arlington. In her mind they were already married though the Joining had been put on hold until he could stand at the altar to accept her as his wife.

Not that he ever would. Now more than ever he was determined not to go through with the actual wedding. He didn't deserve a woman as good, as kind and loyal as Althea. She did not deserve a lying, cheating bastard like him.

"I hear you're awake," Jack said from the doorway. "Can I come in?"

"I don't know," he mumbled. "Can you?"

Jack rolled his eyes. "Don't start that correct Serenian to me, Farrell. Can I come in or not?"

"Why?"

That stopped Jack in mid-step. "Whatcha mean why?"

His throat was so dry he could barely get the words out, the sounds raspy even to his own ears.

"Are you here to rail against me for going after the redcoats by myself?"

"You know you were a fucking fool," Jack said, coming to the bed. He wrapped his large hand around the tall cherry wood four-poster. "Reminding you of it seems pointless."

"I wasn't in my right mind," he replied.

"When have you *ever* been in your right mind?" Jack queried.

Althea came bustling in with a tray upon which sat a bowl and a cup. "Here we go. I brought chicken broth and hot tea. The healer said if you keep them down, you can have soft-scrambled eggs and toast tomorrow morn."

"Whoopie," he said with a grunt.

"Maybe you should throw in some pablum as well, Your Grace," Jack quipped.

"What did I tell you, Jackie?" she said as she put the tray down on Declan's bedside table. "My name is Thea."

That surprised Declan and he turned his eyes up to Jack, raised a brow and silently mouthed '*Jackie?*'

"We had a long talk, milady and me," Jack said with a smirk.

"Milady and I," she corrected.

"Milady and I," Jack repeated dutifully.

Althea frowned. "We will need to lift you to a sitting position, Dec," she said. "Do you think you can endure that?"

Over her head Jack grinned and silently mouthed the nickname then had to purse his lips together tightly to keep from laughing.

"I can try," he told her.

"Jackie, go around on the other side. I'll take this arm and we'll…"

"Let me."

Declan swung his attention to the door. Tim Saur was standing there with a pitcher and basin.

"Oh, Timmy," Althea said. "The water. I had forgotten all about it. Please put it on the table if you will."

"Aye, Thea," he replied and both Dec and Jack exchanged surprised looks.

"I thought since you were awake you might like a sponge bath," Althea told him. "It might help you to sleep better."

"I need a bath," he said.

"Aye, well when you can stand Jack will help you," she said.

Dec scowled. "Not getting naked anywhere with that one," he said.

"Mayhap Meg…" Jack began.

"No," Dec and Althea said at the same time.

Jack held his hands up. "Scratch that, then."

"I'm glad you're here, Tim," Declan told him.

"You remembered him?" Jack asked.

"I heard you and him talking when you thought I was asleep. You said something and I put two and two together," Dec explained. "I'm sorry I didn't recognize you at the stable, Tim."

Tim shrugged as he skirted the bed to join Althea. He smiled at her and although it was a ghastly grin she didn't seem to notice. She patted him on the arm, bid him be careful with their patient then stepped back.

"Gently, lads," she said. "That thigh is the very devil."

Bracing himself as Jack took him under one arm and Tim the other, he sucked in a breath.

"Ready?" Jack asked.

"As I'm ever gonna be," Dec replied.

"On three," Jack said, looking at Tim. "One. Two…"

Before the three was recited the two men hefted him upward in the bed. The pain was horrendous and it was all he could do not to scream as his thigh dragged across the sheet. They steadied him as he sat there panting, sweat pouring off him in just that fraction of a second.

"You said three," he accused.

"Such a baby," Jack said. "Didn't I tell you he was a baby, Tim?"

"You did." Tim agreed and when Dec shot him a narrowed look, the man winked and Dec had to steel himself not to flinch for the wink made the other eye roll in its socket.

He had once been a handsome young man, Dec thought. With his russet hair and bright blue eyes, the camp followers flocked around him like flies to honey. The destruction the Diabolusians wrought upon Timothy Saur was an evil all until itself.

Tim seemed to intercept Dec's thoughts and turned away but not before Althea reached out to wrap her arm through his.

"I have a favor to ask of you, Timmy," she said and when he nodded, she asked if he would fetch her another pillow from the armoire. "It will make it more comfortable for him to sit up if we put a pillow behind his back. Don't you think? I don't want to move him again so I can pull up the ones upon which he's been lying."

"Aye, Thea," Tim said and headed for the armoire.

"Not the thickest one, now," she said. "That would be too much I think."

He wanted to tell her to pull the gods-be-damned things out from under the small of his back for he was bent in such a way it was putting ungodly pressure on his thigh but kept his mouth shut. She was running the show.

"You need help eating?" Jack asked, drawing his attention to him.

"Are you going to spoon-feed me now, too?" Dec grumbled.

"No, I am going to do that," Althea answered, taking the pillow from Tim.

"I can feed myself," he told her.

"I'm sure you can, but humor me," she said.

"She's the boss," Jack said.

"Now, lads, gently lean him forward so I can place the pillow behind him."

Once more preparing himself for the pain, he was surprised when none came.

"That was perfect," she told his friends. "Now, you boys can go."

"Aye, milady," Jack agreed.

After the men left, Althea came around to the other side of the bed, picked up the bowl of broth and the spoon then sat down beside him.

"I can do it," he groused.

"Let me do something for you, Declan," she said. "Let me spoil you."

"Stop," he said.

Her smooth forehead crinkled. "Stop what?" she questioned.

"Stop trying to make it better," he answered. "You can't. I know you want to, but you can't."

She dredged the spoon into the broth, her head down. "Only because you don't want it to be. You take a perverse pleasure in the pain because you believe you deserve it."

That surprised him. She understood what he was feeling. When she lifted the spoon and pushed it toward his mouth, he obediently opened his lips.

"Have you ever had a sour cream tart with plum compote?" she asked in a conversational tone.

"No," he said. The broth was good. Just hot enough and rich with butter.

"I asked Suz if she would prepare one for the noon meal tomorrow. I gave her our cook's recipe."

She was on a first name basis with the staff, he thought. That, too, was a surprise.

"What's in it?" he asked in between spoonfuls of the broth.

"Well, plums, of course," she said.

"Duh," he grumbled.

"You'll like it," she said. "Your father says you are fond of plum brandy and wine so I'm sure you will enjoy the tart."

"Probably," he said.

They didn't speak for a while as he finished off the broth in between sips of the hot tea. She had surprised him again by adding honey, lemon, a stick of cinnamon and a few cloves to the brew.

"Cinnamon and honey have curative powers," she told him.

He thought of the toddy Bess had made for him and his heart twisted brutally in his chest.

"It should also help you sleep," she said, putting the empty bowl on the tray and placing the spoon beside it.

"I sleep well enough," he lied.

She folded her hands in her lap. "I hear you at night, Declan," she stated. "I hear every groan and every gasp."

"Then change rooms if I'm bothering you," he snapped.

"That is not what I meant and you know very well it isn't," she snapped right back at him.

He wanted so badly to rub his thigh but he knew if he did, the pain would only get worse. He needed to lie down again but didn't think he could do it on his own. As though she was inside his head, she got up from the bed.

"I'll send Jack and Tim up to help you," she said. "Obviously I cannot."

He opened his mouth to apologize but she was moving like a force of nature across the room. He had hurt her feelings—again—and felt like a cad.

Reaching up, he scrubbed his hand down his face. The pain was so intense sweat was dripping down his temples. He wondered if she had noticed—figured she most likely had but didn't mention it out of politeness.

Or...

Because she was allowing his male stubbornness without comment.

That was a woman's way.

* * * * *

"How is he today?" Lord Alastair inquired as he took a seat at the dining table to break his fast.

"The healer drained his thigh again," Edward replied. He looked up from scoring the ham steak on his plate. "Did you not hear his bellow?"

"No, thank the gods I did not nor did my daughter," Alastair answered. "We were up early this morn for a ride along the river." He took a sip of his coffee before diving into the vast amount of food he had piled upon his plate. "We had things to discuss."

"Such as the postponement of the wedding," Edward stated. He stuffed the ham into his mouth. "That cannot be helped, Alastair."

"We understand that, Edward, but I believe it is time she returned home and let Declan have his privacy."

"Privacy to do what?" Edward asked.

"To realize where his priorities must lie. He needs to come to terms with the eventuality of the Joining and forget about..." He waved his fork. "Well, you know."

"The dead girl."

"Aye," Alastair agreed. "The dead girl."

"He is in mourning, Lord Alastair," Jamie said from the sideboard where he was filling his plate. "For the girl and his friend."

"I understand that," Lord Alastair acknowledged. "But it has been three weeks and he has made no attempt to get out of bed." He cocked a shoulder. "That can't be good for his recovery."

"It isn't and I have told him as much," his host agreed. "The healer, however, believes he should remain abed for another few days. The wound is not healing as well as it should and he wants to try a poultice that will help to draw out the poisons."

"The boy is in a great deal of discomfort," Jamie reminded him.

"We are aware of that, James," Edward grumbled. "The entire household was more than aware of it this morn."

Jamie pursed his lips as he took his seat and shot his old friend a look that irritated Edward.

"We cannot continue to mollycoddle him, Jamie," Edward declared, putting down his fork. "He is a grown man."

"He is a man in mourning," Althea said as she entered the dining hall. "Allow him his grief and don't add to it by expecting more of him than he is capable of giving at the moment."

"Althea," her father said with a gasp. "That is no way to speak to His Grace."

"Lord Edward knows I mean him no disrespect. On the contrary. I speak to him in the same way I speak to you, Papa," she told him. "He will be, after all, a second father to me just as..." She smiled across the table at Jamie. "Lord James will be a third parental figure as he has been a secondary one to my husband."

"Then what do you suggest we do to tear him out of this mental morbidity into which he has fallen, Althea?" Edward asked.

"Give him time," she replied. "He will rouse himself out of that 'mental morbidity,' as you call it."

"And when he does?" Jamie asked.

"You know well what happens then, Lord Jamie," she answered with a long sigh.

"He'll set out after Penry," Edward said.

Iverson came into the dining hall and over to Lord Edward. He leaned down to whisper in his master's ear. What he said sent a tremor of worry through Edward. He looked up at the servant as Iverson straightened.

"Show him to my study and tell him I will be with him shortly," he ordered.

"Aye, Your Grace," Iverson replied.

Edward picked up his napkin to wipe his lips.

"Has something happened?" Jamie asked.

"It seems we have a guest from the garrison at Gilhaven," Edward replied, pushing his chair back.

"Penry is here?" Lord Alastair asked. His beefy face had turned pale.

"No," Edward replied. "He announced himself as Captain Gunderson of the Governmental Regiment Military Tribunal."

"Want me to accompany you?" Jamie inquired. "As your personal assistant, of course."

Edward nodded. "That might be best." He glanced at Althea and saw that her face was even paler than her father's. "I'm sure this is nothing."

Althea's bottom lip trembled. "Protect him, Your Grace."

"With my last breath, milady," Edward replied.

Walking beside his friend, Jamie lowered his voice. "Do you think this man is here to question the boy?"

"I pray not for one look at that wound and we will have a hard time explaining how he came by it," Edward replied.

"A hunting accident?"

"Mayhap or a misfire while cleaning his weapon."

"Aye, that would work as well," Jamie said. "Should I go apprise him of this?"

"Let's wait until we see what the captain wants," Edward answered.

The young man waiting in Edward's study was tall, well built and quite good looking. He had thick dark brown hair and intelligent green eyes. He had excellent posture and as soon as Edward entered the room, he clicked the heels of his highly polished black boots together and bowed crisply.

"Captain Rand Gunderson at your service, Your Grace. It is an honor to make your acquaintance," he said in a thick Uigingeach accent.

"Welcome to Arlington Castle, Captain Gunderson," Edward said. He held out his hand to indicate Jamie. "May I present my personal assistant, Lord James Giddens?"

Another clicking of the heels, another bow. "Lord James, a pleasure."

"Please, sit," Edward said, going to his favorite chair in this room.

"Thank you," the captain replied and perched on the edge of the seat he took.

"I hope you had a pleasant ride from Gilhaven," Edward told him.

"Most pleasant, thank you. This area of Bhreatain is quite lovely and the keep is an architectural beauty. You must be proud of your ancestral home."

"We are," Edward replied. "May I offer you some refreshment?"

"I appreciate your offer but thank you, no. I am here on official business," Gunderson explained.

"Then how may we help?" Edward asked, trying not to let his worry show.

"You are familiar with a man by the name of Royce Penry?" Gunderson inquired.

"Aye," Edward said. "I've known the Marquis since he was a boy. My son attended the same boarding school with Captain Penry. Why do you ask?"

"I'm afraid he is no longer Captain Penry," Gunderson told him. "Penry is a fugitive from justice."

"Beg pardon?" Edward asked, sitting forward in his chair.

"He was relieved of his duty when he failed to report back to the garrison after a failed attempt to arrest the man the locals are calling the Gypsy," Gunderson explained. "I have it on good authority that Penry set a trap for the highwayman with the full intention of executing him rather than taking him into custody to stand trial."

"I had heard that as well," Jamie put in.

"Aye, well, that is not the way things are done. Had he succeeded in his ill-advised plan he would have been arrested himself for ordering the thief's murder," Gunderson said. "As it was, he was responsible for the unfortunate demise of a civilian."

"The landlord's daughter at the Hound and Stag," Jamie said.

Gunderson turned to look at Jamie. "You seem to know a lot about this."

"Servants gossip, Captain," Jamie told him. "But I did not know Penry had gone missing."

"Do you think mayhap he met with foul play?" Edward asked, hoping that was the case.

"One of his soldiers came forward to tell us about what happened at the inn," Gunderson replied. "He told us Penry had been acting irrationally for quite some time. Apparently he was obsessed with the highwayman, intent on catching him. Told several of his men that he knew who the Gypsy was and that the county would be shocked when they learned his identity. Penry suspected the landlord's daughter and the thief were lovers and that was the reason he set the trap for him that evening."

"Did Penry tell anyone the name of the man he suspected?" Edward asked.

"Regrettably he did not."

"More's the pity, eh?" Edward queried.

"True."

"So what do you think happened to Penry?" Jamie questioned.

"Here's what we know," Gunderson said. "He tied the young woman to her bed with a musket beside her and positioned two soldiers—including the one who came forward to tell us of the incident—at her windows. She must have loved the highwayman dearly for as soon as he was spotted riding toward the inn, she managed to get her finger on the trigger of the musket. She fired, warning away her lover."

"Dying to protect him," Edward said quietly.

"She did. Penry then dispatched all but one of his men to go after the highwayman. The one left behind apparently was ordered to dig a grave for the young woman." Gunderson shook his head. "That, in itself, is a vile thing to do. No proper burial, no prayers spoken over her body. Just a tumble into the wet ground to be covered with mud. Disgraceful."

"He was covering up evidence," Jamie said.

"Was the soldier who dug the grave the same one who came to tell you of this nefarious business?" Edward asked.

"No and we can't find that man, either. Apparently he fled along with Penry."

"Have you any idea where Penry might have gone?"

"We know he visited his family home at Norus Keep but only to steal money and valuables from his father's safe. We tracked him from Norus to Carbondale. From there, we lost him. He could be anywhere in the world by now."

"How can we help?" Edward asked.

"I was told Lady Althea Standfield is staying with you," Gunderson stated.

"She is," Edward replied. "I'm sure you know she and my son, Declan, are betrothed."

"I do know that, Your Grace, and I also know there was no love lost between your son and Penry."

"Far from it," Jamie mumbled.

"Why are you asking after Lady Althea?" Edward queried.

"When questioned, Penry's former aide-de-camp, Sergeant Vincent Breslyn, informed us Penry had gone to Standfield Hall to ask for Her Grace's hand," Gunderson replied. "He also indicated Penry was rather severely rebuffed."

"That's putting it mildly," Edward said. "Lord Alastair was aghast at the man's ridiculous assumption that he was worthy of Lady Althea."

"Quite so," Gunderson said, coughing into his hand.

"I still fail to see why you are bringing her into the matter," Edward told him. "She barely knows the man."

"We believe he may try to contact her," Gunderson answered.

"Why would he?" Jamie asked. "As His Grace just told you, she hardly knows Penry."

"I understand, Lord James, but bear with me as I explain my thought processes. He's a man on the run," Gunderson said. "Deep in his cups, he expressed more than once his admiration and esteem for milady. Sergeant Breslin tells me Penry mumbled something about taking the girl away from him. I assume he was referring to Lady Althea and the 'him' would have been your son. In his present state of mind, he might well try to reach out to her." He spread his hands. "At this point, I know it seems as though we are grasping at straws but I want to catch him before he does anything else."

"Anything else?" Edward repeated. "What does that mean?"

"I am not at liberty to say at this time. We are looking into another matter that I believe ties in with Penry's disappearance."

"I see," Edward said. "So you would like to speak with Lady Althea?"

"If that wouldn't be too much trouble," Gunderson answered.

"No trouble at all," Edward said and looked to Jamie. "Would you fetch Her Grace for Captain Gunderson, James?"

"Of course, Your Grace," Jamie replied.

Watching his friend leave the study, Edward said, "I do hope she will be of some assistance to you."

"So do I, milord," Gunderson agreed.

* * * * *

Althea paced the solarium with the book she'd been reading pinched closed on her index finger. She had been nervous speaking to the captain but he had been respectful and did not seem in the least suspicious. He had, however, asked after her betrothed.

"Declan?" she'd asked, clutching the book tight to her bosom as she sat in the study with the soldier. "Do you needs speak to him, as well?"

"Only if you think he can shed any light on Penry's location."

She'd shaken her head. "No, he and Royce Penry are not on speaking terms. I'm sure he would have no idea where the man could have gone."

"Is he here at Arlington?"

"Penry?" she'd gasped.

The captain had smiled. "No, Your Grace. Lord Declan. Is he here?"

"Aye," she said. "But he has one of his migraines and…"

"Say no more," the captain said, holding up his hand. "I, too, suffer from that demonic malady. I feel for him."

"I wish I could be of more help to you," she said. She wanted to get rid of him before she said something to give herself away.

"Myself, as well," he acknowledged. "It was a long shot but it had to be taken."

She flinched and hoped he hadn't noticed. Her mind went back to the soldier she had killed in the meadow. Had to bite her tongue to keep from whimpering at the memory.

"Well, I thank you, Your Grace," he said, getting to his feet. He bowed slightly, clicked his heels then reached for her hand. The light kiss he pressed to the back of hand was fleeing and polite. "Please extend my sympathies to Lord Declan."

"Sympathies?" she echoed as her heart did a wild jerk in her chest.

"About the migraine," he said smoothly but there was a shadow in his eye that gave her pause.

She eased her hand out of his grip. "I will be sure to tell him."

Now making a circuit of the solarium, she went back over everything that said time and time again—looking for any hint she might have given the man that would make him suspicious.

"There you are," Lord Edward said. "I've been looking all over for you, girl. Tell me what transpired between you and the captain."

Althea put the base of her free hand to her forehead and groaned. "I think he suspects," she said.

"Suspects what?" Lord Edward asked with force.

"That Declan is the Gypsy," she said.

"Why do you think this?" he demanded.

"It was something he said," she replied then shook her head. "No, it was more the way he said it."

"Said what, girl?" Edward snapped. "Tell me."

"He inquired after Declan and I attempted to deflect his query so I could have time to think, but he persisted in wanting to know where Declan was. I told him he was in bed sick with a migraine. He said he well understood the illness for he suffered from them, too. He asked me to extend his sympathy to Declan."

"That would be a normal response, Althea," her future father-in-law reminded her.

"Aye, but it was the way he said it," she told him. "The way he looked at me as he said it. Your Grace, he knows."

"Mayhap he suspects, girl, but he does not know. If he knew for a certainty, he would have insisted on speaking to Declan."

She sank into one of the wicker chairs by the shelves of orchids. "I hope you're right. I hope they find Penry soon."

"I am rather hoping they don't," Edward said.

"Why would you hope such a thing?" she asked.

"It is my fondest wish the bastard is either dead or in a country where he can't be found. Either way, that would prevent my son—your future husband—from ever confronting him. In the condition he is in now, Declan would be no match for a man in his prime."

Chapter Twelve

Jack and Tim rode to the Hound and Stag to see how its landlord was faring. Tim felt guilty for having abandoned the man but the first thing Patrick Arbra told him was that he understood why Tim had left.

"He is your friend," Paddy said. "I would have expected no less of you, lad. How is he?"

"Not good," Jack replied then went on to explain to Bess's father what had transpired that day in the meadow. "The wound in his thigh gives him a lot of pain."

"The gods love him," Paddy replied. "Will he be all right?"

"There's every reason to believe so," Jack said.

"Going to the barn. Feed the horses," Tim said and left before either man could stop him.

"That's the most words I've ever heard that boy string together at one time," Paddy said, watching Tim leave.

"He's getting better," Jack said. "No one at the keep pays any attention to his disfigurement." He smiled. "Especially not Lady Althea. She's gone out of her way to treat him as bossily as she does the rest of us."

"That's good," Paddy said. "All the people who come to the inn can do is stare at him."

"He wants to stay with you," Jack said. "He feels he let you down."

"He's welcome to stay, but he doesn't owe me anything," Paddy replied.

"He feels he does, so if it's all right…?"

"Of course," Paddy agreed.

"Is there anything you need?" Jack asked.

"No," Paddy answered, shaking his head. "But I would ask one thing of you."

"Name it," Jack told him.

"Tell him I do not hold him to blame for what happened to Bess. I wanted to blame him. I wanted to hate him for ever having come into our lives but she loved him." His voice broke. "Enough to give her life for him."

"In his way, he loved her, Paddy," Jack said. "And he will 'til the day he dies." He reached out to put a hand on the older man's arm. "Would you mind if I go out to pay my respects to her? For him and for myself?"

"Not at all. She would like that," Paddy replied. "There's a marker there now. I put fresh flowers on her grave every day."

"If you need anything—anything at all—just send Tim to us and it'll be seen to."

"I appreciate that, Jackson."

"One other thing," Jack said. "Has there been any talk of Penry? Any gossip that might not have been reported to the Royal Marines?"

"There's always talk, son, but most of it is just speculation. The lad who was here that night—Jeremy Belk by name—felt so bad about what happened he came to ask my forgiveness. The lad was so distraught I couldn't send him away although the sight of him made me want to run my blade through his heart."

"That's understandable," Jack said.

"He was a part of it, but I heard most of what went on in here. He tried to talk sense into Penry but that bastard wouldn't listen."

"Has there been any talk about the man that was with Penry? The one who I'm sure dug Bess's grave."

"All I know is his name is Jonas. I'm guessing that's a last name but I don't know for sure. He was a mean son of a bitch; I do know that much. There was a horse left behind when he took my wagon but there was nothing in the saddlebags to tell me who it belonged to."

"Wait," Jack said. "Why would he have taken your wagon?"

"I have no idea, son, unless…"

"Unless what?" Jack pressed.

"Well, there was some talk of a killing over toward Richter's Creek. A healer was done in by a soldier. Seems to me a young boy saw him taking someone out of a wagon and in to the healer. Said the soldier wore the chevron of a private and that was what Jonas was."

"Could the person he took in to the healer have been Penry?"

"I don't know but I do know I heard a shot out front about half an hour or so before the wagon left. I'm sure Tim told you how they'd knocked him out."

"Aye, when he'd come in to check on you and Bess."

"I know now she was probably dead before Tim woke up. Two nasty smashes to the head kept him down a good long while. As soon as he came to, he stumbled to my room. He untied me and I ran to her room. When I saw all that blood…" Paddy swiped his hand over his face. "We followed a trail of it down the stairs and out the front door, around the side of the inn until we came to the grave. I'm thinking the shot I heard came after the grave was dug."

"You think Jonas shot Penry then put him in the wagon and took him to a healer forty miles from here?" Jack asked. He shook his head. "That wouldn't make sense."

"Not unless it was an accident and he didn't mean to shoot him."

Tim came into the taproom and leaned against the door frame. He cocked his head to one side as though he was thinking hard.

"But if he did and he took him to a healer who mayhap wouldn't know either of them and Penry died while the healer was seeing to him. That being the case, Jonas wouldn't want to leave a witness to what he'd done. It's not a farfetched notion."

"Not farfetched at all," Paddy agreed.

"So Jonas could be out there somewhere and Penry could be dead."

"What about the safe?" Tim asked.

"Safe?" Jack asked then snapped his fingers. "That's right. Captain Gunderson told Lord Edward that Penry had gone to Norus to steal money and valuables. He would have been the only one who knew where to find the safe and its combination."

"Then Penry's still alive," Paddy said. "So who was in the wagon?"

"It had to be the other way around. Penry shot Jonas and if that's the case he's a murderer," Jack replied. He grabbed his hat.

"Where you going?" Tim asked.

"To Richter's Creek," Jack told him.

But as he galloped down the coach road Jack couldn't help but wonder why Penry would go to the trouble of trying to save a man he'd shot. That didn't sound like the Royce Penry he knew. Anyone who was nothing more than a commoner or a peasant did not warrant a second thought.

"So who were you seeking help for?" he mumbled.

* * * * *

The morning after her husband came back from his trip to Richter's Creek, Fairling saw him sitting on a rock beside the stream that ran behind their cottage. Last night he had fallen upon her like a rutting stag less than a minute after he'd entered their home. Not a word had passed his lips then and not one word had he said after his forceful lovemaking that—gods willing—she was sure would lead to the child they both wanted so desperately. When he rose just before dawn's first light, he had kissed her, but still said nothing. Stuffing his legs into his breeches, he had gone out the door as silently as a field mouse.

Something was troubling her stalwart husband but she had known Jackson McGregor since she was old enough for him to pull her pigtails and push her into mud puddles. He had been a prankster, a jokester even then and had never outgrown it. There were deep laugh lines around his mouth and at the corners of his eyes because he had earned them like a badge of courage with his happy-go-lucky view of life. He took few things seriously—it simply wasn't his way to be morose and glum like his beloved Declan. When he grew quiet, as he had now, whatever was bothering him was bad.

Very bad.

And he was struggling to cope with it.

Slipping a gown over her nakedness she walked out their back door and followed the dirt trail to where he was sitting. She knew he was aware of her the moment she had opened the door but he gave no sign she was approaching him. Her bare feet made no sound but they did not need to. Her husband was so attuned to the things around him that the misplacement of even one breath of air would come to his attention.

She came up behind him and wrapped her arms around his broad shoulders, resting her chin on the top of his head, but he kept the silence in which he had cloaked himself. Staring over his head at the slow-moving stream where the early morning sunlight had threaded a chain of sparkling crystals across the surface of the water, she smiled as he reached up to cover her crossed hands with one of his. He leaned back so he was pressed against her and she felt his shoulders sag beneath the weight of the thing disturbing him.

When at last he spoke, he sounded tired and infinitely sad.

"I have a tough decision to make," he told her.

"Umm," she said. It was as much a commitment as a statement. She was ready to listen and she knew he understood she would not interrupt until he had said his piece.

He was caressing her hand gently, lovingly. The tension in his body was almost palpable and he was transmitting it to her in the way he stroked her flesh. It was a habit he had when he was trying to come to terms with unsettling thoughts.

"On the one hand, I want him to be happy," he said.

Ah, she thought. She should have known it would be about Declan.

"He deserves to be happy. The gods know he's had enough pain and misery and loss in his life."

She made no comment but she agreed with what he said.

"He doesn't want to marry Lady Althea. Didn't right from the start. I don't think it was as much her as just not wanting to be responsible for another human being." He sighed deeply. "He doesn't trust himself to be able to take care of those entrusted in his care, and a wife? How important is it for a man to protect his wife and keep her from harm?"

"Very," she said quietly.

"Aye," he agreed.

He was silent for a moment then brought one of her hands up to his lips and kissed it.

"I believe he was searching for something to care for. He just didn't realize it. From the moment he saw Bess at the Hound and Stag, he felt a pull he could not deny." He craned his head to look up at her. "I think it started that first night when he saw her lurking on the stairs."

Fairling knew the tale. Her husband shared everything with her—no matter how sordid or evil. He never kept anything from her.

"Here she was this peasant girl, working in her father's taproom, serving coarse and often rude men—like Penry—and he must have felt the need to protect her. Of course her beauty had a lot to do with the way he saw her. Her flirting with him certainly caught his attention and held it. Not to put too fine a point on it but she was available and willing and we both know those are qualities he cherishes in a conquest."

"Aye, we do," she replied.

"So, he fancied himself falling in love with her and also saw her as a way out of a marriage he did not want and was being forced into. We also know he is a stubborn little prick and if you tell him no, that he can't do something or he has to do something, he'll bend over backward just to spite you."

She smiled. That was the essence of Declan Farrell in a nutshell.

He lifted her hand and waved it around as though using it to make his point.

"So, on this hand we have concluded that one, he needs someone to care for and to care for him, that he deserves to be happy. Two, that he had no intention of getting married—no matter who the woman was—and was digging his heels in in protest. Three, he found Bess to be beautiful, willing and accommodating so he took advantage of what she offered and was quite pleased with himself for having done so. Four, he felt an urge to protect her so he convinced himself the best way to do that would be to marry her—although I fail to see the reasoning in that, I believe that was his addle-minded decision—and five, he is a stubborn prick who will do just the opposite of what anyone tells him he should do."

He brought her hand to his mouth and kissed her palm once again then lifted her other hand.

"Now on this hand, we have a woman who loved him from the moment she saw him at her cousin's pretentious ball. She found him handsome, witty and incredibly dangerous."

"Which he is," Fairling reminded him.

"True, but these are things that seem to make the bastard irresistible to every woman he meets. This woman in particular. She is rich, beautiful and will inherit even more riches when her father dies. He is rich, handsome and will inherit even more riches when his father dies. It is a match made in heaven."

"So you would think," Fairling said, playing devil's advocate.

"Precisely. They are both graced with wicked senses of humor, bravery in the face of overwhelming odds—she proved that on the meadow with that steady aim of hers—and a propensity for telling believable lies."

"Propensity?" she echoed.

"I'm learning new words from Lord Jamie," he explained. He tapped the side of his head with his index finger. "I listen, I learn."

"Ah," she said. "Go on."

"Also on this hand we have the other woman. She is beautiful, earthy, and hot-blooded. She gives him what he needs as a man but their clandestine, somewhat forbidden romance makes him feel like the rash young man he was years ago. She brings out the boy in him. She takes him back to a time before his mother and Eion were taken from him. Before he took on dangerous responsibilities that set him on a collision course with the law."

"She made him feel alive."

"Aye," he said. "That is exactly how she made him feel. She brought out his even wilder side and made him think he could do whatever he wanted—gods-be-damn the consequences."

"A dangerous thing," Fairling observed.

"It was."

"And the dirty little nail on this hand is Penry who posed a threat not only to the landlord's daughter but to Lady Althea. He was a thorn that needed to be plucked."

He lowered his head and she eased one hand from his grip to stroke his hair, to give him time to tell her what decision he needed to make.

"Which of the two women is the right one for him, Fairling?" he asked.

She had been looking down at his hair but his question made her lift her head to look at the stream. The water flowed on as it had for decades and would long after she and he were in their graves. It had listened to many a conversation between her and her husband and—gods willing—would listen to many more.

"You are asking which of the two I would choose for him?" she wanted clarified.

"Aye," he replied. "I've told you the things Lady Althea has done for him before and after he was wounded. How she's stayed at his side and cared lovingly for him even when he tried to push her away."

"She's a fighter and she is fighting for the man she wants," Fairling said. She threaded her fingers through his thick blond hair. "For the man she loves."

"This is so," he agreed.

"Had Bess lived, she would have gone away with him without a backward glance, but I'm not sure she would have been good for him. As you say, she brought out the wilder side of him—the side that could have cost him his life. Had he not been riding to meet with her that night, she would not have died. She gave her life for him and most people would say that is the greater love."

"You don't?" he queried.

"The greater love is the woman who would give him up to keep him safe. Hers would be the harder pain at his loss."

"Lady Althea has no intention of giving him up, sweeting."

"No, but she was willing to share him with another woman to keep him happy." She tugged on his hair. "Unlike this woman who would slit her man's throat if his eyes even roamed in the direction of another woman."

"This man is too terrified of his woman to ever contemplate such a thing," he told her.

She snorted for she knew he looked at comely women as often as any man did and had—without doubt—sinned with them in his mind. That was a man's way.

"So, which one?"

"I would pick the one the gods intended that he have else they would not have placed her within his reach," she answered.

"That doesn't tell me anything, Fairling," he complained.

"Aye, love. I know," she said, bending over to kiss him on the head.

* * * * *

As far as he knew everyone in the keep was sound asleep. Jack had finally gone home to the woman he needed to be with. Tim had gone back to the inn where he no doubt thought he needed to be. His father and Jamie were long ago in their beds and from the horrendous sounds coming from his father's suite of rooms, the old man was cutting down an entire forest of trees.

As for Althea? She would never venture from her cozy bedchamber once the clock struck the midnight hour.

"Afraid she'll turn into a pumpkin," he mumbled.

There were no guards outside his door.

There were no guards beneath his window or atop the roof because no one thought he could move about well enough to slip away from their notice.

Warlock was safely ensconced in his warm, dry stall—as were all the worthy steeds of Arlington Castle.

The drawbridge was raised, the portcullis down.

"All is locked and barred," he said as he hobbled his way through the secret passageway behind the wall in his father's office. It was slow going and he was hurting but he pushed the pain aside— as he did many a night—to make this trek through the dusty, winding corridor that led to the postern gate. He doubted his father even remembered the gate existed or that his son knew how to access it. He knew no one in the keep would believe it possible for him to wobble his way along the hidden passage to the outside world.

In his left hand was a lit lantern and in his right the crossbar of a crutch that was torturing his underarm with every slow, laborious step he took.

But he had somewhere he needed to be. Had to be and not even the pouring rain that awaited him beyond the postern gate would deter him.

Once he reached the end of the dark corridor, he hung the lantern on a peg by the gate then quietly opened the well-oiled portal he'd made sure wouldn't squeak. As soon as the gate opened, he blew out the lantern, stepped outside into the rain then pulled the gate closed behind him. It was a matter of limping a hundred yards to the thicket and the little lean-to where he had paid Meg to bring a horse for him. She would be waiting there to help him mount and would be there when he returned to help him down again. Her dislike of Althea was all the incentive she needed to do his bidding without question or censure and for that he was grateful. She had no idea where he went or what he did nor would she ever reveal what she did know to another living soul. Of that he was sure.

Or at least he prayed that was the case.

The tip of his crutch sank into the spongy ground and that made it even more torturous going for him, but he clenched his teeth and tried to force his mind away from the fire in his thigh.

She was waiting right where he expected her. They didn't speak—never did—but she took the crutch from him, stood it against the lean-to then held the roan mare still for him to put his left foot into the stirrup. That meant putting his entire weight on his right leg in order to do so. The pain was so acute he had to bite the inside of his mouth to keep from crying out. She snaked her arm around him to steady him until he could pull himself up and swing his injured leg over the horse.

"Fucking shit," he said under his breath for he hadn't cleared the animal's rump and his thigh had dragged across it. He had to clasp the pommel in a death grip to keep from tumbling off the horse's back. Over the saddle was a thick cape that would help to keep some of the rain at bay and his hands shook as he picked it up and swung it around him. That only added to the agony spearing through his thigh and he groaned.

"Deckie?" she questioned and in the sudden flash of lightning overhead he looked down into her worried eyes.

"I'm all right," he swore. He straightened in the saddle—desperately trying to ignore the pain in his leg—then took up the reins. "Get in out of the rain, sweeting."

He clucked his tongue and the mare moved forward at a gentle gait. Meg had chosen the nag well—with the help of her brother Tomas—and made sure it was taken care of.

Riding into the rain-drenched night, he huddled into his cape, pulled the wide brim of his cavalier hat down over his eyes and urged the little mare into a faster pace.

An hour later, the animal was picking its way through a thick copse of trees to which he directed it. He reined the beast in beside the remains of a large tree that had been chopped down within two feet of the ground. It would serve as a good stepping stool when he dismounted. Once more bracing himself for the agony that was to come, he pulled his feet from the stirrups, swung his right leg over the mare's flanks and dropped to his left foot on the wide trunk. Keeping tight hold on the pommel until he could put some weight on his right leg, he took a deep breath then stepped backward onto the mushy ground. His right boot sank into the mud, but the excruciating pain he had been expecting did not come.

The mate to the crutch he had left at the lean-to was lying on the ground beside the tree trunk. He cursed for he had propped it against a neighboring tree but either the wind or the rain had caused it to fall. Bending over to retrieve it gave him a whole other reason to curse and sweat but once in hand, he braced himself against it and closed his eyes, drawing deep breaths into his lungs.

His destination was another fifty or so feet ahead of him. From where he stood he could see the slight mound and above him the snow-white marker that wasn't there when he'd come to this place three days earlier. The sight of the simple Chalean cross brought such god-awful grief to his soul it nearly drove him to his knees. He stared at it for a long time until he found the courage to move forward.

To the south of the marker the inn sat like a beached whale on a darkened shore. A single light burned in the window of the landlord's bedchamber, but even as he watched, the light went out.

"All is locked and barred," he whispered.

From his vantage point he could not see the front of the inn. Her window. The casement window where she had watched for him that fateful night. That one dark window to which death had come.

He shook himself, hissed at the discomfort that wrought then began to make his way to the grave.

For one brief moment he thought he felt eyes upon him but it didn't matter. It could be Paddy. It could be Tim. If it was either of them, neither would interfere. If it was Penry, let him come. The pistol in his belt was primed and ready.

And so was he.

As he neared the grave, the rain slowed to a gentle mist but he was already soaked. The weather was beginning to cool but he didn't care. The slight chill felt good on his face.

He stopped ten feet away to catch his breath; again he felt as though he was being watched then shrugged it off. He took a deep breath and stepped up to the grave.

Elizabeth Maire Arbra, the marker below the Chalean cross read. Beneath that were the years 2518-2537 A.A.

He wavered there on his crutch and could not seem to take his eyes from the date. Nineteen years, he thought. She was only nineteen years old. Five years younger than he. A year younger than Althea.

Too young—much too young—to die.

He pulled his arm from the top of the crutch and hanging onto it slowly lowered himself—inch by agonizing inch—to the muddy ground. The pain was a prayer, a litany to his lost Bess. It was his hair shirt. His cilice. His punishment.

"Hello, my beauty," he said. "I'm here."

He put his fingers to his lips then placed them to the top of the mound.

"May I sit with you a while?"

He eased to a sitting position beside the grave then began to talk to her. He told her of what had happened between that time and the time he had visited her last. Long into the night he poured his soul out to her as the rain poured over him. Somewhere around three of the clock, he stretched out beside the mound and draped his arm over it. He did then what he could not, would not do at the keep: he began to cry. The sound of his sobbing was pitiful even to his own ears.

* * * * *

Two months had passed since Declan was shot. The through and through wound in his thigh had closed and no longer oozed fluid, but he still could not walk all that well on his right leg for any pressure he put on it hurt. Sometimes more than most. But that was okay. He wanted his family and friends to believe he was helpless, obstinate and intractable.

There was a method to his madness.

To that end he no longer refrained from speaking. He indulged his meaner side by voicing his frustrations, irritations and objections every chance he got—at the top of his lungs on most occasions. He was every inch the spoiled, obnoxious and ill-tempered brat. His surly attitude had finally pushed his father past the point of allowing it to continue.

When his bedchamber door crashed open, he lifted his head and scowled to find his father standing in the doorway.

"Get out of the bed," his father ordered.

"No," Dec said and lay back down.

"Either get up or, by the gods, you'll be lying in a pool of iced water."

"Leave me be," Dec growled at him and pulled the coverlet over his head. "I'm staying where I am."

"No, hell you aren't," his father declared and Dec heard his heavy footsteps stomping from the room.

Groaning, he knew the old man wasn't going to leave him alone so he tossed back the covers and eased his legs from the bed—his breath catching at the fiery pain that burned in his thigh. Hanging onto the four-poster at the top of the bed, he pulled himself up. Gritting his teeth he struggled to stand, wobbled for a moment then took a few tentative steps. Better he be sitting when his father came back than lying helpless in the bed.

It took him a few moments but the pain finally began to decrease in his leg and he hobbled to the chair. He was about to sit down when his father unceremoniously returned. He dipped his eyes to the bucket in the older man's hand then raised his chin. "You were really going to do it," he accused.

"Did you doubt I would?" his father asked. "I am sick of your shit, Declan James, and it will stop. Today."

"Why can't you just leave me alone? Why can't you let me grieve in peace?" he snapped. When his father didn't reply, Dec repeated his words in a bellow. "Will you please let me grieve in peace?"

"Where did you go last eve?" Edward questioned.

Ah, well, the ruse is done, he thought. His madness would now be locked away.

When Dec didn't answer, his father reached out to grab his arm. "I asked you where the hell you went last eve."

Might as well tell him, a voice whispered, the jig is up now.

"I can't stay cooped up in here forever," Dec told him.

"Where did you go?" Edward demanded. The blood drained from his face. "Have you learned where Penry...?" He stopped when Dec shook his head. "Then where, boy?"

"To the Hound and Stag," Dec shouted. He shook off his father's arm and limped to the bed. He sat down heavily—trying not to let the pain show on his face.

Edward stared at him. "By the gods, Declan. Do you know how foolish that was? What if that beast of yours had thrown you? What in the name of the Triune Goddess possessed you to do such a stupid thing?"

"I went to her grave," Dec said as tears pricked hot behind his eyes. "I needed to see it. I needed to..." He struggled to keep his emotions in check. "I needed to talk to her. To beg her forgiveness for being the cause of her death."

Edward lowered his head. He was silent a long time then he sighed deeply. "I understand."

"Do you?" Dec asked in a snide tone.

"Aye, son, I do," Edward replied. He looked up. "I would give anything to be able to visit the graves of your mother and brother but that wasn't an option for me."

"I'm sorry," Declan said. "I'm sorry I couldn't bring them home to you."

"Stop that," Edward hissed. "You are not to blame for their deaths, boy. You are not to blame for your inability to save them. I have never blamed you. Stop blaming yourself."

"It was my fault they were on the *Molly Celeste*."

"Declan..."

"If they hadn't have come to see me graduate, none of it would have happened." He scraped a hand through his hair. "Everyone I love dies because of me," he said. "Bess killed herself to save me. Danny died to protect me." He drew in a shaky breath. "Who's next, Father? Who's the next person to give their life for Declan Farrell?" He dropped to the bed then covered his face with his hands.

He could feel his father looking at him. Prayed the man would just leave.

"Look at me, Declan," his father said softly.

Groaning with frustration for he knew his father wasn't finished lecturing him, Dec lowered his hands.

The old man smiled. "You need to get out in the sun for a while. You are too pale and the warmth will be good for you," he said. "Get dressed and come out to the garden. I will be waiting for you."

After his father left, the room seemed too quiet. It began to close in on him. He took a deep breath and reached for the four-poster.

It took him a while to get dressed in just a shirt and breeches. He didn't bother with underpants, socks or boots for that had nearly cost him his consciousness the night before. He was—he thought—

nothing if not teachable. When he opened his door, he found a carved cane standing against the wall beside his chamber.

"Tim," he mumbled.

As much as it unmanned him, made him look helpless, he picked up the cane and leaned his weight into it. Much to his surprise, bracing himself on the cane helped ease the ache in his thigh. Moving slowly, cautiously he made his way to the stairs.

No one looked twice at him as he gingerly descended the stairs. Servants greeted him with a smile, a slight bow, a curtsey but none of them dropped their curious gaze to the cane and for that he was grateful. He didn't feel quite the full brunt of being an invalid. Hobbling along, he saw Althea watching him from the solarium. She smiled then returned her attention to the book in her lap.

He found his father sitting in one of the two large wicker chairs that faced the bubbling fountain. Neither of them spoke as Dec eased himself into the other chair, laid the cane over his lap then stretched out his right leg.

"May I?" his father asked, looking at the cane.

Dec handed it to him.

"A fine piece of work," his father said, turning the cane over and over to see the intricate carvings etched into the dark wood. "These are Chalean symbols." He glanced at Dec. "Do you know what they mean?"

"I haven't had a chance to look at it," Dec replied. "I think Tim carved it."

"I saw him working on it," his father replied. He traced one symbol. "This stands for bravery." He traced another. "And this for life-long friendship." His fingers moved across each symbol in turn, recounting their meaning. He handed the cane back to Dec. "Very find work, indeed, and lovingly wrought."

"Aye," Dec said and felt the treacherous burning behind his eyes again.

They were silent for a long time—each lost in his own thoughts—then his father chuckled.

Dec looked over at him. "What are you thinking?" he asked.

"I remember when you were about four years old," his father replied. "You had this hellion of a little puppy you named Speckles." He shook his head. "I have no earthly idea why you named him that for the dog was jet black without a single speckle."

"I remember him."

"Why did you give that particular name to the mutt?"

Dec laughed. "Because he had these spots on his belly. They looked like speckles to me."

"Ah," his father said, drawing out the word. "That explains it then."

"He seemed to like it," Dec acknowledged.

"We were sitting in the garden—your mother and I—and you were over there." He pointed to a large bush.

Turning to look where his father indicated, Dec nodded. "That was my fort."

"Your mighty castle, you called it. Once you were under that bush no one was supposed to be able to see you."

"The castle was magical," Dec reminded him. "It had a cloaking spell put on it by a great wizard."

"To protect you," his father said.

"Didn't protect me from spankings," Dec said drily.

"You got more than your fair share, I venture to say," his father agreed.

"I got several boys' fair shares if memory serves," Dec grumbled.

"You were a precocious little bastard even then," his father told him. "That day, more than any other up until then."

"How so?"

"You were under there and we were—as we were supposed to—ignoring you though your mother was watching every move you made. You were playing with the mutt. He was slobbering all over you but you didn't seem to mind. Iverson was a young man, of course, and all of a sudden he came rushing up to us."

"I wasn't aware he had such a speed among his gears," Dec joked.

"He was fairly adroit in his day—though just as stuffy—but on that occasion he was as white as a sheet, shaking as though with the ague and he stammered, 'The k...king is here, Your G...grace.'"

Dec grunted. "Nor was I aware he could ever lose his dignity enough to stammer."

"The poor man was terrified. I jumped up. Your mother jumped up. We were going to run into the keep but when we turned, there was the king coming toward us with his entourage."

"Which king was this?" Dec asked, for there had been a civil war when he was a child. The monarchy changed hands more than a few times.

"King Seamus," Ned replied. "A real ballbreaker that one. At any rate he comes over, we're bowing and scraping and he plops his arse down right where you are sitting and tells me he has a private matter to discuss with me. Your mother excuses herself and in her fluster she completely forgets you're still over there with your pup. Truth told, I had forgotten about you, too, until the king looks over and frowns. I follow his line of sight and order you to go into the keep.

"'No,' the king says. 'Come here, boy.' He crooks his finger at you. You don't move a muscle. You're just squatting there holding the puppy in your arms but the king waves you over. 'Come and let me see that fine hound of yours,' he says.

"Well, you come over—slower than I believe I had ever seen you move—with your bottom lip thrust out and your eyes narrowed. When you reach us, the king holds out his hands and says, 'Let me see that most handsome animal.'

"You hesitated so I reached out and tugged the pup from you and handed it to the king.

"'My,' he says, 'but I believe I would like to have this good-looking canine in my kennel at Boreas. He will make a fine hunting dog.'"

Ned chuckled.

"What did I do?" Dec asked.

"Before I could stop you, you grabbed the pup and moved back, glaring at the king. You said, 'You can't have my dog, you stinky man.' No, no. That's not what you said. You said, 'You can't have my dog, you stinky *fat old* man.' Then you ran off with the mutt clutched so tightly in your arms it yelped."

Dec groaned. "It's a wonder King Seamus didn't confiscate our properties."

"He found it amusing," Ned told him. "He laughed so hard tears ran down his cheeks. He looked over at me and said, 'that one is going to give us a run for our money, eh, Farrell? Something tells me he's going to be a thorn in my side one day.'"

"Not in his but in yours," Dec said quietly.

"Aye, that you have most assuredly been." He sobered. "But that needs to stop."

Dec rubbed his thigh. "My highwayman days are over, Father,"

"I sincerely hope so."

They sat there for a long moment, saying nothing, watching the peacocks strutting about the far edge of the lawn then Ned reached over to put his hand on Dec's, gaining his son's attention.

"You have a good woman who loves you, son. A decent, gods-fearing, loyal woman who would do anything in this world for you."

"I know," Dec whispered.

"She was willing to go to jail to protect you that day in Penry's office. She lied for you. Had she been caught in that lie, the Standfields would have lost everything they own and been tossed into prison alongside you."

"I did not ask her to lie for me, Father," Dec said, his conscience burning him like acid.

"And she killed a man that day in the meadow."

"Something I wish to the gods she had not done," Dec whispered.

"You couldn't have stopped her. No one could have. That is what one does for the person one loves. She deserves so much more than you have given her, son."

"Aye, she does, but she doesn't deserve me."

"Declan..."

"No, Father. She doesn't. You have no idea how low I sank. How despicable a man I truly am."

"What are you talking about?"

"That morning when I left here with Jack, I set into motion a plan that would have shamed Thea to the core had she known what I intended. I sent Jack to fetch Danny Rees. They were going to intercept the priest that would come to perform the ceremony. I was going to replace him with Danny."

"But wasn't he defrocked?"

"Aye." He looked his father in the eye. "That was the whole point. The Joining would not have been legal. My plan was to marry her, wait a week or so then pick a fight with her. Say things that would make her despise me then storm out of Standfield Hall. I was going to make it look as though I had fallen into the river at Dead

Man's Crossing and drowned. My body would never have been found."

"Dear gods," Edward whispered.

"As I said, she doesn't deserve me. Mayhap she would have grieved..."

"Mayhap?" Edward asked. "For the love of Alel, Declan, the woman loves you. Of course she would have grieved!"

"But I would have left her a wealthy widow."

"And you? What would you have done then?"

"Left the country."

"Never to return," his father said.

"Never to return."

"Leaving us all to grieve for you," his father accused.

"As I said, I am a despicable man," Declan said. "I deserve all the misery I've been handed."

"Don't you realize you would have destroyed Althea's life?"

"I was setting her free, Father. She might have mourned for me but then she would have gone on to choose a man she loved. A man who would love her in return."

"There you are wrong."

Both men turned to find Althea standing a few feet away.

"Thea, I..."

"I would have mourned for you until the day I died," she interrupted. "And there would have been no other man for me. I would never have married again. The man I want—the only man I will *ever* want—is sitting right where you are sitting, Declan Farrell."

"I am not the man for you, Thea," he said.

"I would have died for you, too," Althea told him. "Do you know that?"

"Thea, don't say that."

Althea looked at Edward. "Your Grace, may I have a moment with your son in private?"

Edward looked at Declan then back to her before getting to his feet. "Of course, my dear." He patted her arm as he walked past her.

Althea took the seat he had vacated. "I know your heart, Declan Farrell," she said. "I know there is no place in it for me."

"I care for you, Thea."

"But you don't love me and you never will. You will go to your grave missing the only woman you truly want just as you go to her grave every night to mourn her. Last night was not the first time. It was just the first time you were caught."

He looked around her, stunned that she knew he slipped out at night.

"I follow you. I do every time you go to Wixenstead. I stand in the trees as you kneel down beside her grave and I listen to the words you say to her. I watch as you lie down beside her and put your arm over the mound as though you are holding her in sleep and it tears the heart out of me."

"I'm sorry."

"It has to stop."

"Don't ask me to..."

"It has to stop because she is not dead, Declan. She is alive and with Penry."

Chapter Thirteen

"What the hell do you mean?" he roared.

He had never been so enraged in his life. The six words he had bellowed at the top of his lungs brought his father, Lord Jamie, Jasper and four guards running to the garden. They were greeted with the sight of him standing in front of his chair with his fists doubled and his face no doubt infused with fury.

"Explain yourself," he yelled at Althea.

"What's going on here?" his father demanded.

"This is between me and her," Declan snarled. "Stay out of it." He was so angry he was shaking.

"You have made it between all of us with your disgraceful shouting," his father stated. "What is the meaning of this?"

"You do not raise your voice to your wife, Declan," Lord James had the nerve to say.

Declan rounded on him and would have lost his balance if Althea hadn't shot up from her chair and grabbed him.

"Get your gods-be-damned hands off me," he hissed.

"Calm down or you are going to have a stroke," she said evenly but she released him, holding her hands up to show she would not touch him again.

"Don't tell me what to do," he spat. "Don't you ever tell me what to do." He turned the full force of his rage on Jamie. "And she's not my wife."

"She is your betrothed," his father said. "You will treat her with the respect she is due."

He ignored those words and turned back to Althea. "Who told you?"

"Jack."

That was no surprise, but it hurt like hell to hear her say it.

"How the hell does he know?"

"He went to Richter's Creek and talked to someone there."

"Who?"

"I don't know. He didn't say. I don't suppose he thought it important."

"The person could have been lying."

"He doesn't believe that is the case."

"Because?"

"There are too many extenuating circumstances, too many clues."

His father and Jamie might as well have been at a wiffle match for they were switching their stares back and forth between him and Althea. In any other situation, he might have found humor in their perplexed, confused looks and the way their heads swung from him to her and back again. At that moment, all he could find was fury. He ground his teeth, speaking around the constriction.

"How long has he known?"

"Known what?" his father asked. "What is this all about?"

She hesitated then raised her chin. "A month now."

That stunned him so badly he staggered back from her, knocking aside Lord James's outstretched hand. All he could do was stare at her. To give her her due, she did not look away. Did not flinch. She just stood there with her hands clasped in front of her.

"A month," he repeated, his voice as soft as mist on a rose.

"He didn't know how to tell you."

"Tell him what?" his father demanded.

"So he told you instead and between the two of you, you decided to keep it from me until now?" he snapped.

"We thought it best, aye."

"You thought it…"

That was the last straw. The betrayal he was feeling was scalding him alive.

"You gods-be-damned bitch," he whispered.

"Declan!" his father said with a gasp of outrage.

"You lying, conniving, deceitful *bitch*."

"That is quite enough, young man," his father warned. "Get your ass to your room and stay there until…"

"I am not a gods-be-damned teenager for you to order about," Declan shouted.

"You're acting like one," Lord Jamie told him.

Declan pointed a shaking finger at his godfather. "You keep the hell out of this. It doesn't concern you."

"Declan, listen to me," Althea said. "We don't know where he is. Where he took her. As soon as Jack told me what he had found out in Richter's Creek I hired a private investigator. All the investigator was able to find out was that he was last seen on the docks at Carbondale with a woman in a wheelchair. There were two dozen ships anchored in the harbor that day. He's been tracking down the passenger manifests for each of them but it is taking time. Those ships sailed to the four corners of our world. Trust me; we have not been idle in this."

"Trust you?" Declan sneered. "Woman, I no longer trust either you or my so-called friend Jack."

"We are trying to find her for you, Declan," she said. "You must believe that."

"Who in the name of the Father God are you talking about?" his father bellowed.

"Bess," Declan answered.

The shocked looks that replaced the perplexed and confused ones on his father's and godfather's faces were priceless.

"The tavern girl is alive?" his father questioned.

Althea nodded. "Jack believes so."

"And apparently with Penry," Lord James put in.

"That appears to be the case, aye," she replied.

"And they've known for a month and never said one word to me," Declan accused.

"We were..." she began but he literally growled at her and pushed past her.

"Where do you think you're going?" his father snapped.

"Let him go, Ned," Lord James advised. "Now is not the time to press the issue. He's just had a terrific blow."

He could feel their eyes on him as he hobbled his way back into the keep. All he wanted to do was get to his father's study and into the passageway that would take him far from Arlington Castle. It wasn't until his bare feet touched the cold stone of the steps that he realized that wasn't such a good idea. He wasn't dressed to go streaking across the countryside—which had been his intent.

Cursing bitterly, he limped to the stairs, stopped before lifting his foot to the first step and let his shoulders drop. He stood there with his eyes closed, steeling himself to make the climb.

"Do you need help getting up the stairs, Your Grace?"

It was Iverson—helpful as ever—whose gentle voice spoke to him.

"No," he said, opening his eyes. "But thank you, Iverson."

The older man bowed. "You are most welcome, Lord Declan. Would it be all right with you if I walked with you to the top of the stairs?"

Polite, helpful and concerned about him, he thought. He turned to look at the servant. "I would like the company," he said and was rewarded by a crinkling of the wrinkled face of George Iverson.

* * * * *

He should have known someone would come to bother him. The soft knock on the door told him precisely who it was. For a moment he stood there glaring at the portal, not wanting company, not inclined to talk to anyone but when that gentle knock came again, he growled.

"What?" he called out.

"May I come in?"

It was her, the gods-be-damn it, and she was the last of the bunch he wanted to see at that moment and he sure as hell didn't want to talk to her.

"Declan, please," Althea said. "I need to explain to you why Jack and I did not tell you. What he found out in Richter's Creek."

Well, he thought that should prove interesting.

"Come," he barked.

The door opened slowly as though she expected him to throw something at her.

"Close the door," he ordered.

She nodded and did as he asked then took a deep breath before turning to face him where he stood at the window. "May I sit?"

He shrugged. "Suit yourself."

"Will you sit with me?"

Folding his arms over his chest, he leaned his hip against the window sill. "I'm fine right where I am."

She pursed her lips and he knew she wanted to argue the matter but obviously thought better of it. She lifted her chin.

"When Jack rode with Tim back to the inn, he spent quite a bit of time speaking with the landlord. He learned something that made him begin to question the sequence of events that happened that night," she said.

"Such as?"

"First the landlord told him after the young woman..."

"Her name is Bess," he interrupted.

"After Bess shot herself to warn you, Penry sent all his men save one to ride after you."

"Tell me something I don't know," he ordered.

"That soldier would have been the one to dig the grave," she said.

Declan snorted. "Penry sure as hell didn't do it."

"The landlord says he heard a shot in front of the inn and that when Tim woke and untied him, the two of them followed a blood trail down the stairs. Jack believes that was Bess's blood."

"Who was shot outside the inn?"

"Jack thinks it must have been the soldier who dug the grave. He said the landlord told him there was more blood leading from the front door, around the side of the inn and to the grave. If Penry shot the man to keep him from talking then it would make sense that he then dragged the poor man to the grave and tossed him inside."

"And where does Jack think Bess was all this time?"

"The landlord said a wagon was taken from the stable. He heard the rattle of it and Jack said when he and your friend Daniel arrived at the inn they noticed wheel ruts in the mud."

"So Penry placed Bess in the wagon and took off with her," he said. "Ostensibly to Richter's Creek."

"And to a healer there."

"So it was the healer to whom Jack spoke."

She shook her head. "No, Penry cut the healer's throat. We believe to keep him from telling anyone he had seen him. Whoever it was that Jack spoke to there told him he saw a soldier wearing a private's uniform carrying a young woman into the healer's cottage."

"A private's uniform?" Declan questioned.

"Most likely the coat belonging to the man Penry buried at the inn."

"And this witness saw Penry leaving the healer's with the woman?"

"He did."

He narrowed his eyes. "Does the new captain at Gilhaven know this?"

"I imagine he does. The day he was here he hinted that there was more to Penry's disappearance that he was not at liberty to discuss. It would stand to reason that might well be what he meant. If so, he has kept the knowledge to himself."

"And you and Jack did the same gods-be-damned thing to me," he accused.

"We didn't want to tell you until we knew something for sure. To get your hopes up. Until we had unimpeachable information about their whereabouts. You were in such a foul mood; we didn't want to make it any worse."

"And you think by keeping that knowledge from me it was going to make my mood any less foul?" he demanded.

"We knew you were in no condition to go after Penry. By the gods, Declan, you could barely stand a month ago." She swept a hand toward him. "You're not that much better now. Do you really believe yourself capable of going up against a trained military man as you are now?"

"I was a trained military man as well, or have you forgotten that?" he snapped.

"Aye you are but I know how hard it is for you to sit astride horse. To walk. To stand for very long. How could you possibly fight Penry and hope to win?"

"Who says I was going to fight him?" he challenged.

"What were you going to do?" she asked. "Shoot him in the back?"

"You know better than that," he said, stung by such a question.

"Ten paces at dawn, then?" she queried. "You turn, lose your balance and his shot hits you in the chest as you go down?"

She took a few steps closer to him.

"Or were you planning on using rapiers instead? That would work equally well, would it not? You clumsily parrying his thrusts. Hobbling along the floor. I'm sure he would wait for you to right yourself before he ran you through the heart."

"I didn't think you had a mean bone in your body, Thea, but I can see I misjudged you," he replied.

"We were trying to protect you. Don't you see that?"

"This is my life you are trifling with," he shouted.

"My life, too," she shot back.

Exasperated, he uncrossed his arms and raised them to his shoulders, flexing his fingers into fists as he spoke. "Will you please, please stop thinking we are going to be married? We are not. Not now, not ever. Especially not now."

"I refuse to accept that," she said.

"You'd better, for I have no intention of ever Joining with you, Althea," he told her.

"What of the marriage contracts?" she asked.

"Let them put me in jail for breach of contract. What the hell do I care?"

"And Bess?" she asked. "If you are locked in prison will you allow her to remain with Penry?"

It was a low blow and one that made him itch to slap her beautiful face. Instead, he did the next best thing.

"I want you gone from here. Go back to Standfield Hall. Go to hell; I don't care which. I want you out of my home. Out of my life. I don't want to see your face ever again."

She was stricken by his words. "Does it matter at all to you that I love you?"

"No."

That one word seemed to hurt her more than any blow could have. He watched a single tear fall slowly down her cheek.

"Then I am sorry I bothered you," she said. She turned to the door.

"And don't come back," he told her.

She didn't look around, didn't stop as she opened the door.

"You need have no fear on that account, Lord Declan," she said.

After she was gone he expected his father to come annoy him, but he didn't. No one came. He stood at the window until his leg would not allow him to remain upright so he wove his way over to the chair and sat down. He was hungry but had no desire to go downstairs for he didn't want to see anyone or argue with them. He half expected to have his door thrown open and Jack stomp in to confront him, but that didn't happen, either. As the sun began to lower in the sky, he remained in his chair with his face turned toward the window.

"She's alive," he said.

Aye, he thought. Alive and with his mortal enemy. Which raised the question: who the hell was buried in the grave at the Hound and Stag?

And why was he not overjoyed to learn Bess had not died that night at the inn? Shouldn't he be shouting his happiness to his rooftops? Falling about the room trying to dance a jig over the news?

Of course he was happy to know she was alive, although just thinking of her with Penry made his blood run cold.

Then a brutal, wicked thought slithered its way through his mind.

Why was she with Penry? Why had he taken her from the inn in the first place? Had the bastard staged the whole scenario to make him think his lover was dead? Surely that wasn't the case else the soldier who had reported what had happened that night would have been privy to the deception. How could he not have been? That soldier had believed the landlord's daughter had shot herself to warn the highwayman he was riding into a trap. There was blood pooled on the floor at the foot of her bed. Tim had spoken to her and knew she had been shot. He had seen the blood himself.

So why pretend she was buried behind it?

Two reasons, that mean little inner voice whispered. To hurt you and to make you think she was dead. For what purpose?

So she could disappear with Penry?

Had Bess played him for a fool? Been stringing him along the whole time? Had she been in league with Penry? Had she been the bait in his trap and when the trap backfired had the gun at her breast accidentally discharged, wounding her? If that were the case, it would make sense that he took her from the inn, made it look as though she had died and was buried there then taken her to a healer.

And the healer had to die lest he betray the fact she wasn't dead.

"No," he whispered. "That can't be what happened."

Such evil considerations cut into him so deeply his very soul was bleeding.

* * * * *

"What the *hell* is the matter with you?"

Jack's unceremoniously invasion of his bedchamber didn't surprise him. He'd been expecting it all day the day before but it hadn't come. He'd gone to bed expecting to be dragged out of his sleep by the same irate man who was hovering in his doorway glowering at him this morn.

Eight days later than Declan had expected, but here now to fuck up his day.

"You are not welcome in my room, McGregor," he said. "Leave."

"You go to hell," Jack snapped and slammed the door shut behind him. "What the fuck is wrong with you?"

"Nothing a loaded pistol aimed at your crotch wouldn't cure," Declan replied dryly.

Jack snorted.

Ignoring Jack, he limped into the bathing chamber and to the porcelain bowl.

"Where's the cane Tim whittled for you?" Jack demanded, stalking behind him.

"Most likely in the garden where I left it," he replied as he pulled up his nightshirt and took hold of his cock to piss. He glanced around at Jack. "Tell you what. Why don't you fetch it and I'll shove it up your arse so you'll know right where it is at all times."

"Do you have any idea how badly you hurt Althea?" Jack countered.

"Do you have any idea how badly the two of you hurt *me*?" he asked, watching the stream of urine flowing into the bowl.

"If we did it was not intentional or done apurpose. You, my poggleheaded friend, cannot say the same," Jack stated. "You meant to hurt her and you did."

"Such is life," Declan said. He shook his cock then stepped back, letting the nightshirt fall over his nakedness.

"If you weren't a fucking invalid, I'd make you one for what you did to her," Jack said through his teeth.

Turning to the vanity, Declan poured water into the ewer then washed his hands. "Why let that stop you?"

"Oh, you'd like that, wouldn't you?" Jack questioned, leaning his shoulder against the doorjamb, blocking exit.

Declan dried his hands then faced Jack. "You think I enjoy being crippled, McGregor?"

Jack kicked his chin up. "I think you are playing it to the hilt is what I think. Hiding up here in your room like a mole in its tunnel prevents you from living life, don't it?"

"You call this living?" he asked. "Not hardly." He stepped forward. "Now get the fuck out of my way."

"Or what?" Jack challenged, not moving. "Stomp your good leg and hold your breath until you turn blue?" He raked his eyes down Declan. "That's about all you're good for at the moment."

Declan felt that insult go through him like a sharp knife. It hurt. Gods, how it hurt, but he kept his mouth shut although he knew he couldn't hide the deep wound those words caused for his eyes watered.

"You hurt her, Declan," Jack said quietly, stepping back to allow him to leave the bathing chamber.

"Aye, well, it is what it is," he replied.

"Do you know everyone in this keep adores her?" Jack asked. "They believe she walks on water. Especially Tim."

Declan had guessed as much from things the maids said outside his door—things they intended for him to hear. The little bitches sang Thea's praises every chance they got.

"From the moment she first laid eyes on Tim she never once flinched. She doesn't see the horror the greasers made of his face. She reaches out and touches him when she speaks to him, hooks her arm through his and walks with him as though they've been friends for years. Makes him smile. Hell, she makes the bastard laugh.

"She sees him no differently, treats him no differently than she does any of the rest of us. She's the first woman to show him such compassion since he fell into the Diabolusian's hands. She is a good woman."

"A woman you think I should have as my wife," Declan accused.

"Aye, I do," Jack agreed. "As does your father and Lord James, Tim, Fairling, Suz. Everyone here does. They were sorry to see her leave because they had come to gladly, happily accept her as the future mistress of Arlington Castle. They knew they could count on her. They love her. They respect her and now—thanks to you—they pity her."

Declan flinched as he sat down on the bed to pull on his breeches.

"You told your father she didn't deserve you?" Jack questioned. "Well you don't deserve her."

"Do you think Bess was working for Penry?" Declan asked.

Jack was about to say something else but that question made him snap his mouth shut. He stared at him as Dec pulled himself to his feet gripping the four-poster.

"Where the hell did that come from?" he asked.

"Could he have used her to keep me coming back to the inn so he knew where I would be in order to take me down?"

Jack blinked then his eyebrows drew together. He reached up to scrub his hand down his face. "Is that what you think?" he asked.

"I've considered it," Declan said, relieved to push the topic of Althea and his treatment of her from the conversation. "How could I not?"

"Well, I hadn't considered it," Jack told him. "Not for a second."

"Why not?"

"Because she loved you," Jack said.

"Or pretended to," Declan said softly. It hurt to speak the words but they needed to be said.

"No," Jack said, shaking his head. "She loved you. She pulled that trigger apurpose to warn you. I rode to Gilhaven to find that soldier who had confessed to Gunderson. As luck would have it I got to him a few days before he deserted."

"A deserter? Not the kind of man who would be honest with you. So what did he tell you?" He peeled the nightshirt from his chest and tossed it aside.

"That he believed Bess was dead. She had shown nothing but contempt for Penry. This soldier, Belk, kept an eye on her much of the time and he said he could see her distress, her fear. She was terrified for you. The other soldier—Jonas—warned her the musket had a hair trigger. She knew it, so if you're thinking it was an accident that the musket went off, that wasn't the case."

Declan leaned over to pick up his shirt, almost lost his balance, saw Jack start forward then stop.

"Penry faked the burial," Jack said, staying where he was. "He killed the healer so no one would know he had Bess with him. He stole the money from his family home then went to Carbondale. He was seen with a woman in a wheelchair—a woman the witness told the investigator seemed either drugged or unconscious. Our man is trying to find which ship they boarded and where it went. He's narrowed it down to five."

Dragging the shirt over his head, he asked why it was taking so long to check manifests.

"Two of the ships have offices that are open only when the ship is in port. Their records are locked in safes to which our man has no access. The other three bring their offices with them aboard ship. The harbormaster recorded those ships leaving Carbondale for Ionary, Oceania and Necroman. We doubt Penry would go to Necroman so our investigator left for Ionary a week ago."

"Then it could be another week—even two—before you hear from him," Declan said.

"I imagine so."

"I want to know as soon as you hear anything." Jack didn't reply so he looked over at him. "Did you hear me?"

"You hurt her," Jack said. "Needlessly and cruelly."

They were back to Althea, he thought and sat down on the bed.

"She is better off with me out of her life."

"Arguably that's true," Jack acknowledged. "But the silly woman happens to be in love with you and you broke her heart."

Declan looked down at his thigh. "She'll get over it."

"I'm sure she will since there's been a development you should like," Jack told him.

"What development?" he asked.

"Your father will tell you," Jack said. He turned to go.

"Why don't you save him the trouble and tell me?"

"Because I don't want to see the look on your face when you hear the words," Jack replied. He snatched open the door and stomped out, leaving the portal open behind him.

"What look?" he yelled after Jack. "*What* fucking look, Jack?"

* * * * *

Edward paused on his way up the stairs to wait for Jack to join him. "Did you tell him?" he asked.

"I'll leave that honor to you," Jack grumbled. "If I'd stayed in there much longer, I'd have smashed him in those pearly whites."

"Wait for me in the study, if you will. Pay no attention to the workmen."

"Workmen?" Jack questioned.

"That's how the little bastard got out of the keep unnoticed," Edward said. "Through that secret corridor behind the painting of his great-grandfather."

"I had forgotten about that passageway," Jack said.

"As had I, but I am having a lock placed on the postern gate."

"Just one more way to tweak his nose, eh, Your Grace?" Jack asked with a laugh.

"If he weren't grown, I'd take his ass over my knee, but what I have to tell him will be punishment enough."

"You think he'll consider it in that light?"

"Mayhap not when I tell him or even this day, but when it sinks in, he will," Edward replied and continued up the stairs.

Not bothering with knocking, he opened his son's bedchamber door and entered. Declan was sitting on the bed with his shoulders slumped and his head down.

"Come to the desk," Edward ordered.

He expected a protest from his son but Declan surprised him. The boy put a hand on the four-poster and levered himself to his feet. He limped over to the desk and stood there silently.

"Sit," Edward told him.

Declan pulled out the chair and sat with barely a wince as his knees bent.

Reaching into the pocket of his coat, Edward withdrew an envelope, opened it, unfolded its contents then slapped them down on the desktop. He leaned over, picked up a pen and extended it to his son.

"Sign."

Declan glanced up at him, frowned then looked down at the papers.

"No need to read them," Edward snapped. "Just sign and let us be done with this."

Still looking at the papers but making no move to read them, Declan shook his head. "With all due respect, Father, I'm not signing anything until I know what it is."

"It's what you've wanted all these months," Edward told him. "'Tis the nullification of the marriage contract." He shoved the pen into Declan's hand. "Now sign."

"Nullification?" Declan repeated.

"I've not all day to fool with you, Declan James," Edward said. "Sign the bloody paper."

He realized his son's eyes were scanning the document before him. There were only two pages. The first was all the legal mumbo-jumbo the king's solicitor had drawn up rendering the marriage contract null and void. The second contained the signatures of the parties involved: Lord Alastair Standfield, Duke of Oxmoor; Lord Edward Farrell, Duke of Arlington; Lady Althea Standfield, Countess of Edgerton. The only signature remaining to be penned was his son's. At the bottom of the page was a place for His Majesty's grandiose scrawl and seal. When Declan flipped the first page over and saw the signatures, he released a long breath. He laid the pen down.

"No," he said. "I'm not signing this."

"Aye, you will," Edward told him. "Lord Alastair hiked himself to Boreas to have this paper drawn up and spent an hour groveling at the king's feet before his petition to have the contract voided was granted. The poor man was humiliated, shamed when His Majesty asked him what was so wrong with his daughter that even a black sheep like you did not want her. You will sign it."

"I'll not sign it for I'll not have anyone—including the king—think anything is wrong with Thea," Declan said.

"You should have thought of that before you so carelessly discarded her," Edward told him. "Sign the gods-be-damned papers, Declan."

"If I do, she will have trouble finding a man who will vie for her hand and I can't…"

"One has already asked for her hand and Lord Alastair has given his blessing," Edward told him.

Declan looked up at him. "Who?"

"Does it matter?"

"Aye, it does," Declan said. "Who?"

"Captain Rand Gunderson—formerly of the Governmental Regiment Military Tribunal and now commandant of the garrison at Gilhaven," Edward replied.

"A soldier?" Declan scoffed.

"Oh, he is far more than a mere soldier. His mother is the younger sister of High King Rolf of the Uigingeach Royal House of

Bordine. The good captain bears the rank of Duke of Stybiorne, thus he outranks you."

That stung him, Edward thought.

"Bully for him."

"Jealous?"

"No."

Edward smiled. "He will make her a good husband. One deserving of her."

And that one cut.

"Althea is all right with this?" Declan questioned.

"It would seem so since she has received him at Standfield Hall and he is escorting her to the Harvest Ball at the palace tomorrow evening."

"So much for there never being another man for her," Declan grumbled.

"It is what it is," Edward said and when his son glared at him, he shrugged. "One of your sayings I have adopted for my own." He nudged his chin toward the paper. "Now sign. I will be attending the ball at Boreas and wish to be leaving shortly."

"You didn't think to ask me to join you?" Declan complained.

"What?" Edward asked, feigning shock. "You would want to leave your room and venture out with the other living beings in our world?"

"Mayhap I am tired of my room."

"Then sign the paper and I will have Iverson come pack a weekend bag for you."

"I'll not sign that paper until I speak with Althea," Declan stated.

"She has no desire to either speak to you or see you, Declan James. Sign the gods-be-damned papers."

"No."

Edward locked what he hoped was his sternest glower upon his son but Declan withstood it. The boy's jaw was clenched, his fists doubled on the desk but he did not blink. His unwavering stare was a good sign.

"All right. Have it your way. If you wish for Althea and her father to embarrass you at court, so be it." He snatched up the papers, refolded them and stuffed them back in the envelope. "I'll send Iverson to see to your packing."

That said, he spun on his heel and trying not to allow the triumphant grin from stretching across his lips, leaving his son to do the brooding at which the boy was so professionally good.

Chapter Fourteen

The carriage ride to the Serenian capitol of Boreas was an agony unto itself. Wheels never missing a single rock or rut, the vehicle rambled along at a pace any tortoise could outrun. With the suspension squeaking like a banshee and the ripe smell of horse shit that wafted into the window, it made for a particularly unpleasant journey.

"How is your leg doing?" Lord James inquired. He was sitting beside Declan's father for they had reasoned he might need the room to stretch out.

"It only hurts when I flex my knee," Declan answered. He wasn't in the mood for small talk but that was all of which Lord James seemed capable.

"Then don't flex your knee," his father said drolly.

Grinding his teeth, Declan laid his head back on the seat and closed his eyes. Mayhap he could sleep now that the sun was down and the air cooler. They were two hours or more from Boreas and he was surprised at how tiring the trip was proving to be.

* * * * *

Althea stared at herself in the mirror and hated what she saw. She didn't like the hairdo for it made her face look too plump. She didn't like the color of the gown for it made her look too pale. The cut of the gown was worse for it made her look as though she was with child.

Which she was.

Her eyes grew bright with the tears that seemed to come at the drop of a hat these days.

She'd thought her monthly had been delayed because of the stress of Declan nearly getting killed, of helping to care for him, of having him reject her so brutally. The fatigue was easily explainable because she'd spent many a sleepless night worrying about him then crying over his refusal to accept her love. She'd barely paid attention to her tender, swollen breasts or the need to make more visits than normal to relieve herself. There'd been no morning sickness to alarm her. It wasn't until the strange cravings for food she'd never liked began that she started to worry. She devoured kumquats and sour pickles by the bowlful. Tossed down candy and inhaled pastries by the dozens. Such gluttony had surely caused the weight gain that made most of her gowns unwearable. But it was the sudden aversion to foods she'd always enjoyed immensely that sent her to the healer.

Five months, Your Grace, the healer announced with a grimace.

But how can that be? she'd asked.

There is only one way I know that would cause a pregnancy, Your Grace, he stated.

Sweet Merciful Morrigunia, she'd said with a groan and put her hands over her face.

She'd told no one, though she was sure her lady's maid, Ermaline, knew. How could she not?

That one time. One time, she thought, that she had lain with Declan.

That was all it took, Your Grace, the healer said on a long sigh.

The conversation she'd had with Declan at Jack's cottage came back to taunt her:

What is this liquid at the tip?

Semen. The seed of life.

Your seed. Seed that would get me with child. I am not ready yet for a child, Highwayman.

Then when the time comes, I will not spend my seed within you. On my honor, I will not.

That would work?

For centuries that is all that has been used by many couples, he replied. *I cannot swear it works every time but it is my understanding that it does most times.*

It is the chance we take. It will not matter once we are wed.

What?

We will marry eventually.

Milady, I have no inclination to marry.

No, indeed, he did not. At least no inclination to marry her. Bess? Well, that was another matter altogether, now, wasn't it?

She lowered her hands and looked at the missive she had received from the man she had put on Penry's trail. He'd found Penry.

And the woman who was living with him.

* * * * *

He was dreaming of that first night—that only night—he had held Althea in his arms. The night she had given herself to him. The night he had taken the most precious of gifts from her. He had been her first and she had wanted him to be her last.

We will marry eventually, she'd said.

Time swirled forward—capturing them in its vortex and when the spinning stopped he knew her words were coming to fruition this dreamed night.

Gone was the cottage and in its place the chapel at Boreas Keep where dozens of celebrants had gathered to witness the Joining of Declan Farrell and Althea Standfield.

Standing beside him on his left side were his father and mother—back from the watery depths and smiling happily upon him. Jack was on his right—which was proper for the best man.

Suddenly there came the soft tinkle of silver bells. He turned his head to look up the aisle and there she was—so beautiful she took his breath away.

In a sparkling silver gown upon which row after row of diamonds had been stitched in chains from high bodice to hem. With soft silver-colored slippers peeking out from beneath that scalloped hem with each step she took toward him.

Toward him.

No other.

Him.

What a lucky man he was to have this beautiful, loving woman smiling upon him, coming to him. Willing to take him as her mate.

Without questions.

Without judgment.

Without regret.

Her slender arm was tucked into the crook of her father's arm and on her other side walked a woman he had never met, never seen, but she, too, had come back from the Afterlife to celebrate her daughter's Joining day.

"It is now the designated hour of Joining," the emissary called out. "Who comes to seek the blessings of the gods on this ritual?"

"I, Lord Declan James Farrell, Duke of Dungannon, have come to seek the gods' blessings," he stated.

The emissary nodded. "And who has come to Join with this man?"

"I, Lady Althea Anne Standfield, Countess of Edgerton have come to the Joining."

Looking to the lovely woman standing beside Althea, the Emissary: "Can you vouch for your purity, Lady Althea Anne?"

"This man is my first," she answered.

The emissary frowned at her choice of words then asked, "Is there anyone who has reason to believe this Joining should not take place or that it would be invalid?"

No one spoke out against the Joining and he breathed a sigh of relief.

"Lord Declan James," the emissary asks. "Do you willingly give yourself to this woman?"

"With all my heart and all my soul and all my being. I pledge myself only unto her. What is mine will be hers."

"Lady Althea Anne, do you willingly give yourself to this man without reservation, without protest?"

"With all my heart and all my soul and all my being. I pledge myself only unto him. What is mine will be his."

"The Questions were asked. The Questions were answered. Now this man and this woman will kneel before us in obedience to the wishes of their gods. Here, before us, they will pledge themselves only unto one another. One flesh, one inseparable entity, until the end of time. Once mated, never separated."

"I speak now to those of you who have come here to bear witness to this Joining. Let those of you who see this ritual know— In the eyes of his god, through dispensation given to him by Tribunal Law, with the permission of his father and King, and the blessings of this woman's parents and sovereigns, in the presence of his peers, and at the jurisdiction of my hands given by authority as a prelate of the Brothers of the Wind, I declare Lord Declan James bound by laws both preternatural and temporal, to submit himself to this Joining."

Jack stepped forward with a silken pillow upon which rested two broad gold bands. After removing his shirt, Declan held his hand out to Althea. She took it and he helped her to kneel at the feet of the emissary before joining her.

"This man and this woman now kneel before the gods and man in obedience to the wishes of Alel. Here, before the gods and man, they will pledge themselves only unto one another. One flesh, one inseparable entity, until the end of their lives."

The emissary lifted the gold bands and held them up for all to see. He smiled down at them.

"The outward sign of your union, your link to one another, your eternal reminder that you are now responsible to another for your actions, is the Band of Devotion that will be placed on each of you by your fathers. With this symbol, you will be joined for all time. Let all who witness the placement of these bands know: You are one to another, forever as one, never to be parted by anything, or anyone, under penalty of death."

The emissary handed him the smaller of the two bands. Althea held out her arm and he slid the golden band onto her arm.

Althea took the larger band and placed it upon his arm.

Holding his hands over their heads, the emissary looked to the heavens.

"As this woman has agreed to become one with this man, a part of him, so shall these bands be a part of you. As your wife and your husband may not be taken from you, so shall these bands never be removed. They are the symbols of eternal union blessed by the gods, sanctioned by ancient law, acknowledged and accepted and witnessed by those gathered and given to you by my own hands as a representative of the gods on this earth."

At a nod from the emissary, he got to his feet and held out his hand to help Althea to hers.

"With all my heart and all my soul and all my being I pledge myself only unto you, Althea Anne. What is mine will be yours. You, I have chosen of mine own freewill and without reservation or protest. I will walk the day and sleep the night at your side and at no other's. I pledge myself only unto you for as long as there is life for us both. I will be, forever, your true mate in word and deed. We are one flesh, one inseparable entity and until the end of time, once mated, never separated."

Althea's smile was the most beautiful thing he'd ever seen. Her low, sweet voice as she repeated the Joining Vows to him brought tears to his eyes.

"With all my heart and all my soul and all my being I pledge myself only unto you, Declan James. What is mine will be yours. You, I have chosen of mine own freewill and without reservation or protest. I will walk the day and sleep the night at your side and at no other's. I pledge myself only unto you for as long as there is life for us both. I will be, forever, your true mate in word and deed. We are one flesh, one inseparable entity and until the end of time, once mated, never separated."

"With the power invested in me by gods and man, it my honor to pronounce you Joined. You may partake of your wife's lips, Lord Declan," the emissary declared.

One moment they were standing in the chapel at Boreas and the next they were in a bedchamber lit by dozens of white tapers. The air was perfumed with gardenia and a fire crackled in the wide hearth. Rose petals adored the pristine white coverlet upon their marriage bed. On the bedside table were two flutes of sparkling Francachi champagne and a bowl of plump red strawberries.

"Milady," he whispered against her lips.

"My husband," she replied.

He lifted her in his arms and carried her to the bed. As he walked her gown simply dissolved—as did his wedding finery. Dipping a knee to the mattress, he laid her down gently then straightened to look down at her lush body.

"Mine," he said.

"Yours," she agreed.

His hand was shaking as he reached down to touch the sweet flesh of her breast. He ran his thumb over the firm peak and his cock leapt with expectation. She turned to her side to face him and patted the bed beside her.

"You were not so shy at the cottage, milord. Why are you now?"

"I'm not, milady," he replied.

She opened her arms to him. "Then come and service your woman, highwayman."

He swung his leg over her, stretched his body atop hers and lowered his head to slant his mouth hungrily across hers. She opened her lips to meet his tongue thrust for thrust as he reached down to take hold of his cock.

"Umm," she said beneath his kiss then arched her hips to meet his firm invasion. When he was inside her—buried deep and throbbing—she lifted her legs to wrap them firmly around his waist.

Slow, easy, swiveling his pelvis against hers, he withdrew and advanced. Withdrew and advanced. Slid his groin up hers, ran his hands under her ass and jerked her to him with one savage, possessive move.

"Declan!"

He snapped his eyes open. For a moment he had no idea where he was. It was dark but all around him was the sound of creaking and some sort of rolling motion.

"Get your hand off your body, boy."

That was his father's demanding voice and he sat up so quickly the pain in his thigh made him cry out.

And his throbbing, hard-as-a-rock cock push painfully against his breeches. He snatched his hand back for it was wrapped around that cock over the shield of the doeskin material.

It took him only a few seconds more to realize he was in a rolling carriage with his father and godfather looking at him with amusement.

"Dear gods," he mumbled, shamed to his very core. He covered his erection as best he could with his crossed palms.

"Happens to the best of us, son," Lord James said—lips twitching—before turning his head to look out the window.

"Of whom were you dreaming, Declan?" his father inquired. He leaned forward. "Or should I ask which one of them glided through your dreams?"

He refused to take the bait. In the darkness he couldn't make out his father's features once the old man leaned back in his seat for he was on the shadowed side of the coach. Lord James's face, however, was lit the rays of the new moon. There was humor lurking there.

"How far do you think we are from Boreas, Lord James?" he inquired.

"A hand pull or two, I should think," his father quipped.

Lord James was chuckling as he kept his profile to Declan.

"I am bored," his father said. "What shall we talk about, Jamie?"

"Whatever pops up," Lord James said.

"All right," Declan hissed. "I've been duly chastised, milords."

"Fair play to you, lad," Lord James replied.

"Needs to get laid," his father stated. "I'm sure there will be ladies at court who will be quite happy to take matters in hand."

"I believe Deckie has that already covered," Lord James said drily.

"The devil take the both of you," Declan snapped and pointedly ignored them the remainder of the way.

* * * * *

The Central Hall of Boreas Keep was a wonder to behold. As Declan looked down on it from the balcony, he marveled at the beauty of the rich tapestries and the intricate marble floor, which bore the Great Seal of the Serenian Kings. Each successive king's name was stamped in gold leaf on individual round stones circling the hallmark and sealed beneath multiple layers of resin. Above the Great Seal was a multi-paned skylight that cast a greenish glow from its stained-glass panels. The furniture was elegant and bold and shone richly with polish. Scattered about the marble floor were expertly crafted Arabach rugs in intricate jewel-hued patterns.

For centuries the magnificent palace had been home to the McGregor Clan. Jack liked to joke that he was one of the many illegitimate sons of the last McGregor king—at last count there were over forty—but in actuality there was no kinship between him and the crown. Each time Declan stepped foot in the keep he thought of Jack sitting upon the great throne and laughed.

"What do you find funny?" his father asked as they were being shown to their suite of rooms.

"I was thinking of Jack," he answered.

A grunt was the only comment his father made.

When they reached the room that had been assigned to him, the servant stopped, opened the portal and bowed. "Your chambers, Your Grace," he stated.

"Be quick about getting ready," his father told him. "I would like to make an entrance with you at my side for a change."

"And please do try not to limp, boy," Declan mumbled under his breath.

"I heard that," his father snapped before waving the servant on.

There was a second servant who entered the room behind Declan. That man was carrying the weekend bag Iverson had packed for him—including the formal attire that would be required for the Harvest Ball.

"I can unpack," Declan told him. He was anxious to be alone and wanted the stranger gone.

"As you wish, Your Grace," the servant said but his pursed lips gave mute evidence of his censure. He quietly withdrew, closing the door gently behind him.

He stared at the weekend bag for a long time then growled. The last thing he wanted to do—felt like doing—was mix and mingle with a bunch of stuffy aristocrats and royalty. But Althea was here and he needed to speak with her. In his father's pocket were the nullification papers that would put an end to their engagement.

And he wasn't altogether sure that was what he wanted.

* * * * *

The perfumes. The colognes. The pomades. The garishly dressed nobles chittering away like anxious squirrels. Liveried servants making the rounds with silver trays upon which sat flutes of champagne and dishes of exotic hors d'oeuvres. A three-string quartet in the corner playing classical pieces as the known gossips milled about from group to group.

Boring, he thought, drawing the word out in his mind.

He'd been surreptitiously searching for Althea among the throng but had yet to spy her. He'd seen her father, but the man had taken one look at him then pointedly turned his back. No wondering what Lord Alastair thought of him.

It was overly warm in the ballroom so the doors to the garden were open wide. A few gentlemen were on the flagstone patio smoking their cheroots, chuckling over the latest folly among the elite or discussing clandestine business affairs.

"Lord Declan, is it?" a man asked.

Declan turned and stiffened as he saw the bright red uniform, the golden epaulets adorning wide shoulders, a pristine white cravat and row upon row of gleaming medals on his chest.

"And you are Captain Rand Gunderson, Duke of Stybiorne," he muttered.

The tall bastard actually clicked the heels of his highly polished black boots together and bowed slightly. "I am, but please, I am not fond of titles. I find them rather silly and pretentious. Don't you?"

Declan shrugged, took a sip of the wine. He looked about the room, hoping the man would take the hint and leave him be. Apparently that wasn't going to be the case.

"I hear you feel the same," Rand pressed. He grinned. "The truth now."

"I suppose I do," Declan reluctantly conceded.

"So please call me Rand. May I call you Declan?"

He shrugged again. "Whatever tugs on your chin strap, old boy," Declan answered.

Laughter parted Gunderson's lips to reveal strong, white teeth. The merriment crinkled the corners of his green eyes.

"I was told you had a wicked sense of humor."

"Glad you found it amusing," Declan muttered.

"Actually, I'm told we have quite a bit in common," Rand stated, folding his arms over his chest full of medals.

Trying not to let his irritation show, Declan turned his eyes to the man. "Is that so?"

"You were a Royal Marine."

"I never considered myself a Royal Marine. I was forced into the military," Declan grumbled, looking toward his father.

"As was I."

Declan shot him a surprised look.

"True," Rand told him, one hand up as though making an oath. "My father thought it would make me grow up. Teach me to be a man. Curb the wild streak he believed might one day be my downfall."

"I've heard that song and dance before," Declan acknowledged with a snort.

"I thought you might have," Rand replied. "We have other things in common as well."

"Do tell," Declan said.

"I have a keen like for cocked hats and velvet coats," Rand said with a lift of his left eyebrow. "Especially those of a darker red hue."

That sent a cautioning tremor through Declan. He narrowed his eyes. "I suggest you be careful in claiming that, milord," he warned.

"May I ask why?"

"People might believe you to be the highwayman who dresses in that fashion," Declan replied.

"But the Gypsy is dead, is he not?" Rand asked. "And buried in your family plot if memory serves."

Declan felt a muscle bunch in his cheek. "Daniel Rees was a good friend."

"Indeed he was. It is a rare and honorable man who would give his life—and reputation—for a friend," Rand said, looking over the rim of his wineglass. "Don't you agree?"

"Where exactly is this conversation heading, Gunderson?" Declan asked.

"Here and there and yonder," Rand replied. "We have so very much in common as we've already discovered." He smiled. "Such as the dual fondness we share for the same beautiful young lady here tonight."

"If you are speaking of Lady Althea..."

"I am," Rand interrupted then grinned. "You know I am."

"If you are asking my permission to call upon the lady..."

"I don't need your permission to court the lady in question. It is my understanding the marriage contract between the two of you has been vacated. That being the case, you no longer have any hold on the lady, but I would like your blessing to court her"

Declan smiled then leaned in close. "Well, you won't get it," he said before bumping his shoulder against the other man's and limping away with his jaw clenched.

* * * * *

Althea had been watching the exchange from the balcony. She had spied Rand's bright red uniform coat among the swarm of russet, green, gold and brown coats and gowns—the colors of harvest required for this particular ball. There were other military men strolling about but none as tall or elegant or wide of shoulder as Rand Gunderson.

Nor could she miss the only man there dressed in his usual jet-black attire from shirt to cravat to coat to breeches. Leaning against the balcony rail she observed the way they responded to one another.

"Not good," she thought.

Though Rand was laughing, seemed perfectly at ease, there was something not quite right about the way he was staring at Declan. As for Declan…

Could a man stand any stiffer? Give off nearly as much animosity and hostility? She'd come to know him rather well over the weeks of his convalescence and thus could tell when he was being antagonistic. Expressing his natural aggression.

Sighing heavily, she turned from the balcony and headed for the stairs. She had to speak to him though it was the last thing she actually wanted to do. She had come to the ball to try to get over him, but after what she had learned from the investigator, he had a right to know the outcome of the search for Penry. That Declan had come to the ball had surprised her when her father told her. His being there seemed as though it was fated.

As she descended the stairs, she saw him slam his shoulder into Rand and mentally groaned. She feared the deliberate insult would anger Rand, but then she saw him turn his head toward Lord James Giddens and grin widely. Lord James laughed and held up a thumb.

"What is that about?" she asked.

"Beg pardon?" a gentleman coming up the stairs inquired.

She forced a smile to herself. "Just talking to myself, Lord Frazier," she said with a slight inclination of her head. She continued down the stairs trying to interpret that look between Lord James and Rand.

Declan had disappeared from view by the time she reached the bottom of the stairs. He had a way of doing that, she thought with exasperation. Like a phantom gliding furtively between the trees in the forest.

"He's on the patio."

She jumped at the voice and jerked around to find Rand standing behind her. He offered her his arm and she took it without thinking. He covered her hand with his and squeezed lightly, his merry green eyes sparkling with mischief.

"Shall we make the foolish twit jealous, milady?" he asked.

"I think not," she said, frowning at him. "It is never wise to poke a bear with a sore paw."

"What harm would it cause?" he inquired. "He has set you free, has he not?"

Hearing him say that hurt so badly she wanted to cry.

"Is that what you and he were discussing when I saw you together?"

"In part," he replied. "I asked for his blessing to court you."

She stared at him. "You did what?"

"I don't believe he took well to my request," he told her.

"Oh?" she asked. Suddenly her heart was pounding as she waited breathlessly for his answer. "What did he say?"

Instead of answering, he began walking her toward the open garden door.

"Milord, I don't think this is such a good idea," she said.

"It is a lovely night," he stated. "Mayhap the last we'll have before the winter winds come howling. We should enjoy every moment of it."

With perfect clarity she knew what he was doing. She suspected he was in league with Lord James but what they were trying to accomplish was sure to backfire. Declan did not want her, did not want the Joining. No doubt he had in his possession the signed papers that vacated the marriage contract. He would most likely present them to the king before he returned the Arlington.

"Relax, milady," Rand said. "You are supposed to be enjoying yourself with a handsome suitor who has eyes only for you."

She looked up at him. "You are the very devil aren't you, Rand Gunderson?"

"I can be," he granted. "And there is our target."

She had already seen Declan standing by himself in the shadows. The light from a torch lit his profile as he leaned negligently against a stone column and stared out into the darkened garden.

"Mayhap a stroll down the pathway to the fountain," Rand suggested and began escorting her in that direction.

From the corner of her eye, she saw Declan look their way and—just like that—the stiffness returned to his stance. He straightened, pulled his shoulders back. She could feel his eyes boring into her.

"He's watching," Rand said quietly.

"What are we doing, Rand?" she whispered.

"I'll show you," he replied and stopped. Before she knew what he was about, he swept his arm around her, pulled her to him and swept his head down to claim her lips.

Even from the distance that separated her and Declan she heard the low growl. Felt Rand's answering chuckle as he thoroughly kissed her. If her heart wasn't already lying at the feet of a certain former highwayman, she could have been swept away with the kiss that had taken possession of her mouth.

There was a clearing of throat then an apologetic voice interrupting the kiss. "Ah, excuse me, Captain Gunderson?"

Gunderson released her and turned. "Aye?" he snapped.

"My apologies, sir, but the king's minister would like a word with you," a man in the dark blue uniform of the king's elite guard replied.

"Now?" Rand demanded. "Can you not see I am having a private discussion with my lady?"

Another low growl from the shadows made Althea look that way. She could not see him, but she knew Declan was there.

"I do apologize, sir, but Lord Wynth intimated it was quite urgent that he speak with you."

"Oh, for the love of the gods," Rand grumbled. "All right. Lead on." Stepping back, he took her hand, kissed it. "Milady, duty calls."

"I understand," she said.

He winked. "I will return as soon as I can."

"I shall be here waiting," she replied.

She watched him walking behind the elite guard and decided to venture further into the depths of the secluded garden. At the end of the lush grounds she spied the sea gate. Beyond the elaborate wrought iron she caught just a glimmer of the North Boreal Sea. Pulling her shawl about her shoulders, she took the path, which led to the gate.

Once there, she reached out to touch a late-blooming rose on one of the twin bushes that flanked the wrought-iron barrier.

"You shouldn't be out here alone."

She hadn't heard him, but she had been expecting him to join her.

"I am not alone," she said though she did not look up at him.

"Your escort has left you so," he reminded her.

"I am not alone because you are with me," she replied softly.

"He was not much of a gentleman to leave you out here to fend for yourself," he snapped and she realized he was clenching and unclenching his fists.

"Mayhap he knew I would be fine until his return," she suggested.

"Nevertheless he should not have…"

"Your thigh is better?" she interrupted, still not looking at him.

"I'm sorry?" he asked.

"I asked if your thigh is better. I see you aren't using your cane."

He put his hand over the area where the wound was. "It pains me from time to time but not enough to warrant the cane."

"That's good to know. I am relieved that is the case."

She was watching the moonlight turning the seashore a beautiful shade of gold but was keenly aware that he had moved closer to her. When he put a hand beside her to grip one of the wrought-iron bars on the sea gate she could almost feel his warm breath on her neck.

"You look lovely tonight," he told her.

"Thank you, milord."

"You are happy?"

She looked up at him. "As happy as a woman can be when her heart is broken."

"Thea, I am…"

"I like the beard you are growing," she interrupted. "It makes you look as dangerous as you really are."

His eyebrows drew together. "Thea, that…"

"Did you sign the papers?" she asked, turning her face to the sea once more. "I did."

"I saw," he said and she thought she heard disapproval in his tone.

Or wanted to hear it.

"Did you bring them with you to present to the king?"

"I didn't sign them," he stated.

Her heart leapt in her chest. "May I ask why not?"

"I wanted to talk to you first," he replied.

"What is there to say?"

"Will you look at me?" he asked.

She steeled herself to look again into that handsome, manly face. What she saw there surprised her.

"I wanted to thank you for helping take care of me when I was so ill," he said.

That wasn't what she was expecting and—truth be told, she thought—it made her gods-be-damned mad.

"It is nothing I wouldn't have done for any other wounded man," she stated, holding his gaze. Not giving anything away as she looked at him.

He actually flinched and his eyes shifted away from hers as though she'd cut him to the core.

"You know how to put a man in his place, don't you, milady?" he asked.

"Is that all you wanted to speak with about, then?" she queried.

He shook his head. "No."

"There is more?"

"I wanted to apologize for what I said to you that day. I ask your forgiveness for my actions. I know it is no excuse for my appalling behavior but I was hurt that you and Jack had not told me about…"

"I actually have information regarding that issue," she said, cutting him off. "When you return to Arlington you will find a letter I wrote to you before we left for Boreas, but since you are here, I will relate what it is in the letter."

"What issue?" he asked, frowning.

"The man I hired to find Penry came to Standfield Hall the morning we were leaving to come to the palace. He found Penry in Ionary at Guilder's Cay."

Declan's eyes widened. "Was he…?"

"She is with him," she told him. "Alive and well as far as the investigator could tell."

That seemed to anger him more than appease his worry. He reached up to rake his free hand through his hair. "Is she happy?"

"I did not ask him if that was the case but he did ascertain through speaking with the villagers that Penry is not mistreating her in any way. They were seen walking along the shore with her arm through his."

In for a penny, in for a pound, she thought.

"There is something you should know," she said. "She is with child."

He jerked and staggered back as though she'd hit him with a wooden club. "What?" he asked.

"I presume it is yours for the investigator said she was showing quite nicely, as he put it," she said and hoped he did not see her digging her fingernails into her palms.

"Pregnant?" he questioned. He let go of the iron bar and turned away from her. "She's pregnant?"

"It would seem so, aye," she said. She wanted desperately to tell him of her own condition but she would not lay that upon his platter now. He seemed stricken hearing of Bess's impending motherhood. At that moment he didn't need to know the tavern girl's child was not the only one of his making coming into the world.

There was a wrought-iron bench sitting cater-cornered to the gate and he sat down heavily upon it with his hand over his mouth as though to keep at bay the words struggling to get out.

"Will you be going to Ionary?" she asked.

"I don't have a choice. I'll not let that bastard raise my child," he said.

"The investigator said he went to the church in the village and spoke to the priest. No banns have been read in regards to the Joining of William Tucker and Maire Belvoir, the names she and Penry are using."

"So he isn't going to marry her," he said.

"I guess not."

"He would let the babe be born a bastard."

"Would you want him to give his name to your child?" she quizzed.

"Hell, no," he snarled.

"Then that leaves you to do the right thing by her and your child," she said, her soul aching so badly it was all she could do not to drop to the ground and wail.

He leaned forward with his elbows on his knees, his hands on his forehead. "This is wrong—so wrong—on so many levels," he whispered.

"When will you be leaving?"

"Tonight," he answered. He lifted his head to look at her and she thought she saw—nay, wanted to see—anguish twisting his features. "I'll sign the papers before I go."

That news nearly dropped her to her knees but she managed to keep her voice steady and the tears from forming in her eyes.

"Then I wish you gods' speed, Declan," she said.

She ran her gaze over his beautiful face then turned and hurried away before the tears could fall.

Chapter Fifteen

He left the keep and went straight to the docks in the hopes of finding a ship that would take him to Ionary. He was inquiring with the third sea captain when he saw Lord James striding toward him down the dock.

"We need to talk," Lord James snapped when he got within speaking distance.

"Don't try to stop me," Declan told him.

"I have no intention of stopping you. I do, however, have a few things to say to you before you do."

"I have found Penry."

"So I've been told," Lord James said.

"You spoke to Thea?"

"I did and right now it's all I can do not to knock your gods-be-damned teeth down your gods-be-damned throat, Declan," Lord James yelled.

That took him back. The man was looking at him as though he were the lowest of the low and from the way he was curling and uncurling his fists, his godfather meant what he said.

"What did I do?" he asked, trying to remember what he'd said to Thea that might have caused her more hurt.

"You're going to Ionary to do what?" Lord James demanded. "Call Penry out? Snatch the girl from his grasp?"

"Find out if she's there willingly," Declan said. He wasn't sure that was not the case all things considered.

They were seen walking along the shore with her arm through his.

"And if she is not?"

"I'll bring her back to Serenia."

"What if she wants to stay?"

"Thea told you Bess is with child?"

Lord James nodded sharply.

"Then if she is there of her own volition, if she wants to stay, I'll take her ass to the priest and have the vows read over us," Declan told him.

The appalled look that crossed over Lord James' face might at any other time made him laugh but when that look was accompanied with the hardest slap he'd ever taken in his life, laughter was the last thing he thought of doing.

"What the *fuck* is the matter with you?" Lord James bellowed at the top of his lungs. "Why in the names of the gods would you want to do such a stupid fucking thing, Declan?"

"To give my child a name," Declan yelled back.

"Which one?"

Now that wasn't a question he was expecting from his godfather.

"What do you mean which one?"

"Just what I said. Which child will you give your name to?"

"She's carrying two?" Declan asked, horrified by the notion.

"Two...?" Lord James slapped him again and this time Declan staggered back. Hand to his stinging cheek he stared wide-eyed at the irate man who jabbed a finger at him. "You are a complete imbecile. Do you know that?"

"My child has a right to my name," Declan told him. He was more than a little alarmed at the fury that was shifting across Lord James's normally placid face. "I would not be much of a man if I did not own up to what I did. It is not the child's fault it was conceived out of wedlock. I would make things right for..."

"For whom?" Lord James snapped.

"For Bess," Declan said. "For our child."

"So you would marry Bess yet leave Althea to suffer the shame of bearing your bastard child? You think marrying a tavern maid cohabiting with another man is more honorable than a woman of substance who loves you with all her being?"

Shock went through him like the rusty blade of a rapier and he had to reach out to grab a nearby wooden stanchion.

"Aye," Lord James hissed. "You got *her* with child as well. Potent little bugger aren't you?" He reached into his pocket and withdrew the nullification papers Declan had signed before leaving the palace, papers Lord James was supposed to take to the king's counselor. "You can take these gods-be-damned things and wipe your ass with them or better yet..." He took the papers in both hands and tore them down the middle. He tore them yet again then threw the pieces at Declan. "Shove them *up* your ass. You'll wed Althea Standfield or I'll see your father slaps you in Baybridge!"

That said, his godfather pivoted on his heel and marched back the way he had come.

Utterly staggered by the revelation, stunned beyond his ability to voice the questions—How? When? Why didn't she tell me?—that were thundering like runaway hooves in his mind, he slid down to the planks and sat there with his mouth ajar.

"Ye be the one lookin' for passage to Ionary?"

He slowly looked up at the sailor who had appeared out of nowhere. "What?"

"Didn't want to bother ye none considerin' what ye was talkin' to the toff about," the man said. He hawked up a wad of phlegm and shot it over the dock and into the water. "But me ship be leavin' with the mornin' tide if'n ye still want to be goin'."

She hadn't told him. She'd had the opportunity to but she hadn't.

Then that leaves you to do the right thing by her and your child.

She'd stepped aside. He knew it as surely as he knew his own name.

As surely as he knew he had to bestow that name upon his child.

Which one? Lord James had asked.

"Sweet Merciful Alel," he said.

"Ye want to be goin' or not?" the sailor asked.

There was only one thing he could do. He had to go to Ionary. He had to know if Bess had been taken there against her will or if she had been in league with Penry. If it was the former, he would bring her and their unborn child back to Serenia. It if were the latter, he'd stay in Ionary until the child was born then take it from her. Either way, the child would be brought up where he or she belonged and given its father's name. He would rather die than leave a child of his at the mercy of Royce Penry.

* * * * *

"You did *what*?" Edward asked.

"Tore the gods-be-damned things up and threw them at him," Jamie replied. "The brat is going to marry Althea. I assure you."

Edward stared at his childhood friend. "How did you accomplish that?"

"I gave him an incentive."

"How so?" Edward asked as he took a sip of brandy.

"She's having your grandchild."

Edward choked on the brandy and went into a fit of coughing as the fiery brew went up his nose. Gasping for breath, he lurched forward as Jamie came over to pound him on his back.

"Enough," he begged off, holding up a hand.

"I would think you'd be pleased that we had our son by the shorthairs," Jamie quipped. "He may not know what he wants but we do."

"He knows," Edward said in between gasps. "He's just not accepted it yet."

"The girl loves him more than anything in this world and she'll make him a fine wife," Jamie said.

"I'm not arguing with you there," Edward said, his lungs burning from the brandy. He laid his head on the back of the chair. "But what if he brings that tavern wench back with him? What if he marries the chit while he's down there?"

"He won't," Jamie replied.

"How can you be so sure?"

"He will do right by Althea. As much as he balks at being a member of the nobility, he will do what is expected of him and…" Jamie shrugged. "It's what he wants anyway." He laughed. "You should have heard that growl when Rand kissed her."

"That was playing with fire," Edward grumbled.

"Rand was most accommodating," Jamie said.

"What if he had decided to go after Althea for himself?"

"Wouldn't have happened," Jamie said. "His jib is not cut from the same cloth as ours."

"His jib…?" Edward frowned then gaped. "Really?"

"Really," Jamie acknowledged.

"You're sure?"

"Positive."

"Now that is something I would never have even considered about him. Not that it matters."

"The important thing is he made our boy jealous as a Diabolusian warthog guarding its sty."

"Good that you hit it off with him when you went to ask for Daniel Rees's body," Edward told him.

"He's a good man and I suspect he knows Dec was the highwayman."

"Dangerous knowledge, that," Edward warned.

"No, I don't think so. Rand has a social conscience and I believe he admired what Declan did. After all, other than winging a man or two Dec never hurt anyone when he was about as the Gypsy. So the rich got a little poorer when the moonlight rider was on the moors and the poor got a little better off."

"True enough, I suppose," Edward agreed. He'd not told Jamie what Jack had confessed to him about the men Declan had killed in the bar. If the boy wanted his godfather to know, he would tell him.

* * * * *

Guilder's Cay was not far from the penal colony at Ghurn. It sat on the southernmost cliff of Ionary overlooking the South Boreal Sea. Wild and beautiful country, but inhospitable once *el mal tiempo* set in. The craggy cliffs jutted out over thunderous waves that crashed upward in powerful bursts. Such a hostile environment made it necessary for the villagers to build strong rock houses that could withstand the torrential rains and mighty hurricane-force winds that pummeled them from June until late November. No ships sailed into the harbor at Guilder's Cay when fog was thick along that stretch of coast for hidden reefs, and sunken boats posed a serious threat to navigation. Not even the sweeping beam from the Meseta lighthouse could penetrate the dense mist.

So it was that Declan stood in the impenetrable fog beyond the rail of the Oceanian ship the *Medea* and brooded as he listened to the creaking of the masts. The captain of the brigantine told him the fog might lift by mid-morning but chances were good it might not. It could be noontime before the sun burned away the mist.

"Such is the climate here," Captain Kyriakos explained. "It is unlike any other save the Sinisters and that's worse yet."

It had taken the *Medea* three days to sail up to then around Hellstrom Point then down the eastern coast of Virago before venturing southward toward Ionary. As they passed around the horn of Virago, Declan got his first—and he hoped last—look at Baybridge Harbor where the infamous insane asylum was located. From his cabin he watched through the porthole as the forbidding black marble construction loomed over the North Boreal Sea. The sight of that grim structure put the fear of the gods in him and sent a cold shiver down his spine.

You'll wed Althea Standfield or I'll see your father slaps you in Baybridge, Lord James had threatened.

That would be a fate far worse than death, he imagined.

Not marrying Althea, he thought, but being locked inside that loathsome institution from which few patients ever left.

Marrying Althea. When, he wondered, had that started to become something he wanted instead of wanting to run from?

Just the thought of marrying her, living—and sparring—with her was almost enough to push the uneasiness he felt at being aboard a ship for the first time since losing his mother and brother. The slap of the water against the hull as the ship cut through the waves made him acutely uncomfortable, but more so when there was nothing but miles and miles of water ahead and behind the vessel. No land, no safety in sight. When they neared the craggy cliffs of Virago, it was all he could do not to tremble. The memories—like the waves over the *Molly Celeste*—came rushing over him.

"Think of Althea," he'd said.

Not Bess but Althea.

Somewhere in the distance a foghorn bellowed and the low skirl of an answering bell replied. The sounds were ghostly, eerie in the white shroud that covered the water lapping at the ship's hull. He could almost imagine watery spirits clawing their way up the sides and slithering over the rail.

"Nice thought to have before hitting the rack, asshole," he said.

He leaned forward and looked over the teakwood rail but he couldn't see anything—thankfully not a skeletal face peering back at him with its ghastly grin.

He knew he couldn't sleep anyway so there'd be no opportunity for spectral water demons to come wriggling under his cabin door to drown him in his bunk. There were other—more uneasy things—to think about than nightmare visitors.

Bess was less than a mile away from where he stood. Come tomorrow, he would be in the same village with her.

And Penry.

* * * * *

His hands were gentle, his lips so soft against her own but his well-honed body was rock hard. She ran her palms up his thick chest—spreading her fingers through the tight curls—then encircled his neck to press close to him. His kiss took her breath away. His body turned her into a wanton strumpet, a purring feline rubbing across his lower body.

He was her friend. Her savior. Her lover. He had become her world here on this wild, rugged coast. Everything that came before him had been wiped away with the trembling touch of his questing fingers.

"I love you," he whispered. "Sweet gods how I love you."

She could not say the words back to him just yet for she had given her heart to a dark highwayman. Though that man was gone, she would love him until the day she died. Until the rivers ran still and the four winds ceased to blow. She would grieve for him for eternity plus a day.

When she had heard the news of his death she had wanted to give in to her pain and die. There had been only one reason—and one alone—that had prevented her from doing so, and that reason was thriving within her.

She was going to tell him that night. Had planned to tell him. Should have told him before he left her that last time, but the timing had been wrong. He had promised her just one more ride and they would leave together to make a new life.

As they had made a new life, which even then moved within her belly.

"She's kicking again," her lover said and reached down to splay his hand across the mound.

"He's kicking again," she corrected and looked up at him.

He laughed—as he always did—and caressing her belly. "We'll know soon enough I guess."

"Three months," she reminded him.

To give him his due, he acted as though the highwayman's bantling was his own. Not once had he made her feel anything but pride in the child she was carrying. For that he would forever hold a special place in her heart. She would be content to spend her life with him. He had proven to be a good man. She did care for him. Greatly cared for him. Mayhap one day she would grow to love him.

Something she had not expected when first she'd met him.

"I should be going," he said. He gave her belly one gentler rub then released her. "That fog is as thick as pea soup, but it'll be lifting soon enough. The watchman will be leaving his post. I don't care to run into that bastard again this week."

"He doesn't care about us," she said. "About what we do."

"No, but he looks at me as though he's trying to remember where he's seen me before. The less I'm around him, the less likely it is he'll place me."

"Take care," she told him. She reached up to lay her palm on his lean cheek. "I worry about you when the weather is so rough. I would be lost if anything happened to you."

"I've learned to be careful at this new occupation of mine," he replied. He cupped her chin, gave her one last kiss then turned to go.

He opened the door and the fog drifted in—bringing with it the scent of the sea. One last wave and he was gone, closing the door softly behind him.

She went to the window and pulled aside the curtain. The mist was pressing against the panes so she could not see him, but she could see the golden glow of the sun that struggled to light the early morning. The fog echoed his footsteps back to her. She heard him greet the chandler.

"New ships out there, sir," the chandler reported.

"More harbor fees for us, eh?" her lover replied with a laugh.

"I wonder how many ships are waiting in the harbor to dock on our little spit of land," she said, rubbing her stomach over and over again. The babe was particularly active this morn.

Her lover was the new harbormaster at Guilder's Cay. It was his job to inspect each ship that docked here. To collect the docking fees and any taxes. He was the law on the Cay and he took his job seriously. His military training had held him in good stead. A few lies to enhance his resume had been necessary to gain the position but that was a small price to pay for such good employment. For the respect the villagers extended to him. For the anonymity. He had changed his looks entirely by growing a beard and he was letting his hair grow. It was amazing how those two such little things could hide who and what he had once been.

She turned away from the window and looked about the stone cottage she now called home. It wasn't a bad place. It was cozy and warm with five rooms—rather large considering the sizes of most of the other cottages along the strand—with indoor plumbing. The walls were a pale blue and the floor dark teak, which made the structure look more like the deck of a ship that a land-based building. On numerous walks along the beach at low tide, she had gathered all manner of treasures from the receding waves. Driftwood, shells, sea glass. She made the pale green gingham curtains with her own two hands and was in the process of crocheting an afghan in bright pastel colors for the loveseat. The place was neat and tidy for that was the way he liked things. She, herself, tended to be a bit messy but for him she was willing to make the effort to make things orderly. After all, without him, she would be in her grave.

Someone was, she thought, but could find no sympathy for Jonas. That man had been a bad one. If someone had to die, best it be a bastard like Jonas.

She looked at the wood-burning stove and decided to start the noon meal early. Though it was only six of the clock she needed to do something to occupy her. That was the bad thing about being so far from home. Away from all she'd ever known. Away from the father she loved so dearly and who she knew would grieve her 'til he left this world to join her mother.

Oh, how she was tempted to write him a letter. To hand it off to a sailor with a coin or two. Just to let Da know she still walked this life.

"That is a dangerous thing to do, wench," her lover had cautioned. "There are those who would come here looking for you. Too many secrets are riding on you not overturning the boat. My life, my freedom depend on your silence, too."

As she sat about putting the fixings for a barley soup and cornbread upon the table, she acknowledged she owed him so much; she would not betray him. He had helped her to regain her sanity after hearing the news of the Gypsy being shot down on the highway.

"They took his body to Arlington Castle for burial," her lover told her. "Laid him to rest in among the Farrell family."

She'd asked one question then wanted to hear no more.

"Will you promise never to mention his name to anyone nor ever to me?"

He'd given her a long look as though considering then nodded. "I swear no one will ever hear his name from my lips."

"That's all I will ever ask of you," she said.

Taking down a large pot from the shelf, she filled it with water then placed it upon the stove. With the babe kicking and bunching inside her, she pulled out a chair and sat down to peel the potatoes, carrots, onions and parsnips that would go into the soup. As she worked, she hummed to the baby.

It was an old, old song. One she had learned at her mother's knee. A sad song of lovers separated by death. He'd liked the song. She'd heard him whistling it many a time as he dressed.

"I know that song," she'd told him. "But I can't remember the name."

"'The Prince's Lost Lady'," he replied. "My father has a cargo ship with that name."

"Aye," she'd said, remembering.

That was what she felt like, she mused as she reached for what her da called a granddaddy onion.

She began to sing the song for her unborn child…

"Where are you going, my lady, my love? Where are you going this day?
Said she to him, 'It shall not take long; For I go but a very short way.'
And how long will you be, my lady, my love, how long will you be gone this day?
Said she, 'I'll be gone a very long while; And will not be back this way.';
'Will she ever return, my lady, my love?' he begged of her mother one night;
Said she, 'I fear my daughter is dead; And will never return to our sight.'

He mourned for the lady, his lady, his love; He wept for her
    night and day;
Said he, 'I will go to meet my love; For I believe I have found
    the way.'
He took to his bed in the fading light; Turned his eyes to the sky
    above;
Said he, 'I seek what I know I shall find; I go to be with my
    love.'
They laid him down in the green, green grass. On the hills
    overlooking the town.
And upon his grave they carved these words: The Prince's Lost
    Lady is found."

It wasn't the onion in her hand that caused the tears to roll down her cheeks. Nor was it the sting of the knife's blade that pricked her finger that caused her heart to seize in her chest.

She laid her hands in her lap, hung her head and mourned anew.

* * * * *

He'd been pacing the deck all night. Not once had he even entertained the thought of going to his cabin to rest. The fog was his enemy as much as the bastard who lurked on the other side of it. With every scrape of his boot heel across the teakwood deck, he cursed that damnable mist that kept him from going ashore.

"Why can't I take a jolly boat and...?"

"Milord, please have patience," Captain Kyriakos advised. "You do not know these waters. They are dangerous. The fog will lift soon."

"When?" he demanded. "It is nine of the clock and still no sign of it lifting."

Captain Kyriakos sighed heavily. "Milord, I told you it might well be noon before the sun burns away the mist. We've a wind starting up. Mayhap it will push the fog inward enough for me to lower a boat for you. I know you are anxious to reach the Cay."

He had no idea just how anxious, Declan thought as he ground his teeth. He stalked to the rail, wrapped his hands around the wood and growled low in his throat. He felt like a shackled animal—a beast baited and ready beyond the ring at a dog fight. His thigh ached from the wet and cold coming off the water, but it was steady. He was steady and his palm itched to circle the grip of his pistol.

"Ye've that look in your eye, milord," the sailor who had come looking for him on the docks at Boreas observed.

"What look is that?" Declan snapped.

"The killing look," the man replied. "I've seen it many a time on the battlefields of Diabolusia."

"Then you know there's a bloodlust that causes it, don't you?" Declan queried.

"I do, but I would caution ye, sir," the sailor said. "Ionary is a strict country for its laws. At Guilder's Cay the law is the harbormaster. If yer going to the Cay to kill a man, I'd advise ye to be careful."

"I aim to call the bastard out," Declan said.

"Dueling on the Cay is forbidden, milord," the sailor warned. "It carries with it a mighty stiff prison sentence for the man who survives. Two years at Ghurn Colony is what I've heard."

"Then I'll just have to make sure I'm not caught, now, won't I?" Declan questioned.

"What did this man do?"

"You've heard of the highwayman they called the Gypsy?"

The sailor nodded.

"Well, the man I'm going after took the Gypsy's woman and tried to make him think she had killed herself because of him."

"He the one responsible for the Gypsy's death?" the man asked, eyes narrowed.

Declan felt the lump rising in his throat whenever he thought of Daniel. "Aye," he said. "He was."

"And he's hiding on the Cay?"

"Aye," Declan told him.

"Then shoot the bastard a second time for me," the sailor stated. "The Gypsy saved my brother's farm from the tax man." He looked around them then lowered his voice. "Hell, I'll help ye kill the son of a bitch and help ye get off'n the Cay without bein' caught."

"I need to bring the Gypsy's woman with me," Declan said, searching the man's eyes.

"That goes without sayin', milord," the sailor agreed.

* * * * *

William Tucker sat in the taproom of the Jolly Mate and finished off the last of his morning meal. The man once known as Royce Penry had been edgy since around seven of the clock. As he ate, he kept watch on the fog that shrouded the window beside his table. He could not shake the feeling that something was amiss. That there was something lurking in the fog that posed a great danger to him and to the woman he called Maire.

Dimly he listened to the blast of the foghorn, heard the answering bells that signaled there were—he listened more closely and counted the clangs of the bell—five ships in the harbor waiting to dock. The Cay was a busy port for its size. The warehouses along the dock would soon be filled to overflowing with whatever cargo was stored in the holds of those five ships.

"The more ships, the more work for me," he mumbled as he picked up his cup of coffee. The brew had grown cold and he grimaced, looked toward the tavern wench who was flirting with a young sailor. "Constance."

She looked toward him. "Right away, governor," she replied as he lifted his cup.

As he waited for her to bring the enamel coffee pot over to him, he swiveled his head to the window again, hunched his shoulders against the bad feeling that was crawling down his spine.

* * * * *

Just before noon, the combination of the sun and the brisk wind that had suddenly come whipping up from the south began to push the fog away until the village of Guilder's Cay appeared ghostlike along the shore.

Red tiled roof and gray stone, white window frames and black doors adorned each and every building. A cobblestone street separated the taller, two-story buildings, which sat on a slight rise above the dockside tavern, warehouses and smithy. While most of the cottages looked as though they had been pressed from one of Suz's cookie cutters, a couple stood out among the shops at one end of the village and the warehouses at the other. It was to the largest of those cottages to which Declan's eye was drawn.

"Who owns the cottage with the flag flying atop?" he asked Captain Kyriakos.

"That would be the new harbormaster," the captain replied.

Declan turned to look at him. "How long has he been here?"

Captain Kyriakos shrugged. "Four, five months now."

"Is his name William Tucker?"

The captain shrugged. "I can't say. My first mate deals with the harbormasters at each port. You would need to ask him."

"Does he have a woman with him?"

"I've no idea, milord."

"Have you ever seen him?" Declan pressed.

"Once or twice. Right nice-looking man with a beard. That's all I can tell you."

"That's enough," Declan told him. It would stand to reason Penry would grow a beard as a disguise.

While he waited impatiently for the jolly boat to be lowered into the water, he kept his eye on the harbormaster's cottage. No one came in or out of the building but there was smoke coming from the chimney. Bess could well be cooking the bastard's food and that set his temper to churning. It was all he could do not to hiss at the sailors who preceded him down the rope ladder and into the jolly boat.

"You do have your papers with you, don't you, milord?" the captain asked from the deck.

"I have what I need," Declan said. Inside his coat was his pistol. He glanced at the sailor who had assigned himself as Declan's shadow.

"Usually the harbormaster doesn't question passengers unless he's on the lookout for them or they act suspicious," the sailor said quietly. "Just pull yer hat down low, act like ye're someone of great importance and he'll ignore ye. It's the cargo he's concerned about."

"Thank you, Whiggins," Declan replied.

Whiggins nodded then picked up an oar and put his back into rowing them to the dock.

The slap of the water against the hull of the boat might have lulled him at any other time but he was so anxious to reach the dock, to find Bess that he was all but jumping up and down on the bench. He could not take his eyes from the gods-be-damned cottage where he believed her to be. The closer the boat came to the long wooden quay, the antsier he got.

"That's a good sign," Whiggins said.

"What?" Declan inquired.

"The harbormaster's apprentice is checking the cargoes," he said. He nudged his chin toward a thin young man with a crop of fiery red hair beneath his short-brimmed uniform cap. "He's a good lad but a bit slow—if ye get me drift. Scared to death of ye toffs."

There were a lot of people milling about on the docks. A couple of them were in uniform. Neither of them looked to be Penry's size and he couldn't tell their hair color beneath the watch caps they wore.

"Do you see the harbormaster?" Declan asked.

Whiggins swept his head back and forth. "No, milord. I don't. I see a couple of his flunkies there but not him." He cleared his throat then spat into the water. "Do see the gods-be-damned watchman coming outta the Jolly Mate. He's a rare piece of work. Best ye stay clear of him. Most folks do."

Declan wasn't interested in the man who kept watch over the cargo in the warehouses. "I've no business with him."

"Just as well," Whiggins said. "They say he ain't right in the head."

The boat moved into a slip alongside the pier. One of the sailors jumped out to secure the dock line around the cleat at the bow. His hands moved expertly as he tied the cleat hitch then ran to the stern to do the same with the stern line. Once the boat was secure, Whiggins motioned for Declan to disembark.

"Just watch yerself now," the sailor warned.

Tendrils of fog drifted past his face as he climbed onto the pier. Around him swirled the hustle and bustle of sailors and merchants going about their business, dockside dollies trying to do theirs by looking coyly at the newcomers, and beggars hovering in the background with their grimy hands extended. Somewhere in the throng was Royce Penry who at that moment might have a pistol aimed at his back. He reached up to unbutton his coat so he would have clear access to his own weapon.

"Want me to go with ye, milord?" Whiggins asked as he came to stand beside him.

"I think not, but I appreciate the offer," Declan told him.

"If'n it's all the same to ye, then, I'll just mosey along behind ye to watch yer back," Whiggins offered, putting his hand on the grip of his pistol. "I'd feel a mite better 'bout things if I was doin' that."

Declan leveled his attention on the sailor. Whiggins was most likely in his mid-fifties with a ridiculous gap-toothed grin. What teeth he had were blackened all the way to the gum line and rotted out. He had a bulbous nose that was red with broken veins and his eyes were watery, bloodshot. His flesh was as weathered as aged leather and the watch cap that now covered his sparse salt-and-pepper gray hair did little to cover up his protruding ears.

But there was something solid and trustworthy about Elias Whiggins that held him in good stead. Dec was a good judge of character and so far Whiggins was proving to be a steadfast friend.

"I'd like that, Whiggins," Declan told him.

The sailor nodded and ran his coat sleeve under his nose. "Consider it done."

Walking just a little ways behind Declan, Whiggins's head was moving back and forth as the sailor took in the scene around them. His grimy hand never left the butt of his weapon though he strolled along as if he didn't have a care in the world.

It was toward the harbormaster's cottage that Declan was headed. No one seemed to be paying any particular attention to him or Whiggins, but he was sure most of them thought the sailor was his bodyguard. That being the case, those passing by gave Dec and Whiggins a wide berth.

Stopping at the black door that was adorned with a knocker fashioned in the form of an anchor, Declan reached up and sharply rapped the brass handle three times. As soon as he lowered his hand, it went to the grip of his pistol. When no one answered, he knocked again.

"Don't believe nobody's home," Whiggins said. He was standing to one side but he was watching the dock, the people strolling across it and now and again he lifted his head to look up at the second story of the harbormaster's cottage.

"That would appear to be the case," Declan said, turning away from the door. He looked both ways along the street, spied the tavern and nodded in that direction. "Let's see what we can find out."

Whiggins fell into step behind him once again as Dec started across the cobblestone street. They had to stop for a buggy passing one way and a wagon passing the other and while they did, each surveyed the village.

"It's a quaint setting," Declan observed.

"Always liked coming here," Whiggins acknowledged.

Continuing on across the street once the slow traffic passed, Declan spied a woman coming down the boardwalk and stopped to look at her. It wasn't Bess but she could have been with her long, unbound black hair and protruding belly. As she walked past him, he tipped the brim of his cavalier hat and she smiled prettily at him. She got about five feet away before it occurred to him she might know Bess.

"Excuse me, milady?" he called out and she turned around. Her smile gave way to a look of unease. He doffed his hat. "Might you be able to help me?"

"To do what, milord?" she asked, suspiciously.

"I am looking for a lady by the name of Maire Belvoir," he said. "Would you by any chance be acquainted with her?"

"I might," she said. "What do you want her for?"

"She's an old friend," Declan said. "I was hoping to look her up while I was at the Cay."

Her eyes roamed down him from head to boot then back again. He tried to put on his most pleasant, unthreatening grin so she would trust him. She seemed to find him acceptable for she lifted her hand and pointed to the second-largest building across the street.

"She lives there," the woman said. "But I wouldn't be bothering her just yet."

Declan took a few steps toward her. "May I ask why not?"

"I just saw her man going in the cottage. He don't like visitors. Best you wait until he leaves."

"Hell's bells, wench, that could be half the day or more," Whiggins complained.

"Could be, but you don't want to be pestering him. He ain't the easiest man by far," she said then sniffed. "But it's your head, not mine, so do as you please." With that, she turned around and continued on her way.

"Easiest man," Whiggins repeated with a snort then spat into the street. "Them's understatement words if'n I ever heard 'em."

"If I go over there, he's going to recognize me and I won't get to talk to her without him being stuck right under my ass," Declan said.

"Or there being some mighty powerful trouble between ye and him," Whiggins reminded him.

"I need to make sure it's her," Declan told him. "Would you go over, knock on the door and stand aside so I can see her when she answers?"

"What if'n the bastard himself answers?" the sailor asked.

"Knowing Penry as I do, answering his own door is beneath him." Declan shook his head. "No, he'll not be the one to open the door. She will."

"Suit yerself," Whiggins said. "But whatcha want me to say to her?"

"Ask for work," Declan said. "Chances are she'll turn you down, but if you hem and haw long enough, get her to stand where I can get a good look at her, that's all that matters."

"Don't ye want me to tell her ye're here?"

"And alert him to the fact?" Dec queried. "Not just yet. I'll write her a note and have you take it back later."

"Might work," Whiggins agreed. He sniffed then headed back across the street to the cottage the woman had pointed out to them.

Declan's palms were sweating. He wiped them down his pants—winced as his right hand dragged over the wound in his thigh. Looking down at the tortured limb he was grateful he no longer needed a cane to walk but the limp was pronounced. The wound still plagued him and especially so in damp weather. His heart was pounding fiercely in his ears as Whiggins stepped up to the door the woman had indicated and rapped his knuckles on the panel.

* * * * *

Bess glanced at Penry as he went into the bathing chamber and shut the door. She could tell something was bothering but did not want to pry. It wasn't like him to come back this early but he had moods she never questioned. He provided a good living, didn't ask that much of her and never raised his hand to her. She figured she should not intrude on his private thoughts.

Wiping her hands on her apron, she went to the stove to stir the pot of soup. As she reached for the spoon, there was a knock at the door.

She frowned. They rarely had visitors, but when they did it was usually because there was a problem on the docks. She glanced at the bathing chamber door then walked to the door. When she opened it, she was surprised to see a man she didn't know standing on her stoop.

"Ye pardon, milady," the man said, pulling off his watch cap. "Me name is Whiggins and I'm new to these parts." He stepped off the stoop and to one side. He coughed then mumbled his next words.

"Beg pardon?" she asked but when he repeated the words again, she still couldn't make them out. "Are you in need of...?" She crossed the threshold to stand on the stoop.

"A job, aye," her visitor said. "I'm in need of a job, milady. Can do just 'bout anythin'."

He looked so eager, so needy that she hated to tell him no but there was nothing that needed doing around the cottage.

"I'll work for a plate of food if'n ye don't got coin to pay me with," he said, looking hopeful.

"You poor man," she said. "I'm sorry but there's no work to be had but if you'll wait right there, I'll get you a cup of soup if that will tide you over."

His bloodshot eyes crinkled at the corners. "Ye are a merciful lady," he said. "Soup would sure hit the spot on these old bones."

"Then stay there and I'll fetch you a cup," she told him. She was about to step back into the cottage when she saw a man across the street staring at her. She couldn't see his face for it was hidden beneath the wide brim of a cavalier hat but there was something about him that made the hair stand up on her arms.

"Ye be all right, milady?" the man asked.

She tore her gaze from the watcher and looked at him. "Whiggins, is it?" she asked.

"Aye, milady," he said, bobbing his head. "Elias Whiggins."

"I'll be right back," she said, feeling a strong need to get into the house and close the door.

Her heart was racing as she hurried inside. As she shut the portal she saw Whiggins glance across the street to the man who was watching her.

"Who was at the door?"

She turned as he came out of the bathing chamber. His face was close shaven and that surprised her. He had also cut his hair. It was as short as it had been when he first arrived.

"Someone looking for work," she replied.

He grunted. "I'm going to bed," he said. "My belly is bothering me."

"Want me to get you something for it?"

"I'm going to bed," he repeated.

She watched him go into the bedchamber and kick the door shut behind him. Something was troubling him but she knew better than to pry.

Hurrying over to the cupboard, she took down a tin cup and plucked a spoon from the jar beside the sink. She filled the cup with a goodly portion of soup, stuck the spoon into the cup then set it down to tear off a chunk of bread. Carrying the meal to the door, she set the cup down on the table beside it and opened the portal. Whiggins was standing where she had left him with an expectant look on his face.

"Beggin' your pardon, milady, but do ye know the man across the street?" he asked quietly.

She looked at the tall man standing across the way and shook her head. "I don't believe so. Do you?"

"He's been staring over this way ever since ye opened the door," he told her. "Just figured he might be yer husband or a friend of yer husband's and thought I was a'flirtin' with ye."

"I'm not married," she told him.

"Pretty lady like ye ought to be," he said with a snaggletooth grin.

"Mayhap one day," she replied.

"From your lips to the goddess's ear, eh?" he asked with a wink.

"Enjoy your soup, Mr. Whiggins. You can leave the cup by the door." She stepped back, cast one final look at the man across the street then closed the door.

* * * * *

He couldn't take his eyes off her. It was Bess.

And she was carrying his child. The mound of her belly made tears gather in his eyes. He longed to put his hand there. Would the babe be kicking by now? He knew absolutely nothing about babes or pregnancy—or pregnant women for that matter. He'd heard of morning sickness. Was she still experiencing that?

"Is Althea?" he asked aloud.

That thought set him back on his heels.

His godfather's words came back to slap him in the face: *You got her with child as well. Potent little bugger aren't you?*

He slumped against the wall behind him—still a bit spooked when he'd realized earlier Bess was looking at him. The breath had stopped in his throat. Whiggins was turned his way, too, and it was obvious they were talking about him. He'd felt a quick surge of nausea bubble up his throat.

"No, no, no, no, no," he'd whispered urgently. He wasn't ready yet to speak with her. "Why did you point me out to her?"

But then she'd turned away, went back inside the cottage and Whiggins sat down on her stoop to wait for whatever she'd gone inside to do.

Declan was grinding his teeth for the sailor was looking at him, grinning like a jackanapes around mouthfuls of what Declan realized must be soup or stew that Bess had given him. He hissed under his breath when Whiggins laughed then turned to watch a rather saucy minx sashaying along the boardwalk.

For what seemed like an hour Whiggins put spoon to cup, spoon to mouth and when he was done he wiped his mouth on his coat sleeve, stood, put the cup beside the door then came sauntering back across the street.

"Why the hell did you draw her attention to me?" he demanded as soon as the sailor reached him. He turned away as though he hadn't spoken to the man.

"She saw ye, milord," Whiggins said, flinging an arm toward the cottage.

"Stop that," Declan ordered. "What if she's looking out the window?"

"Then she'll think I'm asking why ye were spying on her," Whiggins replied. "Don't want her thinkin' I'm in cahoots with ye, do ye? Not if'n I'm to go back with your note."

Declan opened his mouth to reply but Whiggins pushed him then raised his voice.

"Go on with ye, then. Don't be lurking about staring at the missus!"

Stunned by the man's behavior, Dec realized Bess was, indeed, staring out the window, watching them.

"I'll meet ye in the tavern at quarter past," Whiggins said quietly then hitched up his greasy pants and ambled down the boardwalk.

He saw the curtain close and breathed a sigh of relief. His hands were shaking so he jammed them in the pockets of his coat for lack of anything else to do with them. Sweat was dripping down from his temples.

He was just that scared, he realized.

Of a woman carrying his child.

A woman he was going to take back to Serenia with him and...

"And then what?" he asked.

"Did you say something, milord?" a passing gentleman inquired.

Declan felt the heat rush to his cheeks. "Just talking to myself," he said.

The gentleman tipped his uniform had as he walked past.

"Excuse me," Declan said. "Are you with the harbor control?"

The gentleman grinned. "I am."

"Do you know William Tucker?"

The man's grin slipped away. "May I ask why you are asking?"

People of the Cay were a suspicious bunch, he thought.

"I used to know him a long time ago and I heard he was here."

"He is," the man replied. He narrowed his eyes. "Do I know you, milord?"

"I'm sorry," Declan said and stretched out his hand. "Jack. Jack McGregor."

"Good Serenian name," the man said, taking Declan's hand. "Any kin to the king?"

"Wouldn't that be useful?" Declan countered with a laugh.

"Aye, it would." He released Declan's hand. "Tucker has no friends on the Cay or anywhere else I wouldn't imagine so I'm guessing you're not a friend of his, either."

"Not by a long shot," Declan said.

"You here looking for him, milord?" the man queried.

"Looking for the lady he has with him," Declan said and could have kicked himself for giving away such information.

"Ah, the lovely Maire Belvoir," the man said.

"You know her, then?"

"I know everyone on the Cay, milord," the gentleman replied. "It's my job to do so."

"About Tucker..."

"My advice to you, milord, is to tread carefully around that one. He's got the devil's own temper and especially so when it comes to Miss Belvoir. He'll not appreciate anyone coming around asking after her."

Declan narrowed his eyes. "Are you going to report to him, Mr....?" He stared at the insignia on the man's uniform. "Forgive me but I don't know your name nor am I familiar with the maritime ranks."

"Captain Samuel Cean," the man replied with a slight bow.

"A pleasure, Captain," Declan said.

"Mine, as well, and no, I have no use for Tucker, myself," Cean replied. "I would just ask that you be mindful of any business you might find yourself engaged in with the man. Dueling is forbidden on the Cay. It is punishable by imprisonment." He smiled slowly. "That is if you're caught on the field of honor with a dead man at your feet."

Declan smiled. "Duly noted."

"Excellent," Cean said. He put his index finger to the brim of his uniform cap, inclined his head then continued on his way.

"Nice fella," Declan said.

He'd gotten the impression Cean had about as little respect for Penry—or rather Tucker—as he did.

Chapter Sixteen

"Why are ye prodgrasstigating, milord?"

Declan raised an eyebrow. "Why am I doing what?"

"Prodgrasstigating," Whiggins snapped.

"I might tell you if I knew what the hell you were talking about," Declan told him.

Whiggins rolled his eyes. "Prodgrasstigating. Ye know putting off going to see the wench."

"Oh, procrastinating," Declan said then laughed.

"Ain't that what I said?" Whiggins grumbled.

"Not quite."

"Ye know bloody well what I meant."

Declan looked out the window of the tavern. It was misting, but rumbling in the distance heralded a more forceful storm brewing. For the moment, he had a clear line of vision on the cottage where Bess lived. No one had gone in or come out of the building since Whiggins had sauntered away after eating what he called the best soup he'd ever laid to his gums.

The sailor jerked a thumb over his shoulder. "That there tavern wench been givin' us the stinkeye for a while now."

"Then order another round for yourself," he snapped.

"Gotta be a reason ye be stallin'. Ye knows and I knows it. Whatever 'tis, you can speak to me of it."

Declan searched the older man's steady eyes. "Can I trust you, Elias?"

"With ye life, milord Gypsy," Whiggins said without as much as a blink.

"How did you...?" Declan began then snapped his mouth shut. This was dangerous territory.

"I figured it out," Whiggins said. "Don't no mold grow on this boy."

"Apparently not," Dec mumbled.

"Take the knowledge with me to the grave, I will," Whiggins said. "Ye done a lot of good at ye turn as a highwayman, milord. Ain't no man I know what would turn ye in."

"I appreciate that, Elias," Declan said and meant it.

"Then talk to me, milord. Tell me what ails ye." He grinned that picket-fence grin. "The healer be in as such."

Declan liked Whiggins. The man was coarse and smelled like an outhouse badly in need of cleaning but he believed the sailor was as upstanding a man as any he'd ever encountered.

"I'm waiting for him to leave. I'm not ready to confront that bastard yet. Not where she might get hurt in the process."

Whiggins nodded, reached up to scratch at his stubbled cheek. "Could see how's that would be a quarry for ye, milord. Don't want to go scaring the bantling outta her just yet."

"Quandary," Declan corrected absentmindedly.

"That's what I said," Whiggins replied with a sniff.

* * * * *

The man calling himself William Tucker swung his legs from the bed. He listened for a moment to the soft tune his Crónórgan housemate was humming. It was an old Serenian folk song but he couldn't place it. She was crooning to the babe within her and that made him want to cry. His own mother had never—ever—held him when he was a child. She'd never sang or hummed to him. The back of her hand was the only touch he had ever known from her. She left his rearing to the servants and the horrific nanny who had quietly and methodically abused him until he was old enough to put a stop to it. Listening to Bess—nay, Maire—soothing her bantling hurt him so badly he could scarce catch his breath. Why had no one ever loved him? Held him? Sang to him? Fought for his life as Maire had fought for her lover's.

He heard her go out the back door and was fairly sure she was going to uncover the rain barrel for a storm was coming. The Crónórgan segment of the Chalean race were keen preservers of nature. She never threw anything away. Never wasted anything that could be used a while longer. Like all those of her race, she revered the environment and took as diligent care of it as she did the infant growing inside her womb.

He smiled as he heard the rattle of the oaken lid leaving the rain barrel. True to form, she was saving the rain water for whatever purpose she deemed it was needed.

She would be a good mother to the child. He knew that as surely as he sat there with his stomach tied in knots.

He would be as good a surrogate father to that child as he could be despite having hated the baby's father so fiercely.

But Declan Farrell was no more. He was lying in his grave turning to dust. She would mourn him for the rest of her life, but he had made her promise she would never tell the child who his or her father really was.

The only reason she'd stayed with him in the beginning was because she was grieving for Farrell and was almost mindless in that grief. During her convalescence from the musket shot, she'd spoken not a word to Penry for days on end. Had laid like a statue on the bed and stared out the window, silently crying. Even now she rarely spoke to him though she was friendly with everyone else in town.

"I will take care of you," he'd pledged. "I will provide well for you and the babe. All I ask is that you tell those who ask that the babe is mine. Never, ever mention Farrell's name to me or any other."

"I will not marry you," she had countered. "Ever. I will do what you ask, but if you ever, ever say anything bad about Declan Farrell to his child, I will stab you in the heart while you sleep."

He took her at her word. He knew she would do precisely what she threatened. He had caused her untold grief and while he felt no guilt over how that grief had been laid at her doorstep, he would abide by her condition. Farrell's name never left his mouth or hers.

That did not prevent him from thinking about the dead man, though. Farrell was the reason he could not sleep as well as he once did. His dreams were often filled with the smiling image of that handsome man, but the dreams soon turned to nightmares that pushed from sleep with a hard shove. Gasping, sweating, he would sit straight up in bed to plow his shaking hand through his damp hair.

"A guilty conscience," the wench would murmur then turn over to go back to sleep.

He had since learned that Farrell had not been the infamous Gypsy but had been killed the same day the highwayman had met his violent death on the coach road.

Too busy trying to get himself and Bess out of Serenia, he had not kept up with what was going on near Wixenstead. He was running from the Royal Regiment as much as the law for he had killed two men—Private Jonas and the healer—and nearly killed the woman he was taking with him. He did not learn of the death of the highwayman and Farrell until three weeks after the fact.

He had been sitting in the tavern on Guilder's Cay, nursing a tankard of beer and had barely noticed when Samuel Cean walked into the establishment. He didn't like the man though he couldn't exactly say why. There was something about the way Cean looked at him, seemed to be judging him that simply did not set well. The two of them kept as far apart as possible. Never speaking, never interacting and studiously avoiding each another.

"What's this I hear about the Serenian catching the Gypsy?" the publican asked Cean as the younger man took a seat at a table.

"The captain of the Olympus related this news to me this morn," Cean replied.

"So who was he?" someone in the tavern asked.

"A man thought long dead," Cean replied. "A defrocked priest by the name of Daniel Rees."

"That cannot be," William Tucker denied. "I heard the Gypsy was Lord Declan Farrell."

Cean had turned a hard glare upon him. "You heard wrong, sir," Cean said. "Rees was shot down on the coach road by Royal Marine troopers. He was wearing the notorious red velvet coat, cocked hat and in his pocket was a silver dollar. He opened fire upon the troopers trying to escape. He was killed in the attempt."

"So the highwayman is dead," the publican said. "The gods rest his soul. All he was doing was trying to help the poor folk of Serenia."

"My sentiment exactly," Cean stated.

"Not Farrell?" he had whispered.

Cean's eyes narrowed. "Most certainly not, but that good man lost his life less than a hundred yards from where the highwayman went down."

That had made Tucker spill his drink. Made his heart stutter in his chest. "He's dead?"

"I'm sorry to say he is," Cean replied.

"How?" Tucker asked. "Why was he…?"

"Lord Farrell was on his way home to his ancestral estate with his fiancée and his best friend when their paths crossed that of the Gypsy. His Grace was shot three times," Samuel Cean had informed everyone in the tavern that night. "Caught in the crossfire between the troopers and the Gypsy."

"Wrong place at the wrong time," the publican had said, shaking his head.

"Shot down like a dog on the highway," Cean agreed. "He died from massive blood loss before they could get him to Arlington Castle."

The publican raised a tankard of ale. "May the Wind be always at his back," he said.

"May the Wind be always at his back," everyone in the tavern save William Tucker had replied.

William Tucker had walked home that night with tears in his eyes.

As he woke many a night now with tears streaming down his cheeks.

Shaking off the memory of that night in the tavern, he walked to the window to look out. The rain was now coming down hard and by craning his head he could see it falling into Bess's…

He had to stop calling her that, he warned himself. One slip and that could be his undoing.

"Maire," he said. "Her name is Maire." The rain was falling into Maire's rain barrel.

Feeling somewhat better he left the bedchamber and went into the main room. The smell of soup enticed him to the table. He took a seat, threaded his hands together atop the table.

"You want to eat now?" she asked and at his nod, she picked up a cup and filled it with soup.

"Wind's picking up," he said as she placed it in front of him.

"Looked black beyond the common ground," she said, referring to the land behind the cottages where the villagers had a communal garden.

"I'll go out and latch the shutters when it lets up," he said. He scooped up a spoonful of the soup.

"Should have been done an hour ago," she told him.

"I wasn't feeling well an hour ago," he replied. The soup was delicious when it hit his tongue and he looked up at her. "Good as always, wench."

She didn't reply and he knew she was angry he had come home early and gone straight to bed. If there was one thing Maire disliked, it was being ignored.

* * * * *

Samuel Cean loved storms. He had been born on the wild coast of Virago. As a child, he and his five brothers played in the violent rains that swept across their farm. Daring one another to venture close to things that lightning could strike—and potentially themselves as well—had been the most dangerous thing they'd done growing up. Ever since he was old enough to walk, he'd run out into the rain with his arms lifted to the heavens. He was—according to his Ionarian grandmother—a Water Sign, which meant he had a strong affinity for the element. So it was all he could do not to strip down to his underpants and walk through the downpour that was beating at the roof of his cottage.

What he would have liked to do was strip down to nothing and run through that deluge but his position at Guilder's Cay prevented that. A measure of decorum accompanied the captain's bars pinned to the lapel of his uniform jacket.

Instead, he stood—bare chested and barefoot—in the opened doorway that led out to the common ground behind the cottage and let the rain pebble his face with cold droplets that stung but were invigorating. With both hands braced on the lintels he tipped his head up to the violent heavens. He did his best thinking when the wild elements were beating down upon him and although his breeches were soon soaked through, he did not mind the discomfort.

His mind was on the two strangers who had arrived on the *Medea*. Well, he thought, one was a stranger but the other? He smiled slowly. "We've never met, Your Grace, but I know who you are and I know why you're here."

At that moment he knew where Declan Farrell and the older man were. He had set spies to watch them. They were in the Jolly Mate tavern—most likely to stay there until the rain let up.

"Then what will he do?" he asked the pounding rain.

He had yet to visit the woman he had come to Guilder's Cay to find. The old man had made contact with her but from what Cean had observed, nothing seemed to point to her knowing the man she thought dead was alive and right across the street watching her.

"What will you do when you realize he's alive?"

His thoughts shifted to the man now known as William Tucker. Farrell was there not only for the wench, he was there for the bastard who had hounded him and been responsible for him almost being killed. Who had been the cause of Farrell's friend losing his life on the road to Arlington Castle. The bastard who had tied a defenseless woman to her bed with a loaded musket lashed beside her. A vicious killer in his own right who had murdered the healer at Richter's Creek.

"You've a multitude of sins to atone for, Penry," Cean said quietly. "And your judge, jury and executioner has arrived to see you do."

He could interfere and he knew he should. Dueling was a crime for which Farrell could be sent to prison. Out-and-out murder would see him hanged—not as the Gypsy but as a coldblooded killer. Vengeance, revenge were ways of life on Virago. He'd learned that at a young age when he and his brothers had avenged the deaths of their parents. He could not fault Declan Farrell for seeking his own brand of justice.

"But I can't let you shoot a man then go to jail for it," he said.

He sighed, lowered his arms and stepped back to close the door. He was drenched, shivering but felt refreshed, cleansed, his head clear. He knew what he had to do.

* * * * *

"You want anything else, milord?" the publican asked from the bar.

"The storm is getting worse," Whiggins said. "Ain't no way we be goin' back to the ship tonight in this weather."

"Do you have rooms to let?" Declan queried the publican.

The publican shook his head. "No, milord, but there's a boarding house at the end of the street. I'm sure they have a room or two."

Whiggins snorted. "I'm guessing ye want me to get my ass down there to see 'bout some rooms?" he asked.

"Not until the rain lets up," Declan said. "I wouldn't want a man as sweet as you to melt out there in the storm."

"Could happen," Whiggins said with a sniff.

* * * * *

Sitting in her rocking chair, Bess was working on mending as Penry paced from one window to another. Now and again she would look up to see him frowning, running his hand through his hair. His shoulders were hunched, his eyes looked worried and his posture said he had a distinct sense of edginess.

"Is the storm bothering you?" she asked.

"'Tis not the storm that is bothering me, wench," he mumbled. He peeled aside the curtain on the window beside the door and peered into the gathering gloom. It was five of the clock, had been raining for hours and the sky was dark with danger.

"Then what is disturbing you?" she pressed.

"I wish to Alel I knew," he told her. "It almost feels as though there is a disaster awaiting to happen." He looked around at her. "Do you not feel the unease in the air?"

She shook her head. "Truly no, milord," she replied.

"Well, I do," he snapped and turned back to watching the pelting rain slashing at the window panes. "I've felt it all day."

There was nothing to say to that so she looked back down at her work. Sometimes—and apparently this was one of them—he became paranoid, looking over his shoulder and jumping at the slightest noise. She knew why, of course. He had killed two men and was a military deserter. The law, she was sure, was after him in Serenia. Sooner or later they would find him.

"I'm going to the tavern," he said suddenly.

She looked up. "In this weather?"

"I cannot stay here another minute," he said. He reached for his oilskin coat. "I feel as though ants are crawling all over me."

"And ale will help," she said under her breath.

He drank. A lot.

She watched him put on his oilskin then jerk the door open. As she knew he would, he looked both ways as though searching for anyone lurking about to ambush him.

"Don't wait up," he said before venturing onto the stoop and closing the door behind him.

"I won't," she said.

* * * * *

It was close to seven of the clock and the storm had not lessened. If anything, the rain was heavier and the winds stronger. By the time he and Whiggins made a run for the boarding house, lightning was striking behind the cottages with regularity.

"Weather not fit for fishes," Whiggins proclaimed. The old man looked like a drowned rat as they entered the boardinghouse and Dec was fairly sure he looked no better.

Shaking the water from his hat, he was greeted by the innkeeper.

"You're in luck, milord," the man said. "We've two rooms left."

The rooms weren't anything to write home about, Declan thought as he looked at the Spartan furnishings. A bed. A table with a shade-less lamp. A chair. An open closet.

That was it. What passed for a boarding house in Guilder's Cay would be a hovel in Serenia.

"Privy's down the hall on the right," Whiggins said. "Stinks like it ain't been cleaned in a warthog's age."

"Probably hasn't," Declan replied.

"See ye in the morning. Sleep well, milord," Whiggins said, touching his index finger to his head.

"Aye," Declan said. "You, too, Elias."

After the sailor was gone, Declan peeled the covers back on the bed to inspect them. At least the sheets were freshly laundered and smelled of the outdoors. It was a scent he rather liked for it reminded him of sunshine. He prayed there were no critters lurking in the sheets or on the pillow. Lice and bedbugs were not what he cared to take home with him.

Taking off his hat, coat and untying his jabot, he laid the clothing on the chair then sat down on the bed to pull off his boots. He was tired—not having slept the night before—and the mattress didn't seem all that bad. For a reason he couldn't explain he didn't want to take off the rest of his clothes so he lay down, drew his knees up, clasped his hands behind his head on the lumpy pillow and stared at the ceiling.

Fly specks dotted the expanse above him along with two blotches that looked like pee stains. Moving his gaze down the wall opposite the bed he noticed places where the paint was peeling. There were a few places needing to be patched and one long crack that ran horizontally across the entire surface. The Dockside House was in dire need of repair. It was no wonder there was a For Sale sign on the grimy front window.

"What Bess could do with this place," he said quietly.

Paddy had told him everything that had been done at the Hound and Stag had been Bess's idea. From the paint colors to the curtains and quilts—which she'd made by hand—to the color of stain on the bar, tables, chairs and woodwork.

"You have a true knack for this, Bess," he'd told her—awed by her talent.

Her name elicited an image of her lovely dark golden face with its long black eyelashes framing sparkling ebony eyes. The memory of her long hair dragging across his thighs as she tilted her head back while she rode him sent shivers of pleasure through his cock.

He closed his eyes to better savor the remembrances of their wild nights together in her narrow bed, but the pictures faded like dandelion fluff floating away from the stem in a hard wind.

It wasn't Bess's beautiful face that he began to visualize in his mind's eye but Althea's lovely, rosy cheeks and emerald green eyes.

Eyes that were looking at him with such sadness, such hopelessness, such terrible loss. Green eyes that shone bright with unshed tears. Her words came back to taunt him…

The man I want—the only man I will ever want—is sitting right where you are sitting, Declan Farrell.

He should have gone to her. Should have told her he knew she was carrying his child. What a craven coward he was to have left her there at Boreas Keep and taken ship to be with another woman.

But you aren't with that other woman, Farrell, his conscience reminded him. You have yet to even speak with her.

Aye, he thought. He was doubly a coward where both women were concerned. One he couldn't face and the other he couldn't bring himself to seek out.

He withdrew one hand from under his head and flung his arm over his eyes. The lamp he'd lit when he and Whiggins had come to inspect the room was blazing on the table beside him. The scent of the oil was sharp and musty in his nostrils, but he didn't have the energy to get up to blow it out. His eyes were so heavy, his body equally weighty. All he wanted to do was sleep and forget but as the weariness finally took hold of his mind, Althea's wounded eyes followed him into slumber.

And he dreamed.

He climbed the slight rise that wound along the back of the Duke of Oxmoor's property and opened the tall bronze gate that marked the formal lawn. It was a bright, sunny day with not a cloud in the sky. The air was filled with the sensuous scent of gardenia and song birds serenaded themselves in the spreading oak trees.

Taking the cobblestone path that led beside two strutting peacocks that never gave him a second glance, he skirted the pond. He smiled thinking of the night of the masquerade ball when he'd stripped and dived into its murky waters.

As he moved around a huge spreading chestnut tree, he saw her and the breath caught in his throat.

She was sitting beside the pond at Standfield Hall with a green gingham gown spread out upon the darker green lawn. Her hair was down—almost sweeping the plaid blanket upon which she sat. In her lap was a laughing baby boy of about eighteen months. The child had a lock of her long hair wrapped around his little fist and was trying to stuff it into his mouth.

"No, Niall," she said, attempting to extricate her hair from his grasp, but the little boy chuckled and crammed more of the hair into his mouth.

"That's not good for you, son."

A man dressed in the red uniform of a Royal Marine came to hunker down beside her. "Give him to me, milady," he said quietly. He reached out his arms to take the child.

"Keep your hands off my son," Declan growled.

Althea and the man he recognized as Captain Rand Gunderson turned to look at him.

"I fear you are mistaken, Lord Declan," Gunderson said. "This lad is my son, not yours." He took the child from Althea. "Just as the lady is my wife, not yours."

"She is mine," Declan protested, coming toward his rival with fists clenched.

"You did not want her," Gunderson said. He cupped the little boy's head close to his chest. "But I must thank you for that. What you threw away so carelessly has become the greatest gift the gods ever gave to me."

"There was a Joining contract," Declan told the bastard.

"Which was null and void the moment you stepped foot on Ionary," Gunderson replied.

He turned to Althea. "Milady, I love you. I am here to take you to wife."

She shook her head sadly. "It is too late, milord. I have Joined with Captain Gunderson. He is my husband, the man I love."

"You don't love him," he yelled. "You love me. I know you love me."

Her eyes were sad, her lovely face creased with pity for him. "I did once, aye, but you very effectively killed that love when you denied me and our child."

"I never denied him."

"You left that night knowing I was with child," she accused.

"And you never looked back," Gunderson stated.

He pointed a shaking finger at the soldier. "You shut your gods-be-damned mouth." he shouted. "This does not concern you."

"Anything that concerns my lady—my wife—concerns me." He got easily to his feet with the babe still tight to his chest. "Now leave us. You are not welcome at Standfield Hall."

He took a step toward Althea but she shook her head, put out a staying hand.

"Go away, Declan," she said. "You had your chance and you did not take it. Go to your beloved Bess. Make a life with her."

"I don't want her. I want you."

"You will never have me," she said. "I belong to Rand."

"I love you," he told her and felt tears falling down his cheeks.

He watched Gunderson extend a hand to help her stand. When she was on her feet she kept hold of the man's sword hand, brought it to her lips to kiss. She looked up into his green eyes with deep affection.

And longing.

The way she used to look at him.

"Goodbye, Declan," she said.

"I love you," he repeated, his voice and heart breaking.

"I don't care," she said as Gunderson led her up the path toward the keep.

"Althea," he yelled after her. "Althea, don't leave me."

Her image slowly began to fade.

"Althea, please."

He felt to his knees on the grass, bowed his head with his clenched fists on his thighs and sobbed so wretchedly the birds took flight from the oak tree and the peacocks skirled in protest.

"Althea," he cried. "Forgive me."

Chapter Seventeen

A loud crack of lightning shrieked from the sky and the room lit up with garish blue light. He yelped—jerked out of his sleep by the noise. Something popped loudly beyond the window as another strobe of light pulsed through the room. Rain was beating at the windows. The wind was howling fiercely, pushing against the panes. Overhead the roof timbers creaked.

Swinging his legs from the bed, he grabbed his boots and started pulling them on as the building started to shake.

"Milord!" Whiggins's voice was high-pitched as he pounded on the door. "Milord, get up!"

"I'm up," he yelled back. He ran to the door and jerked it open.

"Tornado," Whiggins told him as though it wasn't obvious by the rumbling bearing down on them.

"Aye," he agreed. "Let's get the hell downstairs."

He had barely cleared the door before a tree limb came crashing through the window and landed right in the middle of the bed where he'd been sleeping only moments before. Seeing the heavy limb with its sharp, jagged edge impaling the mattress where his chest would have been, he shuddered violently.

There but by the Grace of Alel…

"Sweet Merciful Morrigunia," Whiggins said then grabbed Declan's arm roughly and pulled him down the hall to the stairs.

Outside things were slammed against the side of the building. The windows were rattling then imploding as they left the last stair.

"Down here," the landlord shouted to be heard over the roar of what sounded like a thundering herd of elephants racing toward them.

The cellar to which the landlord led them was dark and dank and smelled of feces but it looked sturdy enough. Thick beams supported the ceiling. In one corner was a dugout braced with thick blocks of stone where the landlord's wife and their scullery maid were cowering. It was a tight squeeze but the three of them were able to wedge themselves into the safety of the dugout.

"Ain't been a tornado through these parts in nigh on twenty years," the landlord shouted.

"Lucky us," Declan mumbled.

The scullery maid was whimpering and trembling so violently she was sweating. He reached for her, drew her to him to wrap his arms around her.

"It'll be all right, milady," he said in her ear.

She clung to him like a choking vine. Her fingers were digging into his biceps. When the building shook hard enough to make dirt fall from the ceiling she screamed. He put his hand to back of her head, cupped it then folded his body over hers, tucking her head as close to his chest as he could and her still be able to breathe. It was a strained position for him and his thigh was screaming in protest but the girl was terrified. She needed comforting. He wondered if Penry was doing the same with Bess and prayed the bastard was.

* * * * *

Hunkered down in the cellar of their cottage with a quilt wrapped around her, Bess was pressed tightly in a corner. She watched him pacing back and forth as though there was no dangerous storm pummeling the outside of their home. He was mumbling to himself—she could see his lips moving—and wondered what it was he was saying. That was nothing new; he often talked to himself. She marveled that he could be as calm as he was with the thunder booming, lightning crashing and the wind keening like a Chalean banshee. With his hands clasped behind his back, head down as he paced, he might well be taking a turn around the promenade, deep in thought or talking to a ghostly companion.

The babe moved—bunching up just under her ribs to make her gasp. He—she was sure it was a boy—was active and the thought crossed her mind that her child was sensing her fear and reacting to it.

"It will be fine, little one," she whispered to the bantling. She slowly rubbed her belly then began to hum "The Prince's Lost Lady" and the babe quieted down.

As suddenly as the deluge and punishing wind began, it stopped. It was as though a tap had been turned off. The quiet was unnerving.

"I think it's passed," he said, going to the steps. He put a hand on the banister and looked up the stairway.

"Mayhap it is but a lull before the storm strikes again," she said.

He seemed to be listening intently and when she would have spoken again, he shushed her with a hiss and the elevation of his hand. He stood there for a few moments more before climbing the steps. She waited where she was until he'd opened the cellar door and gone into the kitchen. She could hear him walking around upstairs, heard a muffled curse then he appeared in the opened doorway.

"We've one broken window and the rug is soaked but otherwise we're intact on the main of it."

She nodded and pulled the quilt closer around her for there was cold air coming down the stairway. Overhead she could hear the heavy tread of his boots as he moved to the stairs that led to the upper chambers. The hard thunk-thunk-thunk of his uniform boots scraping on the steps seemed overly loud to her. Five or ten minutes later he came back to the doorway of the cellar.

"All is well above stairs," he said. "I think it is safe for you to come up."

It took a bit of angling to pull her heavy body to its feet but she managed after some huffing and puffing. She cast him an irritated look but he stayed where he was. Her struggle to stand upright didn't seem to have any effect on him. Had it been Declan standing there at the top of the stairs…

"Stop it," she hissed. "That part of your life is o'er."

* * * * *

He unwrapped his arms from around the scullery maid, took her chin in his hand and lifted her tear-stained, bloated face. "It's all right now, milady."

Her hesitant, tremulous smile was gratitude in and of itself but her soft thank you made him feel like a decent man again and—for the first time in days—he realized that was what he truly was: a decent man. At some point he had lost faith in himself but he knew he was no coward. He was a good man, an honorable man and needed to do the honorable thing.

Getting to his feet, he held his hand out to help the scullery maid to hers. Once standing, she bobbed him a curtesy and moved away as the landlord and his wife scrambled from the dugout.

"We need to see how much damage has been done," the landlord said.

"Mayhap there be folk what needs our help," Whiggins suggested.

"Aye," Declan agreed. He stepped aside to allow the landlord's thin-as–a-rail wife to precede him to the stairs but put out a hand to stop her husband. "A rather large tree branch is taking a nap in the middle of my bed. It's going to take several strong men to remove it."

The landlord sighed. "Just one more thing I don't have the coin to repair," he complained.

"I may be able to help," Declan said. "Depending on how much damage has been done to your establishment. Let's hope that branch is the only destruction the storm wrought."

"From your lips to Alel's ear," the landlord said. "Thank you, milord. Any help would be greatly appreciated."

"I've a question you might be able to answer for me," Declan said.

"I'll do my best, milord."

"What do you know of William Tucker?"

The landlord's lips pursed. "Enough to know the man ain't right in the head. Keeps to himself, he does, which is fine by the folks of the Cay."

"And the lady living with him?"

His wife turned to look at Declan. "Maire?" she asked.

"Aye."

"Oh, she's a right sweet girl, she is," the woman said. "Gentle as the day is long. Good with the children hereabouts. Got one of her own coming soon enough."

"Have you heard any rumors that Tucker and she might marry?" he asked. "Do you have any notion how close they are?"

"They're polite enough when…"

The door opened and Captain Samuel Cean entered. He doffed his uniform hat, nodded politely to the landlord's wife then looked to her husband. "Anyone hurt, Carlton?" he inquired.

"No, thank the gods," the landlord replied. "Although there be a big tree trunk in the bed where this gentleman was a-lyin'."

Cean turned his gaze to Declan. "You look none the worse for having a midnight visitor, milord. I take it you were out of that bed before the tree arrived."

Declan liked the man. He was pleasant, helpful and there was something merry in the way his eyes sparkled.

"Another minute or two and I'd have an unhappy fellow, captain," he replied.

"Please, call me Sam," Cean replied. He grinned. "May I call you Jack or is there a title in there somewhere?"

Declan saw Whiggins's eyebrows shoot up.

"Jack is fine," Declan said. "I assume you're checking on the townsfolk. Was anyone hurt?"

"Nothing serious so far," Cean answered. "A few cuts and bruises, a sprain or two."

"Was there much damage done?" the landlord queried.

"We've had more than our rightly share," Cean told him. "There's a need for able-bodied folk to help out."

"Let me get my coat," the landlord said. "Me and the missus will see what we can do."

"That will be greatly appreciated, Carlton," Cean stated.

"Whiggins and I will also help," Declan said as the landlord and his wife went out the door.

"Thank you, Jack. I was sure I could count on you," Cean said and turned to go. He looked around when Declan called his name. "Aye?"

"How did the harbormaster and his lady fair?" Declan had to ask.

Cean smiled slowly. "I can tell you the harbormaster is in good health."

"And his lady?"

"I'm on my way to check on her now," Cean responded. "Would you like to accompany me?"

"Ah, not right now," Declan replied.

"Then I'll be on my way," Cean told him.

After Cean left, Declan found Whiggins glaring at him. "What?"

"Don't ye go volunteering my old bones to be lifting wreckage, and what's this about yer name being Jack?" Whiggins demanded with his hands on his hips.

"I didn't want to give the man my true name," Declan replied. "Not considering I'm here to kill a man."

"Huh," Whiggins said with a grunt. He squinted. "Just when do you plan on doing that anyways?"

"I need to talk to Bess first," Declan answered.

"And just when will that be?" The sailor nudged his chin toward the harbor. "Ye know I got a job on the *Medea* or have ye forgotten that? She'll be sailing in two days times. I can't be staying here with ye and not making any money."

"Then what if I pay you to stay with me?" Declan countered. "To become my..." He threw out his hand, unable to find the right word.

"Manservant?" Whiggins asked with a low growl.

"No, of course not. More along the lines of a companion."

Whiggins sniffed. "How much ye offering to pay me?"

"How much do you want?"

"Depends on what ye want me to do."

"Watch my back as you've already offered to do. Accompany me back to Serenia. I'm sure I can find you a better paying job on one of our ships."

The rheumy, bloodshot eyes lit up. "A better paying job aboard a Farrell Lines ship?" he asked in an awe voice. He came over, spit in his hand then held it out to Declan. "Ye got yerself a deal, milord!"

Grimacing as he spit in his own palm then clasped the other man's rough palm, Declan had an idea. "You said you liked it here at the Cay," he said.

"Good place to retire when the time comes, aye," Whiggins said.

"Ever thought about running a boarding house?"

Whiggins's bushy brows shot up almost under his watch cap. "Oh, hell no."

* * * * *

After he'd made his rounds of the other cottages and shops, Samuel Cean made his way to the cottage he'd saved for last. There was a broken window beside the door but there didn't appear to be any structural damage that he could see. He climbed the stoop and rapped smartly on the panel.

It was Tucker who answered the door.

"What you want?" the bastard asked.

"Just wanted to check to see if everything was good here," Cean told him.

"Everything is as it should be," Tucker said. He stepped back and started to close the door but Cean wedged his boot in the opening.

"Is she all right?" Cean queried.

"Right as rain."

"Where is she?"

A muscle ground in Tucker's cheek. He swiveled his head and yelled, "Maire."

Leaving the door open, Tucker turned to go.

"We could use your help clearing the debris," Cean called after him.

"Got a bad back," Tucker snapped and continued walking.

"Bad back my hairy ass," Cean said under his breath then smiled as the woman who lived with Tucker appeared at the door. "You all right?" he questioned.

"I'm fine, Samuel," she said. "Thank you for asking." She stuck her head beyond the door to look up and down the street. "Was anyone hurt?"

"Nothing to be concerned about. I'm assembling a crew to help clear away the rubble. Do you think you could make some coffee and sandwiches for the workers? Help to serve them?"

"I would be happy to," she said. "I'll get right to it."

"I'm going to use the boarding house as my command center," he said.

"Don't want muddy boots tracking up the fine carpet in your cottage," she accused with a smile.

"True enough. Just yell when you've got things ready and I'll send someone over to fetch it."

"Then I'll see you at the boarding house," she said.

"Aye, you will."

* * * * *

Bess made as many sandwiches as she could with what was in their cupboard—despite the fact that Penry was glaring at her from the table. She'd poured him some coffee and he was sitting there with his hands cupped around the mug.

"It almost came to me tonight," he said.

She looked around. "What did?"

"Where I've seen that bastard before," he answered.

"Who are you talking about?" she asked, tensing.

"Cean," he said. "I know him. I just can't quite put my finger on where and when we met."

"He has that kind of face," she said. She hid her hands in the pockets of her apron for they were shaking.

"It'll come to me," he said. "I never forget a face."

"I'm going to the boarding house now," she said. "Would you bring the sandwiches over for me?"

"Do it yourself," he said. "I'm not your fucking servant."

He pushed up from the table and stalked back through the living area and went into the bedchamber, slamming the door behind him.

He was getting worse, she thought. One moment he could be civilized and gentle—even accommodating—but the next he was a mean, hateful bastard intent on insulting her every chance he got.

Deciding she would send someone back for the sandwiches, she took her shawl from the peg by the kitchen door and left the cottage.

All around her was debris from the storm. The street was littered with small branches, pieces of tin and tile from the roofs, paper and more clothing than she could fathom being left out on clotheslines with a storm coming. She kept her head down so she could locate the obstacles in her path—a difficult prospect considering it was the dead of night and the street lamps provided little illumination. Holding the hem of her shirt up, she picked her way gingerly through the trash. It would not do to fall amid the rumble.

A hand suddenly appeared in front of her.

"Here, let me help you."

She stopped—still looking down—as her heart sped up. Slowly she lifted her head. Past a pair of muddy knee-high boots to a pair of russet doeskin breeches. Past the tail of a dark brown coat. Up a black vest that had been left unbuttoned to reveal the white shirt beneath. Up further still until a strong chin covered in dark whiskers appeared.

"Give me your hand, Bess."

She slowly closed her eyes as her heart leapt in her chest and her mouth went dry.

"It cannot be," she whispered.

She felt a hand close around her own. The touch sent a shiver of emotion all the way through her.

"Look at me, sweeting," he said quietly.

She shook her head. "You're not here. I'm dreaming this."

"I'm here," he replied.

Just as slowly as she'd closed them she opened her eyes and raised her head until she was looking in his beloved face. He was standing there—right before her with her hand clasped in his—and he was smiling gently at her.

"Hello," he said.

"You're alive." Her head was spinning as she stood there in the middle of the street, in the middle of the debris left by the storm, in the middle of the destruction that had once been her life, and then she felt herself falling.

* * * * *

"See? See?" he demanded of Whiggins. "This is why I didn't want to just show up on her doorstep."

"Well, 'tweren't her doorstep you showed up at," Whiggins reminded him. "'Twas the street where you…"

"Oh shut up," Declan snapped.

"Just sayin'," Whiggins said with a sniff.

They were standing beside the bed where Declan had brought her when she fainted. He'd taken the stairs two at a time despite the agony ripping through his thigh and kicked open the first door he came to. That nearly cost him his own consciousness but he clenched his teeth and struggled through the pain. Gently laying her on the chenille spread, he bellowed for someone to fetch the healer. Ten minutes later and that help had not arrived but the landlord's wife had come up to help.

"Women in her condition are prone to fainting, milord," the landlord's wife said as she put a cool cloth on Bess's forehead. "Don't mean nothin', you know."

"Where the hell is that healer?" Declan pressed.

"He's been sent for," she told him. "You need to be patient, milord."

"I tell him that all the time," Whiggins put in.

Grinding his teeth, Declan shoved his hands in his pockets so he would not grab the cloth from the woman and tend to Bess himself.

"Is she pale?" he asked. "Does she look pale to you?"

"She has a glow about her," Whiggins said. "Like most women with child."

"She looks pale," he said, ignoring the sailor.

The healer entered the room then and ordered everyone out.

"I'm not going anywhere," Declan told him.

"Aye, well unless you are the father of the babe she is carrying..."

"I am," Declan stated.

The healer looked at him. "Don't you be lying to me, son," he said, dark eyes narrowed.

"It is my child," he acknowledged. "I am the father."

It was the first time he'd said it aloud and the words humbled him.

"I am the father," he repeated.

"Ain't that a kick in the teeth?" the landlord's wife mumbled.

"A kick in something," Whiggins said, shooing the nosy woman ahead of him out the door.

Once the door closed behind them, the healer turned his full attention on Declan. "I thought William Tucker was the father of this child."

"You thought wrong," Declan said, barely able to contain the anger in his voice.

"That's good to know because I sincerely do not like William Tucker," the healer told him.

"That puts you in good company," Declan replied.

"I would imagine so," the healer agreed before leaning over his patient. "She fainted?"

"Aye."

"Anything untoward happen beforehand?"

"You mean other than me scaring her into passing out?"

The healer twisted his head around and cocked an eyebrow.

"She thought I was dead," Declan admitted. "I...I was trying to be gentle with her but the shock..." He shrugged helplessly.

"Aye," the healer said. "That would do it."

"Is she going to be all right?"

"She is having a healthy pregnancy. Right on target for where she should be at the stage of motherhood. I have been taking good care of her."

"That's a relief," he said. "I was worried Tucker might..." He shrugged again.

"Mistreat her?" the healer inquired.

"Aye."

"He hasn't. She would have told me or I would have seen evidence of it. Believe me. The Cay is a tightly knit community. Things get noticed here and to be honest, people watch him." He gave Declan a long look. "Closely."

"Why?"

"He's a stranger. An unknown commodity. And there is something not quite right about him."

"More than you can imagine," Declan said under his breath.

"So are you here to claim her, then?" the healer questioned.

"That is my intention, aye."

"Then if you are going to travel with her, it should be within the next week or so. After that, travel is not recommended."

"I understand. We'll be leaving as soon as I can arrange passage with a ship heading back to Serenia."

"That would be the *Shield Maiden*, one of the larger Uigingeachian ships. She sails into port tomorrow night and will be leaving on Friday's morning tide."

"I'll have my man book passage for us."

"Shouldn't you wait and ask the lady if she wants to accompany you?" the healer asked.

"Why wouldn't she?" Declan countered.

"Well, there is the harbormaster to consider. He..."

"Declan?"

Both men snapped their eyes to the bed. Bess was looking up at them with wonder on her face. "It is you," she said. "I thought I was dreaming or seeing a ghost."

"I'm very much alive, sweeting," he said. He took the healer's place at the side of the bed then hunkered down beside her—ignoring the protest of his painful thigh.

"It's really you and you're here." Tears filled her eyes. "You came for me."

"I did," he said, gently caressing her cheek.

"Oh, Declan..." she whispered then broke down into harsh sobbing.

He gritted his teeth, pushed up from the floor and sat down beside her, took her into his arms.

"It's all right," he said. "Everything is going to be all right now."

"I will leave you two alone," the healer said. He inclined his head when Declan thanked him for his help.

He held her against him—cooing to her, rocking her—until the sobs became dry hitches. When her tears were spent, he lowered her to the bed and pushed a strand of hair from her eyes. She looked so pale to him, so small and vulnerable and the image of her slumped over the barrel of a musket, drenched in her own blood hurt him so deeply he could barely draw breath.

She put up a shaking hand to touch his cheek and he leaned into the heat of her palm, turning his mouth to put a soft kiss in the center. "I thought I had lost you," she said. "He told me you were dead."

"As I was told you were dead," he said.

"It is a soldier he put into the grave the soldier dug for me," she told him.

"We figured as much," he replied.

"We?"

"Althea," he said and regretted saying the name the moment it left his tongue for it hurt him and put pain in her eyes.

"She is well?" she asked softly.

"She is..." He lowered his gaze to her belly. "She was when last I saw her," he finished.

Bess laid her hand on her stomach. "The babe is yours," she told him.

He nodded. "I know and I am sorry, milady. It was certainly not my intent to..."

She put her fingertips to his lips. "There is nothing for you to apologize for," she said. "If it hadn't have been for our son, I would have taken my life long before now. I was happy when I learned I was with child because a part of you had been left behind."

He took her hand in his, kissed the palm then laid it to his chest. "Our son?" he questioned.

"I know it as surely as I lay here," she replied.

"And he is well?" he queried.

"The healer says he is," she answered. "And you? You were wounded."

"Aye, but I was told you were shot at the inn." He searched her face. "That you lost a lot of blood."

Her face darkened. "The iron ball went through my breast and into my shoulder, barely missing the bone when it exited," she told him. "I know now the musket wasn't lashed to me so it would kill me but to keep me from trying to get away. Had it been one of the longer muskets the shot would have missed me altogether. I was gagged so I could not call out to you but I knew you would hear the musket fire. That was all the help I could give you."

"You could have died," he said, his throat clogging up. "I thought you had." He would never tell her about the men he had killed in the tavern when he'd heard the news.

"There is something I must tell you," she said.

"And there is something I must tell you," he admitted. "Althea..."

Bess looked past Declan's shoulder—her eyes going wide, her lips parting in shock—a moment before Declan felt the cold press of a pistol barrel pressed to the back of his neck.

"Not a word out of either of you or I'll splatter his brains here and now," Penry said, digging the pistol into Declan's flesh.

* * * * *

It was only by sheer luck—or the grace of the Triune Goddess, Herself—that Samuel Cean had seen the man calling himself William Tucker sneaking up the stairs. The bastard was almost to the landing when he caught Cean's eye. There was no doubt who he was looking for.

Fear soaked up all the moisture in his mouth as he left the table where he was helping to roll bandages and quickly made his way to the stairs. Heart in his throat, he hurried up the steps, pulling his pistol from his holster as he went.

When he reached the landing, he saw Tucker opening one of the doors at the far end of the corridor, saw the pistol in the man's hand and felt the world shift around him. He lifted his weapon, aimed—intent on winging the son of a bitch—but his target moved into the room.

"Shit!" Cean hissed.

Pistol pointed upward, he moved silently down the corridor.

* * * * *

"Are you armed?" Penry demanded.

Declan still had possession of Bess's hand. It was pressed to his chest—right over his heart. He tried to calculate how many seconds it would take to release her hand, drop his to the butt of his weapon. By then, he reasoned, Penry would have put an iron ball through him.

"Are. You. Armed?" Penry asked again, twisting the barrel against Declan's neck.

"Aye," Declan said through clenched teeth. "You know gods-be-damned well I am."

"Let go of her hand and slowly raise yours," Penry ordered him. "Wench, take the pistol and toss it away. One false move and I will kill him where he sits."

There was pleading in Bess's eyes as Declan released her hand and lifted his to shoulder height. She reached down to pull the pistol from his waistband. It shook in her hand as she stared at Declan. Her fingers tightened around the grip.

"Don't do it," Penry warned. "I've never shot an unarmed man in the back before but I will make an exception for this one. Throw the pistol, wench."

Declan gave her a slight nod and she did as Penry demanded.

Penry eased the barrel from Dec's flesh. "Now get up," he said as he backed away then sidestepped into the center of the room—out of Declan's reach.

As he got to his feet, he faltered for his thigh reminded him it was not entirely healed.

"Face me."

Wincing, he slowly turned around and looked down the barrel of the pistol pointed at him.

"I'm going to kill you and then her," Penry said. He cocked the pistol.

"In cold blood?" Declan asked. "Not the first time you've done it but you won't get away with it this time."

"I'll put your pistol in your hand," Penry said. "When they come to investigate the shot, they'll believe me when I tell them you tried to kill me and I shot you first. You'll stay dead this time."

Declan saw movement at the door a second before Captain Cean appeared in the opening.

"Drop your weapon, Penry," the man ordered.

Royce Penry flinched, spun around with his pistol aimed at the newcomer but never got a chance to pull the trigger of the three-shot weapon. Cean's own weapon barked and the iron ball hit its target dead center. A dark crimson stain blossomed on the front of Penry's white shirt.

"You bastard," Penry said as his knees gave way and he fell to the floor. He tried to turn, to aim at Declan but Cean fired again. This time the shot went into Penry's temple and the dead man pitched forward onto the floor.

Chapter Eighteen

He stood at the window of the harbormaster's cottage as the first rays of sunlight lit the new day. Below he could see the litter that had yet to be removed from the street. Scanning the rooftops, he spied missing shingles and tiles, a few bare rafters and knew the cleanup was going to take more than a day or two. Luckily no one had been hurt too badly and no life had been lost. The only citizen of Guilder's Cay who had been killed was William Tucker and he had died at the hands of the harbormaster.

"I thought Penry was the harbormaster," Declan said, not looking around.

"He was the night watchman," Cean told him. "I am the law in the Cay. My dispatching him was a legal act. Had you done it…"

"You would have arrested me."

Cean smiled. "Precisely."

"Samuel has been good to me, Declan," Bess said. She was sitting on the loveseat with her hand on her stomach—gently rubbing.

"You can imagine my surprise when I arrived here to find Bess alive and well but under the control of Royce Penry," Cean said.

That remark puzzled Declan and he turned to face Cean. "You knew her from before?"

"Samuel was at the inn that night," Bess replied for him. "He did what he could to help me, but he, too, thought I had died that night."

"You were there?" Declan pressed.

"You can't tell anyone, Declan," Bess said, her eyes begging him for understanding. "They are looking for him in Serenia."

The truth hit Declan like a heavy iron mallet. "By the gods, you are the man who testified against Penry. Belk is it?"

Cean nodded. "Private Jeremy Belk," he replied. "A deserter from His Majesty's Royal Marines."

Declan was floored and he walked to the man's desk and sat down heavily in the chair facing him. "How the hell did you get to be harbormaster here?" he asked. "How did you get from soldier to harbormaster?"

Cean shrugged. "I am from Virago, milord," he replied. "My family has lived off the sea for generations. I know a thing or two about maritime law and what it takes to hold my position."

"But how did you get that position?" Declan queried. "Surely you had to have credentials."

"My family is Rom," Cean told him. "There isn't a document out there my people can't forge. I needed to get away from Serenia, start a new life, have a job. When I landed here after stowing away on the *Andrea Nell* out of Chale, the former harbormaster had been arrested for corruption." He cocked a shoulder. "I decided that job would suit me just fine. I broke into the harbormaster's office, found his file. I took it to the boarding house and copied everything but replaced his name with mine. Gave myself some good references, too. Not a soul questioned the papers." He grinned. "They were that good."

"His first day here, he spied me walking along the beach," Bess said. "He followed me home."

"I wanted to make sure she was all right," Cean said. "That Penry hadn't hurt her more than she'd been hurt that night at the inn. I was relieved to see he hadn't. I was going to arrest him as soon as I got the job but she asked me not to."

"Why?" Declan asked, turning to look at her. "Why not let the bastard be arrested? Why stay with him, Bess?"

"He didn't abuse her," Cean stated. "I would have killed him if he had."

"I owed him my life," she answered. "In his way, he saved me. He took me to the healer that night."

"Whom he killed," Declan stated.

"Aye, he did do that," she acknowledged. "But I had made a bargain with him. I knew I was pregnant. I was going to tell you that night. I made him promise to look after me and your child in exchange for not telling the world who he was. I had no one else to turn to. I had no way to get hold of you and my father was made to believe I was dead."

"I imagine he knows better now," Declan said. "My friend Jack would have told him."

"Jack McGregor, I take it?" Cean asked with a grin.

"Aye," Declan admitted.

"I knew who you were the minute I laid eyes on you, Your Grace," Cean told him. "And I knew why you were here. I couldn't let you kill Penry outright but I knew sooner or later the two of you would meet and one of you was going to die. I wanted it to be Penry so I kept watch o'er you as I have o'er my woman."

That stunned Declan. "*Your* woman?" he questioned.

"We've been lovers for some time now," Cean answered. "I love her more than life itself and I intend to take care of her. I want to marry her."

Bess blinked. "Marry?" she said.

"I do love you," Cean said. "You know I do and I will be a good father to your son."

"My son has a father," she said, looking from Declan to Cean and back again.

"Althea is carrying my child, as well."

"Whoa," Cean said. "Didn't see that coming." He leaned back in his desk chair and from the look on his face, he knew he had won.

"I will take care of you, Bess," Declan said. "I will take care of our child."

"How?" Cean asked.

"I will provide for her," Declan told him. "I will provide for our child. She will not want for anything that is within my power to give her."

"Like what?" Cean pressed.

"What is it to you?" Declan queried.

"I assume you'll give her money," Cean said. "She will own the cottage where she and Penry lived together now that he is gone." He steepled his fingers. "The bastard paid cash money for the place so it is free and clear."

"I had thought perhaps once Penry was out of the picture I would take her back to her father," Dec told him.

"I can't go back to Serenia," she said. "I don't want to go back there. That place has brought me nothing but misery. My father can come here."

"What of the Hound and Stag?" Declan asked. "He loves that place and…"

"You can buy the boarding house for her," Cean said and when Declan snapped his eyes to the man, Cean nodded. "Buy it as a gift for your son, put it in his name and let her and her father run it. Buy the inn from her father and find someone else to run it for you."

"What of Tim? Would he be interested in running it?" Bess asked.

Declan opened his mouth to protest but everything Cean had suggested would work—and work well—for the situation. He had thought earlier of what Bess could do to the rundown boarding house if it belonged to her. Rewarding Tim for his help by deeding the Hound and Stag over to him would be a way to pay the good man back for all he'd done.

"Would any of that be of interest to you, Bess?" he asked. It would be a good solution all the way around.

"Maybe," she said with a sniff. She looked to Cean. "Are you serious about the marriage?"

"As serious as any man has ever been," he said.

"Then get down on your knee and propose to her," Declan told him.

"What?" Bess and Cean asked at the same time.

"I didn't stutter," Declan said.

"Samuel?" she asked.

Cean sat forward in his chair, got up and skirted the desk. He came to the loveseat, went to one knee and reached for her hand—clasping it between both of his.

"Milady," he said. "Would you do me the great honor of becoming my wife?"

"I would," she said.

"I'll have the banns posted today," Cean told her.

Declan breathed a sigh of relief. He hadn't meant that sigh to be audible but it was and both Cean and Bess looked over at him. He felt the heat pulse in his cheeks.

"Glad you're off the hook, Your Grace?" Cean asked with a bit of a sneer.

"I want to know Bess will be well cared for," Declan replied.

"You can count on it," Cean said and got to his feet, helping Bess to hers. "Milady, I believe you should rest now. It's been a long night and you need to sleep."

"But I…"

"You should go rest now," Cean insisted. "His Grace and I have some things we need to discuss."

Bess looked at Declan and when he nodded and smiled, she left them alone together in Cean's office.

"Please, have a seat, milord," Cean said. "This may take a while."

* * * * *

When Declan left Cean, he went straight to the tavern, sat down and ordered an ale. He had a lot to think about—the least of which being the request Cean had made of him—and wanted to be alone while he thought over everything.

Whiggins followed him into the tavern but took a seat at the bar. Already the sailor was beginning to pick up on his moods and must have decided leaving him alone to brood was the best decision.

When the publican brought him his ale, Dec turned to look at Whiggins. "If you can keep your bloody mouth shut, you can sit with me," he called out and Whiggins got up to join him after ordering ale for himself.

"I'll speak only when spoken to," Whiggins replied as he sat down.

"That'll be a nice change," he mumbled.

"For me, too," Whiggins said, taking a long draft of his ale.

Staring down into the amber liquid in the tankard, Declan was finding it hard to live with himself at the moment. A part of him had wanted to insist Bess go back to Serenia with him on the Uigingeachian ship the *Shield Maiden*. Another part of him was glad that she had decided to stay at Guilder's Cay and was glad she had accepted Cean's proposal.

"I will be giving the boy—or girl—my name," Cean had told him. "Do you have a problem with that?"

"The child is mine," he'd replied. "The duty is mine."

"Bess will be taking my name," Cean declared. "The child should as well."

"A false name."

"It isn't a false name," Cean said. "My real name is Jeremy Samuel Belk. My mother's maiden name was Cean. It's not uncommon among the Rom for a man to take his mother's last name."

"When he's hiding from the law," Declan said. "A deserter from His Majesty's Royal Marines."

"You can fix that," Cean said.

"How?"

"Have them grant me an honorable discharge for apprehending a known fugitive from the Governmental Regiment law and pardon me for leaving my post."

"And just how the hell am I supposed to do that?"

"You are an earl, are you not? A member of the peerage. Use your influence with the king's men. Speak to Captain Gunderson for me. Have him go to bat for me. He will. I know he will."

"I'd rather pull my tongue out at the root than talk to that woman-stealing bastard," Declan groused.

"Have you *met* Captain Gunderson?" Cean asked. "He dances with his own kind, milord. Stealing a woman isn't something he would do."

Declan had been astonished by the news but tried not to let it show. The dream he'd had of Althea and Gunderson at Standfield Hall couldn't possibly come true.

"I'll see what I can do," he told Cean.

"One last thing."

"That being what?"

"Don't come back to Guilder's Cay."

"Bess is having my son. I have a right to see him."

"She loves you," Cean said. "I suspect she always will. She knows the two of you can never be together. You being with any other woman is going to hurt her deeply. Seeing you will only make it worse."

"I am going to provide for my child," Declan stated.

"You can do that, but the boy should never know you are his father. Let him believe that honor is mine. Being a bastard is a burden I would not have him carry. Would you?"

There had been strong sentiment in Cean's eyes. He was willing to fight to make the child his own. He made a good point and even though it went against the grain, Declan had nodded his acceptance of the proposal.

"I will write to you to keep you abreast of how the child is doing," Cean said. "I would rather Bess not do so but I won't stop her if she feels the need. Truthfully, I don't believe she will. Once you sail out of this harbor, you will be nothing but a heartbreaking memory for her."

"I never meant to hurt her."

"She knows that," Cean said. "I know that. Let her get on with her life. Let me make her happy. I can. I will."

Bess deserved to be happy. With a heavy heart, Declan forfeited one of his children.

"She ain't goin' with us, is she?" Whiggins asked.

"I thought you said you could keep your mouth shut," Declan grumbled.

"I lied," the sailor replied. "'Sides, ye told me I could have the boardin' house then ye turn around and gives it to the wench."

"You didn't want it and you know you didn't," Declan scoffed.

"Neither here nor there," Whiggins said with a grunt.

"You want it?"

"No," Whiggins replied.

"Then shut up about it."

"Anyone ever tell ye that ye are a rude little son of a bitch?" Whiggins queried, then tossed an irreverent "...milord" in for good measure.

"No one needed to tell me," Declan said. He leaned back in his chair and scrubbed his hands down his face. "I've known it for years."

"So is that offer to work for the Farrell Line still on the table or not?"

"It is," Declan said tiredly, shoulders slumping. He closed his eyes, sighed heavily, let his head fall back and his hands drop to his lap.

"Is that why one of yer ships docked in the harbor this morn?"

He opened his eyes, raised his head. "There's one of our ships here?"

"The *WindLass*," Whiggins told him. "Captained by a man named Bartholomew Tarnes."

"Do you know where Captain Tarnes is now?"

"Was with the harbormaster last I saw of him. They be offloading molasses and sugar from Diabolusia I heard. They'll be sailing on the evening tide."

"For where?"

"How the shit would I know?" Whiggins grumbled.

Declan scraped back his chair and stood, his ale untouched.

"You ain't gonna drink that?" Whiggins asked, reaching for the tankard.

"No and neither are you," Declan told him. "Did you give notice to Captain Kyriakos?"

"Wouldn't matter if'n I did or not considering he sailed outta here this morn," Whiggins answered. "But I be a man of honor and I did what I was suppose to."

"Then let's go," Declan said. "If Tarnes is headed home, I'm going to be on that ship."

* * * * *

Samuel Cean signed off on the cargo from the *WindLass* and handed the paperwork over to her captain. "Fair skies and following seas, Captain Tarnes," he said, saluting the Oceanian.

"Thank you, Captain Cean," Tarnes acknowledged. "May the Wind be always at your back."

"You're headed back to Serenia?" Cean inquired.

"After a brief stop at Derbenille, aye," Tarnes admitted.

"So you're taking the northern route around the Outer Kingdom?" Cean asked, frowning.

"Aye, going straight through the Sinisters. Always a hairy proposition, that one."

"Especially this time of year. Any later and the icebergs would be a problem, I would imagine."

"Even now they can be a hazard but with the gods' help, we'll make it."

"Then I bid you a safe journey," Cean said then looked past Captain Tarnes's shoulder, "for I believe you will be having the Earl of Dungannon among your passengers."

"He will," Declan said as he joined the men.

"Lord Declan?" Tarnes queried. His eyes were like saucers in his suddenly pale face.

"I've never had the pleasure, Captain Tarnes," Declan said, putting out his hand.

Tarnes sputtered but managed to accept the hand extended to him.

"This is Elias Whiggins," Declan said of the man behind him. "He was first mate on the Oceanian brigantine the *Medea* but he'll be going home with us to Serenia."

"Ain't gonna be no working holiday for me, Cap'n, so's don't be tryin' to stick me on yer watch list," Whiggins said, greeting Tarnes with a flick of his index finger from the brim of his watch cap.

"I wouldn't think of it, Mr. Whiggins," Tarnes said, blushing. He gave Declan a worried look. "Are you sure you want to be sailing with us, Your Grace? We're a cargo ship and not fitted for passenger travel. Of course you can have my cabin and I'll bunk with my first mate."

"I wouldn't dream of putting you out, Captain. I can take a berth with your men."

The look of absolute horror that spread over Tarnes's face put an end to that suggestion. He violently shook his head. "Oh, no, Your Grace. Most certainly not."

"He's a right class act, he is, Cap'n," Whiggins said. "But I reckon we'll be takin' yer cabin as ye offered." He clamped a firm hand on Declan's shoulder. "Won't we, Your Grace?"

Declan turned his head and gave Whiggins a narrowed look but the sailor just grinned his picket-fence smirk and said, "A pallet on the floor will be good enough for me."

"Are you sure?" Declan growled.

"Reckon so," Whiggins agreed. "Be a hardship and all but I can make do."

"Sure you wouldn't rather have the captain's bunk?" Declan asked through gritted teeth.

"Nah, I'm good," Whiggins said and squeezed Declan's shoulder before releasing it.

* * * * *

The Sinisters was an evil place. Fog as thick as pea soup was a constant in the narrow strait between the far eastern coast of Chale and the jagged, dangerously rocky cliffs of Outer Kingdom. The crevice through which the ship had to maneuver was only wide enough to accommodate the hull with a foot or so clearance on either side. Many a captain refused to take the northern route through the Sinisters because it was a harrowing experience and not for the faint of heart.

"Ye'll hear the foghorn so don't let it scare ye," Whiggins told Declan. "When you hear it, you can reach through the fog and touch the mountain as we sail through."

That was an unsettling notion. "That close?" Declan asked.

"That close," Whiggins agreed.

When the foghorn sounded, Declan dug his fingernails into the ship's teakwood rail. He could see absolutely nothing but sensed they were within colliding distance to the solid sheet of blackness hidden behind the thick fog. The ship was gliding smoothly through the choppy waters that he had been told were thousands of fathoms deep. A wreck in the Sinisters would be a death knell to the sailors who met their fates within the narrow passage.

"They be ships aplenty o'er which we be passin'. Ships that sank when their hulls were ruptured on the slide across them bastard rocks," Whiggins said. "The bones of hundreds of lost sailors be laying down there."

"Comforting thought," Declan said.

"Ain't it, though?" Whiggins asked with a snicker. "Think of worst ways to meet yer fate."

"Drowning is not a good way to die," Declan said quietly.

"Better than burning to a crisp or being squashed flat as a fritter, I'm reckoning."

"I guess," Declan replied, thinking of his mother and brother and the passengers who had died on the *Molly Celeste*.

The foghorn sounded again to announce the ship had cleared the Sinisters.

"Well, that's it for tonight's entertainment, milord," Whiggins said. "I'm for turning in." He clapped Declan on the shoulder as though they were old friends then disappeared in the fog as he walked to the hatchway that led below deck.

Wishing he had put out his hand to touch the mountain when he had the chance, he extended it now but met only the icy cold of the fog. He pulled the great cape tighter around him for the air was suddenly much chillier than it had been a few minutes before.

It would take the *WindLass* almost a week to sail across the top of the Outer Kingdom and Serenia before it headed south through the North Boreal Sea to Boreas. He had a week of wondering what Althea would say when he went to her. Torturing himself with thinking she might not receive him at all. Worrying that she had found another suitor.

"Lord Jamie tore up the papers that would have nullified the marriage contract," he said aloud. "But does she know I signed them? I told her I was going to before I left."

How was he going to explain himself to her? Would she believe him when he told her he had fallen in love her?

What would he do if she told him she no longer cared? That she wanted nothing to do with him now?

Only time would tell and he had nearly an entire week to worry himself sick over it.

* * * * *

"His Grace, Lord Declan Farrell, Earl of Dungannon to see you, milady," Granger, her father's new butler, said in his haughtiest tone.

Althea felt her heart stutter in her chest. "He's here? Declan is here?"

"Awaiting you in the study, milady," Granger informed her.

She laid aside the book she was reading. Her head was spinning at the news for she had never expected to see him again.

"Should I send him away, Your Grace?" Granger asked.

It was on the tip of her tongue to say yes but her curiosity got the better of her. "No," she replied. "I will meet with him." She got slowly to her feet with a hand to her belly that she could have sworn had doubled in size within the last week. "Did you offer him refreshment?"

"I did, milady, but he declined."

"Then please tell him I will be with him shortly. I would like to freshen up first."

Granger bowed. "Of course, Your Grace."

Her prettiest gown, she thought as she hurried from the solarium to her bedchamber. Her best pair of slippers.

She stopped, pulled the hem of her gown away from her bare feet and groaned. Her ankles were three times their normal size and she knew her face was equally bloated. There wasn't a pretty gown among those that had been made for her advancing pregnancy. None of her slippers fit. Her hair felt—and looked like—straw. She could not possibly receive him looking as she did.

"Why are you here?" she asked and wanted to cry.

Something she did easily and quite often of late.

"Did you bring *her* back with you?" she whispered.

That thought hurt her so badly it nearly took away her breath. She put her hand to her heart where a terrible pain had lodged on the night he had left her at the Harvest Ball at Boreas.

She knew the papers for the nullification of the Joining contract had not been presented for the king's signature but that did not mean Declan had changed his mind about not wanting to marry her. He had made his intentions quite clear by going to Guilder's Cay to find his beloved Bess.

Tears filled her eyes.

"Oh, Declan, why can't you love me as I love you?" she asked.

"He's down below."

She turned to find her father on the landing twenty feet away. He was standing on the top step with his hand on the bannister.

"If you want me to send him away, I shall."

"Have you spoken to him?" she asked.

"No and I have no intention of doing so unless you tell me to send him packing and to never darken our door again. That I will do—and with the greatest of pleasure," her father declared. "Is that what you want, daughter?"

She knew what she wanted and what she wanted was in the study.

"Did he tell Granger why he is here?" she queried.

"I doubt he would state his business to a mere servant, Althea," he replied. He came toward her, his eyes filled with concern. "Tell me what you want done and I will see to it."

"I want him, Papa," she said, unable to keep her bottom lip from trembling. "With all my heart I want him."

"Then shall I have my men wrestle him into chains then toss him into the dungeon?" he asked. "That way you can have him here for the rest of his wretched life. Keep him as a pet. Feed him maggoty gruel and sulfurous water."

"Oh, Papa," she said and tried not to smile at his ridiculous suggestion.

"It's what he deserves," her father said. He opened his arms as he reached her and enfolded her against him. "That and fifty lashes for daring to hurt my little girl."

"I should hear him out," she said.

"You don't have to," he suggested.

"I need this to be over one way or another," she said. "I can't continue to pine for a man who does not want me. Let him say it and we will be done with it once and for all."

"He did say it, Althea. More than once," her father reminded her.

"Then let him say it now that I am carrying his child. Then I will know there is no chance whatsoever for us."

She eased out of his arms, stood on her tiptoes to kiss his cheek.

"Go to him just as you are, then," he told her. "Make no concessions for him. He does not rate them."

Her father was right, but it went against all her feminine instinct not to present herself to him in the best possible light. Yet, if he saw her as he had made her…

She straightened her shoulders. "You are right," she said. "He does not."

* * * * *

Declan was as nervous as a green youth. He had dressed in his finest waistcoat and breeches. Pulled on his best boots. His hands had fumbled so badly with his jabot that Jack had to knock them aside to tie the gods-be-damned thing himself. He had even deigned to splash cologne on his face although the stench of it made his already queasy stomach roil. Not wanting to get dusty on the ride over, he had called for a carriage and he had brought Jack along with him for moral support—although the bastard refused to get out of the carriage to enter Standfield Hall.

"This is for you to do, Dec. No one can do it for you," Jack told him. "Grovel if you must but do not come out of those doors without the lady's promise to give you her hand in Joining."

"What if she…?"

"What if *you*?" Jack countered.

"What if I what?" he'd asked.

"Whatever the fuck you were about to ask of her," Jack said. "Ask it of yourself."

"I doubt I have another man waiting in the wings," he'd mumbled.

"There's always Captain Gunderson," Jack said with a twitch of his lips. "I do believe he fancies you, Declan James. He'd make you a fine husband."

That hadn't deserved an answer so he had stormed out of the carriage and marched up to the door of her father's manor, but as he reached for the lion-headed doorknocker, he froze. His hand shook and his palm was slick with sweat. He had no idea what kind of reception he'd get from her father, the duke, or from the lady, herself.

He almost turned back around to run for the carriage. Instead, he squared his shoulders, took a deep breath and grabbed the brass doorknocker ring.

* * * * *

Jack shook his head. He'd never seen his friend so nervous, so frightened. The poor fool was about to shit his pants.

Or get either his ass or his heart handed to him.

"Don't hurt him, milady," he said softly. "You have no idea what this is doing to him."

He braced his arms on the side of the carriage and lowered his chin atop them. His gaze was steady on Declan as the wretched man just stood there with the brass ring pulled back from the door.

"Slam the thing into the wood, you dolt," he said under his breath.

But Declan just stood there holding the stupid thing. Jack could have sworn the man's knees were shaking.

"Oh for the love of Alel," he snapped and opened the carriage door. He strode up the steps and grabbed Declan's hand—startling his friend and making him cry out with surprise.

"What the hell are you doing?" Declan asked.

"This is how it's done, you idjut." He slammed Declan's hand against the door—three times very hard and very fast.

"Gods-be-damn it, that hurt," Declan complained at he snatched his scraped knuckles back. He shook his head.

"Oh, grow up. A little pain isn't going to kill you. Now stand there and be a man. Don't let the servant see you pouting," Jack ordered then turned and went back to the carriage.

"Fuck you," Declan yelled at him.

"Right back at you," Jack said, flipping him his middle finger.

As he took his seat in the carriage, the door to Standfield Hall opened and a liveried servant appeared.

"There's no turning back now, you stupid little shit," Jack said with a grin.

* * * * *

From the balcony above the front door of his home, Duke Alastair Standfield was watching the scene playing out below. Alerted to the sound of wheels grinding over the cobblestones, he had peered out his window and was surprised to see a carriage with the Farrell crest emblazoned on the side. Thinking it was Lord Edward coming to call, he was infuriated when he saw that it was the whelp instead. Of half a mind take up his musket and put an iron shot through the arrogant little rascal's other thigh, he was curious to know why the earl had come to call. He seriously doubted Althea would approve him shooting the bastard.

So he had gone out on the balcony with the intention of calling down to the man to demand the reason for his visit. But then he noticed the unease in the way the boy walked. Along with the slight limp there was apprehension, nervousness and a marked degree of tension in the way Declan Farrell took the steps up to the door. When he hesitated with the knocker in his hand, Alastair grinned.

"You are scared shitless, you little son of a bitch," he said and nodded. "Well good. You should be."

His attention was caught by the opening of the carriage door as the boy's friend Jack McGregor stormed out of the vehicle and came striding aggressively up the steps.

"This is how it's done, you idjut," McGregor said.

"Scared shitless," Alastair thought then laughed.

* * * * *

Pacing the study from one end of the room to the other, Declan was getting more anxious with every tick of the tall clock in the corner of the room. He was afraid his sour stomach would erupt into full-scale retching if Althea refused to see him. The moment the haughty servant had left him in the study, he'd wanted to run, so he'd forced himself to sit down. That had lasted all of five seconds before he was up and making rapid circuits of the room.

What was taking her so long? He wondered. By the clock it had been…

He had no fucking idea how long it had been.

An hour? Two? Four?

He was in hell and slowly being hoisted upon his own…

His own…

"My own what?" he snapped, unable to hold any thought for long for his mind was seething with absolute terror that she would tell him to go to hell.

And what if she did? What would he do then?

Grovel if you must but do not come out of those doors without the lady's promise to give you her hand in Joining.

Grovel, Jack had suggested. Aye, groveling was good. Groveling might do the trick and especially if he got down on his knees.

He went to the door, stuck his head out.

No sign of her.

No sound of her footsteps.

Or anyone else's for that matter.

Had they all left him there to stew in his own juices?

That would be just like Alastair Standfield, but not like his daughter. She would either face him or send him away. There was never any in between with that strong-willed lass. That was one of the things he loved about her. She could give as good as she got.

He looked both ways down the corridor, groaned then went back to pacing the fine Chrystallusian rug underfoot. Every pass by the clock had him eying it, but it seemed as if the gods-be-damned hands weren't moving even if the pendulum was.

Tick. Tick. Tick.

He ran a hand through his hair.

Tick. Tick. Tick.

He ran his palms down his breeches.

Tick. Tick.

"Hello, Declan."

He turned so quickly he lost his balance and his thigh screamed in protest. He had to reach out to grab the back of a chair to keep his leg from folding beneath him.

There she was standing in the doorway with her hands folded demurely upon the rounded globe of her belly.

The belly where his child—their child—was growing.

He couldn't find his voice. He opened his lips but nothing came out. All the moisture seemed to have evaporated and his tongue was stuck to the roof of his mouth.

"You look well, milord," she said softly. "Your leg has healed?"

Struggling to swallow, he reached down to touch his thigh.

"It pains me at times," he said and could have kicked himself for complaining.

"Then, please," she said. "Sit."

She moved into the room and took a seat in an overstuffed chair beside the fireplace. Though she arranged the hem of her skirt gracefully around her legs, he could see her bare toes peeking out beneath the material. That made him smile—and made that smile widen when he saw her curl them under when she saw where he was looking.

"I like you barefoot," he said then raised his eyes to her face. "You have adorable feet."

"Barefoot and pregnant," she mumbled.

He frowned as he perched on the edge of the loveseat. "Beg pardon?"

She lifted her chin. "My feet are swollen and I cannot wedge them into my slippers."

"Why are they swo…?" Understanding slammed into him and he clamped his stupid mouth shut, felt heat sweep up his face.

"Why are you here, milord?" she asked and he noticed she was twisting her fingers together in her lap. She was as nervous as was he.

Just say it, Farrell, he thought. Say it. Say it. Say it.

"I didn't bring her back with me," he blurted and watched her left eyebrow arch.

She was silent for a moment and when he said nothing else, she cleared her throat. "May I ask why not?"

"She is to be married to a man on Guilder's Cay," he told her.

"Ah," she said. "She met a man there and moved on without you."

"She believed me dead," he explained. "But no. She met him here. At the Hound and Stag."

Her eyes widened. "Oh dear gods, please tell me she isn't marrying Penry!"

"No," he stated firmly. "No, Penry is dead."

She drew in a deep breath then exhaled slowly as her fingers mauled one another, fingernails scratching at knuckles. "Did you kill him?"

"No, the man she is marrying did." He threw out a hand. "It's a long story best told another time."

"Is that what you came to tell me, then?" she asked. "That the woman you love is marrying another man." She tilted her head to one side. "Am I to offer you my sympathy, milord? What of your child?"

He dipped his gaze to her rounded belly. "What of *our* child, milady?" he countered. "Are you in good health?"

She cupped her belly protectively. "I am in excellent health and so is my child."

"Our child, milady," he reminded her.

"I am not asking for you to acknowledge this babe," she said.

That stung but before he could say anything else, she stopped him.

"You went to offer your hand in Joining to the woman you love and your name to her child. I am sorry it did not work out for you, but I am at a loss to understand why you are here before me today. There is nothing here for you, milord."

"My babe is here," he told her. "You are here."

"Neither of which you wanted," she said.

"Thea, that's not fair," he said. "You didn't tell me you were pregnant."

"Yet you were told before you left," she reminded him. "Lord James told you, did he not?"

He flinched. "Aye, he did but…"

"But you went to Guilder's Cay anyway," she said.

"You know why I went. I had to make sure she wasn't in any danger" he protested. "She had been taken against her will by a madman. Only the gods knew what he might be doing to her."

Her eyes flashed green fire. "I told you, Declan, that they were seen walking arm in arm along the beach. Did that sound to you as though he was abusing her?"

"I needed to see for myself, Thea. I needed to talk to her. By all that is holy I swear to you I did not go down there with any purpose other than that."

"Not to offer her your name?" she wanted clarified.

He shook his head. "No."

"Not even to give your child a name?"

"No. I could not."

"Why not?" she demanded.

"Because that name can only go to the child you are carrying. As my lawful heir."

That seemed to infuriate her. Anger flushed her cheeks and she grabbed handfuls of her skirts as though to keep from flying at him to rake her nails down his cheeks.

"I don't need your bloody name for my child, Declan Farrell. I don't need you at all. I will have my child and then I intend to take him to Chale."

"And what name will you give him, Althea?" he queried.

"The Standfield name is an old and honorable one. That is the name he will bear."

"You would tell the world he was conceived out of wedlock?" he pressed. "Born out of wedlock? You would attach that stigma to his name along with the Standfield one? What will you tell him when he asks about his father?"

"I will tell him his father did not want him or his mother," she threw at him.

"That isn't true," he said, his jaw clenched. "I want the both of you."

"Well, you bloody well can't have either of us," she snapped, getting to her feet. She pointed a finger at the door. "Get the hell out of my home." When he didn't move but just stared at her, she stomped her foot. "Get out, Declan, or I will have you thrown out."

"I'm not going anywhere until you listen to reason," he said and knew the moment the words left his mouth he'd said the worst possible thing.

"Get the hell out, you arrogant bastard," she screamed at him.

Two burly servants suddenly entered the room. The looks on their faces did not bode well for his continued good health. He knew he was about to be forcibly ejected from Standfield Hall.

"Sit down, Althea," he said quietly, firmly.

"Don't you tell me what to do," she yelled then turned to the servants. "Pick his ass up and throw it out of my house."

He swung his attention from her to the men. "You do know who I am, do you not?" he asked.

The two—who had started forward at her command—stopped.

"Aye, Your Grace," the shorter of the two replied.

"And you do know that this lady and I are betrothed?"

"Were," she snapped. "Were betrothed."

"Still are," he said, keeping his eyes on the servants. "According to the laws of this country, from the moment she and I became betrothed, she came under my authority. Do you men understand what I am saying?"

The men exchanged uneasy looks.

"Then let me explain it to you in terms you will understand," he said. "She is my property."

Althea's loud hiss sounded like that of a cornered feline. "Declan, I want you out of my…"

"Shut up and sit down, Althea," he ordered.

"I will not…"

"Do as he says, daughter."

Declan looked past the servants to find Lord Alastair leaning against the doorjamb. He nodded to the man then switched his attention to Althea.

"I said sit down," he commanded.

"Papa," she whined.

"He is right," Lord Alastair said. "You are technically under his jurisdiction until such time as the papers are resubmitted for nullification."

"Which they will not be," Declan stated.

"I am reserving judgment on that," Lord Alastair. "I want to hear what you have to say before I make any decision on the matter. You men may go." He glanced briefly at the servants before his stare bored into Declan. "For now."

"Aye, Your Grace," the men said in unison. It was obvious neither of them wanted to be involved in what was happening.

Once they were gone, Lord Alastair came into the room, closed the door then leaned against it with his arms folded.

"All right, boy. Let's hear what you came here to say."

Declan was sitting on the edge of the loveseat with his legs spread, clenched hands dangling between his thighs. When Lord Alastair made no move to join them in the sitting area, he stood out of respect for the man.

"Sit down, Althea," Declan said again.

Snorting with disgust, she dropped back into the chair, glaring at him.

"All right," he said. He leveled his gaze on the duke. "I fully intend to make good on the Joining contract. I would like you to set a date for the ceremony as soon as possible. I…"

"Why?" Lord Alastair interrupted.

Althea looked from her father to him but kept her silence. Her lips were pursed tightly together and her fingers were curled like claws around the arms of her chair.

"Because I love your daughter and want to spend the rest of my life with her and our child."

A simple sentence. A heartfelt confession. An honorable profession of his intent. He didn't expect laughter; he was expecting doubt and received it.

"Just when did you come to this startling revelation, Lord Declan?" her father asked.

Althea's eyes bored into Declan like red-hot pokers. He could almost hear the gnashing of her teeth. Her entire body posture screamed fury at him.

Declan addressed his answer to his intended. "Mayhap it was when you were taking care of me after I was shot. Or mayhap before that, even, when you shot the soldier to protect Jack and me. I know I was already in love with you by the time I went to the ball in Serenia because when I saw you with Gunderson, I wanted to rip his heart out and stomp on it."

"Good thing you didn't," Lord Alastair said drily.

"All I know for a certainty, Althea, is that I do love you. With all my heart and all my soul. I don't want—nay, I won't—live without you. I want to make a home for the three of us and—gods willing—more babes to fill that home with laughter and love."

"Pretty sentiments if they are truthful," Lord Alastair said.

"They are," Declan replied. "I have many faults, Your Grace, but dishonesty is not one of them."

"I see," the duke said. He looked to his daughter. "Are you buying any of this, daughter?"

"Not one copper penny's worth," she sneered. "He can't have the woman he wants so he aims to take me as his consolation prize."

"I can have any woman I want, milady," he said, his ego stinging from the slap.

"Well, you can't have this one," she said. "Go home, Declan Farrell. Go home to Arlington Keep and find you another woman to hurt and shame."

"I'm not going anywhere until you and your father set the Joining date," he told her.

"Would you prefer spending time chained to the wall of my dungeon?" Lord Alastair asked in a pleasant voice. His smile was pure evil.

Declan ground his teeth, struggled to get his anger under control before he said something that would only make matters worse. He turned his gaze to the duke.

"Your daughter is pregnant with my child," he said. "I am offering to make…"

"An honest woman of me?" Althea interrupted with a snort.

He ignored the jibe.

"I am offering to make an honorable place in society for her and our child. To prevent gossipmongers and tongue-waggers from casting aspersions on her or the babe. I never want any man or woman to look upon your daughter and call her a fallen woman. I never want any man or woman to look upon our child and call him or her bastard. I am trying to do the right thing here but I am also struggling to keep what the gods saw fit to put together. Tell me what I need to do to make this right. Tell me what punishment you want me to endure to prove to you that I love her and want to marry her."

Lord Alastair said nothing for a long while.

"Papa?" Althea queried. "Papa, you aren't seriously considering doing this, are you?"

"Since she began showing, only the servants here at the Hall have seen her. They are—to a man and woman—as loyal to the Standfields as any servant ever has been to any employer. They do not nor will not gossip of her condition. This is why once the babe is born, she plans to relocate to Chale. She planned on giving the child the Standfield name and telling those who inquired that her husband—a distant cousin she'd known she'd childhood—was killed in a tragic accident before the babe was born. That would explain the name."

"The babe will bear the Farrell name," Declan said. "Even if I have to take you to court to see it done."

"And risk destroying her reputation and having the child declared a bastard?" Lord Alastair asked. He shook his head. "I think not."

Declan raked his hand through his hair. "For the love of the gods, Your Grace, I love her. I need her. Please don't make this any harder than it has to be."

"Harder on whom, Lord Declan?" her father inquired.

"On her," Declan replied.

"I'm just fine, thank you for asking," Althea snapped. "I can live quite well without you or your help or your bloody name, Declan Farrell."

"But I can't live without you," he shouted. "The gods-be-damn it, woman, I love you. What more do you want me to say? What do you want me to do to prove it?"

Before she could answer, he slid off the loveseat and onto the floor on his knees. He didn't try to hide the pain that action caused as he crawled to her chair.

"I am here, Althea," he said. "On my knees before you. Do you want me on my belly instead? I will do that. Do you want me to kiss your feet? I will do that, too. Tell me what you want me to do and I will do it. I am begging you. Pleading with you. I am dying here, Thea."

Althea was looking at him as though seeing him for the first time. There were tears gathering in her eyes and her chin trembled.

"Do you still reject this man, daughter?" Lord Alastair questioned quietly.

Time stopped as Declan waited for her answer.

"No," she whispered.

Finally. His heart clenched in his chest and he put up a hesitant hand to cover hers. When she allowed the touch, he caressed her flesh.

"I do love you, Thea. As the gods are my witness and on the graves of my mother and brother, I swear it."

Her smile was tremulous. A tear fell slowly from her eye.

"I love you, too, Declan Farrell," she said and reached out her free hand to cup his cheek.

He turned his lips into her palm and kissed her. He looked up at her through blurry vision.

"Never doubt my love for you or our child," he said.

"I won't," she replied then took his hand to move it to her belly.

The babe bunched beneath his touch and he sucked in a surprised breath.

"That is your son greeting you," she said.

"You're sure it's a boy?" he asked and wanted to bite his tongue for he had asked Bess the same thing.

"It's a boy," she stated. "No doubt about it and I have a name picked out for him."

"As long as the last name is Farrell, you can name him whatever pleases you," he said, hoping he wasn't going to hate the name.

"Daniel Rees Standfield Farrell," she said. "How does that sound?"

His blurry vision got blurrier still.

"He would have liked that," he said, his voice breaking.

He laid his head on her lap and she stroked his hair.

"My cue to leave," Lord Alastair said, getting to his feet.

Declan lay with her fingers threading through his hair as she hummed "The Prince's Lost Lady." He forgot all about the pain spiking in his thigh.

Epilogue

Twenty-eight years later

Lenore felt her belly clench as she stared at him.

He towered over her. At least by a good foot and no doubt outweighed her by more than a hundred pounds. His shoulders were so broad they blocked out the light behind him. His chest was thick with muscles lurking beneath his white shirt. Long legs with heavy thighs and lean hips were scant inches from hers. Depthless blue eyes were boring into her and when she looked closely into them she could see red-hot flames leaping there. The rest of him might be cold as ice but his gaze was hotter than the flames of hell. He wanted her. The thick bulge she sensed pressing against the fly of his pants was all the confirmation she needed that he did.

She should move back, she thought. She knew well what he wanted and wasn't sure now was the right time. She needed to put distance between them but his thumb smoothed across her lips in a slow, delectable glide. Tingles wriggled down her sides to pool in her lower abdomen. She felt the tell-tale heaviness between her legs, the moisture easing from her to wet her thong. She knew he could smell the scent of her arousal for his nostrils flared and he inhaled deeply.

"Don't," she said breathlessly.

He slid his hand along her jaw and to the nape of her neck, pulled her face to his. "Don't what?" he whispered as he lowered his mouth to hers.

Just like that—with the touch of his lips—she was lost. All thought of what she had been sent there to do pushed out of her mind. Her world canted to one side, slid out from under her feet. Had it not been for his hand firm at her neck and the brawny arm he slid around her, she might well have gone to her knees.

He drew her up hard against his body, took firm possession of her mouth and slipped his tongue deep inside, a low growl welling up to underscore his need. When he ground his heavy erection against her, she could no longer maintain her impassiveness. She snaked her arms around his waist, splayed her hands over his back and held on tight as he ravaged her senses. She rocked her hips from side to side against his shaft, pressed her tongue past his lips to duel with him, gave back as good as she was getting.

"Hmm," he voiced low in his throat then spread his hand over the back of her head to anchor her, to give him more purchase. She felt the sting of his teeth against her upper lip and clawed at his back.

The taste of him was like nothing she had expected. His body certainly wasn't cold and his mouth was sweet, honeyed heat. The soft breath spreading over her cheek as he kissed her was warm and smelled of lemon.

* * * * *

Daniel wanted to be inside her. He needed to be inside her. Had to be inside her. His hands dropped to her ass and he cupped the taut cheeks—lifting her clear of the floor as easily as if she were a feather. The moment her legs came up to wrap around his waist, all rational sane thought fled his mind. He carried her to the bed across the room and fell with her atop it. Thankfully it was a sturdy piece that had seen many such trysts in its day else his weight would have buckled the legs.

As it was, the bed skidded backward to collide with the stone wall. With one foot on the floor, he levered his body above hers then frantically tore at the waistband of her breeches—dragging them down in quick, brutal jerks. The breeches snagged on her boots, he cursed then jerked at them as well until he could pitch them to the floor. The petticoat came off with them. He growled at the sight of her pantaloons and literally tore them from her hips. Her gasp spurred him harder and he ran his hand between her legs, cupped her then rubbed vigorously. Her female scent was so intoxicating it made his head spin.

Her head whipped back and forth on the dusty bed covers. Her hips arched up to give him leverage to rub her more briskly. The tips of her breasts strained at the uniform shirt and he dropped his mouth to capture one through the crisp cotton.

"Aye," she hissed and buried her hands in his hair to hold his face to her bosom.

Fumbling with his fly, he grunted with each movement until he had freed his cock. It leapt ahead of him like a guided missile and went straight for her wet heat—the heady scent of which was driving him mad. With a savage snap of his hips, he rammed into her. She met him with a fierce upward snap of her own hips and they were locked together in a frenzied battle of groans, grunts, thrusts and outright plunges.

She was gripping him with a hot, velvet fist that slid along his hard length. Tight, slick, greedy little clasps ran up and down his cock as he pummeled her hot channel. Through the fabric of her shirt he found her nipple and clamped his teeth around it. He suckled hard. As he did, her nails raked his scalp, tugged viciously at his hair even as she pulled his mouth harder against her.

He wanted to be fully naked against her. He wanted to lick and suck and nibble at her breasts. He ached to feel her naked belly against his. He wanted—nay, needed—the glide of their flesh against one another.

Her legs clasped him tighter and he knew her release was close at hand. She was straining against him—her heels gouging into the small of his back. His own climax was rushing toward him like a speeding rocket. He dug his hands into the toned flesh of her ass.

"You. Belong. To. Me," he said through clenched teeth, punctuating each word with a savage thrust. "You. Are. Mine."

"Aye," she agreed with a grunt.

The orgasm burst so powerfully he thought the top of his cock would fold back on itself. It was a forceful eruption that poured from him in wave after wave of hot seed. His lower body was jacking like a piston ramming into her. The sound of their bodies slapping together sounded loud to his ears—drowning out the roar of his blood pounding fiercely against his eardrums.

Her hands had gone from his scalp to his back and the savage dig of her nails into his shirt as she held her hips up in offering to him made him growl. He felt the hard quiver of her inner muscles and went still with his cock buried as far as it would go in her body.

"Aye," she shouted as her orgasm rippled fiercely through her wet cavern.

She clung to him so tightly he found it hard to draw breath, but that didn't matter. Her body was his. He had claimed her again, branded her again, spilled his seed into her again and even then the happy little fellas were swimming around inside her with maniacal delight at being given their freedom. He could almost hear them chortling whoopee!

The thought made him giggle and that broke the moment. She stiffened, her head came up and her eyes narrowed.

"You find this amusing?" she demanded, her lips taut.

"Peace, woman," he said, lowering his head to her breast. He swiveled his cheek against her so he could look up at her. "I was just thinking about my seed cavorting inside you and it made me laugh."

"You didn't laugh," she accused. "You giggled." Her eyes narrowed even more. "Like a girl."

"So sue me," he said then winked.

She snorted but threaded her fingers through his hair and gripped it hard. "I'll snatch you baldheaded if you ever do it again. That wasn't a manly sound, highwayman."

"Get up, wench," he said, slapping at her naked ass. "We've a coach to rob tonight."

Lenore McGregor Farrell frowned at her husband. "If my da catches us…"

"Your da and my father are old men. They couldn't catch anything save a cold," he said with a snort. He sprang from the bed and began pulling on his clothes.

"If they ever find out what we've been doing, they'll lock us both in the dungeon at Arlington," she told him. She left the bed and picked up her breeches.

Ten minutes later they were dressed. She in a dark brown coat and breeches. He in a claret-red velvet coat and doeskin breeches— like his namesake the infamous Gypsy robber, Daniel Rees.

He looked about the cottage to make sure they were leaving nothing incriminating behind. One last look at the bed where he had lain with his wife—the same bed where twenty-nine years earlier he had been conceived—and shooed his woman to the door. As she passed him, he reached out to rub her stomach. It was a little ritual they had each time they left her da's cottage.

He loved her flat little tummy—and what was under that flat little tummy—as much as he loved tweaking the ears of the rich people they robbed. That little tummy where chortling little fellas were busy making the acquaintance of a couple of teasing little eggs. Within a few minutes, there would be another rowdy highwayman created to ply his trade upon the coach road.

ABOUT THE AUTHOR

Charlee, as she is known to her readers, is the author of 100 novels, the first ten of which are the WindLegend Saga. She was married 43 years to her high school sweetheart, Tom, until his untimely death in April 2009. She is the mother of two grown sons, Pete and Mike, and the proud grandmother of Preston Alexander and Victoria Ashley and the giddy great-grandmother of Amber Dawn.

A native of Sarasota, Florida, Charlee was adopted at birth and grew up in Colquitt and Albany, Georgia. She says of her heritage: "I was born in Florida and raised in Georgia, so that makes me an official Sunshine Cracker!" She now lives in the Midwest where she enjoys the changing of the seasons.

Her hobbies are reading, writing, and quietly communing with her beloved husband, Buddha Belly, as he guides her gently from somewhere beyond the here and now. She is owned and operated by seven cats who only allow her to leave the house for catnip, kitty kibble, and clumping kitty litter.

She loves to watch *ANYTHING* in which **Allan Hawco**, Michael Trucco, Victor Webster, or Chris Vance have starred, and patterns her heroes after these fine actors as her tribute to the many hours of enjoyment they have given her.

She collects statues of the Grim Reaper, Anubis, gargoyles, and windchimes. One of her prized possessions is a Grim Reaper windchime sent to her by a fan from England.

Her signature Reaper novels have a huge loyal following and currently she is at work on a new dark fantasy set in Australia.

Did you enjoy this book? Drop us a line and say so! We love to hear from readers, and so do our authors. To connect, visit www.boroughspublishinggroup.com online, send comments directly to info@boroughspublishinggroup.com, or friend us on Facebook and Twitter. And be sure to check back regularly for contests and new releases in your favorite subgenres of romance!

Are you an aspiring writer? Check out www.boroughspublishinggroup.com/submit and see if we can help you make your dreams come true.

www.ingramcontent.com/pod-product-compliance
Lightning Source LLC
Chambersburg PA
CBHW060145260626
47160CB00001B/124

* 9 7 8 1 9 4 2 8 8 6 4 7 1 *